The Jerusalem Scroll

Mike Evans and Robert Wise

A JANET THOMA BOOK

THOMAS NELSON PUBLISHERS
Nashville

Published in Nashville, Tennessee, by Thomas Nelson, Inc., Publishers.

This is a work of fiction. The characters, incidents, and dialogues are products of the authors' imagination and are not to be construed as real. Any resemblance to actual events or persons, living or dead, is entirely coincidental.

Library of Congress Cataloging-in-Publication Data

Evans, Mike, 1947–
   The Jerusalem scroll / Mike Evans and Robert Wise.
     p. cm.
   ISBN 0-7852-6915-0
   I. Wise, Robert L. II. Title.
   PS3555.V252J47 1999
   813'.54—dc21   99-19187
                                            CIP

Printed in the United States of America
1 2 3 4 5 6 BVG 04 03 02 01 00 99

כן תדבר ... ...

ירושלם יד ... חר וכוש ...

חרי לורן ... ...

... ... יברעת ...

וחוש ... יוש חלו יזת

... חלו יזת ... וחתוש

ידי י שנרושן ... ...

... דוה ... חסר י

... יוש

שרדו ... ... טירדו ה ישרתו

... ... איות ליהוה וראה

... ... ידכדו אין נעשתה

שכתו וה אכבני ...

... אתה

חכר ה חר

Acknowledgments

The authors wish to thank and acknowledge friends and colleagues who helped with completion of the manuscript. Thanks to Michael Wourms for initial input; to Bruce Barbour, our agent, who went above and beyond the call of duty; to Connie Reece for editorial development; and to Janet Thoma for her always outstanding guiding hand as editor.

Our appreciation also goes to Jerusalem's brightest young journalist with *The Jerusalem Post*, Ilan Chaim; to Jack and Mary Fisher for reading the manuscript; and to Dr. Ray Gannon for his invaluable editorial assistance.

We especially thank Larry Banks, research associate for the Department of Anthropology at the Smithsonian, who directed the excavation at one of the caves in Qumran with the Institute of Judaic Christian Research, and his son, Nathan Banks, a gifted anthropologist, for providing scholarly insights into hieroglyphics and ancient languages.

Dedication

To the precious children of Jerusalem (Jewish, Arab, and Christian)—filled with joyful sounds, innocent smiles, and great hopes, they purely reach out to each other with sincere love and trust in a city polluted with the poison of prejudice. They are the divinely assigned caretakers of the soul of Jerusalem. The fact that they remain true to each other is a mystery much more intriguing than *The Jerusalem Scroll*.

Part
One

1

Saturday, August 1
Dead Sea

A filmy mirage of goats crossing the rugged terrain crept out of the wilderness and then slowly dissolved back into the bleak landscape, shimmering in the quivering heat waves rising up from the barren slopes. The first days of August always brought such things. A breeze swept across the Dead Sea and pushed the desert winds away from Rashid Salah's back. The old man pulled his black-and-white checkered *keffiyeh* more closely around his neck. The long white robe effectively kept the hundred-plus degree heat from his body, but swirling sand still stung his deeply creased face. The Bedouin pulled the edge of the cloth head covering just far enough over his eyes to keep the sun out. Rashid Salah had always considered the land beautiful, filled with colors city dwellers did not notice. He thought about the strange illusions of light and heat.

A generation had passed since Rashid first stood at this exact place, herding his goats and stumbling across the discovery that made him a famous man. Fame was for people who read newspapers and made speeches. His son had become such a man.

Then again, the experts with fancy titles came to *him*, an old desert rat, hanging on his every word, pushing to get his attention, and wanting the secret he would never tell. Rashid chuckled and puffed on his cigarette; the wind immediately swept the smoke toward the sparkling blue water. The Camels were strong and he liked the tobacco's bite. Even though Rashid had not seen it for five decades, what waited in the cave was no phantom of eye or mind.

The story of the Arab shepherd boy was in a thousand guidebooks and the journals of learned men. A footnote to history, perhaps, but still an instrumental part of the revolutionary breakthrough in scholarship. Yes, Rashid was a renowned man of sorts. So what? Was not life little more than an illusion, a mirage in time?

For a moment Rashid Salah closed his eyes and tried to hear the tinkling of little bells around the goats' necks, hoping the carefree life might return when he opened his eyes. But the kids had vanished long ago, stew for a night's supper around a campfire, the single life replaced by a wife, five children, and the end of frivolity. He had been young and hopeful then; now he was wrinkled and sunbaked like bread left in the oven too long. He rubbed his bloodshot, tired eyes and watched the gray van off in the distance, speeding down the highway toward him. Rashid had waited decades for this rendezvous. The time was now.

When Rashid had found the Dead Sea Scrolls in 1947, he could not have conceived in his wildest dreams that seven ancient pottery jars with four hundred worn and tattered manuscripts could be worth a king's ransom. In the late '40s, Jerusalem was still a backwater city with a mixed population of some hundred thousand Jews and sixty thousand Arabs. Tufeili, the dealer in antiquities, had even seemed foolish enough to pay something for the clay vessels. After all these years, Rashid still flinched. A fortune had slipped through his fingers that afternoon. Tufeili had been so sly that as Rashid laid the ancient scrolls before him, the antiquities dealer did not even blink, even though his mind probably whirled like a cash register.

After the deal was struck and a horde of archaeologists descended on the area, Tufeili took on a condescending attitude about the transaction and saw no reason to share his new wealth. "Business is business," he said with a shrug and left Rashid looking like a fool, standing among the staring tourists.

The Jewish lawyer Yitzhak Rosenberg had believed Rashid could successfully sue Tufeili and recover considerable monies. Yet the lawyer's promises had not materialized—not that Rosenberg had not tried hard enough. Their deal was straight-forward. Yitzhak got part of the settlement or nothing. Rashid could envision the bald-headed lawyer with the thin black mustache and gold-rimmed glasses leaning over his desk, poring over documents, grumbling to himself. Rashid Salah came not only to respect Yitzhak but considered him a true friend. Their children even played together. The fact that the Salahs were Arabs meant nothing to Rosenberg, and he had not charged Rashid a shekel for all of his time.

Once Rashid knew the courts would not grant justice, he vowed to wait a lifetime if necessary before he played his one last card. The secret belonged to Musa.

The old man sat down on one of the heavy wooden posts bordering the Qumran community site and looked around the tourist mecca. Fifty years ago nothing was there, just sand and rocks. Then the excavations changed everything. The National Parks Authority kept the ancient Essene Monastery in excellent condition. Perhaps, this place was truly what the ancient ones once called the City of Salt.

Rashid could see the van approaching, far off on the horizon. He thought about Professor Yadin and his army of experts taking the place apart while Rashid and his goats silently watched their frenzied quest. He smiled and swung his worn ivory worry beads back and forth in his left hand.

The large gray vehicle would turn off the highway in a few moments and wind its way up to the tourist parking lot. Rashid was ready.

He watched the van pull up to the end of the lot and a young man wave out the window. From a distance, Musa looked like any son of the desert. One would not suspect him to be a graduate of some far-off place called Cornell University, the only member of the family to ascend to such lofty heights. Rashid still had difficulty seeing him as more than his boy, a Bedouin child; but Western clothes made their own statement. Still, at times, Dr. Musa Salah seemed to be trying to come home again. If he would only find a nice Muslim girl to marry and settle down, everything would be perfect.

"*Abuya!* I hope you've not waited long." Musa slammed the door behind him. Like Rashid, the thirty-eight-year-old son was short and on the slight side, but his black eyes burned with the same intensity that marked the Salah family. "Sorry for the delay."

"No problem." Rashid shook his head. Musa wore one of those strange shirts he called plaids. Khaki pants made him look like the Jewish merchant who ran the Qumran souvenir shop.

"Soldiers set up a checkpoint at the Yericho turnoff," Musa shouted. He opened the rear door and pulled a small spade out of the back. "I got held up." He hurried out of the parking lot, pushing his black hair away from his forehead.

"Time means nothing in the desert." The old man stood up and adjusted his leather thong sandals. "After fifty years, another hour is unimportant." He kept swinging the old beads around his hand.

"How's the rest of the family in Arad?" Musa threw his arm around his father's shoulder and hugged the old man. "I brought the shovel, like you said." He kissed him on both cheeks.

Rashid shrugged. "Your mother blames me for forcing us into city life." He immediately started walking away from the excavations toward the ravine and the caves. "I am the villain . . . always."

Musa laughed. "Arad is barely a village. You have to go all the way to Beersheba to even get close to anything slightly resembling a town. There's no city in sight."

"When you've lived your entire life in a tent, Arad feels crowded."

"Give Mother my love and tell her to watch out for the traffic." Musa laughed again.

"Had to get the family back closer to our people." Rashid lowered his voice. "Anything could happen. Don't trust any of those politicians. Particularly the detestable Zionists in the Knesset. No telling what the settlers or their soldiers might do some dark night out there in the desert."

Musa's countenance fell. "Yes," he said factually. "We must be alert. You used wisdom in protecting the family." He stopped and shielded his eyes. "Why are we here of all places?" He looked toward the caves where Rashid had made his discovery and rested on the shovel.

"You know the area?" Rashid sounded sincere.

"Come on, *abuya*. When I completed my graduate degree in archaeology at Bar-Ilan University, we studied this region so thoroughly, I know it like the back of my hand."

"You *know* the area?"

Musa frowned. "How many times have I stood at this very spot with *you*?"

"So, *you* know the area?"

Rashid watched his son study his face, trying to read the wrinkles as a fortune-teller deciphers tea leaves.

"You are trying to tell me something?" Musa concluded.

Rashid flashed a toothless grin. "I thought *I* was merely asking a question."

Musa rolled his eyes. "Yes, Father. Out here you are still the teacher and I the student. But you know I sat under Professor Yadin and listened to the scholar's endless tales of his finding the papyri written by the messianic fanatic Bar Kochba *right out there*. How can I not know this site?"

"Then you know where I found the first scrolls?"

"Everyone does."

"Why don't you show me the place? I'm getting old."

Musa looked hard at his father and shrugged in exasperation. "I'm not sure what game we're playing, but yes, I'll show you." He lunged forward with large strides, swinging the shovel. "Follow me."

Rashid hung back, grinning as he walked in the footprints left by his son's large hiking boots. He could see no reason for the strange thick shoes. They did not work any better than his simple sandals.

"Of course, over there is Cave Q1." Musa's tone took on a professorial elevation with more than a hint of superiority. "The famous Copper Scroll was located inside." He lectured as if explaining elementary archaeology to a freshman class. "Cave Q11 was the location of the famous Temple Scrolls. The Cave of the Column also proved highly significant."

"You certainly seem to know all about this place." Rashid sounded indifferent but kept grinning sardonically.

"To fully appreciate your discoveries, Father, we must remember what was found in Cave Q3." Musa picked up the pace. "But Cave Q1 is where everything began. You were throwing rocks at your goats grazing in the flat, and a pebble glanced off a boulder and flew into the cave. You heard the jar break."

"You are certain of such a thing?" Rashid flipped the final

piece of his cigarette into a ravine. "Perhaps you can show me exactly where I was standing in 1947."

Musa scratched his head and looked askance at his father. "Sure we're not playing a guessing game?"

"I am simply listening to the great professor refresh my fading memory." The old man shrugged. "By the way, I never threw rocks at my goats. I wouldn't do anything that might possibly hurt them. Maybe you can set the record straight, Doctor. I was bored and simply throwing at caves for target practice." He flashed his toothless smile. "I was trying to hit the entrance. I didn't miss."

Musa squinted and cocked his head quizzically. "That's a new wrinkle to an old story."

"Lead the way." Rashid Salah pointed up the hill.

"About seventy-five feet ahead is the entrance to Cave Q11." Musa started walking again. "The Temple Scroll found there was the document Professor Yadin bought. In a sense, Cave Q11 is what turned this locale into an international sensation."

"You are wrong," Rashid grunted. "They reported everything wrong. Cave Q1 and Q11 are actually the same place."

Musa stopped and turned slowly toward the old man. "The Dominican fathers from the École Biblique in Jerusalem documented the locations of these finds."

"And they're the same people who declared Qumran was the beginning of Christianity," the father shot back. "See. I am not so ignorant as I appear about these things. The Dominicans hung a crucifix on the Qumran Tower to perform their daily masses, did they not? And today everyone knows their claims were nonsense."

Musa's mouth dropped. "Certainly. They were incorrect in their original conjectures."

"Maybe the good Dominicans claimed whatever best served their cause, even if it was not based on facts."

Musa turned and stared. "You never told anyone these things? Why?"

"Maybe I was saving the best secret."

"And what might that be?"

"Show me again the cave where it all began."

Musa started back up the hill. "We'll wind up the slope on our way back to Q1. I'll have to give considerable thought to what you've said about the Q1 and Q11." He rubbed the back of his neck. "You *actually* observed what you've claimed?"

"Over here, son. You're going the wrong way."

"What?" Musa's voice went up an octave. "You're not going to tell me . . ."

"I tell *you*, the expert?" Rashid feigned surprise. "Of course not, but you are walking in the wrong direction." The old man pointed up to the eastern side of a cliff about twelve feet away with a small opening on the side. "I would suggest we try up there."

Musa shielded his eyes and stared up the steep incline. "That's just a hole in the cliff. No one ever worked that little niche."

"Indeed!" The father took the lead, quickly climbing over a pile of debris and bounding up the steep incline. "Let's see if we can still slip inside." He pointed at the entrance.

Musa frowned. He laid the shovel down before he worked his way in and dropped down into the hole.

Rashid kicked the shovel through and quickly followed his son inside. "What do you see?" He squatted down, looking around the dim chamber about seven or eight feet wide and four feet high. "Take a good look."

"Well"—Musa hesitated—"I suppose this is more like a sink-hole, a grotto, than a cave. No one would consider it a storage area."

"The small entrance certainly made a more challenging target than one of the large caves. Don't you think?" Rashid pulled another cigarette from a crumpled package of Camels. "Not much skill required to throw rocks in a mammoth hole." He crawled in ahead of his son.

Musa stared at his father. "I don't think I understand, but I'm getting the strange feeling I know what you're telling me."

"The big shots never gave this place a second glance. 'Not significant enough,' they said. Didn't have the good sense to ask me." He puffed and the strong-smelling smoke curled up and hovered at the top of the cave. "I never told them anything unless they specifically asked."

"Are you telling me this is the cave where you made the original find?" Musa's eyes widened. "*The* place where you found the Copper Scroll?"

Again the old man blew smoke at the ceiling and nodded his head. "It all began here. The only cave that they *never* explored." He swung his worry beads nervously around his hand.

Musa rocked back on his heels and landed in the sand and dust.

"Sure. My rock broke an urn, but that was only the start." Rashid pointed to two large rocks in the center of the chamber. "They are not so heavy as they appear. Probably limestone. The stones lift out." He crawled over to the two flat rocks leaning against each other and touched them respectfully. "I suppose your old father is something of an archaeologist himself." He chuckled, the cigarette dangling from his lips. "I found the Copper Scroll under there."

Musa shook his head and ran his hand nervously through his hair. "You are telling me that all of these years you let the world believe a myth, a wild story?" He blew a mouthful of air toward the ground. "Why would you do a thing like that?"

Rashid shrugged. "*They* could believe whatever made them happy. I said nothing."

His eyes narrowed. "They cheated our family once. I wouldn't give them a second chance." He wiggled the rocks. "I found the first jars under these very stones." He slowly worked the first one out and slung it to one side of the cave. "Over the years I've thought about this cave a thousand times. I concluded it was originally deeper when they stored the jars in here. Part of the ceiling must have gotten soft with time and dropped several feet of dirt. That's how everything got covered up." He started pulling at the second rock.

Musa kept shaking his head in disbelief. "Why did you procrastinate all this time?"

"Such big words!" Rashid Salah threw up his hands. "I thought I'd wait them out and eventually make a private deal with someone like Yadin . . . or maybe through my friend Rosenberg. But there was so much activity going on around here, I didn't dare come back to the cave, lest someone see me. Remember? Time means nothing in the desert."

"Father!" Musa held up his hands in supplication. "You've waited five decades!"

The old man pulled the other rock up and dropped it to one side. He leaned over and peered into the black hole. "See. No one ever looked." He laughed and took one last drag off the cigarette before flipping it out the entrance. He blew smoke in the same direction.

The Bedouin rocked back on his haunches and crossed his arms over his chest. "You know, really . . . your uncle Hassan is responsible for all of this."

"Hassan Salah? In New York City?"

Rashid nodded his head solemnly. "Hassan left as a teenager and wound up in America. For decades we thought he'd disappeared . . . probably died. Then the money started coming back. We couldn't believe it! Poor old dead Hassan turned out to be a rich man." He laughed again. "But he never forgot his family."

"I will always be grateful that he paid my way to go to America and attend college."

"That's what changed my plans." Rashid sighed. "I decided I would wait until you returned." He threw his hands into the air again. "Unbelievable! Then you went to Bar-Ilan to study archaeology! I was dumbfounded."

"Hassan was angry enough," Musa admitted. "He'd planned on my becoming a rich engineer. If nothing else, I should work in his import business. I don't think he's ever forgiven me."

"But when I heard, I rejoiced and cried out, *'Hamdila!'* I thanked Allah that in his gracious will he led you down the right path to fulfill my plans."

"How?"

"You are now completely equipped to reap our revenge." Rashid pointed to the opening in the earth. "This hole is not empty. No mirages and illusions here. Like the Copper Scroll, a treasure has waited for us for centuries. My son, the prize is my secret."

2

Saturday, August 1
Qumran Caves

Musa stared at the black hole, shaking his head and not knowing how to respond. His father had always been a silent man but when he spoke, his words were like iron and as reliable as the sun rising in the east. The desert made one thoughtful; Bedouins were masters of appearing simple while concealing shrewd minds. Musa knew his father was no exception. Something big was hidden at the bottom of the pit.

Musa would not have believed this scenario if he had read it in a novel. Unimaginable. For all these years his father had known one of the most important secrets in modern archaeology and said nothing . . . and he knew exactly what he was doing.

Musa scooted forward and peered down into the dim cavity. Sure. They thought him stupid. Everyone thought Bedouins were backward and illiterate. Fools.

A shot of sunlight poured abruptly into the cave like a giant spotlight highlighting the first act of a play. The father crawled to center stage. "The sun is starting to set." He wiped the perspiration from his brow and looked into the hole. "The original scroll was found here, down in that pit." Rashid pointed to the bottom, four feet below.

Musa cautiously reached into the opening.

"Looks like only yesterday you lifted the first clay vessels out. The outline of the urn against the sand is as pristine as if you were here twenty-four hours ago."

"Like time, change comes slowly in the desert."

Musa looked at his father again. He had the same deceptive, nonplussed look Musa grew up with. What was going on behind that stone face? There was more than he'd said so far.

"Pulling up those bulky three-foot-long urns wasn't easy, but I wouldn't let anything break." Rashid jutted his chin out defiantly. "Took time digging them loose." He swung his worry beads vigorously up and down.

"And something else is down there?"

"I left a little surprise for you to uncover." The father nodded toward the hole.

"Yes?" Musa watched the old man's eyes.

"Americans keep samples of the desert in the backyard for their children to play in. I thought it would be a graduation present if I gave you the most interesting sandbox in the world." He raised his eyebrows. "Your turn."

This time I wait, Musa thought. He's enjoying this cat and mouse chase way too much. He folded his arms across his chest and attempted the most blank stare possible under the circumstances. The smell of tobacco hung in the hot stale air of the cave and made him uncomfortable, but out of respect for his father, Musa said nothing.

The old man sighed and smiled with a look of self-satisfaction. "The hole is not empty," he finally said. "See what you can find." He offered the spade.

Musa dropped on his chest and looked down into the hole,

which was about two and a half feet in diameter and possibly four feet deep. Another scroll in there somewhere? *Allahu akbar!* He reached for the shovel and started scooping the sand back to enlarge the opening.

"I will help," Rashid said resolutely and began pushing the sand back toward the edge of the cave. Dust filled the air.

Musa moved deliberately, with the skillful touch of a trained archaeologist. In a few minutes the mouth of the hole doubled in diameter. He stopped and looked above them. "The sun will be down soon. We don't have much daylight left."

The old man reached beneath his robe and produced two flashlights. "I thought of that possibility, but I don't think we will need much more time." He pointed to the back side of the hole. "Try there."

Musa felt around the edge. "Can't believe it. Feels like the outside edge of a clay vessel."

"It is," Rashid said factually. "Much smaller in size than the others. Probably stored behind them for additional protection."

Musa grabbed the shovel and attacked the back side of the top of the hole. Sand flew in every direction; porous soil crumbled like a disintegrating sand dune. After digging down a foot, he stopped and slipped his legs into the hole. Using his hands alone, Musa carefully dug the sand out around the edge until the complete shape of an urn emerged. Sweat rolled down his face.

"This thing is less than half the size of the jugs the other scrolls were found in." He tilted the jar back out of its place. "Much lighter, too." Musa carefully worked the vessel out of the sand and hoisted it up to the surface.

Rashid slung the worry beads aside and quickly took the urn from his son's hands, placing the clay vessel firmly in the sand. "Musa, you know better than I what will happen if the authorities catch us in an unauthorized dig." He inadvertently kicked the beads into the sand.

"They would confiscate the object immediately and we'd never see it again." Musa crawled out of the hole.

"That's why we came at dusk," the old man explained. "We must leave only under the cover of darkness."

Musa nodded but stared at the jug. He felt his palms perspiring, his heart pounding. "Never, never could I have believed such a discovery possible."

The old Bedouin chuckled. "The father started everything; the son finished it. Don't you think we should look inside at what the ancients left for us?"

Musa ran his hand slowly, cautiously over the smooth surface. "Look outside again," he said without looking up. "Make certain no one is around."

"Hmm," Rashid grunted and stuck his head out the entrance. "Just us. No cars."

Musa Salah carefully maneuvered the clay lid back and forth. It easily came loose. He tenderly laid the top to one side on the sand. "Shine your flashlight inside. I don't want to stick my hand in until I know what's in there. Wouldn't want to wake any sleeping scorpions."

Quickly the old man flicked the light on. "Looks like a small scroll at the bottom," he mused. "Something like the other one, the Copper Scroll."

"I can't believe my eyes," Musa exclaimed. "I believe it's gold."

"Gold!" Rashid's voice danced in glee. "I knew a treasure waited down here!"

"I'm going to tilt the urn enough to let the object slide out." Musa rested the bottom against his leg and slowly lowered the side, listening for the metal scroll to inch forward. "I can reach it now." He nodded toward the sand. "Spread out your *keffiyeh* so we can protect the surface from scratching."

Rashid quickly unfolded the burnoose in a large square. Even at his age, most of his hair was still black. He carefully patted the ground smooth under the black-and-white checkered cloth.

"Here it comes." Musa gingerly lifted the long, narrow gold scroll out of the jar and laid it gently on the headdress. "I can't believe my eyes." He set the urn back upright. A clunking noise echoed from the bottom.

"What's that?" The father flipped on the flashlight again.

"Something else is in there." Musa tilted the jug down.

"Look!" Rashid pointed. "There's a coin of some sort."

Musa stuck his hand in the urn and carefully pulled out a small medallion. "How strange." To avoid damaging it further, he used the edge of his shirt to hold the object. "The thing is copper."

"I can't make sense of it," Rashid mused, peering over his son's shoulder.

Musa held the two-inch disk closer to his eyes. "The coin can be deciphered, but it's going to take some time."

"The object must have been very important to be left in there."

"Yes, Father." Musa turned the medallion over to inspect the reverse. "And it must have some important connection with the scroll." He pulled a handkerchief from his pocket and wrapped the coin carefully before slipping it in his shirt pocket. "I'll have to get more information before I work on this piece."

Rashid dropped down on all fours and stared at the scroll, his face only inches from the metal roll. "A gold scroll must be much more important than the copper."

"You have no idea." Musa held the scroll carefully. "Around 1680 a book was published in the Netherlands containing twelve *mishnayot*, the records of what happened to many of the items in the Temple when Jerusalem fell because of Nebuchadnezzar's attack. Objects like the Ark, the Menorah, and the curtain separating the Holy of Holies were all hidden. Understand?"

"Of course." The old man nodded his head emphatically.

"The book spoke of the existence of a copper scroll, two marble tablets, an ibex scroll, and one more thing . . . a gold scroll."

Rashid rubbed his chin and narrowed his eyes.

"The marble tablets were found in the basement of a museum in Beirut, Lebanon, in 1952. You know about the Copper Scroll. The ibex scroll also turned up out here and, of course, was what Yigal Yadin published and called the Temple Scroll. The only thing still missing is the gold scroll, and we may be looking at it. There is no way to calculate how big this find is, Father."

The Bedouin only reached out to run his fingers gently down the length of the metal. He rocked back and forth almost as if doing obeisance to the scroll.

"You hit the clay pot, and I burst you with my stick!"

"In America they would say we've hit the jackpot." Musa pulled several small orange sticks from his pocket. One had a pointed edge, the other was shaped like a paddle. "I've got to determine how substantial this thing is." He gently stuck the flat stick between the edges of the scroll and probed. "Excellent. The gold is thick enough to have good tensile strength."

"Tensile?"

"Means the scroll isn't brittle," Musa explained. "We can eventually unroll the whole thing without danger of destroying it."

"Excellent!" The old man beamed. "I knew you'd know what to do."

The archaeologist slid down on his side. "I wonder if I can

open it just enough to get a peek inside." He ran the stick down the length of the edge and gently pulled up. "Ah, I think I can get a look." He got closer to the surface.

"You always had excellent eyes." The old man sat back up. "And an even more exceptional memory."

Musa read, mumbling to himself, his head bobbing back and forth scrutinizing the scroll. "Absolutely astonishing," he spoke more to himself. "I can see both Hebrew and Greek." Musa pulled the side back slightly to see farther inside. "This thing also has Egyptian hieroglyphics . . . and ancient Akkadian characters. I've never heard of anything like this one . . . except the Rosetta stone."

"What do you make of it?" The old man hovered above his son.

"The gold . . . the many languages . . . would have to be extremely significant." He stopped abruptly and looked even more closely. "Also Sumerian, I think. Five languages in all! Unbelievable!"

"No one ever had a memory like yours, son. Everything stayed in your head. Like grain in a silo, you stored whatever your eyes and ears poured in."

"Got to open the scroll a tad more," Musa spoke to himself, ignoring his father's ramblings.

"You heard a language, you never forgot it," the old man pontificated. "I'm sure that's why your uncle Hassan helped with college expenses. Of course, I never read much, but you read enough for our entire family. Allah blessed me with an amazing son, reading before you ran."

"Father," Musa cut him off, "I can make out *Urusalim*, the term used in the Egyptian execration texts. Probably material from the twentieth or nineteenth centuries BCE . . . Staggering."

"Ur-usa-lim?" Rashid frowned.

"Jerusalem," Mesa retorted. "This particular spelling is the exact form of the word the first time the city was ever mentioned anywhere."

"I don't understand."

"The word *Urusalim* reflects a primitive context we can corroborate with the most ancient Egyptian documents. The place, Urusalim, or Jerusalem, comes into historical view because a wandering tribal herdsman came out of the Syrian desert to this hill town. His arrival turned out to be a time of great meaning. The inhabitants greeted him with offerings of corn and wine. Even the Egyptians took note."

"Who was this man?"

"His name was Abram or Abraham."

Rashid's eyes narrowed. "You don't mean our Father Abraham?"

"Exactly."

"O-o-o-o-h," the old man gasped.

Musa nodded his head several times. "Yes, Father. We are on to something that far exceeds even your wildest expectations."

The Bedouin leaped to his feet and looked out the entrance again. "We are still safe," he concluded. "No people, no traffic anywhere."

"I'm going to try to make a little sense out of the hieroglyphics. Ancient Egyptian was one of my strong suits." Musa pulled a small lighted magnifying glass from a leather pouch hanging on his belt and leaned closer to the gold sheet.

"Before you were born, it was foretold you would have eyes like an eagle and a tongue as clever as a fox. But no fox understood languages like you." He shrugged and pulled out another cigarette and lit it while Musa pored over the scroll.

For several minutes Musa said nothing. As each of the strange shapes yielded meaning, he felt tension building within. His heart beat faster and his palms perspired. Musa took a deep breath and tried to steady his shaking hands.

"Father," he whispered, "I want you to listen carefully to what I'm going to read." He cleared his throat. "The scroll begins, 'The Inheritance of Melchizedek to the Son of Abraham.'" Musa looked at his father. *This scroll is the title deed to the city of Jerusalem.*"

Rashid shook his head uncomprehendingly. He puffed several times on the cigarette. "I don't understand."

"Every archaeologist dreams of finding something spectacular like the Ark of the Covenant, maybe the metal serpent Moses made during the desert wandering period. These objects are the stuff of legend, even fantasy." Musa wrung his hands. "In addition to those two great objects, there has always been a third one everyone yearned to find. The legendary scroll called the Donation of Melchizedek."

The old man pursed his lips and rolled his eyes. "I see." He clearly didn't.

"The scroll was rumored to have been hidden in the archives of the First Temple. The Jews were always nervous about its contents, but its existence was confirmed in the Tel el-Amarna find." Musa reached over and put his hand on the old man's shoulder. "If this is authentic, I have in my hands the eternal title deed to the city of Jerusalem . . . the greatest discovery of the twentieth century . . . maybe ever. This day will be recorded in stone monuments across the Arab world. Songs will be sung, prayers chanted to Allah because of this find."

Rashid took a long drag from his cigarette and thought on what he had heard. Musa watched the old man stare at the scroll in silence. Still trying to absorb the shock of the inscription, Musa said nothing. Suddenly the old man stamped up and down on the sand. He chanted, "Ishmael! Ishmael!"

Finally, the old man put the cigarette out in the sand. "Exactly who is this 'son of Abraham'?"

Musa smiled. "You will always be a shrewd son of the desert.

That, my father, may prove to be the question of the centuries. Who do you say is *the* son of Abraham?"

"Ishmael!" Rashid snapped.

"And the Jews would say Isaac," Musa fired back.

"Maybe this deed will tell us once and for all." The Bedouin's voice was dry, cynical.

"Exactly, Father. Possibly the Jews never said much about it publicly lest the world discover the true preeminence of Ishmael, the firstborn."

"Yes!" The old man clapped his hands. "This document could seal the fate of the Zionists by proving the Arabs as the rightful owners of Jerusalem. The Arab League will ride the white horse of Rashid into the Holy City of Jerusalem once more. Allah will prevail!"

Musa grinned like an assassin closing in on his victim. "This scroll may prove to be far more than an archaeological find. We might just have given our people the political leverage to persuade the nations to line up with us. Jewish claims of biblical and historical rights to the city will be destroyed."

Rashid's eyes widened in awe. "My son would be remembered for all time as the greatest benefactor of our people." He fell into the sand with his face in his hands. "Allah be praised! Allah be blessed."

Musa closed the magnifying glass and stared at his discovery. The fading light of day cast one final beam across the scroll as the light dimmed.

"I hate the Jews," the old man said decisively. "Zionists pushed their way in here, and with the help of the Americans, chased our people away from their ancient heritage. How sweet it will be to see their heads hanging in shame, relinquishing claim to something that was never rightfully theirs," the old man exclaimed.

Musa carefully pushed the edge of the scroll shut and gently slipped the roll back into the urn. "You have given me a great gift, Father." He carefully set the vase upright. "And a staggering problem. We now have far more to fear than the Antiquities Authority."

"My son, you must be more prudent than I was." Rashid hoisted himself out of the cave and reached back to take the urn from Musa. "Yes, we must think long and carefully."

Musa eased through the opening and looked out over the Dead Sea. The setting summer sun cast a long bloodred reflection across the salty water. He looked down the shoreline toward Masada, towering over the terrain, and remembered the Jewish survivors making their last stand in 73 BCE, during the Roman War. "Would it not be the ultimate irony and justice of history, if the Jews met their final defeat out here in this same wilderness?" He threw back his head and declared, "*Allahu akbar!* God is great!"

3

Tuesday, September 1
Tel Aviv

Monday's El Al 06 from Geneva, Switzerland, slowed to a final halt at Ben-Gurion Airport in the outskirts of Lod, just beyond Tel Aviv. Shuttle buses immediately pulled alongside the 757's sleek white-and-blue hull to take passengers to the great arrival hall. Excited tourists chattered and gathered their belongings while a small stout man inched to the front of the plane as if he wanted to distance himself from them. The balding forty-five-year-old, dressed in an open-collared white shirt, seemed annoyed at the giddiness of the Christian tour groups. His simple black leather briefcase clearly separated the round-faced Israeli from the Americans with badges identifying them as members of a tour group. Because he was far too plain for the Baptists from Cincinnati to notice, no one seemed to mind his cutting to the head of the line.

Daniel Levy glared at the pilgrims as if they were a grudgingly welcomed intrusion in his land. The plain monocolored shirt, pants, and no-nonsense attitude marked him as a typical *sabra*, a native-born Israeli, although he might equally have passed for a baker from Krakow or a lawyer from Warsaw. When the airplane door opened, he hurried down the metal steps and positioned himself in the front of the bus terminal so that he would be among the first off. The arrival of September had not brought relief from the summer heat. Any hope the air-conditioning offered was quickly dissipated by old ladies straggling up the bus steps with the rest of Ophir Tours. Levy mopped the perspiration from the top of his forehead and shook his head.

While not a sentimentalist, Levy still got a lump in his throat when he approached the glass doors where thousands of Jews made *aliya*, returning to their homeland. His last name marked him as a descendant of the ancient tribe of Levi, the sacrifice makers and caretakers of the last Great Temple. Since all of that was two thousand years ago and Levy was not a religious man, he did not think on such things. Yet every time he walked through the arrival entrance, Daniel felt he knew what it must have been like to enter the Holy Land with Joshua. Even the inane tourists could be tolerated under such moving circumstances.

The bus slowed to a stop; Levy was out in a second. He bounded up the stairs well ahead of the slower horde oozing out of the buses. An earlier passenger load had just cleared customs, and he could go immediately to the Diplomatic Immigration and Security desks.

Levy flashed a diplomatic passport, and the officer nodded him on without hesitation. He paused to put the passport back in his briefcase with the other six passports. The Canadian one identified him as Joseph Weiss; an American passport pictured him as Alexander Kline; but the German passport for Herr Dobbelmeister was Levy's favorite. He liked anything that had the potential to misuse Germans. The rest of the passports were throwaways, used only for a onetime ploy in an emergency, because they would not stand up to a thorough security check. Daniel Levy was anything but a plain man.

He stopped at the luggage conveyor belts even though Levy knew his haste had far outstripped the bag handler's capacities. Recent immigrants who could not get a job anywhere else were funneled into these baggage jobs. Their lack of motivation was legendary. Yet the wait gave him time to order his thoughts and take a quick, careful survey of who was going by.

Daniel had grown up with the habit of watching everyone suspiciously. In childhood he had picked up the tendency from his father, Ya'acov. The elder Levy graduated from Auschwitz, class of 1945. After the liberation of the camp, Ya'acov immigrated to Israel because he had no place else to go. Ya'acov was the sole survivor of his family; distrust burned in his soul. Daniel grew up watching his father watch people . . . suspecting everyone. Good preparation for his lifework.

The conveyor started. Service was improving. Daniel shifted his position so he could alternately watch the belt and the crowd. When the lone overnight bag came through, Levy grabbed it and was on his way through the customs exit. The diplomatic passport made answering questions unnecessary.

The usual mob of gawkers hovered outside: vendors, tourists, tour guides, relatives, and locals with nothing better to do than watch strangers. The smell of exhaust fumes, greasy food, and cigarette smoke hung in the sultry air. Reflecting that at least Joshua did not have to put up with *that* smell, Daniel Levy barged through the crowd.

An old Arab woman stumbled in front of him. Levy kept her from falling. "*Keef halik?*" he asked in perfect Arabic. "How are you?"

"*Shukran.* Thank you." She smiled and walked on.

Daniel understood the children of Ishmael, their ways, their disposition. He tended to like Arabs. Ya'acov Levy had settled in the village of Abu Ghosh, a few kilometers away from Jerusalem. Known as Kiryat Ye'arim, the Ark of the Covenant had rested there until King David brought the sacred box to Jerusalem. In the days when Ya'acov Levy first arrived, there was not much tension between Jews and the local Arabs, so Daniel had grown up speaking the local Arabic dialect.

A bank of pay telephones waited fifteen feet on the other side of the swarming horde. The area provided an open space where he could talk without being drowned out by the crowd. Levy always checked in immediately after he reentered the country. While it was possible to receive messages through a secret radio transmitter, the transmission came at fixed times and he usually picked up the messages through a receiver hidden in his home. He did not want to wait for the hour-long trip to his apartment, so Levy kept a mobile phone with a secured number for such purposes. At the dial tone, he punched in the top secret number.

"*Shalom,*" a woman's voiced answered.

"*Alayich shalom.* Daniel L. here." He spoke so low he almost breathed the information into the phone. "I'm back in the country and signing in with the office."

No Mossad officer ever used the official name. Israel's top secret intelligence organization was simply referred to as "the office." Only a top-ranking *sochen,* or case officer, had the number of the agency's chief. The vast worldwide spy network was actually maintained through a unique system of *ozrim,* Jewish volunteers with fierce loyalty to the state of Israel even though they were citizens of other nations. Consequently, at most, there were only thirty-five case officers at any time. Levy considered himself to be in the top 2 percent of the group. The phone number supported his self-serving personal assessment.

"We've been expecting you," the woman responded. "Any problems coming through?"

"None."

"Agent G is waiting to speak with you. Just a moment." The phone was silent.

Levy shot a glance around the area. Nothing much going on. A young woman looked as if she were coming over to make a phone call. The petite blonde appeared to be around twenty-five. Levy liked what he saw. She was not paying any attention whatsoever to him. Unfortunate.

"G here," a man's gravelly voice answered.

"Daniel L. back in town, sir." He could tell the girl was going to make a call. The closer she got, the better she looked. The woman glanced at him as if he weren't there. Being plain had its disadvantages but, then again, no one ever thought of him as a spy.

"How did it go in Geneva?"

Daniel watched the girl fumbling for coins in her purse. She had gorgeous blue eyes. "Getting a little crowded out here," he said slowly, "but you'll be pleased to know our major business deal was consummated."

The man cursed. "I wish you'd quit checking in when there are people in the area. Go to your car and call me on the special frequency. We've just checked out the system. You can say anything you want. I'll be waiting."

"Yes, sir." Levy sounded as if he'd just saluted. He hung up and studied the girl for a moment. He liked blondes, but G couldn't be kept waiting, so he refrained from speaking to her.

Five minutes later Levy found his car in the parking garage. He quickly drove out of the airport parking area and on to the road that led away from Lod and eventually ran into the main highway to Jerusalem. He chuckled when he thought about the agency chief's condescending manner. G did not intimidate him with his brusque tone and demanding demeanor. He had known him since army days. Probably no more than a dozen people knew that the head of the intelligence agency was actually Avraham Halevy. The simple designation "G" was what everyone got. Levy would never have used any other name even though he and Halevy once hobnobbed socially. The first-name business ended when the prime minister appointed Halevy to head the Mossad. Daniel dialed in the special number.

"Continue with the report," G answered without ceremony.

"We now have Abdul Al-Amid working for us as a double agent. He took the money."

"Excellent!" Halevy nearly shouted over the phone. "Good work! How'd you do it?"

Levy chuckled again. "Some of our people tailed him for about four months, until we had every detail of his relationship with his wife and the mistress that he's been keeping in the south of Geneva. A little French fireball that puts sparkles in his eyes. We established the fact that his wife had no idea the woman existed."

"Did the information we sent on his financial losses in oil investments help?" Halevy's enthusiasm died quickly, and he returned to his ticker-tape voice.

Levy watched the cars speeding toward him. The road's incline was obviously increasing, and the pine forests were ahead. "Your data was the clincher. When I knew we had him in economic vise grips, our people left a few tip-offs about the girlfriend with his wife to increase the pressure on our buddy Abdul. He was already sweating it when I played our top card."

"And that was?" Halevy sounded like a computerized voice.

By the side of the road Daniel noticed the old hull of a troop carrier destroyed in the War of Independence. The casualty had been turned into a war memorial. "I'm the only one who knew the mistress was actually our plant. The woman was Jewish, acting as a *sochenet*. She started making increasing financial demands for support as well as spying for me. Al-Amid had no idea what hit him, but he was very clear that the world had fallen on his head. When I offered him money to work for us, our friend Abdul didn't have much of a choice. He grabbed the bait."

"The fact you speak flawless Arabic is always significant in these cases." G clipped his words as if he were typing them on a computer. "He assumed you were of Arab descent."

"I think so." Levy negotiated a curve as the increasingly winding road wrapped around the mountainside. "The big breakthrough came just before I left. Al-Amid passed information that a major new terrorist plot is unfolding. We're going to get our money's worth."

"Highly significant. Fits what's coming in from Syria. When's your next contact?"

"Al-Amid has been reassigned to Washington, and he's ready to run out of Geneva. I will need to contact him in America in a month or so. I am to identify myself as a cousin from Syria."

"I am very pleased." Again Halevy was suddenly uncharacteristically enthusiastic. "You've done extremely well, Danny. We've bagged another desert rat. Badly needed a black agent at that level. Got plenty of whites with brains. The Arabs are always no-brainers."

Levy rolled his eyes at the slur. Mossad officers generally had a low estimate of all the sons of Ishmael. When Arabs became double agents, they were always called blacks in contrast to all other compromised informants, who were known as whites. Daniel had a much higher opinion of Arabs than Halevy did.

"All I have to do is clock in with Al-Amid as his cousin from Syria."

"Okay, Daniel, I want you to go home and sit tight while the rest of the pieces in the puzzle come together. We could give you a new assignment, but I don't want you flying around the world when we may need you at a moment's notice. I believe this thing will open up faster than we might expect. Can't tell about these operations."

"Yes," Levy answered thoughtfully. "We're on to a big operation that is not predictable." He could see the little village houses of Abu Ghosh down in the valley. Jersualem was not far ahead. "Whole thing's a stick of dynamite."

"I want you to take a little mini-vacation, Danny. Put your feet up and wait for me to call you. Read a book, some technical manuals. Stay around town and keep us informed on where we can find you quickly."

"I'll make sure the office knows where I am at all times."

"Good. Good." Halevy returned to his automaton sound. "I'll be back in touch." The phone clicked off.

As Daniel pulled into the outlying district, he felt as if he had truly gone up the 2,400 feet from the coastal plain to the Holy City. To Levy's right, a new large white stone-block wall rose up a terraced hill, forming a retainer for the expansion of the city's main cemetery.

Traffic was crowded as usual but, then again, Jerusalem's population of nearly 500,000 was continually growing. The old roads once fit sheepherders and camels. No one expected the world to move in. Even the improved four lanes were not made for endless lines of Egged buses and irate taxi drivers fighting for space with commuters. Ignoring the snares, he was soon on his way down Herzl Boulevard toward his apartment. Ten minutes later Levy found the back street lined with conventional apartments and duplexes.

His apartment, nestled among trees in the Kiryat Moshe tract just off Herzl Boulevard, was quite plain. Quickly constructed three decades earlier to accommodate immigrants, each unit in the development looked essentially the same. The area was not far from an industrial zone and the Post Office Authority building. Not an exclusive area.

4

Tuesday, September 1
Jerusalem, Kiryat Wolfson

Father north on Herzl Boulevard were more promising quarters for Jerusalem residents. The broad boulevard
wound around the edge of the Kiryat Ben-Gurion government
complex, skirting the Hebrew University, the prime minister's
office, and the Knesset until the street finally emptied into
Sderot Ben-Zvi. Apartments on the east side were considerably
more expensive.

David and Leah Rosenberg lived about half a mile away, on
the other side of the government compound, in the Kiryat
Wolfson neighborhood. Unlike Kiryat Moshe, it was not a plain
area.

A protective wall along the front of the Rosenbergs' two-story
white stone home hid shrubs, flowers, and pomegranate trees,
shielding the second-story windows from direct sunlight. The
final rays of the setting sun pierced the branches, casting long
shadows across the master bedroom.

David relaxed in a lounger, watching his wife finish dressing for the evening. Tuesday, September 1, was a special day of

celebration. Each year on this special night they dined at the Hassan Effendi across from Herod's Gate in the Old City. Leah liked the opulent furnishings and the mood of the posh restaurant. Of all their excellent Arab offerings, minuscule roast pigeon was her predictable choice. Since tonight was their fifteenth wedding anniversary, nothing would be spared.

Leah methodically put on her completing touches, fixing her tiny diamond earrings. Her jet-black hair sparkled with a purple cast against the flawless olive skin of her bare shoulders. Leah's dark almond-shaped eyes were large, mysterious, and when she was upset, fiercely penetrating. Her thin, perfectly shaped lips and finely chiseled nose were clearly Sephardic, but with a universal appeal. She did not look forty.

David almost chuckled aloud when he thought of how most men were so beguiled by Leah, they often failed to recognize they were dealing with a shrewd businesswoman . . . until the deal was done. A very competent amateur archaeologist as well as an attorney, she was indispensable to their law practice.

Like his father, Yitzhak, David helped clients struggle with government bureaucracy. After Yitzhak's death, the entire practice fell to the son, and soon David was well established as the man to see when haggling with the Antiquities Authority or trying to ship quarantined archaeological discoveries out of the country. Leah's extensive knowledge of the value of ancient objects was always the Rosenbergs' trump card. No one stayed more current on what was happening in the digs around the country and what was being sold to the museums than Leah.

"Leah, you are reaching perfection." David got up from the chair and checked his tie in the mirror. "Hate wearing these things," he groused. "Only put it on because it's our anniversary and you want me to."

Leah spun on her heels and kissed him quickly on the cheek. "Oh, you lucky man." She sighed. "The maître d' will swoon, envying you this evening." Leah winked and slightly adjusted his tie. "But, then again, am I not with the most handsome and intelligent lawyer in all of Israel?" She sauntered across the room and picked up her sequined purse. Leah wore her short black evening dress with the flair of a Parisian model.

"We *really* ought to do this more often." Leah raised an eyebrow. "We haven't decked out like this since we were in Rome last year. No one in Jerusalem ever dresses up much," she lamented. Leah whirled and struck a pose like a cover girl with one hand on her hip and a high heel extended. "I like a little class now and then."

"Class, you've got." David offered his hand. "After you, *ma chère.*"

The Rosenbergs took their usual route through the elegant Rehavia neighborhood and down Agron Street east toward the Old City. Passing Independence Park, they could see the new Mamilla Project rising ahead beyond King David Street and the massive ramparts abutting the Jaffa Gate. The black Mercedes turned left onto King Solomon Street and climbed to Paratroopers Road, zooming past the ancient yellowish gray walls of the Old City's New Gate.

"David, I ran across a fascinating report today." She looked at the halogen lights springing on around the walls of the Old City. "This afternoon one of the men at the Antiquities Authority was rather agitated. Someone has been carrying on an unauthorized dig out in the same cave region where the Dead Sea Scrolls were found. One of their employees found a new hole dug in one of the smaller caves. In the corner of the grotto, they discovered a worn set of worry beads the culprit must have accidentally dropped. Looks like a Bedouin was rooting around in there and found something."

September 1 was nothing more than any other Tuesday in Arad. Night settled over the quiet village like a blanket tucking in a sleepy child. The Salah family gathered around the supper table as they did every evening. Plain was too elaborate a word to describe the austerity of the Salah home, mirroring the stuccoed flat one-story dwellings of all of the Arad neighborhoods. Drabness made it impossible to estimate age. Perhaps the bungalows were all built last year, but they looked as if it were two hundred years ago. Little distinguished one house from the other.

The Salah abode was just another stop on a side street. Only the grapevine winding up and through a trellis over the front door set the house apart from its neighbors. Inside the four-room dwelling, a small fireplace dotted the far wall of the living room to help break the chill of a winter day or the desert night. Suha Salah cooked in the makeshift kitchen, a smaller room with pots dangling over an open fire. Two bedrooms completed the mud brown Bedouin home.

"My overly educated son hasn't outgrown his mother's cooking?" Suha chided her son, dishing out the remainder of the *felafel* on his plate and ladling the last of the *shurbit* in the soup bowl. "You still eat like a son of the desert?" The traditional long brown skirt embroidered with strips of soiled lace hung down to her sandals. Her matching bodice covered a baggy red blouse. As was expected of all good Muslim women, a long flowing white scarf covered Suha's head. "And what do you think of the *kufta*?"

Musa nodded approvingly. "The goat meat is excellent as always. My little mother is still the greatest cook in the world. Whether it's an open fire or an oven in a house, you excel at them all."

"I would prefer the campfire." Suha shot a hard look at her husband. "But we have no choice now. We must live like the big-city people."

Musa glanced knowingly at his father, who did not look up but kept eating. He smiled out of the corner of his mouth. "I am sure it is a comfort to my mother to be surrounded by so many friends."

"Hmmph." Suha tossed her head defiantly and marched off to the kitchen. "Sounds like your father."

Rashid winked at his son. "In the old days, a man was the unquestioned master of his house. Wives held their tongues. Today we simply try to survive women."

"As a matter of fact . . ." Musa lowered his voice and leaned closer to his father. "Survival is what I have on my mind this evening. Our treasure has been buried behind your house for a month. Time is not on our side. We must do something."

Rashid shrugged.

"Father, you know that if the Israeli Antiquities Authority ever gets a smell of this thing, they'll descend on us like a hawk swooping down on a rabbit. We can't go on sitting on this treasure."

"Why would they find out?" The old man stuck out his lip indifferently.

"Many reasons, *abuya*. Perhaps, the Israeli soldiers might raid our village after a skirmish with Hamas. Or an archaeologist could discover the hole we left in that cave." He threw his hands up in the air. "Perhaps some snoop in the village saw us digging the hole behind the house. People talk. Villagers gossip."

Rashid pulled out his crumpled cigarette pack and flipped out a slightly bent cigarette. "What is a little time?" He lit up.

"For you, nothing," Musa conceded. "For the rest of the world, much more."

The Bedouin rubbed the scrubby stubble of beard on his chin. "What do you suggest, my son?"

"Father, I have done some preliminary study on the ancient message, but I need help. The ancient languages are filled with complications. The scroll must be placed in a scholarly, scientific environment for research to go forward. Other people must observe my work and verify the finding. Understand?"

Rashid blew smoke toward the ceiling. "More or less." He shrugged.

"The scroll and the medallion must be moved to a place where there will be security." Musa leaned his chair back. "The objects would be best transported to Jerusalem."

"Finish your *felafel* and soup." Rashid pointed at Musa's plate. "You know how your mother is."

"*Abuya*, we are sitting on a political bombshell. Everyone in our family could end up in serious trouble."

Rashid rolled the cigarette across his lips to a space where a tooth had once stood. "You really think there is danger?"

"Trust me . . . as the Americans say."

The old man took a deep drag on the cigarette and filled the table with the stale smell of strong tobacco. "Yes. Of course, you are right. I've known all along this is so. I just don't like to think about such things." He pushed the wing of his *keffiyeh* back over his shoulder. The white scarf and black cord tilted on his head. "I knew in the beginning the seriousness of the matter, but I like the feeling of having a great treasure in my backyard. The world must come to Salah once again for answers. I just didn't want to deal with it this soon."

"Well, we must." Musa leaned over the table and scooped up the last of the *felafel*. "We have to face the issue immediately."

"Hmm," the Bedouin groaned. "You are right . . . as always."

"I've been thinking about where to go for help."

"Listen to me." Rashid pointed his finger in his son's face.

"Long ago I settled that matter. Remember Yitzhak Rosenberg? You played with his son, David."

"Of course."

"Everyone knows the Rosenbergs oppose the injustices heaped on our people. They're big in the Peace Now movement. They are Jews we can trust, and we owe the family more than a small favor. The old man treated me well."

"I don't know . . ."

"I do," Rashid insisted.

Musa nodded. "Actually, David Rosenberg is known in my circles. He has powerful contacts with important people and a reputation for fairness and evenhandedness."

"More important, you can trust him." The Bedouin blew smoke at his son. "Go to Jerusalem and find David Rosenberg. He will know how to protect our treasure."

5

Saturday, September 5
Jerusalem, Elisha Street

The fifth day of September brought an unexpected break in the summer heat. A shift in the winds aired out the city, and people seemed in better sorts. Maybe fall would be unusually early. No rock-throwing incidents marred commuting in and out of Jerusalem. Gaza Strip and West Bank communities did not seem to be particularly upset for the moment. All in all, everything pointed to a good day for the Rosenberg law firm.

Located on Elisha Street just off Shivtei Yisrael, not far from the Old City, David and Leah's business occupied the same building and quarters that had been in the family for sixty years. The stone front on the two-story office building had been added to a much older structure at around the turn of the century. Exterior signs came and went, but nothing much else changed except the tenants on the second floor. The export company had been up there for two decades.

The interior remained a strange mixture of 1940s fixtures, Yitzhak Rosenberg's original rolltop desk, an ancient steel safe, and two vintage desks from the '70s. Three recently added leather-covered chairs sat in the waiting area. The Rosenbergs did not keep a permanent employee but pulled in temporary help when the press of business was heavy. A secretary's desk and chair waited near the front window but were only used periodically. The wooden files and bookcases made antique collectors covet.

"When will they be here?" Leah asked from her desk.

"Huh?" David stirred.

"The Salahs." Leah sounded slightly irritated. "Who else?"

"Oh, yes. Well, any minute." He went back to the article in *Ha'aretz.*

Leah shook her head at David's remarkable powers of concentration. While his capacity to shut out everything annoyed her when Leah was trying to get his attention, she also admired David's faculty to absorb large amounts of knowledge and forget nothing. His ability to come up with creative, innovative approaches to legal problems always fascinated her.

"And you knew Musa Salah as a boy?" The question was only meant to heckle.

"Sure." He didn't look up.

"Bright boy?" Another innocent-sounding distraction.

"Very."

Leah studied her husband's face. When David's hair had begun turning slightly gray around the temples, she loved the effect that only troubled her husband. Although a mite vain, he *was* striking. Even though Rosenberg was a typical Ashkenazi name, probably German, both of their families were actually of Sephardic origin and naturally tended toward coal black hair, dark skin and eyes. Since the first day she had seen David, when he was no more than a gangly, awkward teenager, Leah thought him to be the most handsome boy in Jerusalem. Time had only reinforced her opinion.

Both of their families had immigrated early in the century

and were practically indigenous to the city by the time David and Leah were born. The Rosenbergs came from France with the early Zionists, who acquired land when the country was little more than desert and swamp. Yitzhak Rosenberg's father suffered greatly, trying to make stony soil grow something, anything. He determined his son would follow an easier path. Thus began the tradition of a Rosenberg law practice in Jerusalem.

"Did you know old man Salah very well?"

David finally glanced in her direction with a look that said plenty. "As I told you earlier, my father insisted I mix with Arab boys so I would know their people, but I didn't spend much time around Rashid Salah. *No*. I didn't have any idea of the importance of his find. *Yes*. Soccer was more fascinating than a bunch of old manuscripts." He raised an eyebrow and returned to the newspaper.

Leah grinned, satisfied she was winning her secret game. She looked down at the picture of her mother and father on the corner of the desk. The Shamir tribe came from Damascus in the '20s, planting her parents in one of the experimental kibbutzim in the Galilee. In those days parents and children were separated most of the week. Leah thought the effect on her father disastrous and vowed never to live with the dispassionate distance so natural to this emotionally shut-down man. By age six she was sure that whatever the future held, it would not be life with a husband who could shut her out as her father did everyone else.

"I just don't think you've told me everything about this case," Leah persisted. "You've left big blank spaces."

David folded the paper and dropped it in the trash can. "My, aren't we the detective today."

"I knew it! You never use that phrase unless you're hiding something!" She stood up. "Come clean with me, David." Leah marched across the room and sat down in the old chair in front of his desk. "You obviously wanted me here to evaluate something."

David grinned. He had beautiful teeth, a strong cleft chin. "I omitted a few things." He chuckled. "Partly because Musa Salah strongly emphasized this is a confidential meeting . . . and he's bringing the old man along. You'll get to meet the notorious Rashid Salah of Dead Sea Scroll fame."

"Anything else you conveniently forgot to mention?"

"Oh, I forgot to mention that I noticed my hair is getting rather thin on top, but why bring it up? Who needs fat hair?"

Leah smirked. "Bad, David. Comedians are out of work because of telling better jokes than that one."

"Then let me tell you something that is not a joke. Musa made an important discovery that he's keeping secret from the Antiquities Authority. This complication could turn our negotiations into a real cloak-and-dagger case."

Leah stared for several seconds. "David, you never cease to amaze me."

"Look." David pointed to the window. "It's been a long time, but I'm sure that's Rashid and Musa." He immediately jumped from his chair and rushed toward the door. "Yes, it must be! He is carrying a package under his arm."

Before the father and son were inside, David was pumping their hands and welcoming them. "*Ahlan! Ahlan wa sahlan!*" he greeted them in Arabic. "*Keef halak?*" he asked the old man.

Rashid kept flashing his almost toothless grin and nodding. Leah quickly joined the trio and David enthusiastically introduced her.

"See?" Rashid said to his son. "We are truly among friends."

"I trust so." Musa looked deeply into David's eyes. "It's been a long time." He thought for a moment and said again, "I trust so."

"Please come over and let us talk." David dragged the two leather chairs toward his desk. "Just like old times."

Musa laughed. "We did have fun as boys, didn't we? You could turn a side street into a playground in those days."

"Jerusalem was more like a big town," David said as he sat down behind his desk. "Things were simple then."

"And happier," Musa added.

"Ah, yes. Yes. Regrettably so." David smiled sadly.

"Can I get you some tea? Turkish coffee?" Leah offered. "Mineral water?"

The two Arabs nodded.

"You've discussed our problem with your wife?" Musa asked. Rashid sat at his side with his hands folded in his lap, appearing deceptively disconnected from the conversation. "She knows?"

"My wife and I have no secrets from each other." David smiled at Leah.

She raised an eyebrow as if to say, "At least not in the last five minutes."

"You will excuse me if I get right to the point," Musa began quickly. "We will make time for good conversation when we have these business matters out of the way." He looked at his father. The old man seemed lost in thought.

"We all know my father's role in the discovery of the Dead Sea Scrolls, but only recently have I learned that he did not disclose everything about those finds." Musa again looked at Rashid but got no response. The Bedouin slouched even farther back in the chair as if he might drop off in disinterested slumber. "For fifty years he's been hibernating, vegetating, and playing a joke of sorts on the world of scholarship."

Leah scooted to the edge of her chair. "What do you mean?"

"The original find was not in the cave that everyone assumes was Q1." Musa looked uncomfortable. "My father actually found the scrolls in a small obscure cave that no one ever fully investigated. We have now made a second find in the exact location."

"So that's what the people at the Antiquities Authority were upset about!" Leah exclaimed.

"What?" The old man bolted straight up in his chair. "What are you talking about?"

Musa stared at Leah in dumbfounded amazement.

"One of their people found a fresh hole in that area and discovered worry beads dropped in the sand. Even came up with cigarette butts they're checking for DNA traces. They thought—"

"Worry beads!" Musa reached for his father's arm.

Rashid swore in Arabic and smashed his fist into his palm. "A-h-h," he gasped under his breath. "N-o-o-o."

Leah could see color draining from Musa's face. "No one knows what actually happened," she tried to reassure the young man. "They don't know for sure if anything was removed."

Musa closed his eyes and rubbed his temples. "Just as I feared, even worse."

Rashid fumbled for a cigarette. "I couldn't find them," he mumbled. "Thought maybe they were left . . . somewhere."

Musa slowly turned toward Leah. "How is it that you should know all this inside information?" His eyes narrowed. "A very strange coincidence."

"My wife does not have a graduate degree in archaeology, as you do, Musa, but she is a recognized expert on antiquities." David turned uncomfortably in his chair. "Through the years Leah has cultivated important relationships within the Antiquities Authority. Her contacts constantly provide us with insider information."

"I see," Musa said slowly. "This whole thing is making me edgy, turning into my worst nightmare." Musa looked up at

David like a schoolboy searching for an excuse for being tardy. "Obviously we didn't come any too soon."

"The most important step is to make sure your find is secure," Leah said. "We have no reason to believe anyone has the slightest idea of your connection to the new dig. We simply must keep ahead of any possible inquiries."

Rashid nervously fumbled with his cigarette until he finally lit up. "All of these years I think about this thing and then do such a dumb thing."

Musa patted his father's arm. "It's okay. We all make mistakes. Look. I am also going to need assistance translating the scroll. I'm not good in some of the languages. Part of the message is in Akkadian, Sumerian—the oldest recorded language—and Egyptian hieroglyphics. Ancient Greek and Hebrew are not my strong suit. Everyone needs help occasionally."

David laughed. "Musa, have you ever come to the right place! Leah is excellent in Akkadian. Not many people even know where to start on that language."

Leah scooted her chair toward Musa and his father. "Musa, you don't know me, but you've got a long history with David's family. You can trust all of us."

Rashid pulled at his bottom lip. "You might not like what you find in this message." He jabbed at her with his index finger. "You may find a big surprise."

"I think of myself as a scientist," Leah retorted. "David and I aren't observant Jews. We're not religious, but we hate prejudice. I can't imagine how any discovery from the past could offend us." She looked at her husband and smiled. "David is even accused of being an enemy of Judaism because he's so liberal toward your people's rights."

Musa nodded his head slowly. "If I keep the scroll in my possession, I am courting disaster." He shrugged. "Additional experts must be involved in exploring this message if my discovery is to have credibility."

"We must leave it here," Rashid broke in. "No more mistakes. Musa, give them the package and let's go home."

The young Arab took a deep breath. He looked back and forth between the husband and wife. "You're sure of the security?"

"Been doing business for years," David answered and grinned. "Haven't lost anything yet."

Musa turned to Leah. "Then, you must know that what I have found possibly dates to the First Temple period, much older than the Dead Sea Scrolls. I believe this document may well prove to be the long-rumored Donation of Melchizedek." He carefully picked up the string-tied brown package and slid it across David's desk.

Leah swallowed hard. "You're serious?"

"Serious as death itself."

6

Saturday, September 5
Jerusalem, Elisha Street

David waited until the Salahs crossed the street and disappeared around the corner before turning to the butcher paper–wrapped box, which was sitting innocuously in the middle of his desk like a time bomb hidden in a bus station locker. He gently shook the package. It rattled. "What are we going to do with this thing?"

"We'd best pay careful attention." Leah ran her hand slowly across the brown paper. "What we have here is no run-of-the-mill counterfeit oil lamp swiped by some opportunist for a small museum in Detroit."

David thumped the top of the package with a ballpoint pen. "Tell me about the Donation of Melchizedek. What is it?"

"For generations scholars debated whether it was legend or fact. Same issue as the so-called lost books of the Bible. Supposedly this ancient document bequeathed ownership of Jerusalem to Abraham and his heirs. The deed was rumored to have been kept in the Temple with the Ark of the Covenant or at least somewhere in the environs. History is vague about the contents because no one apparently wanted to disclose exactly what it said, but Jews generally believed it granted them all rights to the city."

David slowly turned the box around in front of him. "Unfortunately, the package is just larger than a shoe box; it won't fit in our safety deposit box. We obviously can't entrust it to any of your colleagues over at the Rockefeller Museum."

Leah gently tilted the box and listened to the sound of an object sliding. "David, if the age is even close to the antiquity Musa claims, we can't use anything less than the most formidable security. What does that suggest to you?"

"I think . . . maybe . . . I'm going to call in a favor." He tapped on his lips with the pen. "You probably don't remember Avraham Halevy, but he once worked with army intelligence and security. I've known Avraham for years. Done him a few favors. I'm sure he'd know where the best place is to keep these treasures."

"You trust him?"

"He owes me a big one. During a training exercise years ago, I kept him from stepping on a land mine. After that, Halevy always thought of me more like a brother."

"Don't you think we ought to take a look inside?"

"Of course not." David tossed his head indifferently.

"Don't give me that smug look. You're just as curious as I am."

"Not me." David got up from his chair and walked toward the front door. "It's none of my business."

"Well, it's mine," Leah asserted defiantly.

"We have to rise above mundane curiosity." David reached for the doorknob and shot a sly glance over his shoulder. "You need a more professional attitude, dear." He flipped the lock on the door and pulled the long shade down. "Rip it open!"

Leah instantly snipped the string and broke the adhesive

tape on the sides. Carefully separating the paper, she opened the box cautiously. "He's got packing on top and bottom . . . something is wrapped in strips of gauze."

"When Musa first called me, he said the scroll and a medallion were found in a clay urn." He peered over her shoulder. "Obviously, Musa left the jar at home. There's a metal coin of some kind in there. Be cautious."

"Are you kidding? This find is either a hoax or the greatest treasure I'll ever touch." Leah lifted the bundle out and laid it gently on the desk. She slowly unwrapped the gauze until a soft leather pouch emerged. "I feel the scroll inside. About eleven or twelve inches long." Leah peeled back the cover over the end and slowly let the gold cylinder slip onto David's large ink blotter. A copper medallion gently dropped on the cardboard cushion.

David poked at the round coin. "Several different scripts." He flipped it over. "Can't make out anything, but I see the shape of letters." Slowly pushing the medallion aside, David bent over his desk, getting as close as possible to the scroll. "Incredible. It's a continuous sheet of solid gold rolled like a Torah. The outside is smooth as a platter, highly polished, without a mark. Even in its day, it must have been worth a fortune. Never saw anything quite like it . . ." The pale yellow of the high-grade gold seemed to glow in the reflection of the overhead lights.

"We must be very cautious about touching the inside surface." Leah opened the bottom drawer of her desk. "I've got rubber gloves in here somewhere. I used them in translating an old manuscript several weeks ago." She sorted through the contents, found the gloves, then worked the tight latex tips over her fingers and pulled the gloves up to her wrist. "We can't be too careful. We don't want oil from our hands to get on the surface."

"How are we going to look at the inside?" David poked at the scroll.

Leah reached back into the drawer. "Need to soften it up just a smudge with a little assistance from the modern world." Leah pulled out a travel-size hair dryer she kept reserved for unusual occasions, plugged it into the wall, and flipped the switch on. The small electric appliance shot a stream of warm air over the scroll. "We need gentle heat." Leah slowly moved the dryer up and down the length of the scroll. "We must make the gold just a mite more malleable. Hand me a couple of pencils."

David spread a handful of pencils across the top of his desk. "Take your pick."

Leah handed the dryer to her husband. "Keep the dryer about six inches above the scroll. I'm sure Musa already followed the same procedure." Taking a pencil in each hand, Leah gently worked the rubber tip of the eraser under the edge and carefully pushed up. The scroll eased open about half an inch. "Ah, just enough to let me take a peek. See, it's moving easily. Yes. Our Bedouin archaeologist has already been here. You can turn the dryer off."

David stared at the etchings inside the gold scroll. Black markings across the pale yellow surface looked more like scratches than words. "What a challenge. Can't believe you opened it."

Leah carefully tilted the scroll to avoid putting pressure on the open side. "Take the flashlight out of the utility drawer and shine it inside." Using the pencil's rubber tip, she carefully edged open the golden sheet until more writing was discernible.

David held the light over her shoulder. "Hmmm. Strange-looking characters."

"Get that big magnifying glass your father kept in one of those cubbyholes in his desk, David. I'll know in a hurry if this thing has veracity."

With her left hand, Leah held the magnifying glass over the metal sheet. She took a deep breath. "No question about it. The cuneiform letters are Akkadian." Her hand tightened on the magnifying glass's handle. "Yes. Very primitive." She strained forward, the muscles in her jaw flexed. "Going to take some hard work to start reconstructing the syntax." Leah looked up and wiped her forehead with her arm. "I am overwhelmed. Musa wasn't exaggerating the possible age." She bent over the scroll again.

"I recognize some of the Hebrew letters, but it's certainly a strange form." David adjusted the flashlight. "Never seen Hebrew written in such shapes. Must be ancient."

"Look!" Leah used the tip of the pencil as a pointer. "Check out this word. *Jerusalem* is in Greek as well as the ancient Hebrew form *Jebus*. Here is the word *peace* in Akkadian. The mere fact that a document encoded in Akkadian, Hebrew, Egyptian, and Greek is using such a word is absolutely astounding."

"I don't understand."

"I know of no ancient document in this form. As a matter of fact, I don't recall ever seeing anything in this configuration anywhere. I am convinced that these ancient languages are in a mysterious code." Leah straightened up and rubbed her neck. "In the ancient world there wasn't contact across cultures like today. Who could have had such a vast knowledge—to speak these languages fluently and write them—when the cultures were separated by such distance and time? That factor makes everything about this document highly significant.

"It's going to be difficult to translate for that reason alone. No one scholar could do it. I'm not sure about what this says, but the longer I look at the scroll, the more I am inclined to believe Musa knows what he's talking about."

"He certainly has no reason to deceive us." David switched the flashlight off. "I feel he's been forthright."

Leah sat down in the old chair in the front of the desk and started scribbling on a notepad. An old souvenir flag from the 1948 celebration of the nation's birth still stood in a corner against more than slightly yellowing wallpaper. On the back wall, a signed portrait of Golda Meir hung next to a picture of Yitzhak Rosenberg posing with David Ben-Gurion. Stacks of files and papers cluttered the top of every flat surface. Coffee cups dotted the desktop terrain already littered with pictures, pencil holders, and strange mementos garnered over half a century.

"What's this all about? Come on, Leah, you're thinking something."

"David, we've got to take a look at the whole text." Leah tossed the notepad back on the desk. "Get the dryer fired up again. We must open the scroll wide enough for me to take pictures of the entire text."

"We can't do that!"

"Sure we can." Leah picked up the pencils again. "We need to have a copy for security purposes anyway. Can't just release an object of this caliber without a record for verification."

"I don't know." David hesitantly reached for the dryer. "Are you sure . . ."

"Absolutely. Let's go." The dryer whirled and the smell of warm plastic filled the air. "David, pick up a pencil and steady the scroll while I pull the side back farther. Keep the heat on the bend."

For the next ten minutes Leah tediously maneuvered the scroll open. She finally straightened up. "I don't think I ought to go any farther. The scroll might crack. The most important thing is to get a picture of the entire text as best we can. I'll keep the side open while you snap it."

David picked up his digital camera from its usual place in the top shelf of the bookcase behind his desk.

He quickly shot pictures from several different angles. "I think I got it."

"Okay, David. Let's not take any chances. I'll close the scroll again, and you get your buddy Halevy on the phone. I want those pictures developed immediately so I can try to get a read on the message. I'm sure there's something unusual there."

7

Monday, September 7
Jerusalem, Kiryat Moshe

When he was home and not on assignment for the Mossad, Daniel Levy usually walked the backstreets of Kiryat Moshe in the early morning. Taxis did not buzz the residential area, and noise was minimal. Ambling down the block stone pavement, he watched old ladies scurry off to the market in search of bread for breakfast. Occasionally someone rode by on a bicycle. Children were not playing yet, and the streets looked like a Polish neighborhood might have before World War II. Daniel liked to think he would have grown up in such a place if Auschwitz had not happened. Maybe his grandmother . . . grandfather . . . an uncle . . . anyone who perished . . . would step out of an old worn doorway and join the parade to the bakery shop. The fantasy pleased him.

The quiet stillness at sunrise seemed the way he thought Jerusalem should feel. Raucous noise belonged in Tel Aviv, where people played. The faithful prayed here. Of course, Daniel wasn't religious, but he admired the practices of the pious. He even tolerated the Hasidim his friends detested and always smiled when some old man in a black suit and *kippa*, with *tzitziot*, or fringes, dangling beneath his coat, shuffled off toward an obscure synagogue. Tranquillity brought him balance.

And balance did not come easy in the world of spies. Conniving and collusion were not a great formula for mental health. The Mossad's motto, "By way of deception, thou shalt do war," was indelibly etched on anyone working in the intelligence jungle. Deceit made for a hard way of life; at least the delusory lifestyle kept Levy from any sense of well-being. Agents continually endured escalating stress. The split-second timing of operations necessarily pushed a *sochen* to his limits. As their usual reward for faithful duty to their country, undercover officers generally indulged in wild living, heavy drinking, and ulcers. Levy's marriage had been an early casualty. These days he tried to find better solutions. The walk at dawn was one of them.

Daniel rounded the final lap of his neighborhood jaunt when the mobile phone on his belt rang. No one used the number except "the office."

"Levy," he answered immediately.

"Top Dog." It was Agent G's emotionless voice.

"You ready to put me back in action?"

"What's the matter, Danny? Not enjoying your vacation?"

Levy picked up his pace. "I'm caught up on my reading. Okay?"

"Well, we're not on ours." G betrayed no hint of feeling. "A new terrorist initiative is definitely afoot. Getting strong reports from Syria, but we're not ready to pop the cork on your big connection. Sit tight."

Levy slowed down. "I've *been* sitting around here for days." He kicked at a can. "I'd like to hang loose for a change."

"Why don't you put in a little extra time on target practice at the firing range?"

"I have."

"I'm impressed. Now, let's get down to business." Halevy's no-nonsense responses meant discussion ended. "I do have something of an interim assignment for you."

"Interim?

"Remember the security safe in your closet?"

Levy stopped. "The one under the floor? Of course." He instinctively looked around to make sure no one was eavesdropping.

"Amazing what comes up on our computer screens when we punch in questions and answers. Your security system won the contest we're running on storage locations. I have an important package that needs protection."

"You've called to suggest that I sit on the closet floor for the next several weeks?"

"Don't be cute, Danny. An important package is on the way to your house at this very moment. Lock it up until you hear from me."

"Oh, come on."

"Stay in touch." Halevy clicked off.

Levy swore and hurried toward his apartment. When he turned the last corner, he recognized the plain brown car waiting in front. Halevy was not kidding about the timing. The man in the driver's seat immediately got out of the car. He nodded professionally.

"Got something for me?" Levy walked briskly toward the curb.

The operative opened the car door and produced a brown paper–wrapped package slightly larger than a shoe box. "You have a gift from the office." He handed Daniel the parcel. "Must be a big deal. I was told to tell you that it's fragile."

"Hmmph!" Daniel gently shook the box. "Took years of military and intelligence training to handle these assignments!"

"Top brass said you wouldn't be thrilled with this opportunity to advance your career." He smiled cynically and got back in the car, driving away without saying anything more.

Levy hurried into the house and walked immediately to his back bedroom. After pulling the window shades and locking the door behind him, he pushed the contents of the closet out on the bedroom floor and peeled the rug back. The floor swung up against the back wall; wood siding covered a steel plate. The cement box beneath the closet floor contained a large black safe. An electronic lock sealed the door. Daniel punched in the code and quickly opened the safe. At the bottom several brown envelopes, three pistols, and boxes of bullets stood together. Levy carefully set the box on top of the pile and locked the safe again. In a couple of minutes the floor of the closet looked like Daniel's typical mangled mess of mismatched shoes, socks, and dirty clothes.

Levy twisted and turned, running as hard as possible to avoid the hit squad chasing him. No matter which alley he took, the armed attackers stayed close behind. Cold icy terror clutched at his throat. Death seemed imminent when a far-off bell intervened. The scenery scrambled. Daniel fought for self-composure. Only slowly did he realize the phone was ringing.

Throwing back the covers, he sat straight up in bed and tried to clear his head. The digital clock read 3:23 A.M. and the phone would not stop. He fumbled for the receiver.

"Hello." His voice sounded low and raspy.

"Hope I didn't get you off the firing range."

"What?" Daniel's voice raised two octaves.

"Anyone as highly motivated as you are would be out sharpening their skills at this hour of the morning." Agent G spoke in his sarcastic monologue.

"Your wife throw you out and you need a place to stay?" Levy turned on the bedside light. "You can level with an old friend."

"Let's keep it on a professional level," Halevy snapped. "We have business to do."

"I'm already hard at work guarding the package." Daniel propped a pillow behind his back. "But I'm sure I can work something else in."

"In the last eight hours important information came in from Syria and Iran. Terrorists are on the move."

Daniel slung the sheet back and slipped out of bed. "I see." The casual sound was gone. "You need me to contact Al-Amid?"

"The president of the United States called an impromptu conference in Washington, and the prime minister is leaving in the morning. I want you on the airplane with his people."

"What's my M.O. for this trip?" Daniel was already reaching for his pants.

"You'll be with the press corps, in the back of the airplane." Mr. Computer was spitting out instructions again. "Nothing must jeopardize your cover. I don't want you to appear to know anyone. On this trip don't even make eye contact with people from the office. You are now representing the press, so you won't be flagged in the U.S. We'll get you a Nikon 300 millimeter 2.8 camera—it'll shoot more than just pictures!"

"Yes, sir."

"Our man in the brown car will be at your house in approximately fifteen minutes. He's bringing press credentials and a new passport. Don't contact me. I'll contact you."

"Yes, sir." Levy caught his breath and thought for a moment. "By the way, how do I hook up with the prime minister's airplane?"

Agent G cleared his throat and coughed. "I'm getting tired.

Been down here since six yesterday morning." He yawned. "Should have already briefed you. Drive your car to Tel Aviv. Take the usual route through security onto the tarmac. Look for the PM's 707. You already have clearance up and down the line. Just hop the airplane."

"What do you want me to do with my Syrian cousin?" Daniel kept reaching under the bed for his shoes and socks.

"I'm getting sleepy, too." Halevy yawned again. "Should have started with that question." He cleared his throat once more. "From what the CIA tells us, Al-Amid is now working in the center of sensitive communication. Act like you know more than you do. Bluff him into thinking he's just confirming other sources, but zero in on what the terrorists in Syria are planning. The trouble is we're not picking up on the people behind what's coming down. That's the big problem. We want names and faces."

"Rather sketchy assignment." Daniel frowned in the mirror. He could only find one sock and his hair looked terrible.

"That's it for now. I hope to fill in the blanks before you see cousin Al-Amid." Halevy was fading. "I'm currently expecting more data. If I get it, you'll be among the first to know. If not, I'm depending on your ability to work Arabs."

"I'll need grease to get the wheels rolling." Daniel brightened. His sock was on a chair on the other side of the room. "Money puts words in Al-Amid's mouth."

"You're authorized to pay what it takes. We'll wire money to his Swiss bank account after he talks. How much depends on what he knows. You understand the procedure."

"Yes, sir."

Halevy paused and sighed. "Danny, I know I don't need to tell you . . . but we're playing with dynamite . . . maybe even nuclear dynamite."

8

The scorching sun settled over the Siberian mountains, hiding the secret nuclear city, Krasnoyarsk/26. Hidden in a mountain behind barbed wire, with no telephone links to anywhere but the top leadership in Moscow, the city's very existence had been a state secret for over thirty years. Built in a granite peak Moscow believed would withstand a nuclear strike, the seven-square-mile city was still equipped to produce bomb-grade plutonium even after a nuclear war. The three nuclear reactors had produced more than forty tons of plutonium that had in turn equipped a third of the Soviet arsenal.

Since the fall of the Soviet Empire, life had become difficult in Krasnoyarsk/26 as well as in the other seven secret cities. Once-affluent scientists now tried to survive on thirty dollars a month with salary payments often delayed for months. In 1996 the director of the Nuclear Science Center in Chelyabinsk/70 shot himself. But things were decidedly different in the city's cement-hidden offices of Ivan Kremikov, former KGB regional head.

On the top floor of the security offices, thirty-five-year-old Alexei Izhevsk watched his boss, Ivan Kremikov, now head of the area's Russian mafia. The small but athletic-appearing aide studied Kremikov, who was sipping his coffee and listening intently to a small Arab sitting across from him. Ivan's stomach struck Alexei as being worthy of an eight-month pregnancy. A massive black moustache covered his bottom lip, making it impossible to see much of his mouth except when he smiled. Izhevsk stood beside him, waiting in the corner like a menacing phantom.

"The matter is simple." Rafik Khaled talked nonchalantly as if he might be the master of the universe. "You are the true survivors of the Soviet Empire, my friend. Only you, and a few strong men like you, have remained our true friends. We know you will do business with us." He sipped from an ornate coffee cup, another vestige of better days. "We are old friends."

Kremikov had a deceptive way of smiling. His pitted forehead knurled in an understanding frown that seemed to say "of course" but probably meant "definitely not." "Yes. Yes," remained his only response.

Alexei knew Ivan's bored answer implied, "Only a fool would accept this Arab's prattle at face value." Maybe this Khaled was such a fool. Maybe not.

"Both of us know the United States is the Great Satan," Khaled continued. "Remove these obstructionists and we can eradicate the Zionists instantly. In one great sweep, our armies will dispatch the pests." He gestured as if swinging a sword in the air. "Of course, your help is essential for our victory, my brother."

"Yes. Yes." Ivan's smile never changed. He held a Cuban cigar between his thumb and index finger and kept popping it into the black forest above his fat lower lip. The former KGB agent chewed his cigar but said nothing more.

"We would have no problem transporting the bomb south through Afghanistan and then into Iran," Khaled continued. "Our friend Osama bin Laden has already made his facilities in the Kandahar region available to us." He crossed his arms over his chest confidently. "No problem anywhere along the way." He laughed. "The CIA trained and armed his people to fight you in Afghanistan. Now we both win. It's payback time."

Kremikov raised his finger instructively. "Ah, but you see, one issue remains, even with our friends." The artificial smile broadened. "There is the question of money."

"Name your price!" Rafik jutted his chin forward defiantly. "Friends should not even speak of such things for more than a moment."

"But the question is, how will we be paid?" Ivan Kremikov smiled pleasantly. "And when? We don't take American Express."

"Terms can be worked out." Khaled shifted his sales job downward toward vagueness. "These matters will all fall into place once we have the bomb. You know the great colonel of Libya stands good for everything."

Kremikov abruptly smashed the cigar in an ash tray. "Don't toy with me." His demeanor turned hard, unflinching. "Yes, of course, my people have these weapons." He laughed. "We have everything. The Westerners like to call us 'the Russian mafia,' the new rich." He leaned over the table. "You listen to me, Khaled. I've been financing and running terrorism for three decades. I made the name of the KGB a thing of terror across all of Kazakhstan. Now I am about other things. Today I work only for money. Lots of money!"

"I understand," Khaled acknowledged the reality. "I expected such to be the case." He no longer looked so happy.

"Understand me." Ivan thumped on the table with hard jabs. "We get paid in cash *first*, before anything happens." Ivan glared. "I don't believe in nationalism, political parties, God, or anything else under the sun but money! Are we clear?"

Khaled's ingratiating manner dissolved and another mask emerged. No longer the flamboyant Arab aristocrat, the hardened terrorist had obviously known the terms of the deal before he arrived. "I assumed we shared a common enemy and goal," he said coldly. "My people are motivated by a high idealism, by their faith. However, we understand the power of gold. You will be paid well enough."

The former KGB officer cursed. "Your so-called idealism bores me, Rafik. Kremikov sees no Allah in the sky. I expect twenty million American dollars delivered to me personally. Then I will make arrangements for the nuclear device to show up at any place you desire."

"Twenty million is considerably above the market." Khaled looked angry.

"I am the market," Kremikov shouted and might as well have added the "stupid" he implied. "Who's your alternative? The British?" He laughed again. "Maybe you could cut a better deal with the Israelis?" Ivan turned to his aide and winked.

Rafik Khaled stood up. "The price is too high. I must pursue further consultations with other leaders of the Islamic Revolutionary Front."

"Then don't come back." Ivan tossed his head indifferently. "If you don't do business in this moment, I am through with the hot air blowing in from the desert. Tomorrow I am to meet secretly with Taliban leaders from Afghanistan. They will probably bring the twenty million with them." Kremikov stood up. "All success in your endeavors, Khaled. Good-bye."

"Wait!" The terrorist held up his hand. "We will meet the price and the conditions." His hand trembled slightly.

"Oh?" Ivan puckered his lip nonchalantly. "Whatever you say." The enormous belly shifted slightly.

"We want the nuclear device in one month. Is that possible?"

"Anything is possible for Ivan Kremikov." Alexei Izhevsk spoke for the first time. "I will give you the proper bank account information for the transfer. We will move the money instantly, sending it through two countries. You have the money here in twenty days, and ten days later you have the bomb."

"What guarantees do we have of delivery after payment?" Khaled's eyes narrowed, becoming black and sullen. "We will only pay 40 percent before delivery."

"I ask you again, Rafik. Who else had you planned to do business with?" The meaningless smile returned. "It's all or nothing."

The terrorist looked at Kremikov and his aide with total contempt. "Allah's will be done. The deal is struck." He did not extend his hand.

Ivan Kremikov shook the Arab's hand anyway and gestured toward the door. Khaled quickly disappeared down a long dingy corridor. The burly Russian turned to his aide and continued to smile. "What do you think, Alexei?"

"They'll not like it, but this new Islamic Revolutionary Front organization will pay on time."

"Yes, you are correct. Now it is time for us to do business, Alexei." Kremikov settled back in his chair and sipped the thick black coffee. "We are going to make our own little deal on the side? No?"

"Deal?" the aide asked.

"Alexei, Alexei, you Jews are all the same." The smile never changed. "Businessmen to the core. That's why I like having you around. Your father endured what put many under the ground, into the bosom of Mother Russia." Ivan frowned and gestured apologetically. "Of course, the days of Stalin, Khrushchev, the whole rotten bunch, were a most unfortunate time. We all did what was necessary to survive." Ivan Kremikov shrugged. "It's good you understand, accept, and forgive. You and I rise beyond the past and recognize the present realities." He held up his coffee cup in a toast. "Besides all that, you're smarter than everyone else in my organization."

Kremikov's mention of the past made Alexei want to put a bullet in the back of this pig's head, but more important things were afoot than simple revenge. "Even when we are in private, we should not mention my unusual Jewish heritage." Alexei Izhevsk was polite but emphatic. "Anti-Semitism still reigns, and many are not as magnanimous as you, my friend." Alexei knew this was the best protest he could settle for.

Ivan smiled. "Alexei, my son. Of course, you are no Zionist, but I've sniffed out that you're not so happy with my giving away these atomic toys to people who might use them on your distant relatives." Kremikov winked. "I've picked up on your hints. I think you'd like to offer me a little deal."

Alexei Izhevsk nodded his head casually. "Possibly." He inhaled deeply. The moment was at hand.

Ivan Kremikov chuckled. "You don't fool me. Okay, how much will you pay me to let you make sure this great bomb never goes off?"

"We are friends," Alexei began slowly. "Comrades in the great class struggle."

Kremikov exploded in a belly laugh. "That's why I like you so much. What a joker you are." He abruptly stopped laughing. "I think you know the way to Tel Aviv." Ivan shook his finger back and forth like the dial on a metronome. "Five million would be sufficient to allow you to fix this bomb to go off in their faces. You can charge Tel Aviv seven million and take home two in your pocket. We both win."

"I am only the humble servant of my master, Kremikov. How could I possibly make such arrangements?" Alexei returned the coffee-cup salute. "Where would I make such a contact with the Israelis, with their Mossad?" He tried to sound innocent.

Ivan pointed toward the floor. "Everything down there is at your disposal. You know that. We have floors of equipment waiting for your use. The computers, transmitters, decoders—use what you choose. No one will bother you. Ring them up in Tel Aviv. Make a deal."

"I can try." Izhevsk fought to look indifferent.

Ivan Kremikov leaned forward. "Remember the extra five million remains completely confidential between us," the big man growled. "No one, and I mean no one, must get a whiff that I am dealing from both sides of the deck."

"That I can absolutely guarantee!" Alexei Izhevsk genuinely smiled. "We both must keep our little secrets."

9

Monday, September 7
Jerusalem, Kiryat Wolfson

Like smoke lingering after a fire, an uncomfortable silence settled ominously over the tense atmosphere in the Rosenberg law office. David avoided conversation. The twenty-four hours following Musa's visit and their reception of the scroll had been filled with constant confrontation. Leah stared at papers on her desk. No one spoke except to answer the telephone. Time crawled by.

Leah glanced at the antique wall clock above Yitzhak's old rolltop desk. "You said Musa would be here in ten minutes?"

David drummed on his desk with his fingers. "I don't want to argue about this matter again."

Leah glared. "Let me explain my position one more time." She crossed her arms over her chest. No man was going to ignore her, much less the one to whom she was married.

"I understand your position fully." David spun around in his desk chair to face the computer screen behind him.

"Don't you dare turn your back on me." Leah stood up and

leaned over her desk. "We're dealing with a much larger issue than a slight difference of opinion between us."

"Still playing the detective." David shook his head. "If we're not careful with what is said, Musa will think I am betraying him. Everything depends on trust in these sensitive matters."

"David." Leah shifted gears down to pleading speed. "I've worked all night on the translation of this scroll. The message will prove to be political dynamite one way or the other. I understand why the old man hinted we may not like the contents."

"I'm a lawyer, not a politician. I'm not interested in speculations about how this or that might play in the newspapers." He kept his back to her.

Leah shook her head emphatically. "Israel is a powder keg right now. We're coming down to critical negotiations with the Palestinians. Anything could tip the balance scale of world opinion in the wrong direction. Think of the political ramifications of the most ancient manuscript ever found indicating the true ownership of this city."

"You don't let up, do you?" He pulled at the corner of his mouth and rubbed his chin. "We've had this scroll in our possession twenty-four hours, and it's caused me nothing but misery.

"First, Halevy doesn't want to help us, and I have to pull out all the stops, telling him more than I should before he'd take it off my hands. Next, you stay up half the night toying with this thing, and I don't get any rest. Then, the remainder of this morning you've been on my case. I'm not in a great mood for you to push me any further."

Leah took a deep breath. "If Musa runs with the scroll or ultimately turns it over to the wrong sources, there's no telling what could happen. We've got to maintain some control over the destiny of this document."

"You simply want to make sure that you're included in the translation. That's the bottom line."

Leah rolled her eyes. "Of course, I want to be included, but that's not everything. If I'm involved, we will have strings attached to what follows. You can negotiate an agreement with Musa to count me in . . . if you *want* to."

David threw up his hands. "Okay. I'll try. That's all I can promise." He turned back to the computer. "I'll talk to Musa, but only on the condition I don't hear one more word out of you." He pointed his finger at her. "Got it? Not *one more word.*"

Leah turned back to her desk. "Whatever you say, David." She fought to keep from smiling. The issue was too large to gloat over a tactical victory.

Five minutes later Leah saw a gray van pull into a parking place on the other side of the street. Musa Salah got out and worked his way through the traffic. David shot a stern look at his wife and bolted toward the door.

"David, where are you . . ."

"We're going to get a cup of coffee." He shut the door before Leah could answer.

"Oh, no!" Leah pounded on her desk. "Outflanked."

Musa Salah carefully eyed a taxi flying down the street before negotiating the oncoming traffic. One could never be too cautious of crazy drivers. He could see inside the front windows of the law firm. Everything looked acceptable, but he felt apprehensive.

David Rosenberg came out the front door. "Hey, let's grab a cup of Turkish coffee," he shouted and pointed up the street. "Good little place up here."

Musa caught up with David as he bounded up the street and

shook hands. "Had to drive my father back to Arad last night. Took a while to get in today."

"How is he today?"

"Still upset. Thinks he's blown the whole thing."

"Too bad." David pointed to a sidewalk cafe just a few feet ahead. "The worry beads don't amount to anything."

Musa nodded. "Probably a thousand worry beads just like his in every Arab village in the West Bank."

David opened the door to a small cafe sandwiched between a dealer in Holy Land souvenirs and a pharmacy. The restaurant smelled of pastries and spices. All but one of the eight tables scattered around the room were filled. The proprietor smiled at David and gave a friendly wave. They sat down near a back wall.

Musa immediately noticed that the *matam* was Arab owned and most of the customers were Palestinian. The wall menu reflected Muslim tastes. A good sign. Musa relaxed.

"Give us two regulars," David called to the waiter. "And some of the *baklava*." He smiled. "I eat in here all the time," he confided. "Good folks."

"How have you been?" Musa smiled but carefully watched David's eyes. The Jew seemed at ease and made strong eye contact. No hint of guile. So far so good.

For the next few minutes David rambled on about where he'd been over the last twenty years. Family. Marriage. No children. Law school. The usual summary of the journey from adolescence to adulthood. His voice sounded the same as in the old days. No hint of condescension.

"Like I said on the phone," Musa picked up his end of the conversation, "when I went to America to attend college, my world changed radically. From Bedouin boy to preppy."

"Really made the leap?"

"No." Musa shook his head. "Learned the talk but never got

the walk, as the Americans say." He sipped the cup of coffee. "Americans scared me. Too fast. Too materialistic. Too obsessed with money. Too obsessed . . . period. Couldn't ever become one of them."

"Yeah." David nodded enthusiastically. "Know exactly what you mean. Look at how they lean on Israel to negotiate. Power-hungry maniacs." He stopped and grimaced. "Guess that wasn't the best example I might have offered." He looked embarrassed.

Musa smiled. Surprisingly, David's politics didn't irritate him. The comment was honest. Musa didn't trust American politicians either. Everything about the conversation felt right. He laughed. "Sure. Good point. The Americans do it to you today. Do it to us tomorrow. All the same."

"Well." David smiled and his voice changed—"I guess you want to know what I've worked out."

"Sure."

"I have an absolutely secure safe. We photographed the text of the scroll to document the find for our future verification and security purposes."

Musa felt uncomfortable. "You're certain?"

"Absolutely."

"No problem getting the scroll back whenever I want it?" Musa kept watching David's eyes.

"Absolutely not a problem. We're in very good shape."

"But how could you possibly photograph the text?"

"Like I told you yesterday, my wife is a good archaeologist. She used a hair dryer to loosen the metal enough for us to get an adequate look inside."

David's eyes were telling the truth. Musa again relaxed.

"But there is one thing I really need to talk with you about," David hedged and sounded apologetic. "My wife is also very good with languages. She already took a hard look at the

Akkadian in the text and has made some headway. I'd like to request that you include her in the translation."

Musa studied David's face carefully. "There may be political ramifications to what we decipher. Could be a problem."

"We are aware of that issue." David kept smiling. "Leah's an archaeologist, not a politician."

David stopped and cleared his throat suddenly. Not a good sign.

"Can you guarantee she will keep things on a scholarly basis?" Musa pushed. "That's the critical issue."

"Absolutely! I pride myself on keeping my wife under control," he lied.

David's answers came too quickly; he was too certain. Musa immediately felt hustled. The wife issue was moving way too fast.

"Let's go talk with her." Musa abruptly stood up. "I'd like to hear her thoughts."

"Right now?" David looked up in surprise. "Before we're finished with coffee?"

"Why not?" Musa smiled deceptively and gestured toward the door. He walked through the doorway, hurrying up the street. Out of the corner of his eye he could see David scurrying behind him.

"Perhaps I should speak for both of us." David caught up. "Makes it simpler with one person negotiating."

"But she is the one I would need to work with." Musa felt a sense of growing irritation. David was pressuring him for some reason. When they reached the door to the law firm, Musa walked in without breaking stride.

Leah looked up from her desk in the back. "My, that was a fast coffee break." She glared at David.

"I understand you want to be in on the translation," Musa began immediately.

"I insist," Leah said bluntly.

Musa saw David put his hand on his forehead and close his eyes. "Our Bedouin women do not speak so bluntly." Musa was surprised his words came out so forcefully. He only intended to provoke Leah to test her metal.

"I'm not one of your women," Leah shot back. "And I have some sense of the potential political significance of this document. I couldn't walk away from this project if I wanted to."

Musa slowly turned to David. "You said she wasn't politically motivated." He held up his hands in consternation. "If not, I'd certainly hate to get caught in the cross fire when Leah *did* develop a political conviction."

David looked at Leah with a glance that might cut her in two pieces. "A few seconds ago I assured Musa your only interest in working on the translation was for scholarly reasons." He sounded exasperated.

"But now I am hearing threats." Musa edged away from the woman's desk. "The husband and the wife do not seem to be telling me the same story." He crossed his arms over his chest. "And then I also discover *my* scroll is stashed away somewhere. The original harmony in our agreement suddenly turns into a storm of contradictions. I am not comfortable with any of this."

David's face had taken on a decidedly red cast and he was shaking his head emphatically. "Musa, I am sorry. Matters are being blown way out of proportion. My wife has spoken out of turn." He looked very upset.

"Perhaps I have completely misjudged you." Musa looked hard at Leah. "Maybe I should take my scroll back and leave at once." He stopped and his voice became hard. "Unless you have no intention of giving it back to me."

"Oh, no!" David agonized. "Musa, no one has any such an idea. No matter what occurs, we would never violate an agreement."

Leah's countenance fell. Her mouth dropped. "Oh, my, what have I done?" she groaned.

"Possibly you have come to think of yourselves as pharaohs and my people as your brick builders," Musa answered. "You expect to order me around as the slave." He looked at Leah. "You think of me as an inferior to be commanded like a dog. Huh? Is this what I am to you?"

Leah hung her head. "David, you warned me." She held out her hands to Musa. "The politics, the confrontation, the strife . . . it makes us all a little crazy."

"Musa, I do know how important this find could be. That's why I want to be involved so badly. Please forgive my brashness. I did not mean to offend you."

"Please," David begged, "I can better represent you if we're in on the translation. My wife sometimes oversteps her boundaries, but she is a quite competent archaeologist and linguist. Her zeal caused her to be too forward."

Musa watched the faces of the husband and wife carefully. Both were visibly shaken. Leah had turned 180 degrees in a few minutes, but he did not like the pushiness that most Jews exhibited toward his people.

"You are sure that I can pick up my scroll at any moment I should choose?"

"Absolutely." David nodded up and down emphatically. "No one is going to keep you from anything that is yours."

"I apologize for my attitude." Leah sounded in full retreat. "I simply can't express how much I want to help in the translation."

"I will think about it." Musa put her off. "Next time we might discuss it." He worked at sounding difficult. At least he felt as if he had the situation back under control.

"We need each other," David persisted. "The most important ingredient in our relationship must be trust. I pledge to you that my wife and I will be worthy of your utmost confidence."

Musa took a deep breath and exhaled. "Don't ever threaten me." He tried to sound firm but not confrontational. "Okay?"

"I really didn't mean to come across that way," Leah pleaded.

"The truth is, I will need help on the translation," Musa conceded. "In addition to problems with Akkadian, I don't know ancient Greek well." He cleared his throat. "But trust is *everything*."

"Certainly," David agreed immediately. "As a matter of fact, I know an excellent translator who absolutely fills the bill. A Roman Catholic priest and scholar. Because of a vow of poverty, money isn't an issue. As a Christian, he wouldn't be caught in the Jewish-Arab political vise. We've worked with the man before and he's very good, as well as completely trustworthy."

"Who is he?" Musa asked skeptically.

David smiled for the first time since they had entered the law firm. "His name is Kelly. Father Michael Kelly."

"He's internationally known," Leah added. "His credentials are impeccable: Ph.D. from the Pontifical Academy in Rome."

Musa brightened. "I know of his work. Read him in some scholarly journals."

"We could contact him for you and arrange an interview," David added.

"Perhaps." Musa shrugged. "You've given me much to think about today. I must sleep on all of these matters before I can answer. I will call you in the morning." He walked quickly to the front door. "Good day." He smiled politely and shut the door behind him.

Musa did not look back until he crossed the street and was in his old gray van. Only then did he glance through the front window into the law firm. He could see David angrily lecturing his wife. Leah appeared to have no response. Musa switched on the ignition and smiled. "My, my, how the high and mighty have fallen," he said to himself and chuckled as he drove away.

10

Tuesday, September 8
Over the Atlantic

The back section of the prime minister's modified Boeing 707 was full. Support personnel, advisers, and the press corps were crowded together on the airplane. As usual, the prime minister kept his cabinet officers sequestered up front in specially constructed quarters. Limited space in the coach made it impossible to lie across the seats and sleep. Daniel Levy popped a sleeping pill and settled in for the night.

Halevy's call at 3:00 A.M. along with leaving immediately for the early morning flight had made a big gap in Daniel Levy's night. After a much better breakfast than the usual bill of fare on commercial flights, he stretched out across several seats in the back. As per G's instructions, Daniel had isolated himself in the last rows away from everyone else. The flight attendants closed the windows along the sides of the plane, and the movie started. The cabin became quiet and dark.

Daniel reasoned that a good solid, long sleep would also help get him past jet lag, and he could hit the ground running when they landed in Washington. He put on a sleeping mask and had no trouble drifting off.

The usual cast of attackers returned in battle attire. In short order, the chase was on. Roaring jet engines seemed to provide a new dimension of background sound to this dream. The steady hum of flying objects rushed through his mind. Suddenly he was standing in a black room with a sniper's laser sight beaming a red dot on his body. No matter how he dodged or ran, the deadly dot followed, sometimes over his heart, other times on his head. No matter what he tried, no reprieve was possible.

Daniel stirred from his dream. Pursuit always made for fitful sleep, but the pattern remained the same virtually every night. When the repetitive nocturnal scenes came to mind during waking moments, Daniel often wondered if these nighttime assaults were his unconscious mind's attempts at sharpening his survival skills.

Something grabbed his foot, and Daniel tried to kick. When he hit the seat in front of him, he assumed the flight attendant must have bumped him with the service cart. Levy pulled the blanket farther over his head, but the next tug was harder. Propping himself up on an elbow, he pulled off the mask and realized a shadowy figure stood above him. Daniel bolted upright.

The close-cropped gray crew cut was all too familiar. Small wire-rimmed glasses and the scar across the man's right cheek made it clear that Agent G had come on board with the PM's personal staff. Daniel rubbed his eyes to make sure Avraham Halevy was not part of the dream.

Agent G stared intensely at Daniel and then glanced toward the rear of the airplane. With his hand near his chest, he flipped his thumb in the same direction and moved on.

Daniel slung the blanket aside and slipped his shoes on. He quickly ran his fingers through his hair as if they were a makeshift comb. When he stood up, Daniel noticed the flight attendants walking up the aisle toward the nose of the airplane. He hurried to the back.

G waited in the food galley. As soon as Daniel entered, the Mossad chief closed the curtain and snapped it shut.

"I sent the girls to check on things up front," G stated with his usual detachment. "They'll be gone for a few minutes."

"Surprised to see you."

"Surprised to be here. Hadn't planned to come." Black circles ringed Halevy's eyes and the whites looked like a road map to blood vessel city. His face sagged. "Last-minute interruptions."

"Yes." Daniel remembered he should be standing at attention and straightened in a rigid military posture. "Sir."

"Relax." G swore. "We've all been up too long and late for the formal stuff." He fished out a cigarette and lit up. "Fortunately, I make the rules on this airplane and can smoke whenever I choose." He smiled slyly. "Just don't you try it."

Levy chuckled. "Ah, the perks one gets at the top leave the little folks in total envy."

G moaned and blew smoke toward the ceiling. "Here's the inside story, which came in after you left your place." He leaned against the side of the kitchen serving area. "Uncle Sam is bigtime unhappy with our front man because we're not jumping through Yankee political hoops quite like they think we should. The Americans are turning up the heat. The story just hasn't hit the papers yet and may not for several days."

"I don't understand."

Halevy leaned forward into Daniel's face. His stare was grave, angry with steely determination. "The Americans may be about to betray us. Looks like the president is jumping back with the United Nations over Resolutions 242 and 338. In addition, he's pulled the Russians back in to the peace process. It seems like

Jerusalem is going on the negotiating table. Might return the city to partition status in order to accommodate Palestinian claims for locating their own capital there. It's hardball time."

Levy felt his jaw tighten. Cold fear gripped him. "The Americans are playing both sides of the table again?"

"The president has sent the first signals that they'd go for a Palestinian state with full autonomy. His statements tipped us off that something new was in the mill. Then the secretary of state wired a veiled ultimatum. We're highly concerned."

"How does Al-Amid fit into the picture?"

Halevy nodded his head back and forth like a semaphore at a train crossing. "The CIA is now part of the pressure game. Suddenly they're not sharing critical information with us. Their well has gone dry. Seems like they are siding with many of our adversaries. They may be betraying us."

"You're serious?" Levy's voice raised an octave.

"That's when we know the USA really means business." G put out the cigarette in a half-empty cup of coffee standing among the dirty dishes and immediately lit another one. "The CIA has much more data on this new terrorist group than they are giving us."

"So, Al-Amid's information becomes twice as important to us."

"And you can bet we won't be sharing it with them," G grumbled. "Right now we need to be in a position to know more than they do . . . or at least make sure they think we do."

"What's going to happen if the Americans keep up the pressure?"

The Mossad chief swore vehemently. "We're not backing down an inch on Jerusalem, and I don't think we're manufacturing any more land that we'll be giving away. They've completely underestimated our determination."

"I can pay Al-Amid more than the going rate?"

"Your judgment will not be questioned by anyone, Levy. Do what you have to; get all the facts. We suspect that the rise of the new terrorist organization might be linked with an overall Arab strategy to pressure the Americans by blackmail with an 'increased' oil supply." He puffed hard on the cigarette. "Sort of a one-two punch in a technological war. In addition to the oil supply, we're talking about over a trillion and a half dollars that could either make or break the American stock market, depending on how the oil countries want to use their huge reserves. If that kind of money started whipping through Wall Street, the rest of the world investors would grab what they had left and run. In four or five days America would be in the greatest economic crisis in fifty years or maybe ever. You can see the chaos such a strategy would create."

"And then the American public squeals like wounded pigs."

"American political opinion swings like a gate in a windstorm. Most don't relate to Israel on the basis of principle, just convenience. A shift in their foreign policy right now could be disastrous for us. I don't need to tell you any of these facts."

G put his hand on Levy's shoulder. "Danny, I'm talking to you for a very personal reason. I don't have any confidence in what the CIA is up to. I'm also worried about the possibilities that Al-Amid may be under surveillance from Syria. If they've found out he's talking, Al-Amid's life isn't worth birdseed."

Levy nodded.

"And yours isn't either."

11

Tuesday, September 8
Jerusalem, Dormition Abbey

A cool breeze swept down from the heights of the Old City wall and spilled over Mount Zion, signaling autumn's approach. The rains would come soon. David Rosenberg hurried down the cobblestone street beneath the stone walls surrounding the Armenian Quarter of the Old City. Within thirty minutes of Musa's departure from the Rosenbergs' office the day before, David was on the phone with Father Michael Kelly. Now he was on his way to see the priest.

Still thinking about Musa's phone call only two hours earlier, he left Armenian Patriarchate Street and exited through the Zion Gate, heading to the Dormition Abbey. The archaeologist was not a man to be manipulated. When Musa had finally called after making him wait twenty-four hours, David felt a profound sense of relief; Musa had agreed that Leah could work on the translation, and he also invited Michael Kelly to join the effort.

Leah's silence from the moment Musa left their meeting had been somewhat refreshing. David deeply loved his wife and admired her intelligence, but he did not like obstinacy, and

Leah's persistence could be maddening when she fixed her mind on some impossible objective. Maybe this time she had learned a lesson.

A large tour group ambled out of the entry to the Dormition Abbey and the lawyer had to wait for the pilgrims to clear away. Old ladies chattered in German and pulled their bored husbands along. Germans particularly liked the Abbey because they tended to be Roman Catholics, and the Benedictines who maintained the traditional site of Mary's death were mostly German. David finally inched his way through the dawdling tourists and entered the stone edifice.

Rather than stay on the visitors' route through the gift shop, David opened a door clearly marked No Entrance and went inside. In sharp contrast to the babbling tourists and the noisy press of the crowd, he was immediately engulfed in monastic quiet. The granite walls and floors echoed every sound his shoes made. An overpowering sense of the majesty of silence settled over him. David's usual hostility toward Christians subsided in the environment of sober sanctity inside the Abbey.

At the end of the hall, he entered a large room clearly arranged as a gathering place. The high vaulted ceiling and large Gothic candelabra now converted into an electric chandelier made it feel appropriate to speak only in whispers. A gigantic oil painting of the Madonna and Child hung over a natural rock fireplace. If the painting had not been done by a medieval master, it was an expensive imitation. In the corner a monk wearing plain leather sandals and the usual dark brown vestment of a Benedictine appeared completely absorbed in his book. David slipped across the room toward Father Michael Kelly.

The priest looked to be in his mid to late fifties. His half-glasses clung to the end of a large nose, and his white hair was closely cropped, causing him to look like he had just awakened. Kelly wore a graying goatee. Pale skin reflected what one might expect of a scholar always buried in books. His features and small blue eyes suggested Michael Kelly must have been an unusually handsome young man, but time had fattened his nose and puffed his eyes.

"Excuse me, Father." David always began formally even though they were good friends.

Kelly looked startled and then smiled broadly. "David! Shalom!" He closed the book. "How good to see you."

"Sorry to interrupt."

"Not at all." Michael Kelly stood up and laid the scholarly tome aside.

"Forgive me for calling on such short notice."

Kelly gestured toward the door. "No problem. I'm glad you could have lunch with us today. We have some very important guests I'm quite sure you will enjoy, and then we'll have plenty of time to talk."

David fell in step alongside his friend. "When I first called, I was concerned that you'd be off on some scholarly conference on the other side of the world. After all, an hour's notice is hardly polite."

"You certainly got my attention with your description of an important new find. A little sketchy, but I'm intrigued." Kelly ushered David down a long corridor. At the other end a dining hall was in view. "Actually, I'm somewhat between assignments right now, and it's a good time to entertain the possibility of a new project. I want to hear every detail." He stepped aside so David could enter the hall.

Monks and priests drifted toward the tables. The Benedictines were easily identified by their brown robes and hoods. Most were old men. Other priests in the dining hall wore white robes with black scapulars. Bishops in black cassocks with purple cinctures and zucchettos stood out among the more bland colors and carried themselves with an air of importance and self-appointed dignity. Conversation sounded formal and proper.

David felt overpowered by such an august assembly, as if he were the shoeshine boy at a convention of heads of state. Their intimidating appearance did not bother him as much as the realization they all were speaking German, which he neither understood nor liked. Even though David prided himself on having a liberal, unbiased mind, he recognized his distinct prejudice against Germans . . . and German Christians most of all.

He followed Michael to a massive wood table where three bishops and monks from the Dormition community held two chairs in reserve. Some clerics smiled, others looked somewhat askance at him. David seldom wore a tie as was the general business practice of most Israelis. He wondered if the church big guns thought him to be the gardener or a cleanup man invited for lunch as an act of charity.

"I believe you've met our abbot before." Michael deferred to a large man standing in the center of a group of clergy. "Abbot Friedrich Hoffman is our spiritual leader."

"Good to see you again, Abbot Hoffman." David offered his hand. "It's been a while."

"Welcome to the Abbey." Father Hoffman shook hands warmly.

Father Kelly launched into a rapid-fire discourse in German. David caught the word *juden* and suspected he was being explained. The group began nodding pleasantly. Hands were extended. The priest's countenance brightened.

"We shall attempt to speak English," one of the bishops said almost without an accent, "although we have limitations. I apologize that the entire group doesn't speak Hebrew. Please allow me to introduce myself. I am Father August Beck." The large overweight German extended his hand. His fat neck rolled over the stiff clerical collar. Near absence of hair made his large round face look like a bowling ball. "I am a papal nuncio." He looked around the group. "We are very interested in Israel and Jerusalem. It will be a pleasure to talk to a lawyer." A large gold crucifix hung around his neck.

At once a monk in a plain, unadorned robe began ladling out hot soup, and David's presence was almost immediately forgotten. Bishop Beck obviously guided the discussion around topics that interested him, and he was particularly concerned with what he kept calling "the new situation" in Russia.

"But can we *actually* work with the Russian Orthodox Church?" one of the Benedictines asked. "Is it possible to help them at this critical moment in history?"

Two of the bishops shook their heads vigorously and looked sour.

Bishop Beck smiled slyly. "Some of us think not, some of us think so." He looked at one of the dissenting bishops. "Why not?"

While older than Beck, the aged bishop was much smaller in size. He fired off a rapid response in German. The prelate sounded angry, militant, and kept jabbing with a long bony index finger to make his points.

David felt exceedingly uncomfortable and buried his face in the steamy aroma of the hot chicken soup. The pungent, delicious smell helped compensate.

"So much for the situation in the former Soviet Union," Kelly broke through in English. "We live in a fascinating time. Yes?" He seemed to be wresting control of the conversation from Beck. Kelly obviously had significant stature with the group. "I understand the American church, with its problems with vocations, is pushing the envelope on marriage for clergy."

The group broke into raucous laughter. "Can you imagine women living here?" a Benedictine joked.

"The pope and his wife make a Holy Land visit?" Abbot Hoffman quipped. The clerics continued to snicker.

"You don't fool me, Father Kelly," Bishop Beck answered. "Underneath those robes, you're as liberal as they come. You're part of that Yankee agenda to make the Roman Church smell American."

Kelly's eyes twinkled. He was clearly in his element, exchanging witty repartee with ecclesiastical bigwigs. "Come now." Kelly feigned a pained look. "I am no more than a humble scholar, seeking only to serve the Holy Father."

The group hooted. Someone started passing a platter of roast beef around. Steaming potatoes followed. A monk brought in a large wooden bowl of salad.

"You should know the Vatican is aware of your membership in that awful American symposium called the Jesus Seminar," Beck countered. "The Holy Office says they are nothing but a collection of the worst heretics assembled since the Reformation." He fiddled with the pectoral cross dangling from a hook on the buttons of his cassock. "Frightening lot."

"I am only trying to guide them into the true faith." Kelly's voice reeked with the sound of contrived innocence. "After all, someone must be the light in a dark night."

A bishop who had said virtually nothing during the conversation tore off a chunk of meat and suddenly spoke in threatening tones. "If your scholarship wasn't so highly recognized, you'd be in trouble." He made his point with a jab of the fork. "Cardinal Ratsinger is deeply disturbed that your name is even associated with that pack of fools."

Father Kelly's eyes narrowed. He smiled at David and answered the bishop in German. The priest sounded firm and uncompromising. David watched the exchange and realized he had never seen this side of Kelly. The mild and unassuming scholar was no mean church politician. A game was being played out in these German conversations. While David had no idea what it was, Kelly was clearly a master player. Bishop Beck's eyes reflected approval of how the priest handled himself. In turn, Michael Kelly was alive and energized in a way David had not previously observed. The scholar had political ambition and friends in high places. Perhaps these connections would yet prove useful to a lawyer dealing in antiquities and sensitive international negotiations.

Use of the English language evaporated like steam from the soup pot. German drifted into Latin and David waited silently in the backwaters of a conversation that did not involve him. By the end of the meal, Beck and Kelly were obviously locked in a good-natured struggle to dominate the group. The bishop appeared to have the edge by virtue of his office, but Kelly's intelligence seemed to successfully challenge the pecking order. David watched the other clerics' acquiescence to a lesser role not much better than his own. In spite of the bishop's original assertion, no one asked him a single question about Jerusalem, Israel, or the Jewish world.

Once the meal was finished, Kelly excused himself and took David back to the sitting room.

"Quite a conversation," David observed. "Sounded significant."

Father Kelly nodded as he walked. "These men are pipelines to the Holy Father himself." The priest smiled with a self-satisfied look. "You don't get much higher. People at the top know who I am." He raised his eyebrow and winked. "Not a bad place to be."

Kelly opened the heavy wooden door and ushered David into the large conference room with a massive fireplace in the center. He pushed up two chairs near the fireplace and suggested David sit down. The priest closed the ancient wooden door; the stone-walled room felt quite soundproof. He sat down and rested his head on one hand in a pose reminiscent of a priest about to begin the rite of reconciliation.

"Let me get to the point," David began. "Anything I tell you must be kept in total and strict confidence."

"All is 'under the stole,' as we say about confession."

"We may have in our possession either the legendary Donation of Melchizedek or an exact copy."

Kelly's mouth dropped. "You're not serious?"

"And the copy is in five ancient languages, including a form of ancient Greek. That's where you come in."

Kelly pulled at his lip, his eyes narrowed. "I'm sure you are fully aware of the significance of what you are suggesting."

"I think so." David tried to sound condescending to counter any hint of limitations. "Do you think you have the capacity to work with such antiquity?" A little tit for tat.

"Look," Father Kelly answered bluntly. "After an outstanding career in an American seminary, I finished a Ph.D. at the Pontifical Academy in Rome. I probably would have entered the office of the secretariat and the field of diplomacy if I hadn't done so well in ancient language study. Vatican politics became a hobby, not a career. I distinguished myself by archaeological research in Galilee. Does that answer your question?"

"You would be part of a team, including my wife, Leah, and Dr. Musa Salah, whose father was the Bedouin who originally discovered the Dead Sea Scrolls."

"Agreed," Kelly snapped.

"You don't have to think about the proposal?"

"If you're even close, I want in on this action."

"Again, all attempts at translation must be clandestine and confidential to the group."

"Agreed," the priest answered again.

David extended his hand. "Let's shake on it."

Father Kelly immediately responded.

"I suggest we meet in our home tomorrow night." David stood up. "Perhaps a light supper to get everyone acquainted and then a discussion of how to proceed. You know where we live."

Michael Kelly nodded and slowly rose from his chair. "I'll be there. Even the pope couldn't keep me from coming."

12

Musa shot a quick glance around the Rosenbergs' home. The severe modernistic style with clean sharp lines reflected sophisticated tastes. Plain furniture and pale colors highlighted the numerous artifacts. Original oil paintings, reminiscent of the work of Modigliani and Cézanne, contrasted artistically with the extraordinary archaeological discoveries displayed around the living room. Halogen lamps accentuated the nuances of shadow and form in each of the antiquities. By Jerusalem standards the home was elegant; by desert standards, palatial.

He ran his hands over the smooth surface of the polished marble table. Making the leap into the modern world had never been easy. Life in a dormitory at Cornell University was equally disconcerting. No one understood the simple joys of sleeping under the stars at night, eating around an open fire, running barefoot in the sand, and watching people who said little but communicated volumes. Time had pushed one foot into this world of noise, cement, asphalt, nonrepresentational paintings, and grotesque statues; but the other foot remained firmly planted in the desert wilderness.

"Please try one of the hors d'oeuvres." Leah offered a plate of crackers and black Russian caviar, obviously trying hard to please.

"Thank you." Musa made eye contact and smiled pleasantly. Leah seemed genuine enough tonight.

"Father Kelly should be here any moment," Leah called over her shoulder and returned to the kitchen. "Make yourself at home. Enjoy the relics."

Musa nibbled on the cracker and bent down to inspect what was obviously an ancient Canaanite-period clay deity encased in a glass box. Although museums would kill for such a piece, his thoughts were elsewhere. He felt comfortable with David because he still seemed to be the good childhood friend, but Leah was a different matter. Aggressive women made him uncomfortable, and he could not help feeling apprehensive. No matter how hard she tried, Leah was simply too up front and blunt for his tastes.

The doorbell rang and David immediately appeared from the kitchen to answer it.

"Father Kelly!" He swung the door open. "Come in, come in." David welcomed his friend.

Musa braced himself. He had not met many Catholic priests, but the ones Musa knew seemed foreboding and condescending. Scholarly types had to be even worse.

"I want you to meet Dr. Musa Salah." David introduced the two men. "You're both fascinating people. You'll enjoy each other's company." The negotiator inched away, having done his job.

Musa extended his hand. "Father Kelly, glad to meet you."

"Just call me Michael and dispense with the Father business," he quipped good-naturedly. Surprisingly, the priest wore a short-sleeved shirt and might have passed for the average Ashkenazi on the streets of Jerusalem. "I'd much prefer to work on a first-name basis." He shook Musa's hand warmly. "Friendship counts with me."

Musa was so taken aback, he was not sure how to respond. He fumbled hesitantly. "Fine. Please, call me Musa."

"Good. Good!" Kelly exuded an all-encompassing warmth. "Sounds like we'll get along famously." He tapped Musa gently on the shoulder.

Musa watched Kelly turn to Leah with the ease of a diplomat moving down a receiving line in an embassy. A Jesuit named Father O'Neal at Cornell had tried to convert him to Christianity. His specialty was Islamic studies, and Musa became another challenge for the Jesuit evangelist. O'Neal's class in paleontology made him a captive to the man's influence. Vastly superior in training and education, the Jesuit descended on the Muslim student like a vulture swooping down on a desert kill. Musa finally dropped the class and usually ran from men with white collars around their necks.

"A little caviar?" Leah returned from the kitchen. "We're so delighted you could come this evening, Father Kelly."

"Please, just Michael." Kelly radiated natural charm. "We know each other far too well." He kissed her hand and took a cracker in one grand sweep.

Musa listened carefully as the priest and the Jewish couple exchanged pleasantries. He sensed a level of diplomatic grace and social facility far beyond his capacities. They were masters of small talk; Musa was not. But he liked what he saw of the priest. The man had none of the pompous arrogance Musa expected. His down-to-earth qualities felt right. The longer he listened, the more Musa relaxed. Maybe the man had possibilities. Musa munched an hors d'oeuvre and listened.

After ten minutes of social conversation, Leah moved the

group into the dining area. Musa stared in amazement. Around each place Leah had arranged special dishes filled with appetizers. *Tahina* and *humus* were favorites. Musa especially enjoyed the sesame seed paste and chickpeas. Arab dishes clearly signaled a gesture of goodwill in Musa's direction. He appreciated the attempt in preparing *kufta*. Leah had done well with the spiced meat. Adding roast lamb to the already sumptuous menu was more than Musa could ever have expected.

"Far exceeds what we eat at the monastery," Kelly commented halfway through the supper. "We only serve the meat-and-potatoes stuff Germans exist on. Bland. Not much spice. And the heavy starch has the capacity to turn one into a beach ball. But this is wonderful. Leah, you are a great cook."

"Thank you." She smiled modestly.

Michael turned to Musa. "Ever worked with one of us priest types before?"

"Once or twice." He grinned politely. "Mostly from a distance."

"We can be a bunch of overbearing bores," Kelly conceded. "Difficult and demanding. I hope your experience wasn't too bad."

"We all have our moments," Musa answered cordially.

Kelly immediately launched into a self-deprecatory joke about priests. Everyone laughed. Musa felt his doubts fading. Yes, this Kelly was a very different sort. Not like the Jesuits or his American language professors who often seemed condescending because of his Palestinian background . . . or so he had felt.

"Let's move into the living room for dessert," Leah suggested. "We can talk around the coffee table."

When they had reassembled she announced, "I'm switching menus on you. I have a nice Swiss chocolate torte." She nodded pleasantly at Musa. "If my sources are correct, you've always had a weakness for *shokolada*."

Musa beamed. With a culinary tour de force, Leah had broken through his defenses. "Your intelligence gathering is astonishing." The path to his heart was paved with chocolate. Perhaps, he reflected, he had been too hasty in all of his judgments. Leah's delectable cake more than touched his nerve center. The atmosphere felt charmed. Musa took a second helping of the rich dessert.

"I think we should talk about our project." David shifted the conversation. "As you know, Musa discovered a medallion and a gold scroll that appears to be the text of the legendary Donation of Melchizedek. We moved the objects to a secure location but photographed the script to inspect before we start the actual task of translation. Leah, please get the photograph." He nodded and Leah compliantly went to the back of the house. "I know you'll want to work from the original, but we have a decent copy to start with tonight."

Leah returned and spread an eight-by-ten-inch picture on the coffee table in front of them. The photograph left much to be desired but gave a clear indication of the script.

Kelly the priest instantly became Kelly the scholar. Any hint of glibness disappeared with the intense silence of deep thought. His countenance changed; he locked onto the manuscript as if everything else in the room had disappeared. The priest picked up the photo reproduction and held it close so no one else could see. He mumbled to himself while he scrutinized the document, scanning each line with his index finger. His eyes darted back and forth over every inch of the picture.

"What do you think?" Musa broke the scholar's concentration.

Michael blinked several times as if returning from a state of altered reality. "Absolutely amazing! Of course, one must be cautious in assessing such a matter, but you have definitely come up with something most worthy."

Musa smiled at the Rosenbergs. "We think so."

"What do you make of it?" David asked.

Kelly's eyes narrowed, and he studied the script once more. "The issue is not just that the same meaning is conveyed in a number of different languages, as was true of the Rosetta stone. The meaning of the message is interwoven through all of the languages, more like a modern crossword puzzle. To get the point, one must understand how it fits within the total picture."

Musa's mouth dropped. Kelly was more than good. With one observation the priest had come up with a brilliant insight. Musa had not made any headway sorting out the syntax.

"Isn't that strange?" David persisted.

"Beyond strange," Michael answered soberly. "I know of nothing like it." He thought for a moment. "But it's like the message has been encoded in this form because it has universal significance . . . or at the least is intended to extend beyond one group of peoples. After all, the five languages represent highly diverse segments of the ancient world." The priest picked up the manuscript and started studying it again.

This man is even better than his reputation, Musa thought. David was right. Including him might be one of the most important decisions they had made.

"We believe the structure and early components in the message definitely point to the strong possibility this is either a copy of or the preserved form of the Donation of Melchizedek," Leah spoke for the first time since the discussion of the scroll began. "You can see our line of reasoning."

"Y—e—s," Kelly exhaled. "We have in our possession a most extraordinary document, regardless of what it is finally judged to be. I can tell you the Greek is of the most ancient of origins."

"For these reasons," Leah continued, "the contents could have highly significant political consequences."

"Why?" Kelly puzzled. "I don't follow your reasoning on that one."

"Well." Leah sounded more assertive. "If this is the actual Donation it will be a strong determining factor in whether Arabs or Jews have the ultimate right of ownership to this city."

"Oh, come now," Kelly scoffed. "An ancient document would have no bearing on the present status of this place. That's a political issue to be solved by contemporary people. Actually, the issue is much larger than a Jewish and Arab decision anyway."

"I don't think you understand," Leah shot back. "The relationship of Jews and Arabs to everything in this land is based on what occurred centuries ago. Claims and rights are based on decisions and agreements made by our ancestors."

Kelly grinned slyly and shrugged his shoulders. "That's why you people can't get your political problems solved. Modern diplomacy doesn't have a chance in a nation ruled by prejudice."

Musa felt his newly formed optimism draining away. In seconds, Kelly had made a 180-degree switch. Musa looked at the empty dessert plate on the coffee table. *I've let myself get sidetracked*, he realized. *Better pay attention to this man's ideas.*

Leah crossed her arms over her chest and dropped back in her chair. "And just how would you solve the current tensions and disagreements over the status of Jerusalem, Father Kelly?"

"Oh, we're getting formal now." Michael sounded smug. "Good. That's the best atmosphere for a political discussion." He cleared his throat. "I believe the Vatican has already staked out the high ground. We have what will ultimately be found as the best solution. The only hope is the internationalization of the city with oversight from an international tribunal. The offices of the pope would be an excellent starting place."

David and Leah exchanged looks of consternation, then turned to Musa with a similar look of dismay.

He caught their glance. Kelly had started taking on the air and sound of the Cornell Jesuit. For all his social facility, Kelly had no idea of the depth of his own prejudice, and he also missed the obvious fact that Leah was offended. Musa watched her face carefully. It appeared to be frozen in ice. Something more lingered there besides a difference of social opinion. He saw pain beneath the anger.

"Come now," Kelly persisted. "We are people of science. Modern scholarship has given us the tools to rise above petty nationalism. We meet on the higher plain of superior reason. Surely some political slant in this document could not divide us against each other."

"Excuse me," Leah interrupted. "You don't think *you* came here tonight with your own political agenda? Surely what you just suggested is as biased as anything we believe as Semitic peoples."

"What?" Kelly gnarled his forehead. "You must be kidding."

"You are the pope's boy," Leah fired back. "The only difference between you and Musa and us is that you're pushing a Western solution for a Middle Eastern problem."

Kelly's fair skin took on a decidedly pink color. "That's only because you people think you own the history of this land."

"You think you've got a claim to a piece of it?" Leah sounded tough. "What do you hang your hat on? The Crusaders' invasion, the most terrible bloodbath in the history of the region? Remember the Christians rounding up the Jews in Jerusalem and burning them in their own synagogues? Is that the logic of your warranty deed?"

The priest clearly looked miffed. "Our Lord was crucified here," he sounded defensive. "Because He died for the world, the world has a right to this place."

Leah swore. "The world doesn't live here day after day. The world only comes for ten-day tourist visits. Let me tell you something, Father Kelly. It was the shed blood of *our* families that obtained access to this land, not the death of one of our ancestors centuries ago. Families like Musa's and our own must carve out an existence in this place by the sweat of our brow while the pope and his buddies at the United Nations are discussing the future over vintage wine."

"I see we have very different points of view." Icicles hung from Kelly's words.

"Excuse me." David, the negotiator, interrupted. "We must do everything possible to avoid the natural political minefield that is inherent in this document. I ask that each of us set aside our strong feelings about contemporary issues. We must stick with what is in this manuscript."

As David continued to plead for tolerance, Musa studied the face of the priest. His mind was now clear. Not only had his all-accepting view of Kelly changed, Musa now felt strangely closer to Leah than he had at any time. She had spoken well in answering this arrogant presumptuous tool of Rome. He could not have said it any better.

Kelly was a very skillful scholar, Musa concluded. No question about it. But he was about as neutral as the chief rabbi of Israel. Father Kelly would yet prove to be a problem.

Leah worked at the sink, finishing up the dishes from the evening meal. What was left of the meat went into a plastic dish for the refrigerator. She put the last of the glassware back in the cupboard above the cabinet.

What if her husband was displeased because she said too much? She'd had every intention of keeping her mouth shut through the entire evening, but Kelly's comments hit every button. Her rebuttal had simply popped out.

At that moment Leah became aware of how much anger stayed bottled up in the depths of her soul. An image emerged.

Six-year-old Leah's mother, Yanait, stood frozen in place at the sink in the simple kitchen in their small house. From the child's vantage point, the little woman looked six feet tall. Yanni's faded housedress hung limply nearly down to her ankles; the leather on her thick-soled shoes cracked on the sides. Words had been said that kept her from moving.

Leah looked again at the voice coming from behind her. Mrs. Bazak remained the steady fixture in their neighborhood. People moved in and out, but the tattered refugee from Hungary stayed. To Leah's eyes, Mrs. Bazak was old enough to be in a class with Noah. The old woman waved her arms frantically and cried.

Mrs. Bazak's mouth kept moving, but Leah could not hear the sounds coming out. Even though Yanait's arms tensed to the point of trembling, she did not move. The silence inside Leah's head seemed so intense that something might explode. Only very slowly did she let Mrs. Bazak's words tune back in. At first they came so softly, the woman might have been at the end of the block whispering. Then, like a radio slowly turned up, the sound became clearer. Leah's mind could not accept what she clearly heard.

"He's dead!" Mrs. Bazak kept saying between sobs. "They shot him. A sniper shot from the top of a building. Dead!"

Yanait finally broke out of the emotional bands locking her in place. When she turned, Leah could see her *Ima*'s face twisted in grief and pain. The corner of her mouth dropped and quivered. Yanait's eyes widened in horror as if she were already looking at the bullet-punctured body. The tense arms and hands found life again and shook violently.

"Your boy!" Mrs. Bazak wailed. "The Arabs shot and killed your little Zvi. He's lying in the marketplace."

Yanait slowly crumpled to the floor in a silent heap. Leah rushed to grab her. *"Ima! Ima!"* she cried in the pale white face. Leah's small hands could not move her mother. Suddenly, Mrs. Bazak was in the middle of everything. Crying, wailing, and trying to wake up Yanait, finally pouring water in her face.

Only after Leah's mother was seated at the table again, lost in grief, could Leah let the meaning of Mrs. Bazak's words fully sink in. "Zvi is dead," she had said. The teenage brother Leah adored was what the big people called dead. The meaning of death was not clear, but Leah knew it meant they did not come back again. They didn't play with the dreidel at Hanukkah ever again. They didn't tell you stories ever again. There would be no more agains, ever again.

Leah, the housewife, stared at a folded white linen napkin on the kitchen counter and saw Zvi's shrouded body being laid in the square hole in the hard ground. After they had each thrown a handful of dirt in the grave, men from the neighborhood shoveled dirt on top of Zvi. Leah remembered standing there, staring at the dirt on her small palms, worrying if Zvi would have dirt in his eyes, his nose, his mouth. She wanted to jump in the hole and throw her body on top to protect her helpless brother from the dirt. Anguish swelled up in her with such intensity, Leah thought she would leap. In fact, she wanted to be buried. Just curled up on top of her brother's final bed, gently protecting him from any further hurt from the horrible Arabs.

Leah looked at the napkin and realized her enormous anger was only a shield. Hidden at the very bottom of her soul was sheer pain. Agony that had begun on her mother's kitchen floor and never left her. Years had passed, but her own kitchen was now filled with grief every bit as severe as if she were again standing by Zvi's open grave.

Leah wept silently. She did not want David to see. The suffering remained too private, too immediate, too personal. Leah dabbed at her eyes with a dish towel.

"Just wanted to tell you," David said from the door to the kitchen, "I appreciated what you said tonight."

Leah did not turn around. "Thank you."

"You spoke well. Kelly was an insensitive fool."

"I'm glad you approved." Leah smiled at the carefully folded napkin and placed it gently back in the drawer.

13

Wednesday, September 9
Washington, D.C.

On the other side of the world, dawn was breaking over America's capital. The sun, yet hidden below the horizon, slowly spread light across the face of night. Thousands of commuters jockeyed in the dimness for the best position on the beltway, pouring an endless line of bureaucrats into the Federal District. Like ants scurrying off to another day's toil in the world's most significant ant bed, workers paced themselves against the rising sun. The Washington Monument glistened in the first rays of the day, the shimmering image stretching down the Mall's long reflection pool. Sunlight caught the spire on the nation's capitol, and the aurora slowly crossed the great city until the splendor peered into the windows of the Mayflower Hotel, where the prime minister's entourage slept, struggling to overcome jet lag. The building, which had been modified to accommodate the security needs of their government, was home away from home for Israeli diplomats.

In a small room on the hotel's top floor, Daniel Levy had been at work for some time. Hovering over his desk in his underwear, he was closing out the coded messages his computer picked up from the special phone number the Mossad used for relaying information to *sochnim* around the world. Using a special software system, implemented only for these limited occasions, the computer quickly turned the symbols into hard data.

Mossad used a double coding system with phonetic sounds having numerical value. The name *Abdul* broke into two parts with *Ab* having the value of seven and *dul* twenty-one. However, a second system was in place assigning each number to yet another code system, which changed weekly. The double system made it impossible to decipher a message without the sophisticated software.

Daniel knew he must quickly digest the relevant material before destroying every trace of the transcription. With his usual intensity, he devoured the communiqué. The "office" update had everything Levy needed to know. He electronically accessed the file on his so-called long-lost relative Abdul. The update sheet laid out a step-by-step description of events. Earlier, in late July, Mossad agents had faxed Al-Amid's secret phone number to his mistress in Switzerland. In turn, she was pressuring the Syrian, accusing him of a hasty departure from Geneva in an attempt to ditch her. Her threats to call Al-Amid's wife had worked. He was afraid of not being able to meet her financial demands; Abdul had cratered under the pressure and become an informer. Everything was now in place for Daniel's call and *tachless*, or genuine business, as the agents called an approach. When the day's work was done, Levy would type in the results and send the information back to Israel.

Daniel hit the delete button and the screen blanked out once again. He carefully stored the top secret computer unit in a hidden side pocket in his suitcase, taking out a tiny remote transmitter and a small Beretta pistol. *Sichlut*, the agency's recording unit, would be ready to record every word during the contact.

Levy glanced at the digital radio clock by his bed. "Ten after six," he mumbled to himself. "Cousin Abdul should be waking up about now. Let's give him a little cheer to help his day start nicely."

He punched in the diplomat's home phone number and waited. The phone rang five times.

"*Ahlan*," a man's groggy voice groaned.

"*Keef halak?*" Levy spoke loudly, hoping his voice would be recognized.

After a long pause, the man said in excellent English, "Just a moment."

Daniel listened intently. A phone was picked up. After a few seconds another phone clicked off. Moments later the second phone was picked up again. "Speak English," Al-Amid said. "My wife doesn't understand." After a long pause, he added, "so I won't wake her up."

"Welcome to America," Levy began. "This is your cousin from Syria."

"Yes. Yes. I know." Abdul forcefully cleared his throat.

"I am in Washington now," Levy began. "I felt it would be good to see family in this strange land. Might we have breakfast together?"

Al-Amid waited a long time. "This morning?" he finally answered.

"Why not?"

"Yes, it will be good to see you. Where?"

"Perhaps the Washington Hilton, in an hour."

"Make it an hour and a half." The Syrian sounded flustered.

"Okay, eight o'clock sharp in the coffee shop."

"Yes. Fine."

"It will be good for old times' sake," Daniel added. "We can talk about family matters."

The phone clicked off.

Daniel grinned. His "cousin" seemed somewhat distressed, he thought. Maybe a little *ahwa* would wake him up. *Some of the strong black coffee wouldn't hurt me either,* he said to himself.

The agent opened the back side of his black suitcase, pulling out an old shirt and pants. The well-worn twenty-year-old clothes were meant to reflect vintage immigrant style. A Syrian cousin should not look too prosperous. He slipped on the pants, exposing his knee through a tear in the jeans.

Moments later Levy was back on the phone to the *tzevet*, the security team. He began without ceremony. "I will be at the Hilton Hotel coffee shop at eight o'clock. I want electronic sur-veillance of the conversation and backup in case our friends from the north try to ambush me. Got it?"

"Sit in the back if possible," the anonymous voice instructed. "Wear your wire in case we have any complications."

"I will."

"Hitting someone at the Hilton is unlikely, but Reagan got popped there. We'll be watching your back."

"Good." Levy hung up and put on the blue flannel shirt. He lit a cigarette and lay back on the bed, feeling fully satisfied. With the cigarette dangling from the corner of his mouth, Daniel began writing out his "want list" for Al-Amid.

At 7:45 A.M., Levy walked briskly into the Hilton's first-floor coffee shop. Winding his way to a rear table, he took a chair with his back to the wall. The rough clothing was somewhat out of character for the professional atmosphere of the hotel, but he was not obvious, looking more like one of the maintenance per-sonnel.

After ordering coffee and a bagel, Daniel carefully surveyed the rest of the customers. Seated halfway in the middle of the restaurant, a man in a business suit read his newspaper while aiming his attaché case at Daniel. They made brief eye contact, and Daniel knew the electronic surveillance equipment inside the case was on. Outside the restaurant window, an old brown van pulled up to the curb in the no-parking area, and window washers got out. The men certainly were not in a hurry to get down to business. Daniel relaxed. The backup muscle was in place.

At 8:05 Abdul Al-Amid entered from the hotel side of the coffee shop and looked around nervously. Daniel saw him but made no movement. Al-Amid quickly identified Levy and hurried to the table.

"Good morning." The diplomat embraced Levy and kissed him on both cheeks in the typical Arab manner.

"*Marhaba*," Daniel welcomed Al-Amid.

"We should speak English to be less obvious." Al-Amid pulled at his collar and wrung his hands. "We don't want to draw more attention to ourselves than is necessary."

"Fine." Daniel smiled. "Good to see you again so soon."

"The woman is squeezing me," Abdul began at once without the usual formalities. "I can't afford problems at home. Matters could get out of hand quickly."

"I know. I know." Levy shook his head. "The way of the world is hard. You are a good, industrious husband who deserves understanding."

Abdul looked pained. "My wife's family has connections with President Assad. Nothing must leak out."

"I am glad you came to me, my friend." Levy patted the Arab on the hand. "I know how to handle these matters." He looked around for the waitress and snapped his fingers in a gauche manner. "Coffee for my friend!"

The waitress gave him a look of disdain and turned toward the coffee machine.

"You simply need some financial help," Levy continued. "How can I be of service?"

The waitress placed a cup of coffee before Abdul. Levy did not look up, his attention riveted on the Arab.

"She wants to live like a queen in Switzerland," Abdul groaned. "If I cut her off now, the woman will call my wife."

"What will it take? Five thousand? Ten?"

Abdul settled back in his chair and stared at Daniel. The Syrian picked up the coffee without looking away. He took a long sip and put the cup down on the tablecloth, missing the saucer. For a moment Abdul rubbed the bridge of his nose. "What do *you* want?" he finally asked.

"First, I just want to be your friend." Levy worked at his most sincere expression. "I sympathize with your people, and we're both concerned about the same objectives for our countries." Abdul did not look convinced, so Daniel pressed on. "However, I do need some information. My ability to obtain the kind of money you need has to be based on something. Information is the commodity."

Al-Amid looked nervously around the room. "What do you *want*?"

"A new terrorist initiative is under way." Levy chose his words carefully. "You know about these people. I need to know who they are and where they're coming from."

Al-Amid did not blink. Good sign, Levy thought. Abdul simply looked straight ahead.

"I must know what these people are about." The buddy-buddy act was over. *Tachless* time. Levy meant business now.

"Islamic Revolutionary Front." Abdul's mouth barely moved. "Some old leaders banded together in a new organization." Al-Amid clenched his jaw. "The rest costs you forty thousand. Not a penny less." The friendship act was over. Everyone was doing business now.

"Forty's a lot."

"I know a lot," Al-Amid countered.

Levy sucked on the inside of his cheek. "The office" would not be thrilled with this figure, but G had said no one would question his decision. "The last time we met I asked for information. You said a microfilm would be forthcoming."

"I have it with me." Abdul sounded ill.

"Okay. I've got you covered *if* you have the microfilm today."

Al-Amid slowly nodded his head in agreement. "We have a deal."

"The money will be wired to my Swiss bank account," Abdul dictated. "And it must be there in twenty-four hours."

Levy shook his head and frowned. He did not want to appear too eager or as if he had bottomless pockets. "I will try," he sighed.

"I must know you will, or I have nothing to say." Al-Amid's eyes looked desperate.

"We are friends. I will obtain the money even if I must take some of it from my own account." Of course, the Syrian did not believe it, but Daniel's statement had the nuance of great sincerity.

"I can expect the money to be in Geneva by noon tomorrow?"

"Absolutely." Levy threw in the towel.

"The Islamic Revolutionary Front has achieved a level of cooperation previous terrorist organizations have not had. Usually everyone fights with everyone else, but the IRF has been able to sidestep the old irritations. They're funded by four Arab nations."

Daniel tried to look deadpan, but the significance hit him like a board in the face. "Who's the leadership?"

"You know Osama bin Laden, the Saudi multimillionaire operating out of Afghanistan?" He did not wait for a response.

"After the Americans bombed his training facility, he gained even greater stature and was able to use his influence to bring various factions together. Then Hamas brought in some of their best-trained terrorists. In Libya Muammar Gaddafi sent two of his best people. The leadership is formidable."

"Where does Syria fit in?"

"Syria is pouring in enormous amounts of money," Al-Amid replied. "They are infiltrating agents from governments throughout the world into Jordan. In addition, they have cleared the IRF to bring their weapons of mass destruction in through Lebanon."

"I see," Levy mused thoughtfully. "Therefore, money is no object."

Al-Amid kept glancing nervously around the restaurant and nodding his head.

"What is their prime objective?"

Abdul took a deep breath. "The code name for their plan is 'The Road to Jerusalem.' The group shares the common belief that the rightful owner of Jerusalem is the prophet Muhammad, and they intend to return control of the city to Islam. If nuclear response is required to do so, they are prepared ultimately to take such action."

Daniel's face froze. He felt a hard knot form in his stomach. He knew Jerusalem was more than a holy city to Muslim radicals; it was a political as well as a religious symbol. He pressed Al-Amid harder. "Why is control of Jerusalem so important to them?"

"The IRF believes Jerusalem is the wedge that can split world opinion and tip the balance of support toward the Arab world. Jews get too much propaganda mileage out of their absolute control of the city. Any and all means will be used to end their reign of terror."

The Mossad agent scrutinized the face of the frightened man

sitting across from him. Something was not quite right in the eyes. "You have more to tell me," Levy concluded.

Al-Amid licked his lips and glanced at the floor. "The IRF has VX-type nerve gas, and they also have the missiles to drop the gas on Jerusalem."

Levy tried not to look surprised and only shook his head. "The microfilm?"

Al-Amid pulled a small matchbook from his pocket and laid it on the table. "Why should I trust you?"

"You're on the payroll already. And besides, we are not through doing business with each other."

The Arab stared at Levy with cold, hard eyes. "Just don't miss a payment."

"The money's on the way as soon as the film is in my hand."

"Inside the cover."

"I will pick it up after you leave."

Abdul's hand trembled when he dropped the matches on the tablecloth. The diplomat quickly put his hand back in his pocket.

Daniel picked up the matches and lit a cigarette, laying the little pack back on the tablecloth. "Looks a little more convincing if I light up," he smiled. "I'm going to put a small piece of paper on the table. A sort of grocery list. You may need more financial assistance. Answering these questions will help me get you more money."

"I—I—don't know." Al-Amid's color was not improving. "I want out of this business."

"We are friends." Levy put his hand on top of Abdul's and smiled broadly. When he took his hand away, the piece of paper remained in the Arab's palm. "Do not worry. I will protect you at all costs."

The diplomat took a long deep breath. "I must make sure the money is in Switzerland before I make any decisions."

"I may not be here long on this visit, but I will be in contact," Levy concluded. "My number in Jerusalem is on that piece of paper. For the next several days I will be at the Mayflower Hotel."

Abdul abruptly stood up and embraced Levy in the usual Arab manner. Moments later the diplomat disappeared out the side door of the restaurant and was gone.

Daniel finished his cigarette and nodded to the man in the middle of the restaurant. The Mossad plant picked up the briefcase and left. The workmen finally finished the front window and began putting the buckets and squeegees back in the truck. The *sochen* put out the cigarette in the ashtray, blew a long breath across the table, and slipped the matchbook into the palm of his hand. He walked out the door of the coffee shop and into the hotel lobby.

Only after Levy was completely out of sight did a woman at another side table pull a cell phone from her purse and begin talking. "They're gone," she said in Arabic. "All of them, including the agent with the briefcase."

14

Wednesday, September 9
Jerusalem, Dormition Abbey

As noon passed in Washington, D.C., evening was falling in Jerusalem. From minarets across the Holy City, singsong voices called the faithful to prayer, and Muslims fell to their knees with faces on the ground. Tourists returned to their hotels as shadows drifted across the alleys and cobblestone streets of the Old City. Supper dishes were cleared away at the Dormition Abbey, and the monks prepared for evening prayers.

Father Michael Kelly sat in the large gathering room reserved for visitors, making polite conversation with Dr. Salah and detailing the history of the Abbey, killing time until the Rosenbergs arrived. The thick brown Benedictine robe contrasted sharply with Musa's casual khaki pants and pullover shirt.

"Of course, the Church of the Dormition is the very crown on Mount Zion," Kelly explained with more than a small hint of pride in his voice. "The land was presented much earlier by a Turkish sultan to the German emperor, although the present structures were dedicated at the beginning of the twentieth century. The crypt has a stone sculpture to represent the blessed Virgin's last sleep at this very spot before she was assumed bodily into heaven. Or so the dogma goes." He filled the Arab's glass with more Liebfraumilch.

Musa nodded politely with a hint he already knew the story well. "Yes. So I understand," he said politely.

"One of our chapels was a donation of the Austrians in memory of Prime Minister Dollfuss, a victim of Nazi persecution." Kelly continued his monologue. "Other chapels came from various nations in honor of Mary."

The door opened. "Sorry we are late." David Rosenberg hurried into the room. Leah trailed behind. "Got delayed at the office. Last-minute nonsense."

"We were just reviewing the history of my ancient home." Kelly stood, and Salah followed suit. "An opportunity to tell Musa something of our past."

"Good. Good." David stood back to allow his wife to sit down first. "The time was not lost then."

"Hardly." Musa again smiled perfunctorily. "The Dormition Church is a fascinating place."

"I know everyone is eager to begin the translation," David started at once. "Of course, we also want to work from the scroll. I think the first order of business is to decide where the operation will occur, so we are assured the scroll is stored in a protected environment."

Kelly smiled deceptively and settled back in his chair. *The lawyer is all business tonight and ready to take over. If there's anything more pushy than a lawyer,* the priest thought, *it's a Jewish lawyer. Going to have a little tug-of-war before the day is over.*

"Perhaps we might share our opinions about the possibilities for an acceptable site." David kept smiling at everyone. The good humor felt a bit contrived.

The priest waited. Let them play their cards first. Who will start the game?

The group looked at one another, attempting to be pleasant, nonchalant. Like children playing drop-the-hanky, the foursome was circling.

"Perhaps we should allow ladies to be first," Musa broke the silence. "Leah must have an opinion we should weigh."

Leah looked surprised at his suggestion. She cleared her throat. "Well," she hedged, "I had thought earlier that the Shrine of the Book might be a good historical location. After all, the Dead Sea Scrolls are on display there. The adjacent Bible Lands Museum is well equipped for such a purpose. What do you think, Michael?"

"Interesting," the priest murmured.

"How does that sound to you, Musa?" David Rosenberg jumped at the idea, sounding as if he'd come with the matter settled. He was trying to drop the handkerchief.

"We do well to remember the reputation of the scholars identified with that project." Musa was not playing the game. "The original recipients of the scrolls concealed them for years. Literally hid them from the rest of the academic community. If clandestine copies of the manuscripts had not been released in Pasadena, California, the entire collection of documents would still not be available. People of that ilk frighten me."

David's face fell.

"I see," Leah said slowly.

"Frankly, I would prefer more neutral ground," Salah pressed on. "The entire area is in Israeli control."

"I see your point." Kelly quickly intervened to push the conversation in another direction. "What would be more suitable to you, Musa?"

The archaeologist frowned. "I suppose we should keep the work here in Jerusalem. No one wants to travel to Tel Aviv." He seemed to talk more to himself. "I have been associated with the Rockefeller Museum on Sultan Suleiman Street. East Jerusalem has some advantages. For one, the museum staff are excellent people. But we should only tell them enough to use their facilities."

"But they have such limited security," Leah objected. "Their building is equipped to prevent petty theft but hardly to stop a serious onslaught. If news of the find gets out, politicization will surely follow. The Rockefeller wouldn't stand an assault. Any storage area in that museum would be vulnerable."

Salah reluctantly agreed.

"You, Michael?" David sounded far less assured. "Something to add?"

Kelly looked thoughtfully at the floor. Mustn't sound eager. Play his cards slow and easy. Give it some time as if this idea were his reaction.

"Have you worked at any of the universities in the area?" Musa probed.

"Their libraries would give us immediate access to linguistic materials," he continued.

The priest stood up. He did not want them going down that alley. "Perhaps I should show you something. It just occurred to me that you might find an aspect of the Abbey interesting." He pointed toward the door. "Follow me."

Kelly led the trio down the hall in the opposite direction of the dining hall until they came to a large wooden door with heavy black metal hinges. The portal's size and rough surface looked far more fitting to a medieval castle than a church.

"I've never been this way," David observed. "Michael, you've shown me some unusual back halls before, but this is quite different."

The priest pulled a large old key from beneath his brown robe. "No one ever opens this up." He slowly turned the key until the lock clicked. "Most of the monks aren't even aware of what's beyond the door. They simply assume it's a janitor's closet or something of the sort." When Kelly pulled the door open, the hinges squeaked a high-pitched squeal. Steps disappeared down into pitch-black darkness.

"We just happen to keep a light inside the door." Kelly reached to the exact spot where an amazingly clean, shiny flashlight waited. "I'll see if it still works." The light was bright and sharp.

"What's down there?" Leah peered into the blackness.

"Let's find out." The priest started down the steps. "Allow me to lead the way. Just watch the light beam ahead of me." He picked his way down the broad wooden steps.

At the bottom, Michael aimed the flashlight around a large oblong chamber until he spotted a breaker switch on the wall. The air smelled damp and cool. "Stay put." He quickly crossed the room and threw the switch.

Light sprang up, revealing a long rectangular room that had not been used for a long time. Cobwebs crisscrossed the far corners and unadorned walls. Long tables and a few chairs were stored around the edges. Heavy wooden ceiling beams and the square, smooth granite blocks covering the floor made the place feel like a fortress. Cement slab walls only added to the austere feeling of being trapped in a dungeon.

"Your monks ever put people on a rack?" David joked with less tact than usual. "This would be a great place for an inquisition."

Musa laughed, but the comment obviously did not set well with the priest. "Wine was once stored down here," he answered bluntly.

"I'm not sure that even a bomb would shake this place," Musa added. "You people built these things as if you planned to sit out Armageddon down here."

Leah laughed nervously. "Certainly wouldn't want to get locked in."

"On the other side of that wall are the crypts." The priest sounded like the tour director again. "Might say the room is a hedge against a population explosion. Should we run out of burial plots, we can knock the wall down and this space is available."

"You're suggesting the group work here?" David sounded skeptical.

"We'll air the place out and get heaters in here if necessary. I promise to keep the project secret from the monks and monastery staff. So many tourists come and go every day, no one would notice you entering. And you could slip out at any time without being recognized."

"But entry?" Leah protested. "You don't allow people to wander around the Abbey as they please."

"I can arrange for each of you to have keys both to the building and to this door." Kelly bore down. "There couldn't be a more secure arrangement that allows you better access at any time of your choosing."

"Very interesting." Musa looked around the vast chamber. "We could bring in additional lamps for the best possible illumination. Tables are certainly already here."

Kelly adjusted a chair. Getting there. The Arab is crossing the line. Got to add a little something more to hook the Rosenbergs once and for all.

"Virtually no one knows about this cellar?" David looked doubtful.

"Exactly," Kelly insisted. "Probably only two or three members of our community know what's behind the door. Maybe only one other person besides myself has been down here."

"The Armenian Library is only a stone's throw away," Musa added. "They have excellent material on ancient languages."

David and Leah looked silently around the room as if searching for, but not finding, new reservations to suggest.

"I can have our kitchen staff prepare extra food on the days when supper or lunch would be an encouragement." Kelly pointed toward the ceiling. "I could bring the meal down here, or we could eat at a private table in the dining hall."

"Excellent." Salah nodded agreement.

"But where would the scroll actually be kept when we aren't working?" Leah questioned.

The priest walked to the front wall. Ah, the final question he was hoping for. The last trap sprung.

An indentation in the wall appeared to have been planned as a niche for a shrine or, perhaps, a statue. The three-by-four-foot opening was about window height. The priest reached into the center and slowly worked a square stone loose. About the size of a cinder block, the piece slid forward, revealing a large black hole.

Kelly looked around the group triumphantly. "Discovered this little secret by pure accident once when I was doing an archaeological exploration of the building." He stuck his hand inside the hole, running his arm in nearly up to his elbow. "Don't know if it was an accident or designed on purpose. This room dates back to nearly the turn of the century, so there's no telling how the hiding place began."

"Well, the Abbey is outside the Old City walls and has a sort of neutral character." Leah appeared to have decided that the game was over.

"I must say that if any word of this project leaks out, we could be faced with serious harassment." David sounded like a stern judge. "I suppose it goes without saying, but we'd best be highly circumspect."

"Couldn't agree more." Kelly was equally emphatic.

"As soon as the scroll is delivered, we can begin." Musa crossed his arms over his chest and pulled at his lips. "I am anxious to see my find again."

"I'll begin to make the room more comfortable," Leah added. "Get a coffeepot in here. Several genuinely comfortable chairs."

The priest looked thoughtfully around the room as if contemplating other helpful changes. He had done it. He fought to keep from smiling. Yes! The find would be on his turf. Should anything go wrong, he would be the one to make sure the scroll stayed in the right hands.

Once agreement was struck the group quickly dispersed. Father Kelly locked the door and slowly walked back down the long silent corridor. Most of the monks were nourished by silence, but Michael Kelly only tolerated what seemed to him to be a vast emptiness. In the early years Michael had tried to pursue the disciplines of Benedictine spirituality, but his mind always drifted toward the more scholarly matters. After years of technical study in philosophical theology and form criticism, the critical issues generated a profound skepticism that caused him to doubt if anyone inhabited the silence. By that time he had invested too much time to leave the priestly life and continued on his way more out of rote habit than commitment. No longer merely empty, the silence had become long and endless.

He thought about the Rosenbergs, hurrying off together, happy with each other, confidants, obviously friends as well as lovers. Such moments of reflection always turned painful and he did not allow them to linger beyond a point. His introspection always ended up in the same place. He next remembered the conversations, the banter, the give-and-take of debate with other scholars during the years he studied and taught at the Pontifical Academy. Those were good days, filled with camaraderie, friendship, and exciting evenings packed with stimulating exchange. The glory of the Vatican still beckoned to him with enticing promise.

"Maybe this project will be my ticket back to Rome," Father Kelly said to himself and closed the door to his small room behind him.

15

Thursday, September 10
Washington, D.C.

"Maintenance!" A caller knocked on Daniel Levy's hotel door a second time. "Room check."

Levy thought for a moment and quickly looked around his room in the Mayflower. The green light on the black device attached to the ceiling meant the system was on. Nothing appeared out of order. Everything was working. "I didn't call for service."

"Routine safety check. Looking at all smoke detectors."

Levy cracked the door. The blue jumpsuit and leather belt full of tools looked legit. The small man appeared to be a typical immigrant filling the area's low-paying grunt jobs. Daniel's natural skepticism was allayed by the fact that the Mayflower had been practically taken over by Israeli security. The man at the door could have passed for a repairman at any hotel in Tel Aviv.

"Sorry to bother." His English wasn't bad. "Need to make sure the smoke detector is functionary. Okay?" English test flunked.

The Mossad agent looked the man over carefully. He remembered the window washers working outside the Hilton while he had met with Al-Amid. Yeah, the guy must be an Israeli.

"Just a moment." Daniel left on the safety chain and quickly pulled his pistol from a shoulder holster on the chair. Sticking the .22 caliber Beretta in the small of his back between his belt and shirt, he opened the door. "Make it quick," he demanded.

The man smiled politely and sauntered in. When the door clicked shut, the maintenance man quickly turned around. His entire countenance changed immediately. "Security breach." The immigrant look was gone, replaced by a hard I'm-in-control demeanor. "Abdul Al-Amid's wife found out everything. She's gone to officials. Nothing is certain now."

"Who are you?" Daniel's hand slowly moved toward the gun behind him. The room was suddenly getting warm.

"The 'office' sent me because discovery is too sensitive to send through normal channels." The man's eyes burned with fierce intensity. "Syrian is marked man, and you must leave country immediately. He probably go down today."

"What?" Levy's voice raised the usual octave.

The interloper reached inside the jumpsuit and pulled out an airline ticket. "We made all arrangements. If you leave in fifteen minutes, you can be on the night flight back to Israel. We can't afford to have you in United States if this hits papers." The small man leaned menacingly close to Levy's face. "Particularly, if Al-Amid assassinated in the next twelve hours."

"I want to know more details about what happened."

"I'm not authorized to say more." The contact man started toward the door. "Just be on the flight."

"But how did she find out?" Daniel caught the sleeve of his blue jumpsuit.

"Al-Amid stupid and sloppy." The small man pulled away. "Fool make one too many mistakes." He let himself out.

For a full minute, Daniel stared at the ticket jacket. Agent G had warned something of this order was possible, but how could the setup have gone sour so quickly? He glanced at his watch. Time was of the essence. Questions could be sorted out on the airplane. No alternative but to rush like mad.

Levy grabbed the first cab in front of the hotel door, but traffic proved to be a problem. He screamed at the driver, threatened, and demanded. The cabbie suddenly cursed him in Arabic.

"You from Arabia?" Daniel asked in Arabic.

The driver abruptly smiled in the mirror. "No, Iraq. Why didn't you just say you were a brother?"

Levy forced a smile. "Sorry. I didn't recognize you. I'm in something of a bind." He waved a fistful of bills in the air. "Really under a deadline."

"Hey, no problem for one of our own." The driver hit the gas.

Daniel slipped the money back in his pocket. *Can't believe it. A thousand taxis in Washington and I get this guy. With my luck, he'll turn out to be one of Saddam's agents.*

No matter what the cabbie did, cars were stacked up clear out to Dulles Airport, and the driver could only maneuver so far. Security regulations made access all the more difficult. If Daniel had not run through the airport, he'd have been late for the flight.

Among the last passengers to be seated in the 747, he sank into his business-class accommodations and stared at the back of the seat in front of him. Levy inhaled deeply. The smell of food was already in the air. He watched flight attendants shuffle the final passengers to their seats. The uniformed mother hens helped stragglers get their belongings stored overhead, admonishing the disobedient to put the luggage carriers under their seats.

He swore under his breath. All that work for months only to have Al-Amid's cover blown! The pigheaded idiot! No telling what we've lost. He ground his fist in his palm. At least the microfilm information was secured and intact.

"The film!" he exclaimed.

The passenger next to him turned and looked at Daniel out of the corner of his eye. "Excuse me."

Levy smiled apologetically and silently cursed himself for letting his shock at the day's events cause a slip of the tongue. "Just something I forgot."

The man looked away nonchalantly. "Always happens."

Daniel grimaced and shrugged. Strange that the agent at the hotel did not have any instruction about the microfilm. G should have given some indication of how disposal should proceed. Maybe things happened too fast. Perhaps he should make sure nothing had been overlooked, Daniel decided.

"Please tighten your seat belts." The flight attendant gave the final instructions. "All electronic devices must be turned off until after we have been in flight at least ten minutes. We are leaving momentarily." The mother hens scurried to get strapped into their nests.

Levy watched their final dash to secure the flight and decided to contact "the office" as soon as the plane was in the air. He would leave an inquiry about the microfilm and then check back in later.

Flight 289 left without incident and the phone on the back of the seat worked well. Daniel left his carefully worded inquiry and hung up. The usual airline peas-and-carrots mishmash was served quickly, and Daniel settled in for a nap. When he awoke, the in-flight movie was going full tilt. One look at his wristwatch made it clear Daniel had slept two hours longer than he thought possible. Jet lag remained a bummer. Time to see if there was a response from the office.

He dialed in the special set of numbers carried only in his head.

"Shalom," an anonymous voice answered.

"Levy," he responded quietly. The passenger next to him snored softly.

"Just a moment." The line was silent.

Daniel pressed the phone to his ear and waited. Static was bad but did not seem to be insurmountable. He hated making the call in such a public setting, but things were proceeding too fast to wait until he landed. He might need to act quickly.

"Can you hear me clearly?" a new voice answered.

"May lose some of the transmission, but I'll tell you if I miss anything."

"Listen very carefully. The office did not . . . I repeat . . . the office *did not* send a contact person or airline tickets to your room in Washington. Do you understand?"

Levy caught his breath. "You said no one from the office delivered the tickets?"

"That is correct. I am going to give you another number. Call immediately and further instructions will be waiting."

Daniel hastily scribbled the number in the palm of his hand and made the next call.

"Yes," the familiar flat voice of Avraham Halevy answered.

"Levy here. I am on an airplane, returning to Israel," he began.

Agent G cursed violently. "I have no idea what has occurred, but obviously someone intercepted your contact with the Syrian cousin. I don't have to tell you how serious the matter is."

Daniel looked out the window, peering over the towering clouds that covered the ocean thousands of feet below. He suddenly felt small and helpless. "Yes." The best he could muster.

"I don't want you to drive your car out of the airport until we've checked it for explosives." Halevy paused. "And I don't

want you making any phone calls outside the terminal."
Monotone kicked in; the all-business voice had been activated.
"When you exit, look for a man holding a sign saying, 'Ramat
Tours seeking Mr. Goldberg.' He will have a car for you."

"I understand."

"The microfilm is possibly far more significant than we
thought. You will be taken directly to your house. Put the film
with the package I sent before you left. Wait for further instruction concerning disposition."

"I understand."

"Our man at the airport will stay with you until we've sorted
this one out. We can't take any chances with what could happen.
Don't contact me further. We can't be sure where the pieces in
the puzzle are. Suspect everyone. Who knows what group is
behind the contact with you. Maybe the CIA, for all I know. I
will find you."

"I understand." Levy could not come up with any other
response.

For a split second he remembered his training as a cadet at
the Mossad Academy. Levy did not have to think about what
might happen if attacked. Should his brain tell his hand that he
was threatened, Daniel would shoot to kill by sheer reflex. He
would fire the flat-tipped dumdum bullets until the .22 caliber
Beretta was virtually empty. Once the assailant was on the
ground, the last bullet was to be fired into his own temple. The
Mossad taught the boys to always protect Mossad's most valuable property at all costs: their knowledge, themselves.

"Trust no one." Halevy's objective detachment dropped.
The Mossad chief sounded personally concerned. "You're a
very important person to me, Danny."

"I'll try to pay attention." Levy tried to sound lighthearted.

"You do that. Shalom." Halevy hung up.

16

Friday, September 11
Arad

Rashid Salah listened in bored silence. Friday afternoon. Nothing left to do but listen. Brother Hassan continued his endless, mindless description of the glories of New York City. Even as a child, Hassan had always been a pretentious loudmouth. Hitting it rich in the export business only exacerbated the problem of a runaway mouth.

The Bedouin looked around the outdoor restaurant. Simple rusted tables, old chairs, cracked sidewalks. The village of Arad did not compare well with any place in the world. If the wind shifted, the smell of the sewage drain sometimes drifted across town. Typical of the Bedouin towns of the Negev, daily life there reflected Third World conditions. For sure, no great sites to contrast with Hassan's great metropolitan center. Nothing to brag about here.

Late afternoon sunlight bathed the outdoor restaurant in pleasant warmth. A waiter came and went, disappearing back inside where the coffee and a few sticky pastries waited on display. The young man's constant questions and attention annoyed Hassan, and he told the attendant to leave them alone.

Continuing political unrest guaranteed that old men and young boys would spend endless hours discussing and arguing their painful plight. Severe unemployment and economic conditions offered few opportunities for anything more than talk. In order to monitor such discussions, years ago Rashid staked out his own special table against the old faded stucco wall beneath a window opening into the kitchen.

Hassan's visits every couple of years had to be tolerated. Money came in regularly to help the family and Hassan *did* put Musa through college. Even though Hassan remained adamantly opposed to the pursuit of archaeology, without his uncle's help Musa would be feeding goats grazing around rocks rather than looking under boulders for ancient treasures.

Long-suffering Rashid drew long puffs of smoke from the Turkish *nargila* water pipe and tried to pretend an interest in Hassan's recitation of accomplishments since the last visit. Any hint of the customary unassuming humility of the Bedouin people had long since been eroded by affluent American capitalism. Out of the corner of his eye, Rashid watched his brother drum on the table with a finger sporting a large diamond ring. Years ago he had gotten a bellyful of these bragging stories calculated to make his family sound like lazy morons.

"I often speak of my former life in the desert," Hassan reminisced, toying with the end of his bushy mustache. "Americans are fascinated by tales of sleeping under the stars. I remember those nights well."

"I remember them from last week," Rashid mumbled. "Didn't seem particularly romantic. Mainly hot in the day. Cold at night."

Hassan looked slightly annoyed and immediately launched into an explanation of the tastes of the American public. With the subtlety of a bulldozer, he detailed how his grasp of the desires of his adopted country allowed him to buy shrewdly and continue increasing his wealth.

Rashid puffed nonchalantly and listened quietly. He detested the fact his brother had gone through three American wives and no longer practiced their religion except when he was back in the country. Rashid studied the overweight braggart. The pudgy fingers and heavy jowls repulsed him. Too much rich food. Hassan had lost the simplicity of the desert, the strength of a Bedouin. And yet he strutted through Arad as if the Salah family were paupers, lucky to have such a benefactor as a relative. Rashid wondered if another afternoon of Hassan's stories might push him over the edge into murder.

"But I must say," Hassan continued, "I am still disappointed in Musa. I give him a first-rate education and what does he do? He squanders it playing in the dirt!"

Rashid bristled and slowly removed the mouthpiece of the *nargila* from between his teeth. His eyes narrowed. This time the old windbag had crossed the line. No one said a bad word about Musa and went unanswered.

"If the boy would just listen to his uncle, he, too, could become rich." Hassan shook his head. "Instead, he chases after worthless relics from the past." He folded his hands over his large stomach. "Such a waste."

Something snapped. Rashid fought to keep his hands from trembling and ended up hiding them under the table, but his anger would not be denied. Hassan had gone way too far. Like a pump forcing hostility up from his gut, rage throbbed within the old man. No one could say a bad thing about his son and get away with it. For decades he had told no one of the discovery. Now Musa had the treasure, and he could use the secret one more time to defend his boy even as he had rewarded him for his diligent study. And who would know anyway? No one was in sight. Decades of caution were worth throwing to the wind to shut up this old fool once and for all.

Rashid shook his head vigorously. "You are completely wrong," he said forcefully. "My son's career will prove to be more significant than anything anyone has done in this century." Each word became louder. "Musa made a discovery that will liberate every Arab in this land!" He pounded the table. "Understand? Musa will set us free!"

"What?" Hassan blinked several times and frowned. "What is this madness you are spouting?"

"Can you keep a secret, old man?" Rashid leaned over the table, inches from Hassan's nose.

On the other side of the open window, the Hayat brothers leaned against the wall with their ears tuned to the conversation outside. While the teenagers fancied themselves master spies, the sheer boredom of life in a village with unemployment and limited schooling made for exaggerated imaginations. Constantly hoping to stumble onto some tidbit of information useful to Hamas, the boys were forever slinking down alleys, peeping in windows, and eavesdropping. Most of the village considered them a nuisance and underestimated their capacities. Hamas officials listened when they came around with a report.

"Did you hear that?" Kamal Hayat leaned closer to the open window. He beckoned to his brother Hafez and put a finger to his lips. "Listen." The smell of old hot grease drifted past them out the window.

Two years younger than Kamal, Hafez had always been the more aggressive of the brothers. In spite of, or perhaps because of his age, Hafez was already a veteran of Hamas campaigns of terror. Starting with rock throwing during his teenage years, Hafez advanced to firebomb hurling as well as becoming a look-out man for violent attacks on Israeli soldiers. The teenager was always prepared to kill. Hafez inched toward the open window. The wall felt hot and oily.

"That's old man Salah out there," Kamal Hayat spoke under his breath.

"Who's the other guy?"

"His brother. The one from America."

Kamal had worked in the restaurant since he was twelve. After a couple of years, the woman who owned the place taught him to cook. Eventually Kamal ran the place by himself. Eight years of waiting tables and overhearing conversations had turned him into a first-class Hamas informant. He specialized in knowing everything about everyone in the village. No stranger went unobserved or unreported. Kamal picked up information by eavesdropping through the open window.

The Hayat brothers' father had died in the first *Intifada* uprising, hit by gunfire during a running battle with Israeli soldiers. The boys' mother was never the same again. The passing years only made everything worse. Handsome enough, Kamal and Hafez looked like average Palestinians, with coal black hair and olive skin. Weight lifting with rocks and heavy parts of burned-out cars added muscular dimensions to their short statures.

"What'd he say?" Hafez cupped his ear.

"The old fool claims his son's made a secret discovery."

Hafez slipped up under the window ledge. Limited opportunities for anything but trouble made Palestinian life hard for young men. Schools were often closed; the economy stayed depressed. Conquering invaders kept a tight hand to the throats of the locals. Old men who should be leading them proved to be as impotent and powerless as their terrified, whimpering wives. The only emotion sustaining Hafez was pure hate.

"What do you mean 'liberate every Arab'?" The man on the other side of the wall challenged his brother.

"Next time you think my boy is a fool, you'd best remember what I'm about to tell you." Rashid Salah was unusually aggressive. "Musa has always known what he was doing." Salah sounded angry. "But when the history books are written, it will be him they remember, not us."

"What are you saying?" The brother was no longer in control of the conversation.

"Let me ask you again. Can you keep your mouth shut for once?"

"Sure. Of course."

Kamal's feet slipped out from under him and he tumbled to the floor. For a second, he gritted his teeth as if expecting his thump on the tile floor to end the old men's conversation. He cursed the slick surface created by years of cooking meat and bread in boiling oil.

"What I am about to tell you is top secret." The noise in the kitchen had not disturbed Salah. "Hassan, you must swear to tell no one. No one. Understand?"

"Of course, of course."

"Musa is both a son of the desert and a man of learning," Salah boasted. "Say what you will, you are lucky to understand the newspapers while Musa knows the meaning of things."

"But what has he found?" the man sounded a little irritated.

"Musa found a secret ancient scroll that proves Arabs are the true owners of Jerusalem. We have the warranty deed of the first owners."

"What?"

"I said, my son *can prove* the Jews are upstarts!" Salah's voice was low and clear.

Hafez looked at Kamal in puzzled amazement. "What?" he mouthed. "What did he say?"

"Musa and his friends are translating this document even as we speak," Salah bore down. "My son is going to demonstrate that the Jews are thieves and liars. The world will join us in throwing them into the sea."

"You are serious?" Hassan asked in amazement.

"When Egypt and Arabia come to bow at Musa's feet, you will ask forgiveness for what you have said," Salah boasted. "Syria and Jordan will be my boy's servants."

"Where is this thing, this scroll?" Hassan pressed.

"Hidden in Jerusalem," Salah answered, lowering his voice. "Only Musa knows the exact location."

Hafez's eyes widened. He looked at his brother in wonder.

Kamal nodded his head up and down in deliberate sweeps as if telegraphing a plan of action. He pointed across the kitchen.

"Can I see this scroll?" the old man asked.

"Didn't I tell you only Musa knows the location?"

Kamal beckoned for his brother to follow him and slipped across the kitchen. He pointed to the back door and went outside. Hafez followed.

"What do you make of it?" Hafez Hayat shut the door behind them. The air smelled clear, free of the smell of spices and grease. He took a deep breath.

"The Salahs are onto something big." Kamal scratched in the dirt with the toe of his shoe. "They've never been very political, but it sounds like the old man has crossed the line."

"This could be our chance." Hafez jabbed his finger at his brother. "We need something to get the attention of our new leaders."

"You're right." Kamal rubbed his forehead and pulled a cigarette out of his pocket. "If we turned up highly significant information, the Islamic Revolutionary Front would see both of us in a new light. We'd be insiders for a change."

"Exactly! Hamas only treated me like an amateur. This information would guarantee I'd be seen as a professional."

Kamal Hayat leaned against the building and crossed his arms over his chest. "Got to work this angle slowly and carefully. We don't want the local contact to know the whole story. We must take the message to the top personally . . . or as close to the top as we think we can get." He lit the cigarette.

"Nobody knows who that is," Hafez fretted. "They won't let a couple of kids like us get very far."

"Not unless we play our cards right," Kamal countered, dropping down on one knee. "Here's what we must do. Follow old man Salah home. Check around. Find out where his son is living in Jerusalem these days. Do whatever it takes. Get everything we can on this story. That way the big boys will have to listen to us." He inhaled deeply and blew smoke toward the sky.

Hafez cracked his knuckles and popped his fingers together. "We might be able to pump that old windbag from New York City, too. He comes down to the market and talks to anyone who listens."

"Yeah. We can play him like the big shot. Make him think we know things we don't. Maybe he drinks."

Kamal shook his head. "We wouldn't want anyone we know to see us with liquor. Wouldn't set well with the IRF. Good Muslims don't. Remember?"

"But we could let our local man know it's a maneuver. Keep the communication lines clear. I think a little *hamra, wiskee, araq* would oil his tongue plenty."

"You start tailing both of them. Figure out how to get the New Yorker alone." Kamal Hayat stopped and thought for a moment. "I'll work on finding out where Musa is. I know the youngest cousin. I think I can get something out of her."

Hafez beamed. "No one will be able to doubt that we are seasoned spies. Whatever this discovery is, it will be our ticket to the top."

"We must act immediately," Kamal concluded. "I'll see the cousin tonight. You zero in on the New Yorker in the morning. He likes to talk. Let's give him a chance."

17

Sunday, September 13
Jerusalem, Dormition Abbey

While the Bedouin and his brother argued, the translators assembled in the secluded room beneath the Dormition Abbey. The Rosenbergs were again the last to arrive. A large table had been set up in the middle of the room and the place swept clean. The day before Leah brought a coffeemaker and cups. Father Kelly came up with several extra large lamps to highlight the study table.

Leah glanced around the room. Things looked better to her. Not quite as drab and foreboding as before. She felt more optimistic.

"I trust you brought your copy of the scroll," the priest asked the Rosenbergs.

"Yes." Leah opened a small briefcase. "I've blown it up some, but too much enlargement removes some of the detail. Becomes counterproductive."

"We need to get the original back now." Musa sounded quite definite.

"Absolutely," David Rosenberg agreed. "As a matter of fact,

I put in a call to my friend Avraham Halevy." Rosenberg bit at his lip. "We're experiencing a delay."

"Avraham Halevy?" Musa looked at each person. "Who's that?"

"The person that handles security for us," David continued in a business-as-usual tone of voice.

"You said the scroll and medallion were in a safe," Musa bore down.

"Yes, that's correct." David smiled sheepishly. "Actually, the safe belongs to Halevy. You might say he's in the security business."

Musa clenched his fist. "You let this find get out of your hands?" His voice raised. "And you led me to think the objects were in your possession all the time?"

"We simply didn't discuss the details." David sounded defensive. "When an object is worth a great deal of money, I always use better security than my office safe alone."

"This is outrageous!" Musa simmered like a pressure cooker about to blow. "You took my archaeological treasure and turned it over to some Halevy character without my consent?"

"Look!" David shifted back into a defense attorney posture. "I sought the maximum protection for this treasure. Isn't that what you expected of me?"

"I anticipated you'd be completely aboveboard in every aspect of this transaction." Musa dug in his heels. "I don't like surprises."

"Just miscommunication." David didn't give any ground.

Leah tried to catch his eye, but David kept talking directly to Musa. Got to hit his off switch, she thought. David doesn't read emotions well. He's missed how upset Musa is.

Musa crossed his arms over his chest. "Then why aren't the scroll and medallion here today?"

"Turns out Halevy is more involved in national security than

I thought. He grilled me about the package. I had to tell him more than I intended."

"What?" Musa Salah came out of his chair. "This scenario gets worse by the moment."

"Oh, don't worry." David gestured with both hands as if making a closing summation before a jury. "Everything is under control. The scroll and medallion are absolutely secure."

"Why did you tell this Halevy anything?" Musa pursued David.

"The man is involved in the top levels of government security and totally trustworthy," David backpedaled. "I've been a friend of Avraham's forever. You know—old buddies. Apparently, there's some problem with the place where the box is secured."

"Government security?" Musa's voice kept rising. "Problem? Trouble?"

"No, no." David added head shaking to hand waving. "The person in charge of the safe was called out of the country but will be back shortly. A simple delay. That's the only problem."

"But what did you tell this Halevy about my find?" Musa spread his legs and crossed his arms. "If there is anyone I don't trust, it's an official of the Israeli government."

"I told him virtually nothing." David continued his retreat. "Halevy was only concerned to get some idea of the value of the package," he lied. "I simply made it clear that the contents were priceless."

"And why would they be so valuable?" Musa pushed.

"Because of their antiquity." David smiled and shrugged.

Leah glared at her husband. Why in the world did David tell this espionage character everything? And why had this supposedly "good buddy" pumped him like it was a criminal investigation? Musa would go through the roof if he had any idea of the full extent of what David said. David's lying was reprehensible.

"Exactly *when* will I have the scroll back in my hands?" Musa clenched both fists.

"The man in charge of the safe is on his way back to Jerusalem even as we speak." David cleared his throat forcefully. "By tomorrow we will have everything here in this very basement."

"Good. Good." Kelly appeared to be trying to smooth things over. "Today we can work from a copy and tomorrow check everything against the original." He pointed toward the table as if ushering people to their seats. "I'm sure we're all relieved to know the scroll is safe." Kelly cleared his throat. "As scholars, we each know how to consult dictionaries and lexicons to study the languages in which we are not experts. So, I expect each of us will come with insights from our outside study."

Leah watched Musa's face. The usual stoic Bedouin mask had disappeared. No one in the room wanted to recognize the anger sparking in his eyes.

"I'm going to exit and let you experts get down to business." David looked edgy and backed toward the steps as he talked. "A lawyer in a meeting of translators is like a grease monkey in a surgical operating room," he tried to joke. "I'll get out of your way." He feebly waved and hurried out.

Leah watched her husband quickly exit. David obviously did not want more questions. Not a good way to start the job.

"Might I suggest we use this small tape recorder?" Kelly laid a microcassette recorder on the table. "As we develop significant ideas and insights, we can record them for later transcription."

"Certainly," Leah agreed cheerfully. She smiled at Musa. He did not respond. "I'm ready to begin when everyone else is."

"Let's commence!" Kelly beamed confidence, obviously attempting to shore up Salah's reluctance. "Why not sit down on both sides of the table around the copy? I'm sure we've all given preliminary thought to some aspects of the shape of the text."

Leah slipped into a chair at the left side of the table and produced a few pages of notes from her briefcase. She kept smiling at Musa, trying to drive a wedge in the ice.

Musa stared at the top of the table, trying to get a grip on his emotions. The one guy he thought he could trust had misled him. David played the old shell game just like the rest of them. Israelis assume Bedouins are mindless children to be placated, fools to be manipulated. *Father was wrong. We should never have come to these people.*

"I suggest we follow the usual methodology for archaeological research so that all findings can be validated without contradiction." Kelly launched into a discussion of procedure and documentation, sounding as if he owned the project. "Because I've worked on countless projects, I can lay out the correct format and make sure our work is in a form that will lend itself to publication later." His facile social patter became all business. Diplomatic nuances turned into hard scholarly assertions.

Musa drummed on the table with his fingertips as he watched the priest climb into the driver's seat. The man has two sides that he turns on and off like a light switch. The warm diplomatic facade only camouflages a cold calculating personality. He is no different from the rest of the Westerners.

"We must divide up responsibilities for translation according to our individual abilities. Then we will work in tandem when we start trying to match phrases. I am sure each of us will need to do considerable research on our own."

Musa watched Kelly's eyes moving backward and forward behind his reading glasses like the cursor on a printer, mechanically spitting out words. Behind the robes of the good confessor beat the heart of a hard-nosed scientist. He divided up the tasks involved in translation like the president of a corporation giving his staff of peons their daily tasks. *Who appointed him chairman of the board?* Musa wondered. He'd been here less than an hour and already felt pushed too far.

"Excuse me." Leah cut into the dissertation. "I'm wondering how this explanation is sitting with you, Musa?"

Musa jumped. "Thank you," he answered in surprise. "Perhaps I will comment when the good professor is done."

Kelly looked startled. "Yes, of course," he retreated. "Didn't mean to get ahead of anyone. Are we all on the same track?"

"I believe the translation will prove more difficult than first appears." Musa moved in slowly. "Conventional methods aren't going to be adequate." He watched Kelly's eyes. "We will need to evolve an approach tailored to the unique demands of the scroll. The method must arise as we work together. No one person can be in charge," he ended more emphatically.

The priest frowned.

"I strongly agree with Musa," Leah added. "I believe his observations are consistent with the subject matter before us."

"Good. Good." Kelly picked up the reins again. "Then I suppose we are ready to begin the actual task." He again flashed his ingratiating smile. "Let's hit it."

Leah began by making several broad observations about the character of the ancient Hebrew. Kelly followed suit, giving similar responses about the Greek text. Musa mainly listened to the scholarly ping-pong match between the two.

"Then we are in agreement," the priest concluded. "The text is much more complex than anything any of us have seen before. There is no question about the extraordinary antiquity."

"But I recognized these facts the first time I saw the manuscript," Musa countered to make sure he was recognized as a genuine player. "Ancient languages are not my strongest suit, but even I foresaw these issues. I am more impressed with the observations made during the first time we met. The actual meaning is interwoven throughout all of these languages. We must understand everything to understand anything."

"Well put," Leah answered. "We are not only deciphering the meaning of words, but we must put together the entire sentence structure flowing from one language to the other in order to grasp the complete content."

Kelly agreed. "The ancient writer had an extraordinary mind." He chuckled. "Or he was *really* inspired, if you believe such an idea."

"How about a 'her' instead of a 'him'?" Leah feigned innocence. "We don't know the writer was a man."

"We are dealing with the essence of language." Kelly ignored her question. "Words label things, identify them. However, the power of language is its capacity to take us inside meaning. As translators, we will have to be like divers that go down to the deepest depths of the ocean to bring up the treasure."

"I agree with the suggestion we each work separately on the language that we are most competent in and then blend our discoveries," Leah asserted herself. "Obviously, we're going to have to do private research on many of these symbols because they are so peculiar to the ancient world."

Kelly looked up at the ceiling, staring back and forth and pondering the suggestions. "Sounds reasonable," he mused with a hint of condescension. "But we must avoid the danger of fragmentation," he pontificated.

"Sounds excellent," Musa snapped. "What else would *you* suggest, Leah?"

Kelly recoiled in surprise, looking miffed.

Musa smiled. Kelly is a real old-fashioned chauvinist. On a

good day he's probably convinced God is lucky to have the priest on His team.

"I'm sure Leah is well acquainted with these usual approaches to translating papyrus manuscripts and codices." Musa intended a let's-put-you-in-your-place twist to his suggestion.

"Michael was brought on board because of his ability to deal with classical Greek," Leah said. "Seems logical he'd zero in on that target."

Kelly frowned again. He clearly preferred the driver's seat and didn't like to be talked down to.

"You are the person with a grasp of Akkadian and Sumerian." Musa continued talking directly to Leah. "We must depend on your skills with those languages. You also understand hieroglyphics, but so do I. I will work on the Egyptian."

"Excellent," Leah agreed. "I think we have a basis to continue our work. Let's see how much we can get done tonight."

The priest pushed back from the table. "I'm somewhat pressed this evening." He sounded distant and lofty. "I am finishing a paper to be delivered at the Pontifical Academy in Rome." He stood up. "I only had enough time to get this project started this evening." Kelly looked down on the other two as he talked. "Moreover, I can work here after you're gone if you leave the copy." Kelly started up the stairs. "You can let yourselves out."

Musa watched the priest stomp up the stairs. He's angry. Next time Kelly will be a tad more reluctant to hit the gas pedal before he knows we've got our seat belts on.

"When do we gather again?" Leah asked.

"Time is of the essence," Musa added. "I suggest we stay at this task every evening until it's done."

"Tomorrow night?" Kelly continued going up the stairs. "I

suppose. Yes. I will be here at the same time." He disappeared up the stairs.

"I think we need to work as late as possible each evening," Leah called after him. "We're not observant. Don't mind working on the Sabbath."

The large wooden door shut behind the departing priest.

"Something I said?" Leah asked Musa.

Musa grinned. "I think Father Kelly likes to be in complete control." He smiled even more broadly. "And I don't think he's too keen on women with brains."

Leah fought breaking out in an ear-to-ear grin. She pushed her papers together and winked at Musa, "I don't think either of us is a pushover."

"About the scroll, Leah . . ."

"I'm very sorry there was a misunderstanding." Leah sounded urgent and sincere. "We were completely wrong not to have been more explicit. I must ask you to forgive David and me for not considering your feelings."

For a moment Musa did not know how to respond. "Thank you for saying so," he mumbled.

She abruptly reached out and touched his arm. "I don't want you to worry. Everything is safe and will be back in your hands quickly." Leah smiled again and hurried toward the steps. "Again, I apologize for our lack of sensitivity. Hope to see you tomorrow." She hurried away.

Musa watched her disappear through the door at the top of the stairs. He felt baffled and confused. The session had been an emotional roller-coaster ride, swinging him from explosive anger to contempt and back around to an experience of considerateness and compassion. He was not sure what he felt anymore. Consternation was the only word that came to mind.

18

Once the airport buses released the passenger load, Daniel Levy raced into the Ben-Gurion Airport arrivals building, staying well ahead of the pack. For the last three hours the Mossad agent had gone over every step of the procedure in contacting the Syrian diplomat. Somewhere . . . something . . . somehow . . . someway . . . someone . . . The carefully constructed protective conduit had broken down. That's all that counted. Since "they" had succeeded in getting him on a particular airline, "they" certainly planted one of their people on the plane. Daniel knew that mingling with the passengers on the bus, an assassin lurked, prepared and ready to strike.

Minutes later, Levy emerged out the exit and into the crowd waiting for arrivals. He glanced around the predictable scene of chaos. Near the back of the mob, a short scruffy man in casual pants, a lightweight jacket, and an open-neck shirt held the all-important placard: Ramat Tours—Mr. Goldberg.

Daniel walked straight toward the plain-looking agent, straining to make eye contact. Once they connected, the man lowered the sign and nodded toward the parking lot. Daniel fell in alongside without saying a word. His single black bag went in the trunk. Minutes later they pulled out of the parking lot in the man's white Ford Escort.

"Uri Dori." The man extended his hand while he drove. "Your guide while you are in Israel." He grinned slyly and looked in the rearview mirror. "We don't want any unexpected additions to our tour."

"Why the tourist act?" Daniel relaxed for the first time since his second phone call from the airplane.

"The office pulled me in from assignment in Jordan," the round-faced man explained. "Apparently, they didn't want anyone even slightly connected with you to show up. They didn't know how completely you'd been identified and were afraid of you getting close to your car until everything checked out."

"What a security breach!" Daniel swore vehemently.

"By the way, we've already cleared the car. No problem. We hot-wired it and already sent the vehicle on to your place in Jerusalem."

"Glad to hear it. But the tourist sign?"

"We figured the other side would have agents waiting outside the airport but they might not have passed on a clear picture of who you are or what you looked like yet. The tourist ruse would make it harder for them to hook on."

Levy glanced in the side mirror. "Doesn't look like anybody's back there."

"Yes, I think we got a clear break from the airport." Uri's pleasant demeanor quickly faded. "As you're aware, we have a very serious leak."

"Who is it? CIA? Hamas? The new group?"

"Sorry. Don't know. Our people at the top are extremely concerned that you have been compromised beyond repair on this operation."

Daniel grimaced. The worst words he could hear.

"No one's blaming you. Something went wrong in the middle. Probably the whole problem was Al-Amid. The guy's a real piece of work. Typical Arab."

Daniel watched the scenery go by. The road was starting to wind up toward Jerusalem. He would probably be put on permanent vacation again. Plenty of time to look at trees.

"You've got the microfilm?"

"Yeah," Daniel answered grimly. "It's in the usual place." He reached in the backseat and pulled his briefcase over. "I put the piece in the security liner." He flipped open the locks, lifted the lid, and took out a brown leather folder the size of the inside pocket of a man's jacket. "Got the film secured inside."

"Good. I need to keep that thing close to my heart. I'm to take the film from you and deliver it straight downtown as soon as we arrive."

Daniel handed the pouch to the *sochen*. "I can't believe it. Never had anything like this happen to me before." He stared at farmers working the fields. "Sure. The boss thinks I'll get knocked off and no one will know where the film went."

"What'd you do with the information our boy Abdul gave you?" Uri avoided the implications of Daniel's assertion.

"I've already sent in a complete report of the exchange in the restaurant. Names, details, the works. Abdul had important things to tell us. Every detail's on the computer."

"How about the package?"

"Package?"

"Yeah. You know. The brown paper–wrapped box the office sent you?"

"Oh, that thing's been in the safe in my closet for days."

Uri watched the road but kept glancing in the rearview mirror. "Did you look at it?"

"No. Just dropped it in the safe. Why?"

"Turns out the box has important contents." Uri slowed for a pickup. "I'm supposed to pick up the bundle and take it to the office."

"What's that all about? They don't think I can even sit on a package?"

Uri shrugged. "Don't take it so hard. Apparently, a Jewish attorney came into possession of an ancient find that might prove the Arabs have the rights to Jerusalem."

"You're serious?"

"The office is." Uri looked askance with a "know-what-I-mean" look. "Everyone's edgy these days about anything with political significance. The front office doesn't want this parcel to get out of their sight. They've instructed me to get the thing back at once."

Daniel shook his head. Nothing was working right. Uri didn't have to say it. Halevy didn't think he was even capable of keeping a simple box without getting into trouble. Then again, maybe G expected the IRF to blow up his flat . . . or something of that order. He cursed Al-Amid and wished someone *would* shoot the jerk.

Uri Dori knew where Levy's apartment was located. Even though it was not necessary, Daniel directed him down Herzl Boulevard toward the Kiryat Moshe area as if Levy had a need to be back in control of something or the other. The familiar neighborhood was virtually empty of anyone on the streets, except for a few parked cars. People worked, shopped, stayed inside, something, at that hour of the day. Uri pulled up in front of the flat.

"Nothing like home, sweet home," Uri quipped.

"Yeah," Daniel replied glumly.

"I'll grab your bag out of the trunk, and we can get that package you've been keeping."

Levy shook his head in disgust but did not move. Not wanting to get out of the car, he stared at the front door like a prisoner contemplating the gate into a prison.

The popping roar of an engine broke the solitude of the neighborhood. At the other end of the block, a motorcycle turned the corner. Daniel kept looking at the front door to his flat, lost in his thoughts. Rather than slowing, the cyclist sped up as he approached the back of the car. Uri had just opened the trunk when he realized the motorcycle was aiming straight at him, coming at breakneck speed.

"Hey!" Uri yelled at the top of his voice and went for the small gun in a concealed holster at his hip. The bike was flying at full throttle. "Stop," he demanded, drawing the gun and leaping from the back of the car toward the low rock ledge in front of Levy's flat. Uri got off one shot and rolled over the top of the wall. In that second, he saw the rider tumble from the motorcycle, but the vehicle kept coming for his car. Uri erroneously assumed his one shot hit the rider.

Everything turned to slow motion. The rider rolled toward the curb like a professional stunt man. Levy had one leg out of the car and was leaning toward the ground when the motorcycle hit the trunk. The roar of the explosion sent a shock wave that slung Uri back from the wall, across the grass, and into the front wall of the apartment. A ball of orange fire erupted straight up toward the sky. Pieces of metal and glass sprayed in every direction. Uri no longer heard anything but felt something hot slice into his leg, then his arm, maybe his side. The world disappeared in blackness.

When Uri opened his eyes, he saw nothing but a vast expanse of blue above him. The silence was more intense than anything he had known in his life. After a moment, the agent realized he was not immersed in quiet as much as lost in total lack of sound.

He tried to make words but nothing seemed to come out of his mouth. Then the pain set in.

From everywhere below his neck the report was coming through loud and clear. Terrible pain. He moved his fist. Something thick and gooey was running down his arm, covering his hand. Legs. Arms. No response. From somewhere in the center of his being he knew the awful truth. He was dying. The sky quickly faded and the light disappeared. No time was left.

Uri could feel a sensation of movement around his waist. Yes. Someone was doing something down there. He tried to yell, to call, to speak. Nothing.

A face broke into the blue above him. His eyes wouldn't focus. Blood kept blotting out everything in his left eye. The face wasn't clear, but he thought it must be Levy. Daniel Levy. The mouth was moving, but nothing came out. The pain must be drowning him out. Nothing was intelligible.

Uri's trained instincts kicked in. Had to protect the material at all cost. Nothing could be lost, destroyed. He had to get the microfilm back to Levy.

"In my pocket," Uri tried to shout. He had no clue if anything came out. He attempted to call louder. "Hidden in my jacket. Leather pouch. Microfilm."

The policeman squinted. He did not appear to get the message.

"Mossad. Agent. State secrets."

The policeman came closer.

"Inside my coat pocket. Get the billfold to security."

Uri wanted to move his arms but couldn't. Everything was fading. Pain increasing. Nausea welling up.

"Package inside the flat. Archaeological find." Uri's throat filled with something. "Get it out. Jerusalem is in jeopardy."

The policeman got closer. It looked like he was saying, "What?"

"Save the film," Uri tried to yell but felt his energy drying up. "Package in a safe," he pushed with his last effort, "inside the flat. The fate of Jerusalem and our people . . . in your hands." The man's face turned as white as everything else. All-engulfing nausea swallowed his remaining consciousness. Everything disappeared.

The policeman stared at the man who had been shouting in his face. The cop quickly opened the coat and found the blood-smeared billfold. "Medic!" he cried to the man standing behind him while putting the leather pouch in a plastic bag. "Do something. This guy's going fast."

"Over here!" the medic yelled and waved.

A team of paramedics leaped the wall. "Got to get him in an ambulance." The first man rushed past the policeman. "He's losing too much blood." Another aide started checking the tourniquet that was slowing the flow of blood from the thigh.

"You've got to keep this man alive," the policeman demanded. "Something big's going on here."

"Think we're not trying?" the first medic barked out of the side of his mouth. "Keep out of our way."

The policeman stepped back, wondering which house contained this mysterious package. Men carrying a stretcher came over the rock wall. The policeman could see other medics putting whoever the guy in the street was into a body bag. Must have been the passenger. Although the policemen had seen plenty of gruesome sights, he looked away. The bomb really messed that guy up.

"Which place?" he talked to himself. "Which building would they have been going to?" He looked at the angle of the car in relationship to the surrounding apartment buildings.

"We've got you covered," someone spoke behind the policeman.

He turned and found a stout, rather fierce-looking middle-aged man holding an identification badge in his hand. "I'm with the General Security Service. Internal Security will take it from here."

The policeman took a deep breath. GSS had rank. Time to go home.

"We're dealing with a very sensitive matter here," the GSS officer explained. "Anything I should know?"

"You'll want this material." The policeman took the plastic bag from his pocket. "I think there's microfilm hidden in there somewhere."

The security officer took on the poker face of someone who already knows the cards everyone is holding. "Come with me. We need a full report."

Although the police tried to secure the area, too many people had filled the streets before they could take charge. Residents, reporters, the curious, quickly descended on the site of the charred and smoldering automobile hull.

No one had questioned the man who appeared to be a bona fide paramedic working the scene. His disguise gave him access to every aspect of the tragedy, and the reporter from *Ha'olam Hazeh*, a left-wing publication from Tel Aviv, had moved among the medical professionals as if he knew exactly what he was doing. The policeman never questioned the reporter, who listened over the officer's shoulder as Uri Dori died. The ruse had often worked, allowing the journalist to mingle among the authorities, listening, getting every word in his concealed tape recorder.

19

Tuesday, September 15
Jerusalem, Elisha Street

Leah Rosenberg stared at the headlines in *Ha'olam Hazeh*. The story of a terrorist bombing of two Mossad agents touched the worst fears of every Jerusalemite. One man was dead at the scene, the other died on the way to the hospital. Apparently, the bomber escaped.

On to the next column. A report of a secret archaeological find got equal billing. The story said that one of the downed agents was hiding a politically sensitive document that might have bearing on the Arab-Jewish struggle over Jerusalem. Although the report was speculative, the account was well enough written that passions would be inflamed. Police had searched the agent's flat, seeking the hidden package. No indication of what they found. The reporter closed with the conjecture that the Mossad had botched another important assignment. David interrupted her thoughts.

"Yes, I want to speak to him immediately," David shouted in his desk phone. "Don't tell me Halevy isn't in. I know he's there!"

Leah looked up from the paper and watched her husband's red face. His hands trembled. She had seldom seen him so angry.

"You tell Halevy that I expect to hear from him within one hour or I'm going to be over there tearing the place apart. Got it?" He slammed the phone down.

"Avraham Halevy is stonewalling you?"

David shook his head in a rage. "I don't know what's going on, but Halevy looks like a snake." He sat down behind his desk. "Musa will think I'm lying. Things could spin completely out of control." He ran his hands nervously through his hair. "I can't believe any of this."

Leah looked at the headlines again. "Our worst nightmare!" She took a deep breath.

The phone rang, and David grabbed it immediately. "Law Offices."

He listened a moment and rolled his eyes, nodding his head in compliance. "Yes. Yes," he finally answered. "We'll be there as quickly as possible." He hung up.

"Halevy's releasing the scroll?"

David shook his head. "Michael Kelly. He just got off the phone with Musa. Our Arab colleague has gone through the ceiling. We're to come to the monastery as quickly as possible for a meeting. Things aren't good."

Leah bit her lip. "We've tried so hard." Tears welled up in her eyes. She looked at the newspaper again. "Who'd believe anything so bizarre could happen?"

David stared at the top of his desk. "I simply don't understand."

"Why would Halevy avoid you?"

"Oh, no!" A look of insight crossed David's face. "I see it now! Halevy always avoided discussing his agency. Sure. It fits! Dead Mossad agents. One of them storing our package. Get it? Halevy is involved with Mossad."

Leah looked dumbfounded. "We gave the find to the most controversial operation in the whole government!" She paused. "And you told that man everything!"

David grimaced in pain. "The mistake of a lifetime!" He wrung his hands. "I suppose we have no excuse but to go to the Abbey. I didn't want to show up without the scroll, much less explain to Musa that Halevy won't answer my phone calls."

"Look." Leah took her husband firmly by the hand. "I will go by myself and tell them you're getting the scroll back. At least we'll put up a good front for the time being."

David leaned back in his chair and fumed. "I'm not going to be sidestepped by my supposedly good old buddy. I will keep after him until I get the box back."

"I know everything will be okay." Leah hugged her husband. "I'll call you around noon." She grabbed her purse and left the office.

Leah caught a taxi that quickly roared down Hativat Yerushalayim Street running along the walls of the Old City and around Mount Zion to the turnoff into the parking area nearest the Church of the Dormition. A steady flow of tourists had already begun so she could slip into the Abbey virtually unnoticed.

Musa listened to the priest with increasing irritation. Before Leah hit the last step, the archaeologist came out of his chair, charging across the room.

"Have you seen the papers?" Musa made no effort to hide his anger. "Everything is out in the open. Do you understand the seriousness of this disaster?"

"We are as distressed as you are," Leah began, "but—"

"There is no 'but,'" Musa interrupted. "They might as well have published my name."

"We are all equally in jeopardy," Leah countered. "Something is going on here that none of us understand. We must keep cool heads."

"Your husband is at fault," Musa countercharged. "He gave away the find."

"And blaming each other is not productive." Leah held her ground. "Even as we speak, David is hard at work getting the scroll back." She gave Musa a that-puts-you-in-your-place look.

Musa crossed his arms over his chest and looked away. "The next step will be that the Antiquities Authority will start putting two and two together and get Musa, not four."

Father Kelly walked over to the archaeologist and put an arm around his shoulder. "We're all a bit edgy about this story in the papers. However, I'm sure the Rosenbergs had absolutely nothing to do with these headlines. We cannot rightly blame them for anything that has happened in the last twenty-four hours."

Musa puckered his lower lip and jutted his chin out defiantly. "I simply don't understand how any of this nonsense could happen."

The door at the top of the stairs opened, and a monk in a brown robe came down the first steps. "Father Kelly, please excuse the interruption, but you said we could find you down here if we needed you . . . and . . . well, could you come upstairs for a moment?"

"Excuse me." The priest left quickly.

Leah did not say anything but was trying to look pleasant. Musa felt agitated. He finally sat down at the worktable and looked at the copy of the scroll.

"I know how hard it is to trust us," Leah began slowly. "Both of our peoples have been betrayed many times." Leah paused and clenched her jaw. "Certainly we've had our share of reasons to be afraid of Arabs. Our only hope is to forge a new path together. Maybe working on the scroll will help all of us."

Musa looked away from the copy for a moment. "You never cease to surprise me, Leah. You can be tough. You can be gentle." He smiled. "But you are usually right. I trust that is the case this time."

Leah sat down opposite him. "I just want you to know that David is trying to do the right thing. We have no choice but to support each other. We may be all any of us has before this adventure is over."

Musa nodded. *Need to cool it for the moment*, he decided. *Let's see what she does.*

He shook his head. "Everything has become so complicated since I found that thing." He swore under his breath.

Leah relaxed. "Don't worry. Everything is going to work out all right."

They sat silently for a few moments, uncertain whether to try working on the translation while Michael was gone. Then Leah pushed her chair back from the table. "I think I'll make a fresh pot of coffee. You want some?"

"Sure." *She's trying hard to smooth things over*, Musa thought. *Might as well let her try. But no promises.* He was still angry.

Leah searched through the supplies on the table that held the coffeemaker. "Uh-oh. Looks like we're out. Well, since Michael has stepped out for a while, I'll go see if I can find some in the kitchen."

Musa sighed as she headed toward the stairs. *Great. At this rate the scroll will never get translated.*

A few minutes after Leah left, Father Kelly returned, hurrying down the stairs. "Well, the local papers aren't our only problem," he called out before he was halfway down. "We've just hit the tip of the iceberg. Looks like we have more than one person talking."

Michael looked around the room. "Where's Leah?"

"She went to find some coffee . . . What do you mean, someone else is talking?"

The priest sat down at the head of the table and glared at Musa.

"Yes?" The archaeologist frowned.

"A number of our priests help small churches scattered around the countryside. Consequently, some of our community have just returned from the Negev." Kelly stopped in a grand pause. "They've just returned from the little village of Arad. Know the place?"

"What?" Musa's voice slid up to a squeak.

"Yes. I thought you'd know the town." Kelly leaned over the table. "Our people stopped in a restaurant and got to talking with some of the locals." The priest rolled his tongue around his lips. "Seems that an old Arab came back from New York City to see his brother. The uncle's been boasting that his nephew found a manuscript that will set their people free. The whole town's buzzing."

Musa's mouth dropped. "Uncle Hassan!" he gasped.

"Isn't this an interesting paradox?" Kelly bore down. "We have the Jews reading about an assassination and the Arabs talking about 'their find.' Amazing what a difference twenty-four hours can make."

Musa swallowed hard and looked desperate.

"Well, of course, everybody in town knows about the Salah clan and their big find decades ago." The priest took on a casual, sarcastic air. "Lots of talk that this educated son of theirs, the one that went to America, is hiding this great discovery." Kelly leaned over and winked. "People are looking for the lad everywhere, don't you know?"

The color drained from Musa's face, and he choked.

"And you are accusing the Rosenbergs?" Kelly reversed his

good-old-boy imitation, becoming hard and cold. "Sounds like you're the one we had best watch."

"You're sure of what you're saying?" Musa could barely speak.

"My conversation upstairs was with the priest who just returned from Arad. He couldn't possibly have fabricated such a story."

"I told my father how important it was to keep every word secret." Musa remained visibly shaken.

Kelly glared at the archaeologist. "Reporters have identified the village and see a connection with the explosion in the Kiryat Moshe neighborhood. Ink is about to flow like blood."

Musa rubbed his forehead and closed his eyes.

"Not so easy to be on the receiving end, is it?" Kelly sneered.

Musa slowly rose from the table, his eyes widening. Dismay had turned into anger. His lower lip shook. He looked at Michael with seething hostility, and without a further word of explanation, the young man headed for the door.

"I wouldn't show up at Arad," the priest called after him.

Musa slammed the door behind him and hurried out of the Abbey. *Was Kelly lying? Surely the Father would not have told anyone. Maybe Kelly told one of those priests, and he talked. I don't trust any of them. I'm nothing but a pawn, a fool in their eyes,* he thought.

That afternoon in an apartment in Kiryat Arba, outside Hebron, four right-wing radical Jewish leaders gathered around Nahum Mana's desk embroiled in heated conversation in the midst of hovering cigar smoke. Three were heavily bearded, and one was clean-shaven.

"I say the whole story is another propaganda attempt to further confuse the negotiations," Amnon Zichroni argued forcibly. "We ought to blow the whole thing off."

"Good try," a small bald-headed man countered. "But I don't think so. I've heard about this Donation of Melchizedek thing all my life. We can't chance a slipup."

"Killing two of our agents?" Zvi Shavit challenged. "We can't let an attack of this magnitude go unanswered."

Nahum Mana nodded in agreement. "Every now and then someone has to nudge the government along to get them to act as they should. Such is the task the Holy One, blessed be His name, has given us. I vote to strike!"

"But where?" Shavit asked and turned to the bald-headed man. "You're the 'in' with the intelligence people."

The fat man took several hard puffs off his cigar. "A strange story trickled in from a village named Arad. This thing is supposedly linked to the Dead Sea Scrolls find. Same people involved."

"Really?" Mana raised his eyebrows.

"Yeah."

"Old man Tufeili was the connection on that one," Zvi Shavit added. "I used to go by his souvenir shop over there near Al-Asfahani Street before he moved his family to Bethlehem."

"Yeah," the fat man growled. "Stole a fortune and opened a first-class tourist trap to make another bundle."

"The Tufeili family could be in on this?" Shavit looked mean. "I never liked that guy anyway."

Amnon Zichroni shook his head. "As your lawyer, it's my job to warn you that we could all get ourselves in deep trouble."

"Thanks." Nahum winked at Amnon. "Exactly what our counsel is supposed to do. Now it's time for us to take this advice under advisement and drop the bomb."

Everyone laughed except Zichroni. He shook his head.

"We've got to answer with an eye for an eye, a tooth for a

tooth," Mana pressed. "Tufeili's business is as good a target as any."

"Agreed," the fat man concurred. "We've got to move immediately, or we lose our edge."

20

Wednesday, September 16
Bethlehem

The first light of dawn found bus No. 23 making the first run of the day. The usual six-mile trip from the Arab bus station opposite the Damascus Gate down the Hebron Road to Bethlehem took about fifteen minutes. The historic route wound past Kibbutz Ramat Rachel, the last Jewish outpost on the border with Jordan before the Six Day War; the Mar Elias Monastery; and the nearby Bell Position, a fierce bastion of the Arab Legion in that fierce struggle. Tourists often took the bus because of the biblical panorama of the orchards and fields where shepherds watched their flocks by night.

A battered green Volkswagen van sped recklessly around the bus, taking the curve at a high rate of speed. Tinted windows made it impossible to see inside. The bus driver might have noticed there were no license tags on the van. They had been removed just beyond the Israeli checkpoint into Palestinian-controlled territory.

Tourists had not yet begun their daily pilgrimage to Rachel's Tomb, Israel's most sacred shrine next to the Western Wall and the Tomb of the Patriarchs. Because the vehicle's driver did not have to watch for tour buses pulling on or off the two-lane road, it went even faster.

Minutes later, the Volkswagen slowed with the approach of the line of souvenir shops that ringed the outskirts of Bethlehem. Just ahead to the right loomed the plush facilities of a tourist shop, the Bethlehem Star. The large two-story white stucco building sported the biggest bus parking lot on the strip. Tufeili's gold mine was well entrenched with every travel agency in the country.

The green van slowed and swung into the parking lot, making a wide sweep as if completing a U-turn back toward Jerusalem. When the Volkswagen pulled alongside the building's sidewalk, the side door slid open and five men dressed in black T-shirts and dark pants rushed out. With quick precision, each hurled a canister through the nearest window and ducked for cover. Moments later fire and debris exploded in every direction. As soon as the first detonation of glass and smoke cleared, the five stood up and hurled a second round of explosives, then sprayed the building with bullets from their Uzis. A security guard tumbled from the top balcony and hit the cement.

A minute later, as the attack force prepared to load up, one of the crew made an unplanned final swipe at the Bethlehem Star. He left the others and hurried down the side of the building to throw a last hand grenade into the top floor, where people must surely be hiding. His foot slipped on the gravel and the throw was bad. The grenade hit the window ledge and bounced back.

"Look out!" The assailant screamed and ran for the van. "Duck!"

The ping of the little steel bomb bouncing twice on the parking lot disappeared in the wham-boom of the concussion, which sprayed shrapnel in every direction. The full force of the explosion hit the attacker and the back of the van.

The assailant screamed and crumpled to the ground. "My back! My back!" He rolled in the dirt. "I'm down."

"Fool!" The driver ran around the side of the van. "You weren't supposed to hit them again."

"Look!" Another guerrilla pointed at the left rear tire. "We're going flat!"

The driver cursed. "We've got to get out of here." Two shots barely missed the driver's head.

"Watch out!" One of the hit men pointed to the back of the burning building. "There's a security guard over there."

Shots rang out from the other side of the parking lot. One of the crew fell to the ground with a hole in his head.

"Inside! Inside!" the driver screamed. "Let's go."

Bullets flew in every direction. The van started up, but the windows were shot out on all sides. Seconds later the driver hit the gas, but a front tire was now flat, sending the vehicle swerving to the left. Fighting for control, the driver jerked the wheel to the right. At that moment, a bullet hit him in the neck. Seconds later the van crashed into the side of the burning building.

Out of sheer force of habit, Leah flipped on the television set as she dressed. She hoped to catch an early morning news report. David always said little as he finished shaving and dressing. No point talking to him.

The announcer concluded the weather report, and the station broke for a commercial.

"I guess we just missed world news." Leah zipped the back of her dress and slipped into her shoes. "Maybe we can catch something on the radio on the way to work."

David grunted but did not look away from the mirror.

"We have a fast-breaking report," the announcer said as he returned to center screen. "While the full account is still coming in, four deaths are now confirmed in an early morning attack on a well-known business establishment in Bethlehem. At least two Arab security guards died in the exchange of gunfire with terrorists. In reprisal for the death of two Mossad agents, right-wing Jewish extremists attacked the business of the Tufeili family, long-time residents of Bethlehem and the original brokers for the Dead Sea Scrolls."

Leah froze in place, staring at the television. David slowly turned from the mirror.

"Initial evidence indicates the extremists reacted against reports of an ancient Arab document purporting to establish their claims to Jerusalem. It is not clear whether the attackers thought the alleged scroll to be in the Tufeili business building, or whether the Tufeili family was the target because they were believed to be linked to the discovery of the ancient document."

David walked closer to the television, holding a razor in his hand. "No! No!" he gasped.

"It's started," Leah cried. "The war is on." She stiffened.

"Idiots!" David shouted. "These fools didn't even get their target right. Who knows how many innocent people will die."

Leah's hand trembled. "If they'd attack unknown Arabs, what would they do to us if they thought we had the scroll?"

"I've got to get the package back from Halevy today." David threw the razor in the sink. "Time is everything."

"No!" Leah cried. "Our *lives* are everything. Think about what could happen to us."

David wiped the remaining shaving cream from his face without finishing. "Got to see him immediately," he muttered. "Face-to-face. So far he's dodged me. No more!"

Leah looked in the mirror and saw the reflection of Zvi's picture on the opposite wall. The eyes, the mouth, had been so similar to her own. "We've got to get out of this thing. I don't want to end up like my brother."

"Extremist fools!" David grabbed a shirt off the rack. "I've campaigned all my life against these reactionary bigots."

"You're not listening to me." Leah grabbed his unbuttoned shirt with both fists. "We could be next. Do you understand? Next!"

"Look." David retreated. "You're the one who was hopping to get in on this thing. Not me."

"Anyone could find out where we live. We're known all over the Jerusalem area."

"Settle down," David demanded. "You're turning into a sky-rocket. Get a grip."

"Don't placate me." Leah's voice kept getting louder. "Your family were the ones who didn't take a dime from old man Salah. If you didn't have such a guilty conscience, we wouldn't even be in this mess."

"Stop it, Leah. You're jumping to unwarranted conclusions."

"I'm talking about history." She leaned into his face. "Family history. Dead relatives. Don't blame me because you're a soft-hearted and softheaded liberal."

David jerked away. "Cool it. I've got business to take care of."

Leah started crying hysterically. "You don't care!" she called after him as he stormed out of the bedroom.

David slammed the door and rushed down the hall to the phone. He had called Avraham Halevy's number so many times he now knew it by memory. The usual feminine voice answered.

"This is David Rosenberg. You know who I am by now. I demand to speak to Avraham Halevy at once."

"I'm sorry," the woman explained too quickly, "Mr. Halevy is not in the office."

"Listen. I know where you're located, and it's not in some innocuous government building. Believe me, I know who Halevy works for, and I am coming down to Mossad headquarters immediately. If Halevy isn't there to talk to me, I'll be back with reporters. Got it?"

"Yes . . ." The woman hesitated.

David hung up. "Now, let's see what my good old friend does."

Musa was on his way to Arad when he heard the report on the radio. Anger had already turned into fear. He sped up. His only thoughts were for the safety of his family. Hassan had exposed everyone to great danger. Why did he always have to be the arrogant old big shot? His father should never have told him anything. Musa's mind raced back and forth, thinking of a hundred consequences of what could be ahead for all of them.

Realizing that someone might be looking for him, Musa took a side road and parked on a narrow dirt street behind his parents' home. He worked his way through several houses and came in the back door.

The family was sitting in the front room, his mother and sister silently huddled together. A man he did not recognize was going out the front door. Musa waited until Rashid shut the door.

He stepped into the small living room. The plain stucco walls were stained with smoke from an open fireplace. Three chairs, an old couch. The room was as spartan as the desert. "What is going on?"

"Musa!" Suha, his mother, leaped up and embraced him.

"We have been so worried." Baraka joined her mother, clutching her brother's waist.

"Son!" Rashid ran forward with his arms wide open. "Everything's gone crazy."

"Who was that?" Musa asked.

"A reporter from Jerusalem." The old man looked worn and frightened. "He wanted to know about you. I don't know what's happening."

"Sit down. Sit down." Musa pulled up a chair. "I must know everything."

"I'm an old fool." The father shook his head. "Hassan made me angry. I talked too much."

Musa looked at the floor and bit his tongue. "Just tell me what you told the reporter."

"Nothing!" Rashid declared. "Nothing! I swear on the prophet's grave."

"But you had to give him some explanation."

"I told him to get out," the father insisted.

"Where's Hassan?"

"He left," Rashid insisted. "Went back to New York City yesterday when things started getting out of hand."

"That's a relief." Musa sighed. "At least we've got him out of the way."

"But the Hayat boys came to see us," his mother added. "They want to find you to help in the fight to liberate our people."

"Oh, that's all I need."

"They are talking about *jihad* and want you to join their secret army," Suha continued. "I'm very frightened."

"You should be," Musa said sternly. "The situation is extremely serious. Let me repeat what I said earlier. No one, I repeat, no one can be trusted."

"But what can we do?" the old man implored.

"Listen carefully." Musa beckoned them closer. "Your house may be under surveillance. Maybe they've even bugged these rooms and are listening."

Suha grabbed her husband and clutched at him. "Help us." Baraka huddled between them.

"I have a plan." Musa's voice dropped to a whisper. "Gather up your things. Tonight I want you to go back to the wilderness. Get the goats. Food. Tents. And return to the places you know so well, where you will be hard to find. You must leave immediately."

"Yes." His mother clapped. "Yes. I knew my son would know what to do."

Rashid nodded his head slowly. "I agree."

"No one must see you leave. Understand?"

The old man kept wringing his hands. "I should never have told Hassan anything."

"I will know where to find you." Musa brushed his father's comments aside. "Do not come back until I tell you. Agreed?"

"Absolutely," Suha concurred. "*Tayyib.* Okay."

"And what will you do, son?" Rashid asked.

"I'm not sure. I must get the scroll back in my possession. But I don't even know who to trust myself."

"Why?" Suha agonized. "Why has all of this happened?"

Musa hugged his mother. "Fear does terrible things to people," he concluded. "Terrible things."

21

Thursday, September 17
Tel Aviv

The Hadar Dafna Building stood inconspicuously on Tel Aviv's King Saul Boulevard, a gray, bare concrete structure like the average office tower built during the Israeli state's rapid growth and expansion. The ground floor opened into a lobby with a bank on the right and a door on the opposite wall bearing a nondescript sign: Security Service Recruitment. No casual inquirer would suspect they were standing before the entrance to the Mossad's central offices.

While the second-floor cafeteria served the public and small businesses in the area, the entire structure was actually a building within a building. On the other side of the threshold, the heart of the secret intelligence network churned away like a finely tuned racing machine.

Avraham Halevy had been at work in his inner office since dawn, preparing for the executive staff meeting. Assistants shuttled in special reports of the attack in Bethlehem as discussions proceeded on their best response to the killing of *sochnim*

Daniel Levy and Uri Dori. The five top officers were edgy and irritated.

"Let me summarize our conclusions to this point." Halevy read from his notes. "We agree that we must make a substantial response. While we don't know who all the players are in this new Islamic Revolutionary Front, we do believe they are behind the attack as well as the execution of Abdul Al-Amid. We have identified some potential targets in what appears to be their leadership."

The five men nodded concurrence.

"Our old friends in Hamas are probably in on this," the head of operations added. "We should hit their big men hiding out in Amman as well."

"Hear. Hear." Several men agreed.

Halevy frowned. "We can't afford another foul-up in Jordan. The botched attempt to knock out Sheikh Ahmed Yassin was a disaster. Cost us plenty in lost public confidence."

The head of operations looked away. His face reddened slightly. "We've covered our errors in that operation," he grumbled.

"But we do have solid evidence on these two young men from Arad?" Halevy asked the large man sitting at the end of the table.

The stout, white-haired Mossad executive looked like a clone of Ariel Sharon, Prime Minister Benjamin Netanyahu's Minister of Foreign Affairs, and had hawkish views similar to the controversial Israeli politician. "The Hayat brothers are young but still veterans of Hamas attacks," he explained. "Hafez is the firebrand, eager and willing to kill our people. We intercepted his attempts to send information on this scroll business to the top people in the new IRF. Actually, he helped us identify a couple more of the players."

"Do they take these Hayat brothers seriously?" Halevy asked.

"We can't tell for sure," the stout man answered. "But we think the Hayats are trying to become big boys. Just maybe the top people we want to sting are paying attention to these local yokels."

"Shall we hit them?" Halevy asked the group.

The five men looked back and forth at one another. Slowly they began nodding their heads.

"Okay," Halevy summarized again. "We're trading two teenagers for our two seasoned professionals. A poor trade, gentlemen."

"Not if we throw in the likes of Rafik Khaled and Abdi Fatah Ghamen," the Sharon look-alike countered. "We got their names from Daniel Levy's contact with Al-Amid. Knock them off and our trigger-happy friends will have something to meditate on. I move we include them in our hunting list."

"Hear. Hear!" The other three affirmed again.

Halevy raised an eyebrow. "That wouldn't even the score, but it would help. Five hundred of those swine aren't worth one Jew."

"It's a start," the head of operations grunted.

"What about this scroll thing?" another executive asked.

"We took a look at it," Halevy answered. "Photographed the text, but not quite sure what to make of the medallion. We had one scholar study the thing, but he couldn't make much out of it. Too complicated. Like everything else, the problem's going to be more in perception than facts. It's in my office."

"Apparently the Hayat brothers picked up on the fact that your friend Rosenberg is the contact man for the Salahs," the rotund man groused. "Rosenberg's name is circulating in the Arab community."

Halevy swore. "I was afraid something like this might happen. I've tried to distance David Rosenberg from this problem, but I don't think he's going to let me help him. Sooner or later, the package is going back to the Rosenbergs."

The head of operations held up his hand. "I move we hit these Hayat brothers in twenty-four hours with an intent to assassinate Khaled and Ghamen within a month."

"Those are big boys," the hawk objected. "Going to be hard to do anything quick."

"Let's try," the operations chief pushed.

A young woman entered the room and pressed a note in Halevy's hand. He read it and frowned. "Looks like I have a problem downstairs, gentlemen. I think we've come to a conclusion anyway. We get the Hayats today; the top dogs tomorrow. Agreed?" He left the room without further discussion and hurried into the secretary's office.

"He's in the lobby?" Halevy snapped at the secretary.

She looked apprehensive. "Nothing persuaded him to leave."

"I expect more from you people," Halevy barked.

"He's threatening to bring the press." She kept her eyes glued on the computer screen.

Halevy glared. "Have someone bring him up on the elevator to the fourth-floor conference room right now. I'll meet him there."

Minutes later Avraham Halevy walked into the room where David Rosenberg waited at the end of the table.

"David! Old friend." Halevy extended his hand, but Rosenberg did not smile. "Wonderful to see you."

"We have a problem," David said, ignoring the usual formalities. "A serious problem. I can't seem to get you to answer my phone calls."

"So sorry." Halevy feigned a pained look. "Unfortunately, I've been away." Halevy pointed to one of the padded chairs. "Do sit down. It's been so long since we really talked."

"I came to you initially because you were a trusted friend." David bore down. "I knew this archaeological find was important, but I didn't foresee anything like what's happened in the last twenty-four hours."

"You certainly did the right thing by seeking me out." Halevy kept smiling. "Just like in the army days when we had to constantly outflank those Arabs."

"I need it back immediately," David said bluntly. "I must leave here with the package I gave you."

Halevy's smile faded. "David, this little box has taken on political significance. We have to make sure we take each step carefully. I'd hoped to keep you from getting caught up in any cross fire."

"The box is my private possession." David sounded cold and hard. "I have your written receipt." He took a deep breath. "Of course, at the time I didn't know you were working with the Mossad."

Halevy tightened his jaw but did not take the bait. "I can't simply release something that now constitutes a security problem for the state," he explained slowly. "These are matters that require due process."

"I'm a lawyer," David snapped. "I know what constitutes theft and unlawful possession. Don't play word games with me."

"We have our lawyers, too." Halevy forced a smile.

"And I have the power of the press. Either you give me that box or I'll be back with a host of reporters, making sure they know you're an officer of the Mossad and have stolen this archaeological find from us."

"You wouldn't." Halevy tried to take the comment back, but the words had slipped out.

"I have a photocopy of the text," David charged. "You'd be hard-pressed to prove you didn't know what I was talking about." He crossed his arms over his chest. "You really want this much heat from the press right now?"

Halevy stared at David. Agent G knew a standoff when he saw it. Rosenberg was not bluffing. Friendship was strained to the limits, and David would call in the media. They would have a field day with the story. The general public did not know he was the Mossad's director. Maybe the enemy didn't know either, and that fact could not be in jeopardy. Might blow the cover on the impending attack on the IRF. David was creating his own problems.

"In addition," David threatened, "I have a number of prominent people who have also seen the document and are prepared to testify that they knew I entrusted the finds into your keeping. You want to face those charges?"

We have a copy of this thing. He has a copy. No point in risking a PR disaster. Time to fold his cards, Halevy decided.

"I won't leave without it," Rosenberg repeated.

"David. David. This is all a misunderstanding. I have no intention of keeping your property. I simply wanted you to understand how important the matter is, and I was trying to shield you from catching any stray bullets, bombs under the car . . . Once that's clear, I'm delighted to deliver the box back into your hands."

"I fully realize the seriousness of this entire episode." No give in his voice.

Halevy stood up. "Good. I'll send two of our employees down to your law office with the package." He extended his hand. "We must get together socially more often. Leah is such a delightful person."

David glared. "Can I expect the parcel to arrive by five o'clock?"

"Of course."

"I have your word?"

"David!" Halevy pleaded.

"Be aware that I have tape-recorded our conversation," David bluffed. "I will expect the package by five."

Avraham backed toward the door. "The agents will be there as agreed. My best to all concerned." He smiled and hurried out the door. Halevy stomped down the hall, cursing under his breath. "An amateur outflanked me! I can't believe it."

22

Thursday, September 17
Jerusalem, Dormition Abbey

Leah stopped at the entry to the Dormition Abbey and rubbed the side of her face. The escalating strain was simply too much; her neck muscles felt painfully tight. Musa would immediately insist on knowing the status of the scroll. Tension was high enough without any more misunderstandings over getting the find back.

She waited for a group of French-speaking tourists to pass, entered, and quickly found her way down what was becoming a very familiar hallway. Leah glanced at her watch. 1:10. She was not late this time. Well, only a few minutes late. The delay caused by David's recent phone call was worth the lost time. At least, she had something good to report. The box should be back in their hands by 5:00.

Leah could be critical of David, but she would not tolerate anyone else saying anything negative about him. He had made an intelligent decision in trusting the scroll with Halevy, even though things turned sour. Her complaints had only been cannon fodder in a domestic squabble. She did not want him taking any more heat from Kelly, Salah, or anyone else. After all, he had successfully retrieved the find from a no less formidable foe than the Mossad itself.

Leah paused at the basement door and braced herself. The attack in Bethlehem had to be on everybody's mind. The last radio report was terrible; Musa would be very upset. She opened the door and slowly started her descent.

Michael Kelly sat across the table from Musa Salah, talking vociferously as the priest often did. As usual he wore the brown Benedictine habit; Musa looked like a local street vendor. Not much style there. Both men stood when she came down.

"Good afternoon." Leah tried to sound bright, upbeat.

"*Shalom.*" Michael always offered the proper Jewish response, consistently the diplomat.

Musa nodded solemnly.

"I have good news for you." Leah sat down next to the priest. "By late afternoon we will have the scroll and medallion in our law offices. David took care of the problem this morning."

"Good! Good." Kelly sounded buoyant. "Now, Musa, that ought to be a bit of encouragement for you."

The Arab glowered. "Encouraged? How can anyone be reassured on this day?"

"We're getting the scroll back, man." The priest worked the good-ol'-boy angle. "*Now*, we'll be able to get down to business."

"The Tufeilis weren't family friends, but they were human beings. People innocently making a living . . . until this morning."

Leah studied Musa's face carefully. Dark rings circled his eyes. He must not have slept well in some time. Still, he looked more frightened than worried. And anger obviously simmered beneath these emotions. Words had to be chosen carefully.

"Of course," Kelly answered. "The situation is deplorable. Danger lurks everywhere."

Leah shook her head. "Musa, no rational person can condone what happened in Bethlehem. My heart goes out to everyone in the Arab community." She felt Musa scrutinizing her as if searching for some flaw. He was spoiling for a fight.

"Arabs should not have to live under conditions dictated by lynch mobs and terrorists." Musa's words were laden with a nasty tone.

"A terrible time." Kelly sounded like a philosopher pontificating about the weather. "A difficult time to be alive."

"An easy time to die," Musa shot back. "Particularly if you're an Arab." He eyed Leah.

Leah felt the muscles in her neck start to throb again. Her cheek twitched. Mustn't get dragged into an angry exchange. Things aren't going in the right direction. Time to be quiet and just listen.

"I propose we get down to work." Kelly still sounded like the diplomat. "We mustn't let these momentary political interruptions distract us from our important task."

Musa almost had not come to the meeting. Only at the last minute had he thrown in the towel and driven to the Abbey. He had not slept well the night before, worrying continually about his family. Everything about the translation project irritated him, and he had even begun to doubt the validity of the whole thing.

When Leah had opened the door, Musa glanced at his watch. More than ten minutes overdue. The Rosenbergs' habitual tardiness annoyed him. Jews were an inconsiderate lot anyway. He believed them to have a particular talent for being tactless and abrasive. Musa's years of education in the United States had sensitized him to Western punctuality. If the Rosenbergs really cared about his feelings, they would get there promptly like everyone else.

Even Leah's report that the package would be back by late afternoon did not set well. *Only stalling*, he had thought. *Buying time so her incompetent, bungling husband could appear to be doing something. Typical Israeli smoke screen. Say one thing. Do another.*

"So, let's get to work, shall we?" the priest said.

Kelly's babbling did not set any better with Musa than Leah's straggling behind. Americans could be worse than Jews. After all, his family was out there somewhere in the wilderness, maybe being chased by reporters—or worse, police—at this very moment running down a sand dune seeking cover. Kelly, the delegate from the land of plenty, the product of a society obsessed with air-conditioning and vacant parking places, could not possibly understand his family struggling to survive in the barren, arid wilderness.

His mother would be pleased to be out of Arad and back into a tent, but Suha was not young. Since Baraka's birth, her health had suffered. She certainly was not in any shape to be chased up some steep hillside by an attacker. And then, Baraka was only a child. Musa had not been happy when he had heard that his aging parents were taking on another mouth to feed. No one had asked his opinion in the first place. Baraka only made their flight to safety more vulnerable and difficult.

When no one responded to his prodding to start work, Kelly plowed on. "We all know these political flare-ups are going to happen from time to time. Unfortunately, our archaeological discovery coincided with another attack of the 'crazies.' That's all." He stuck out his lip with the indifference of an Englishman casually sipping tea immediately after receiving word that the children of Chinese tea merchants were starving. "Merely a coincidence," Kelly concluded.

"*Our* discovery." Musa clipped his words. "I was under the impression that my father and I found the urn in the sand."

"Figure of speech." Kelly kept that ingratiating smile stretching from cheek to cheek. "You understand. 'We' is simply a collective pronoun."

Musa simmered. If he wanted to get plural about the problem, Kelly could go out to the desert and help his father herd goats. Maybe carrying water up a hill for Musa's mother would prove to be a meaningful task. Kelly's hands were not nearly callused enough. A little back bending might improve his attitude.

"Leah, I'm sure by now you've adjusted to these periodic terrorist attacks," Kelly continued.

Musa caught a look of consternation flash across the woman's face. More than amazed, Leah seemed shocked that the priest suggested such a thing. How could anyone discount the deaths of innocent people as if the situation were no more than a news report interrupting the broadcast of a soccer game?

Musa bit his lip, lest his anger explode like a bomb. He was surrounded by idiots.

"No one acclimates to terrorism." Leah was blunt. "At best we only try to survive."

Kelly took a deep breath and mentally took a step back. Nothing seemed to be working. Everyone was too uptight. The important thing was getting them back to work.

"Americans have little sense of what we live with in this land." Musa sounded as if he were spoiling for a confrontation. "The privileged seldom understand the exploited."

Only a trained response kept the priest's smile in place. Hardball time. This boy had overdosed on self-pity.

"We're all under a great deal of strain," Kelly conceded. "Sure. This is not a good day."

"How would *you* suggest we proceed?" Leah asked Musa.

Good ice breaker, Kelly thought. She seemed to be trying to stay out of the man's line of fire. Kelly watched Musa's face. No signs that he was going to respond. Probably wouldn't like anyone's suggestions.

"I'm sure each of us has been exploring various aspects of the text," Leah continued.

"Definitely." Michael relaxed. "The text almost has a cryptographic quality to it. "

"On the other hand," Leah countered, "it may have been an attempt to put the message in a universal form. Perhaps the structure of the language was intended to suggest that possession of the land had implications that surpassed a time and place."

"A decidedly Jewish perspective." Musa was back in the game. "I know of no ancient people who attempted to spiritualize geography like the Jews did. Sort of a chauvinistic approach to real estate."

The priest flinched. Musa was looking for a fight, and Leah was only going to take so much of this. Keep the balls in the air.

"Yes," Michael drawled, "an interesting approach."

Musa slumped back in his chair and crossed his arms over his chest. "Maybe we've only found a fabrication concealed with Jewish religious documents to shore up their political aims."

"Musa, I don't think so." Leah seemed to be trying to cajole. "Such a scenario wouldn't fit the ancient world. Ownership of Jerusalem is a recent political issue."

"Let's face it," Musa attacked. "You have no interest in this project beyond confirming current Jewish claims to Jerusalem. Admit it."

Michael watched Leah's face harden. He thought he saw her

cheek twitch. This thing was turning out to be harder work than keeping the Curia happy with the pope.

Leah rested her forehead against her hand and looked at the floor. She did not answer.

"Perhaps we ought to avoid getting into the contemporary issues that divide us," the priest suggested. "Let's aim at exploring the scholarly problems."

"Easy for *you* to say," Musa bore in. "You think we ought to bring the pope over here and make him the mayor of Jerusalem."

"Come now," Michael scoffed. "I don't think I even implied such a thing."

Musa glanced back and forth between the priest and the woman. "Obviously I am outnumbered in these discussions . . . but then again, Arabs are always outnumbered . . . and if not, the balance is restored by a good old American-style gangster attack."

Michael took another deep breath. Nothing was going to work with this guy. Musa had slipped off into that predictable Arab irrationality that caused the camel jockeys to shoot themselves in the foot over and over again.

"Perhaps this is not a good moment to work," Michael concluded. "Maybe we should let matters settle overnight and then return to the table."

Leah kept staring at the floor.

"Remember when blacks wanted to ride up front in the buses in Birmingham, Alabama?" Musa asked. "You probably weren't interested at the time, but people marching on Selma, Alabama, were shot for no other reason than that they were ethnically different."

"What?" Michael's voice rose. "What in the world are you talking about? We're working on a scroll thousands of years old, not something even vaguely related to contemporary American politics."

"I'm talking about attitudes." Musa did not retreat. "When I listen to both of you I get nothing but the same old rhetoric forced on my people at every turn." He stood up. "This whole project is a hoax. I want my objects back." Musa stormed up the stairs and was gone.

Kelly clenched his jaw and tried not to speak. The idiot! Unstable as water. He was intelligent enough to know better. So, where was Leah in all this mess?

"I suppose I'll go back to the office." She stood up. "We obviously won't be doing anything much today." Leah picked up her purse and started toward the steps. She looked tired and defeated. "I doubt if Musa will be contacting me. Let me know what happens if he calls you." At the top of the stairs, she turned and called over her shoulder. "Good luck."

Michael did not look up. He drummed on the table with his fingertips and stared into the darkness at the far end of the room. How did he ever let David Rosenberg get him tied up with this bunch of screwballs? Then again, he needed a big breakthrough. A headline grabber. The kind of sensational story that gets Rome's attention. *And that's why I'll go right on tolerating this nonsense,* he told himself.

The priest pushed back and stood up. He walked around the table several times and finally sat down on the edge. He had never gotten the international recognition he thought he deserved. If this thing had any validity at all, it would be his ticket to the top. Can't let their silly ethnic squabbles get in the way. Got to get this project back on track.

The priest trudged back up the stairs and locked the door behind him. He walked slowly down the long hall, realizing what a mistake it had been to become a priest. Predictable adolescent guilt and too much enthusiasm drummed up at youth camps looked like inspiration and a call to a vocation. Now, decades later it all seemed like nonsense. The writer of

Ecclesiastes knew his stuff. "Vanity of vanities," said the preacher. "All is vanity." The sage was no fool. Ah, but there was a cure for his boredom. Nothing was wrong that a good dose of fame would not cure.

23

Thursday, September 17
Jerusalem, Elisha Street

Leah got into her car but did not turn the key. She watched tourist buses come and go from the parking lot accessing the Zion Gate and the Dormition Abbey, but she found it difficult to leave. Everything was so jumbled and confused. She could not believe that what was supposed to be a translation session had turned into a twenty-minute confrontation, accomplishing precisely nothing.

Then again, nothing was going well. The City of Peace was now no more than a city of pieces. Everywhere she turned, people acted edgy and irritable. Fear settled over Jerusalem like fog rolling in from the ocean, drowning out sunlight and hope. Though understandable, Musa's mood still took a toll. Anger worked on Leah's psyche like a boa constrictor squeezing the life out of its prey. The priest's attempt at manipulation only added to the tension.

She reached for the ignition key. Musa had every right to be angry. The Salahs knew the Tufeilis. Just people trying to make a living. Innocent bystanders. Boom! Their business is gone.

People are killed. Lives are ruined. Who can bear such things? She turned the key.

Minutes later Leah was back on Hativat Yerushalayim Street, heading toward the law office. She passed the Damascus Gate and noticed the usual hustle and bustle of crowds streaming into the marketplace. Business looked good. Palestinian women balancing baskets of fruit on their hips or their heads. Shoppers plowed through the mob. Children dashed down the stone steps toward the massive entryway. The little guys waved their postcards and Chiclets at the tourists. Amazing how enduring commerce always remained in the face of adversity.

Two small boys dashed in front of her car even though the light had already turned yellow. Yanait had always urged Leah to have children. The traffic light changed; she hit the gas. As a Zionist, her mother's favorite line from the Torah was, "Be fruitful and multiply." If Yanait had brought it up once, she'd said it a thousand times. "No matter how difficult the times are, we have an obligation to bring children into this world. Jewish survival demands reproduction."

Leah was never quite convinced. She wanted to believe, but Zvi's death canceled the covenant with Yanait, Israel, and God Himself. Even Yanait had never been the same again. Profound grief lurked beneath the surface of every conversation. Sometimes in the middle of the night, Leah heard her mother weeping. On the yearly anniversary of his death, while the Kaddish prayers were said, Yanait seemed near collapse. She wept with such depth of agony, observers might have thought the shooting had only been a day ago, not a decade past. Leah did not believe she could survive such pain. The only guarantee was never to have a child.

David remained ambivalent about children. He liked the idea but retreated from a commitment to the fact. "Someday," he often said. "Yes, someday soon." But time had a way of sweeping all the somedays into a pile and dropping them into the dustbin of yesterday. And now they were getting older.

Leah parked in the reserved place behind their building and went in the back door. She unlocked the front door and turned on the lights. David should be showing up shortly, and there was work to be done. She sat down at her desk.

In the center of the protective desk pad, David had left a note. "With appreciation to the most sensuous woman in Jerusalem. Your lover."

Leah laughed and quickly slipped the pink slip in her desk drawer. She took it out and read it again three times, giggling. The upside of being childless was a relationship filled with many little romantic surprises. They were indeed lovers, companions, colleagues, and most important, best friends.

Hubbub over the translation project had cut into the demands of office work. Of course, David did not complain about the interruptions, but papers had to be filed and several contracts needed to be completed that afternoon. After all, the Salahs were not the only game in town. There were at least two to three hours of work to be done. Leah put the note in the drawer for the last time and got down to business.

When the back door opened, Leah knew it was David. She glanced at her desk clock. 4:14. No question about it, she had made a real dent in the pile of papers.

"I'm back." David locked the door behind him.

Leah stood up. "Great. You'll be pleased with the shape the Al-Habbini contracts are in, and I've finished off those two court petitions that have been pending for a week."

David grabbed her cheeks and gave her a quick kiss. "Always the most efficient of the efficient. Great!" He sat down at his desk. "And how much of the text of the scroll did you get done?"

"Nothing." Leah sighed. "Musa blew up and we left."

"Oh no!"

"Didn't last half an hour. Bad scene."

"Everybody's tense." David settled back in his chair. "People are very upset about the killing of the Mossad agents and the subsequent attack this morning. There's a sense of impending doom everywhere."

"How big a factor is the newspaper story about the discovery of the scroll?"

"People love a good mystery. They're intrigued as much by what they don't know as what the paper has speculated. No question about it, the scroll is politically explosive."

Leah got up and walked over to his desk. She plopped down in David's lap and threw her arms around his neck. "Really think I'm the most sensuous woman in the country?"

"Jerusalem is the best I can do."

"You're rating me slightly above all those fat women down in the market?"

"Okay. I'll throw in the whole West Bank."

She abruptly kissed him passionately. "There!" Leah thumped him on the chest. "How's that fit the rating system?"

"On second thought, I'll throw in Italy and France." David laughed and kissed his wife again. "Well, dear, our precious little package ought to be here any minute."

Leah stood up. "I wonder if this thing has become more trouble than it's worth." She ran her hands nervously through her hair. "What started out as a great adventure has turned into a nightmare. Maybe this thing is jinxed . . . like King Tut's mummy or something."

David's countenance changed. "Strange you'd say that." He pursed his lips pensively. "The confrontation with Halevy was no fun. I can't believe it, but I nearly had to declare World War III to get the guy to cave in. If I hadn't bluffed him with the threat that I recorded our conversation, I don't think he'd have agreed to bring it back."

"Sure he'll keep his word?"

"No." David shook his head. "I won't believe it until the box is sitting on my desk. If Halevy backs out at the last moment, there isn't a lot I can do."

"He didn't seem to want bad press?"

David rubbed his chin. "Well, that's the last lever in my toolbox."

Leah smiled at her husband. "No one could have done any better. And," she paused and raised her eyebrows apologetically, "despite what I said, asking him to protect the box was still the right thing to do under the circumstances."

David rolled his eyes. "That depends on whether we have the box back in the next fifteen minutes."

"Sure." She turned away.

Leah sat back down at her desk and stared out the front window. Several minutes later a brown car pulled into a parking place in front of their building. Two casually dressed men got out. One carried a paper-wrapped parcel.

"The package is here!" Leah jumped up from her chair. "We've won the war of nerves."

David watched the front door intensely.

The pair entered unceremoniously and walked straight toward the Rosenbergs. "I believe this is the Rosenberg law firm," the man with the package stated factually.

"Yes," David answered.

"I have a delivery." The agent placed the box on David's desk. "You'll need to sign for it."

David beamed triumphantly at Leah. "Certainly. Please send my appreciation to Mr. Halevy."

The agents offered no acknowledgment of the name.

"And express my appreciation for his efforts in storing the material for me."

Again no hint of recognition.

David signed his name and handed the paper to Leah. "We'll need a copy for our records, and you gentlemen can be on your way."

"Certainly." The second agent spoke for the first time.

"Should have left it in my office safe in the first place," David said as he picked up the box. He opened a small safe next to his father's old rolltop desk and stuck his hand inside. "Probably saved a considerable amount of trouble if I'd put it here." David realized the agents were watching him open the safe. "I'll move it somewhere more secure later." He pushed a number of envelopes aside and inched the box in. Then he shut the door and whirled the dial on the combination lock. "Takes care of that." He smiled broadly, the relief at having the package back in his possession obvious.

Leah thought the copy machine would take forever. The quicker the men left, the better. "Here's the original back." Leah handed the men the receipt. "We have our copy. You gentlemen can be on your way."

"Let me walk you back to the car." David sounded jubilant, and he had evidently decided to be gracious now that his ordeal with the Mossad was finally over. "I can't tell you how glad I am to have this problem resolved." He uncharacteristically put his arm around one of the men's shoulders as if they were old friends. "We do thank you, boys."

"Glad we could help." The agent lost nothing of his all-business demeanor.

Leah watched David walk the men to the curbside. She mentally ordered her husband to hurry. Okay. Okay. Don't push your luck. The scroll is back in our safe for the night. Cut the buddy-buddy act and get back in here.

David was talking to the agent on the passenger side. The other man started around to the driver's side when the crack of gunfire exploded. The agent slumped into the side of the car. More shots rang out and glass sprayed across the office. Leah saw the old wall clock explode in a shower of metal and glass. She hit the floor under her desk. Bullets ricocheted across the office.

For a few moments Leah cowered beneath the desk, shocked senseless. Gunfire stopped, and she looked out. Large jagged pieces of glass hung from what was left of their front window. Side windows in the brown car were scattered; no one was in sight. People were running in all directions. In that second, Leah realized she could not see David.

She leaped up and charged toward the door. She jerked the door open and saw the second agent twenty feet up the side-walk holding a gun over a man's body. Another agent lay motionless in the street next to the car. But David? Leah turned back toward the office's scattered window.

Curled up against the stone facade beneath a shower of glass slivers, David's crumpled form slumped under the ledge of the empty office window as if a great force had slung him backward into the wall. Blood was already pouring out on the sidewalk beneath his body.

"David!" Leah screamed at the top of her lungs.

His eyes stared straight ahead, glazed, fixed. He did not move.

Part
Two

24

Friday, September 18
Mount of Olives

Shadows stretched behind the stone sarcophagi in long dark jagged lines, lengthening down the steep hillside of the Mount of Olives. The grieving procession hurried to finish their task before sunset, when the Sabbath began. Memorial stones left by mourners dotted the tops of the slab gray monuments jutting up out of the stony ground. As if in a daze, the bereaved ambled in and out among the endless lines of graves, following the journey of the shrouded form on the special Jerusalem burial society stretcher. The Rosenberg plots had been in the family for decades, carefully preserved, the site being coveted by many of Jerusalem's faithful for their final resting place.

The stretcher lumbered along on the shoulders of David's best friends: a member of the Knesset, a lawyer, an army general, one of Israel's largest antiquity dealers, and two aging uncles. The large crowd of friends and family followed the funeral procession down the traditional route of Jesus' Triumphal Entry into the Holy City. Avraham Halevy blended into the throng as simply another son of Israel, bemoaning the loss of a friend. The Benedictine in the brown habit was an unusual addition, as was the Arab standing along the edges of the crowd with the priest. Differences were not noticed on this day.

Always egalitarian about death, Jewish custom dictated one single garment for the dead. David had been wrapped in the simple, handmade white *tachrichim* shroud, purposely without pockets to remind that only the soul counted now. A *tallit*, or prayer shawl, lay over the shroud. Although nonobservant, the Rosenbergs' identity was molded by the ancient traditions, and in their grief they turned instinctively to the faith of their ancestors.

Seven times the procession had paused on their descent to the grave. Seven times for the seven occurrences of *hevel*, the word for utter futility used by the book of Ecclesiastes to describe the ultimate plight of all humanity. Seven seemed particularly appropriate today.

The rabbi stood in front of the rocky soil piled in a dusty chalk heap next to the oblong black hole. The old man's *tallit* hung around his shoulders and disappeared beneath an enormous white beard, his *kippa* sunk into his snow-white hair. Standing next to the grave, he chanted a prayer to the God of all compassion to receive David's soul while the remnant of both families gathered around, weeping, clutching each other. Yanait cried for David and once again for Zvi. She wept for the grandchildren she would never see.

When the men turned the last shovel of dirt and the final symbolic rocks of mourning and respect had been placed, the rabbi made the final pronouncement. "May he come to his place in peace." Then the multitude of mourners began their long slow walk back into the rest of their lives. Leah mechanically trudged on into her worst nightmare. Even though a scant twenty-four hours had passed since David's death, Leah looked two decades older.

As her mother and grandmother before her had done, Leah ate the first meal after the funeral, the *Seudat Havra'a*, the Meal of Consolation, with her family. She ate the hard-boiled eggs in silence, like a prisoner accepting the first day of lifetime imprisonment. The flame of the seven-day candle flickered in the corner of the kitchen. Leah would not bathe, use cosmetics, or sit on a chair until the wax and fire were spent.

Contrary to what Leah felt, time did not stand still. On the day of the funeral, a new terrorist group surfaced and took credit for the assassination of the Mossad agent and the well-known Jerusalem attorney. The Islamic Revolutionary Front also took responsibility for the earlier deaths of the agents in the Kiryat Moshe neighborhood. Spokesmen in Kabul told the world via television they would eventually unleash a nuclear attack on Israel for the state's continuing atrocities against the innocent. Officials of the IRF proclaimed themselves as the new leaders of the Arab world and then promptly disappeared into obscurity. Within forty-eight hours, Israeli military forces responded to their claims by attacking the Arab village of Arad. They claimed solid evidence that the perpetrators of recent terrorist attacks lived there.

The government proclaimed the right to strike based on the previous day's nuclear threats. The reason a remote town like Arad was chosen remained obscure to the general public. In the middle of the night, the Israel Defense Forces hit Arad like a tornado. Resistance proved to be brief and insignificant. A number of young men were killed, among them the Hayat brothers, thought to be local leaders of the new IRF. Bulldozers smashed their home to the ground as well as grinding into rubble the restaurant where they worked. By morning, the little town of Arad looked more like a smoking ruin than a once-struggling center of commerce. When the army withdrew, thick black columns of smoke remained.

For the seven days of the initial *shiva* mourning period, Leah did not come out of her house, while friends and relatives made condolence visits, speaking with her about David. Yanait answered the phone and registered the messages of sympathy that poured in from across Israel. Politicians and the curious, friends and professional acquaintances, all shared a common sense of horror and dread of what lay ahead.

Yet solitude could not isolate the house of David Rosenberg from the storm brewing across the country. The night after the funeral, rioters attacked the Muslim sector of the Old City; hours later yeshiva students were knifed at a bus stop. Additional soldiers began patrolling the streets. Arab men threw rocks from the top of the Temple Mount on Jewish worshipers at the Western Wall. Defense forces responded with rubber bullets, and two Arab boys went to the hospital.

Ancient archetypes of war oozed up from beneath the cracks in the cobblestone streets of the Old City and found reincarnation in children and teenagers. Gog and Magog; Jupiter and Mars; specters from Sheol and the Four Horsemen of the Apocalypse mingled with demons of hell, all surging down the streets and roads, infiltrating the byways and the little alleys, corrupting hearts and minds. The City of Prayer was fast becoming a den of destruction. Rumors of the discovery of an ancient golden scroll containing a deadly secret had been the key that unlocked far more than Pandora's box.

Toward the end of her time of *shiva*, Father Kelly called. Leah had agreed to see him and Musa for the first time since the funeral. With the bedroom door slightly ajar, Leah heard her mother's exchange with her friends. She did not want to talk about their work, to be reminded that it was David who had brought the group together. Yet she knew the time had come to face it. After a quick glance in the mirror, she adjusted her black dress and walked out. Yanait had ushered the two men into the living room and discreetly retired to the back of the house. Both men were dressed casually. They sat down and waited quietly until Yanait had walked out.

"Thank you for coming," Leah said as she entered the living room.

"Thank you for allowing us." Michael stood and extended his hand. "You have been in our thoughts constantly."

Musa nodded his head vigorously and kept his eyes on the floor. "I cannot express my great sorrow over what has happened to your house. I am grieved over the loss of an old friend of my family."

"Your words are a comfort. Gentlemen, please sit down." Leah looked around at the artifacts, the stylish furniture, the oil paintings. Everything was in place; yet the most important part was gone. "Was it just a few weeks ago that we gathered here to discuss our translation project? Everything feels rather disjointed."

"Nothing prepares one for the loss you have experienced." Father Kelly sounded very different today. The diplomat had become a priest again. "The pain of death cuts to the very core of our souls." He reached for Leah's hand. "No words are adequate. Only God can truly comfort us."

The priest's hand was soft, warm, much like David's touch. Michael's gesture helped ease her awkwardness. She squeezed his grip and then let go, settling back in her chair.

"Do you have a rabbi, a spiritual adviser, a friend to talk with?" Michael asked.

"I tend to be a solitary oyster. No, during this past week I have kept my own counsel." She forced a smile. "I've done nothing but think over and over again about why David was killed. How I will go on. What's next? What should I do? These questions haunt me day and night."

"Yes. Of course." Michael looked deeply into her eyes. "Musa and I talked of similar things. David's death has made our petty arguments seem foolish and irrelevant. We, too, have thought a great deal about what is important."

"I must apologize for my behavior the last time we were together," Musa began. "I was very upset because my family was in danger, but I behaved badly."

"Musa." Leah tried to smile again. "Each of us has been under great stress. Let's face it. We are living in the midst of a war zone. It's hard to keep one's balance under those circumstances."

"Are you aware that the Israel Defense Forces attacked the village of Arad?" Kelly asked.

"No!" Leah gasped. "Musa! Was your family hurt?"

Musa shook his head. "They were safe in the wilderness, but people were killed and property destroyed."

Leah felt her stomach tighten and a knot formed in her throat. "It has to stop. The killing has to stop," she anguished. "I don't care what anyone's race, politics, or religion is. This constant bombing and sniping only afflict the innocent. Widows and orphans are left to cry in the night." She bit her lip. "If anything good can come out of David's death, it must be a new resolve to stop this senseless killing."

Michael exhaled deeply and rubbed the side of his face. "Yes. Yes. You are desperately right." He spoke with uncharacteristic intensity. "Our religious communities must find a way to lock arms, not break them."

"David and I weren't observant." Leah tried to keep tears back but couldn't. "Our backgrounds didn't shape us to think much about religious things." She looked pensively at David's picture, which Yanait had placed on a coffee table several days earlier. "He'd be surprised to know that I went to the synagogue on the Sabbath. I bought a prayer book and have been reading the prayers. They help."

The priest nodded knowingly. "Do you have any idea what really happened to David?" Michael's question had a tentative, pensive edge.

"Avraham Halevy, the man who kept the package for David, came to see me. He has, well, let's just say, he has inside information. Avraham said the shooting was probably in reprisal for what happened in Bethlehem."

"But how could the terrorists have known that David was involved with the scroll?" the priest asked.

Leah noticed that Musa recoiled at the question and looked shaken. "The terrorists may have been after the agents that came to our office, and David simply happened to be in the line of fire." She thought Musa had taken on a sick look.

"But weren't they waiting outside?" Michael pushed.

"Yes." Leah hesitated. "Avraham was certain the assassins were waiting in the alley when the package arrived."

"Then they couldn't have been following the people who brought the scroll back," Kelly reasoned. "They would have been there in the first place because of David."

"Yes," she agreed. "I thought the same thing, Michael. An important piece is missing in Halevy's explanation."

Musa kept looking at the floor. Leah couldn't help but notice he avoided all eye contact.

"I suppose these intelligence and terrorist matters are always riddled with inconsistencies," the priest concluded. "But this explanation leaves serious issues unresolved."

Leah looked away from Musa and back at David's picture. "I have come to one conclusion," she stated emphatically. "David hated bigotry and fanaticism. He would not have wanted me to retreat one inch from my commitments because of fear or intimidation. David would have insisted that I go forward with my life just as I planned. Do you understand?"

Both men nodded solemnly.

"The best memorial I can offer to him right now is to finish our translation project regardless of what happens around us. I'm not sure I'm ready to return to the law practice yet, but I must be faithful to the task David and I set out to complete. I will start at once so that it will be clear that nothing has deterred us." She looked hard at both men. "Has either of you become afraid? Want out?"

"No, no," Kelly insisted.

Musa looked frightened but did not say no.

Leah folded her hands in her lap. For a moment she felt her profound sorrow crack and a new surge of strength break through. "I give you my pledge of total commitment to get this thing done as quickly as possible. Can I count on both of you to stand with me in doing everything possible to finish the translation?"

Musa closed his eyes and stopped biting his knuckle. "I will do everything in my power to help and . . ." He seemed to choke on his words. "And I will protect you, Leah. I promise to do whatever is necessary to make sure no one harms you." Tears welled up in his eyes.

The priest reached over for his friend's hand. "We stand together on this pledge. Don't worry, Leah. While we certainly can't replace your husband, we can offer you a bulwark of strength during these difficult days." With his other hand, Michael covered Leah's palm. "Whatever our differences have been, we will stand together. We *will do* this thing *regardless*."

25

Wednesday, September 30
Jerusalem, B'nai Yisrael Synagogue

The Days of Awe were still fresh and the promise of Rosh Hashanah unfolding as Leah had endured her seven days of seclusion following David's murder. Her mourning period extended into the ten days between the New Year and the day of repentance and self-examination. She had not attended Yom Kippur services for many years, but now, as the holy day arrived, she desperately felt the need. When Kaddish prayers would be said for the departed, she yearned for David's name to be remembered in the midst of the congregation of the righteous. Leah felt that upon seeing the Ark containing the Torah, the eternal light burning above it, the faithful praying in their *kippot* and *talitot*, each of the ancient customs would offer new consolation and strength.

Avoiding the more stringent Orthodox synagogue blocks away, Leah tied a scarf on her head and walked into B'nai Yisrael, a Conservative synagogue closer to her home. The Days of Awe would be over with the setting of the sun, but for the next few hours she hoped to soak up prayers like the dry earth receiving the first fall rain.

Finding an empty seat near the back of the small synagogue, she opened the *machzor* prayer book and thumbed through the pages to catch up with the service already in progress for several hours. The smooth flow of holy words felt like a mountain stream meandering over ancient rocks in a creek bed extending back across three millennia to the very foot of Mt. Sinai. She drank the words like a parched horse stumbling into an oasis. Many filed back and forth, leading the reading. One of the congregants ascended to the lectern and offered the assurance of the Psalms. "As tender as a father with his children, the Lord is compassionate with His worshipers." The words washed over her with the cleansing sweep of the ebb tide leaving behind a cleansed beach.

After a short break in the service, prayers resumed and two older men opened the Ark. They removed the large velvet-covered scrolls and hoisted them on the shoulders of a man wearing a multicolored striped *tallit*. In solemn procession he carried the large Torah around the small synagogue as the most treasured of all possessions. Worshipers reached out with prayer books to touch and kiss the honored scroll. Leah simply listened, absorbing the ambience of the service.

An aged and esteemed rabbi, wearing a long white robe and an exceptionally large *tallit* that swept across his shoes, shuffled up to the pulpit to deliver his short sermon on the meaning of the day. Speaking in slow and deliberate tones, he explained that the Holy One governs the world with a mixture of justice and compassion, not unlike a king with expensive fragile glass goblets. If he poured hot water to sterilize them, the cups would be shattered. On the other hand, freezing cold water would crack the glass. Only by mixing cold and hot, mixing compassion with concern, could the vessels endure.

"But!" The rabbi shook his finger toward the sky. "God's love and compassion overwhelm His demand for strict justice! We can eagerly search for forgiveness and trust His mercy."

In the Yom Kippur smorgasbord offering of blessings and judgments, Leah found mercy to be the most encouraging of all the promises. She felt a desperate need for reassurance. Everything in her wanted to believe that David's death did not negate either justice or compassion. Both were certainly in short supply in Jerusalem, in the country, and in the world, for that matter.

The rabbi and the reader restored the Torah to its resting place and closed the Ark. The Musaf service continued; remembrance of the past once again evoked, sacred memory rekindled, the pain of Israel revisited. Abruptly, the words of the prayer took on a biting edge.

The rabbi read slowly, painfully.

"Of steel and iron, cold and hard and numb, now forge yourself a heart and come to walk the world of slaughter. You shall wander in and out of ruins, look in where all the black and gaping holes appear like ragged wounds that neither wait nor hope for healing more in all this world."

Leah caught her breath as if a blade sliced across her palm. The rabbi's recitation of atrocities lumbered on with words matching the cadence of the pallbearers who bore David's body down the Mount of Olives. Stories of Romans decreeing the death of Jews teaching the Torah were followed by the accounts of rabbis executed for reciting the *Sh'ma Yisrael*. Accounts of pogroms preceded the remembrance of Warsaw's Jewish girls, who took poison rather than submit to the Nazis.

The liturgy continued with the story of the young boy Frantisek Bass, deported in 1942, murdered at Auschwitz in 1944, representative of fifteen thousand children who passed into the death camp at Terezin. Frantisek left a poem.

A little garden,
Fragrant and full of roses,
The path is narrow
And a little boy walks along it.
A little boy, a sweet boy,
Like that growing blossom.
When the blossom comes to bloom,
The little boy will be no more.

Leah bit her lip and squeezed her knuckles until they were white.

And then the congregation remembered the six million; no markers to denote where their ashes mingled together with dirt, human beings who disappeared like grains of sand and yet remained ubiquitous in that moment of sacred memory; people whose bones were turned into handles for knives, whose skin was used as lamp shades, whose hair was made into cloth. The words of remembrance lifted from the page and flew to Leah's soul, to the forbidden place where she kept the image of her husband curled up beneath the ledge of their office building, he, too, another victim of hate.

And then the rabbi said a most unexpected thing. "We know that this world will be saved from evil."

The congregation responded. "Should this not be true, may we know nothing further, as nothing will be worth knowing."

Leah began weeping, softly at first and then shaking uncontrollably. As if coming from a far distance, the recitation of the places of pain continued:

"Bergen-Belsen . . ."
"Dachau . . ."
"Buchenwald . . ."
"Hebron . . ."

"Jerusalem . . ."

Yes, Jerusalem. Leah closed her prayer book. Would this world, this place, be saved from evil? Only the Holy One of Israel could accomplish such a thing, but she could deal with the hate and prejudice in her own heart. Regardless of what happened in the streets, she could rise above every impulse of vengeance and revenge. Repentance and remorse had to be genuine. Moments ago the rabbi had asked, "Are our enemies mightier than we?" He answered his own question, "Torah is stronger than their might, and our dream is greater than their night." She would believe this promise. Leah had found ground on which she could stand.

Father Michael Kelly drove the Abbey's beat-up Ford down the same road the terrorists had used in their attack on the Tufeili family's gift shop. The priest glanced to his left out over the traditional sight of Shepherd's Field but did not pause. Father Kelly had seen the place a thousand times, and his scholarly skepticism tended to regard such places with contempt. The pilgrimages of the pious held no fascination for the hardnosed archaeologist. Security had been increased since the terrorist attack by Jewish extremists, and Palestinian police patrolled the area in pairs.

He slowed when he passed the burned-out shell of the Tufeilis' building and then continued on toward Manger Square in the heart of Bethlehem. He pulled into the renowned square, which was as much of a parking lot as anything else, and locked his car. Dressed as a tourist, Kelly concealed any hint that he might be a cleric. The last thing he wanted was to be identified.

As was true of all who entered the Church of the Nativity,

Kelly bent low to cross the aperture into the nave. Such a position was not comfortable and hurt. He straightened and rubbed his back, looking around the eleventh-century church built by Crusaders over the remains of Constantine's edifice from the fourth century. He knew the vast wooden ceiling rested on stout English oak, a gift of King Edward IV. In fact, there was almost nothing he did not know about the ancient church. But Michael had not come on a scholarly errand this time.

Skirting around a slow-moving herd of tourists, the priest cut through the nave and quickly found his way into the Roman Catholic section, maintained by the Franciscan friars. The place had not been chosen casually. He was simply too well known by the priests in the usual churches in Jerusalem. Bethlehem was different because the Franciscan in charge was new in town, and of course, was not of his Order.

Michael stepped into the long stone nave where the traditional Christmas Eve services were beamed around the world. The clean lines and uncluttered walls contrasted strongly with the multiplicity of the smoking lamps dangling on every side in the Orthodox section of the compound. The array of smoke-tainted icons were not particularly impressive to him either. Things were different on this side. Something in the austere stone walls resonated with his own soul.

A day earlier the priest had called to make sure he knew the time when the local boys would be open for business. Of course, the procedure was held in sacred confidence, but Kelly could not quite bring himself to share the intimate truth with anyone who might really know him. The new Franciscan priest would not recognize his voice.

Abbot Hoffman had delivered a homily on the importance of being transparent, but other factors prompted the out-of-the-way trip to Bethlehem. Obviously, such pride and arrogance were other sins to add to the list. The very sins that ought to be at the top of the load, perhaps. By now a considerable load indeed. And it had been a long time since he had dumped the full soul. Bending low was never easy for him under any circumstances; today it would be particularly difficult.

He braced himself and looked around, merely a formality because Father Kelly knew exactly where the wooden booth was. Probably the place did not get that much use, since mostly tourists frequented the church.

Michael glanced at his watch and knew he was on time. Since Vatican II, everyone called it the Rite of Reconciliation. The name was supposed to make the pill much easier to swallow. Still, the result and the effect on him were the same: it was time to make confession.

26

Thursday, October 1
Jerusalem, Dormition Abbey

Leah had intended to request that the police or some law enforcement officers accompany her in moving the scroll from the office safe to the Dormition Abbey. The longer she considered the idea, however, the more this approach seemed a concession to terrorism, and she was determined to give no ground to saboteurs. Actually, escorts might call attention to the fact she had the object. The less fanfare the better.

In the end, Leah went to the law office at the regular hour, opened the safe, and took the cloth-wrapped scroll out of the brown box. In its place she left a souvenir clay lamp and locked the safe. Burglars would get no more than a worthless relic. She put the package in her black leather briefcase and walked out.

To her surprise, Leah arrived in the basement before the other two translators. She flipped the lights on, and with methodical precision unwrapped the scroll and laid it on the table. Only then did she realize something was wrong. Leah picked up the cloth and shook it. Nothing fell out.

"Good heavens! Where is it?"

Leah turned the briefcase upside down and shook it. Nothing came out.

The medallion was gone! Leah sank back in the chair in disbelief. Did Halevy keep it? she wondered. Did he lose it? She rubbed her temples nervously, trying to maintain her composure. What will Musa think? He'll explode.

After several minutes of consternation, she spread a thick soft piece of velvet over the worktable and placed the scroll carefully on top. "I've got to keep going," she muttered to herself. Days earlier she had stored a hair dryer in the basement in anticipation of opening the metal scroll. With gentle patience Leah ran the flow of warm air up and down the length of the scroll. Only after ten minutes did she begin to gently pull the roll apart.

The door opened. "Musa? You down there?"

"No, Michael. It's me."

"Leah?" The priest bounded down the stairs. "You're the first one here?"

"You sound surprised."

"Well, uh . . . I guess . . . I usually expect you to be last to arrive." Kelly looked over her shoulder. "Ah, the precious scroll is finally here."

"But the medallion isn't!" Leah looked at him with desperation in her eyes. "I don't know what's happened, but it didn't come back in the package."

"What?" Kelly frowned. "You're kidding."

"No." Leah shook her head fiercely. "I'm really upset."

The priest pulled at his goatee and took his half glasses off his nose. "You're sure it's not back in your office somewhere?"

"Absolutely not."

"Hmm, not a good sign." Kelly twisted his mouth and looked up at the ceiling. "Musa won't be a happy camper. What a bizarre turn of events." He sat down. "Why don't you keep working on opening the scroll while I think about this little problem that might just blow us out of the room when Musa gets here."

"Okay." Leah kept moving the blower up and down above the bend of the scroll. "I'm making progress. Won't be long until it's completely open."

Michael sat down. "I'm sure each of us is more than ready to get some significant work done. I hope we can move quickly today."

A large section peeled back. "Since we've already given some attention to many of the words, we're in a good position to get on with it."

The door opened again, and someone came down the stairs. "I'm here," Musa called out.

"Good," Kelly answered.

Musa stopped at the bottom of the stairs and stared. "Leah, you're already here?"

"And hard at work." She smiled. "Good morning."

Musa looked surprised. "Hmm, I guess I'm the last one today. We are certainly off to a new start. Good." He sat down and watched Leah. "Good."

"Musa . . ." Leah sounded tentative, unsure of herself. "I have some bad news."

The Arab's brow furled. "What could possibly be bad today? The scroll is back."

"But the coin isn't," Kelly interjected. "It wasn't returned in the package."

"What?" Musa barked.

"I don't know what's happened." Leah's voice sounded shaky. "I didn't discover it was gone until I unwrapped the parcel just minutes ago. It couldn't be back in the safe. I don't know why Halevy would have kept it, but the medallion simply didn't come back from his offices."

Musa wrung his hands. "Oh, no! This is terrible!"

"Look." Kelly put his hand on Musa's shoulder. "I'm sure this isn't Leah's fault. I know she'll keep searching for it, but the scroll is what really counts."

"The medallion is priceless!" Musa charged angrily.

"I know," Leah agonized. "I promise to keep looking. I'll go back to Halevy and—"

"No, not him!" Musa hit the table with his fist. "I want no more contact with government officials. The less we call attention to the fact we have an archaeological find, the better off we are."

"Actually it was so corroded," Kelly broke in again, "we might not have been able to decipher anything." He took on his "I'm-in-charge-of-things" air. "What counts is that we have the scroll."

"What counts?" Musa looked up at the priest with anger flashing in his eyes. "The loss of any portion of this find counts, period." He hit the table again.

"Please don't leave," Leah begged. "We've already had enough losses." Tears ran down her cheeks.

Musa glanced up at her for a moment. His fierce look of anger softened, turning pensive. "I demand that we agree on one thing: the scroll will not leave this room unless I take it out with me. Agreed?" He looked back and forth between Leah and Michael.

"Absolutely!" Kelly shook his head emphatically. "We'll keep it in the hiding place in the wall."

"I concur." Leah inhaled deeply.

Musa looked at the floor. "Let's get on with the task at hand. We can talk more about this problem later."

Leah picked up the hair dryer and continued running it gently down the length of the scroll. Several minutes later the scroll lay flat on the soft cloth. She switched off the dryer and put it aside. "I think we're ready to begin. Take a look."

The two men hovered above the gold document, staring at the symbols and hieroglyphics. Leah took a file folder out of her briefcase and removed several pages. She laid her copious notes out on the table and waited.

Kelly traced the first few lines with his index finger, positioning his hand just above the surface of the gold, without touching the scroll. He straightened up, then sat down, staring thoughtfully at the priceless object. "I am not a person given to mystical experiences," he began thoughtfully. "Things that go bump in the night never held a fascination for me. I'm practical, basic. I tend to believe only in the tangible, the calculable." He ran his hands through his hair. "But ever since I've gotten involved with this thing . . . I don't know . . . it's certainly had a strange effect on me."

"What do you mean?" Leah asked.

"The thing has its own aura. A magnetism of some sort. I can't quite say. Such an attraction is foreign to my experience. I've even been taking my religious life more seriously."

Musa had been unusually quiet. He quit pulling at his chin and shaking his head. "Hard to say about these objects," he finally added. "The past created a unique ambience."

Leah smiled at him. "Ancient objects always had something of a religious effect on me. Touching the far distant past seemed a holy thing."

"Yes, yes," the priest agreed. "For me, the very nature of antiquity is like the substance of truth itself. Augustine taught us that the closer we come to truth, the closer we come to God.

I always considered things of truth to be essentially synonymous with the divine. Ancient artifacts are like that."

Musa pursed his lips and frowned. "Yes," he said slowly, "I suppose so, but let us begin to deal with the words. I brought a laser pointer so we can point to characters without touching the scroll." He ran the laser along the first line. "Much of this initial material is Greek and Hebrew. I would think we could all agree quickly about how the document starts. Let me offer what I have for a benchmark."

"Excellent." Kelly put on his half glasses.

"*Aluw kai tremo haguowyi* is a mixture of Greek and Hebrew of course," Musa began. "My reading is 'behold and tremble the nations.'"

"Yes," Leah answered.

Kelly nodded.

Musa ran the pointer down the line. "In this area we come to some addition of Egyptian hieroglyphics and Akkadian. The latter is not clear to me, but I can take a shot at the rest." He held up his notes. "*Hal.luw* is *come* and *Ierosalein* is Greek for *Jerusalem*, but I am not certain of what follows."

Kelly looked toward Leah and raised his eyebrows quizzically.

"If I anglicize the hieroglyphics, we are dealing with *nety, en,* and *Ir.* Fairly common, they mean 'in order that or which,' 'to,' and 'to make.' The Akkadian addition is the word for *peace.*"

"Very good!" Kelly beamed. "The way I put that passage together would read something like, 'that, which comes to Jerusalem peace to make.'"

Leah nodded. "So, what I have for openers is, 'Behold and tremble when the nations' . . . or . . . 'Behold and tremble, the nations that come to Jerusalem to make peace.'"

Musa's demeanor changed, and he smiled. "Yes, this is excellent. Real progress for a change. I have been worried nothing might happen when we got down to business."

The Arab archaeologist bit his lip. "I have been very concerned about my parents, but they are doing fine." He paused. "Everything is very confusing right now. I must confess that I've been afraid this whole discovery might disappear. Turn out to be a hoax." He took a deep breath. "Or be seized by the authorities." He shrugged his shoulders and held up his hands. "Of course, I'm still concerned about the medallion."

"I understand." Leah sounded sincere. "After all, this is *your* possession. We are only your guests on this project."

Musa looked surprised but pleased. "Thank you," he mumbled. "Let us keep after our task."

Leah returned to her notes. "The Egyptian character *cher* is common for *with* and the *umeis* is the usual Greek form of *you*. Because the syntax doesn't follow the pattern of any one of the other languages involved, we must guess whether the phrase *with you* refers to the sentence that went before or is a part of what follows, but it may well complete the statement 'come to Jerusalem to make peace with you.'"

"Ah!" Kelly the scholar shook his finger in the air. "Or . . . or . . . this may be a brilliant play on words actually applying to both what came before and what follows. A two-edged sword. A two-sided meaning."

"Ah, very insightful." Musa seemed to be moving from the fringe to the center of the discussion. "I grasp that the next part of the phrase means 'will dance.' I don't get the Sumerian or Akkadian, but in between is the Greek *konioron* or 'the dust of.'"

"Let me help." Leah glanced at her notes. "The hieroglyphic is again 'with' and *zaqru* is 'the ridge' or a 'peak mount.' I believe in context it refers to the ridge of Jerusalem."

Kelly clapped. "My friends, I am amazed at the pace we are

moving. Leah, your work is excellent. The two of you have come out at almost the same place where I am. However, I think the problem is syntax, as we recognized earlier. I would put the message together in this way." He read from a page in his notes. "'Come, that which the nations behold. Dance with peace in the dust around Jerusalem's ridge.'"

Leah shook her head. "I don't think so. Because of the manner in which the text is constructed, I believe word order must honor the arrangement of the original text."

"And why?" Kelly took on the condescending look guaranteed to irritate. "All ancient languages have unique structure. Re-e-ally."

Leah's eyes narrowed. She wondered if the other two could see the hair rising on her neck.

Musa waved his hand at them. "No. No. We have come to the real crunch in making sense of this message. Let's face it. We have no precedence to settle this argument. We simply don't know from the shape of the text which way is correct. Probably the path lies in what we must intuitively perceive."

"Not very scientific," Kelly shot back.

"But we have no other evidence to go on," Musa countered.

The priest looked down at his notes quickly, as if to avoid an argument he couldn't win.

"I will go back to my textbooks when I return home," Leah added. "Possibly, I will find the clues we need. I must assume the author is of Jewish origins and would have a natural tilt toward Hebrew grammar."

"Why?" Kelly countered instantly. "We can't make such a leap in judgment. No! We must not operate with such loose assumptions and ill-constructed parsing of verbs or tenses."

Leah felt her face burn, and she worried her anger might be obvious. She took a deep breath to hold her tongue.

"We have two impasses today," Musa said. "I will leave those arguments to both of you for the moment. The next section is much easier for me." He ran the pointer down the line from right to the left. "The Hebrew begins 'and celebrate.' The text gives the number forty-eight. I know from basic Greek study that *menas* is months. The rest is clear, 'from the day Jerusalem is divided.'" He looked up and waved the pointer. "There you have it. 'And celebrate forty-eight months from the day Jerusalem is divided.'" Musa stopped as if something in his own words had suddenly caught up with him.

Leah stared. "The division of Jerusalem?" She sounded incredulous. "Mankind has been consumed with an unholy rage to divide Jerusalem."

Kelly took off his half glasses. "We're staring that one in the face even as we speak."

Leah exchanged a look with Musa. "This sounds almost like a prophecy of something that was to come. Maybe a warning of what must be avoided."

Kelly rubbed his chin. "Something very strange is going on." He held his notepad to the light. "I might even translate the first part like this. 'Behold and tremble! Nations pretend to come to Jerusalem to make peace and dance on the mountains. But forty-eight months later the city is divided.'" He tossed the pad on the table. "Amazing! We've opened a real can of worms."

27

Thursday, October 1
Old City, Muslim Quarter

From the Dormition Abbey Musa walked down Habad Street across most of the Old City until it intersected Ala a-Din. He longed for a secluded restaurant to sit and think. The Muslim Quarter seemed the only appropriate place to settle.

The Quarter abutted *Haram e-Sharif*, the location of the Dome of the Rock, where Muslims believe Muhammad leaped into heaven on the back of his stallion. Jews still called it *Har Habayit*, the Temple Mount. Christians as well as Jews also called it Mount Moriah. A holy site for all three faiths, the north end bordered Sultan Suleiman, the street appropriately named for Suleiman the Magnificent, who four centuries earlier rebuilt the walls ringing the Old City.

The narrow streets meandered in and out between two- and three-story stone buildings. Here and there awnings jutted straight out of the walls. Green doors and shutters lined the way along the ancient stone pavement of the streets and alleys. Smells of spices, cooking meat, sweets, and smoke blended into what seemed to Musa the special perfume of the street, inviting in its own singular way.

Stopping at a kiosk in the Khan al-Sultan souk, he noticed the headlines in *Al-Jihar*, an English-Arabic newspaper. The Mossad had struck again in Jordan. The story was messy, the details gruesome. The headlines made Musa angry, and he did not want to read anymore. He forged ahead in his journey to nowhere. Eventually, he found a small outdoor coffee shop with a vacant table.

Muslim women ambled by, heads covered with scarves, stuffed plastic grocery bags at their sides. Occasionally an old man with his *keffiyeh* thrown over his shoulders bounced down the street on the back of a dilapidated donkey. Across the street, shop owners leaned over a small table, locked in a fierce game of *sheshbesh*, or backgammon, grunting and groaning as if the fate of the city rode on the outcome. A few young men sat at the adjoining tables, reading Arabic newspapers and smoking strong tobacco. Their hair was cropped close, like most young Arabs; their T-shirts and jeans had long passed retread time. Since Jerusalem had been sealed off following the recent attacks, they were lucky to be there at all. Clear glass cups waited for their enjoyment on glass saucers, white foam floating on the thick black coffee.

Musa thought long and hard on the strange message they had found that afternoon: the warning of Jerusalem divided. *What could such a thing have meant in ancient times? The city captured? Yes. Divided? Unthinkable. The 1948 Arab-Jewish War had divided the city for nineteen years with only the Mandelbaum Gate linking the two worlds, but that divider fell when the entire city was captured by the Jews in 1967. Most regrettable*, he reflected.

Musa shook his head and stared at one of the young men laboriously reading the evening paper. The feature story ran alongside a picture taken in Amman of several men lying dead in the street. As was often true of *Al-Jihar*, the featured story asserted that three young men living in Jordan were gunned down by the Mossad, claiming them to be Hamas operatives. During the attack two Palestinians were blinded, with Israeli intelligence leaving behind the unwritten message "an eye for an eye." While there was no proof of Mossad involvement, King Abdullah charged they were responsible. Israel insisted the affair was an internal rivalry within Hamas. The top of the page showed an official reading a statement, demanding an explanation and apology from Israel. The young man appeared to digest the story as if it were supper. No question that he hoped for a change in the status of Jerusalem. His dreams were simple. No division. Total Palestinian control.

Musa sipped his coffee and thought on the strange, convoluted arrangement to which he was now a party. *Who would believe such a thing? On one side, a Christian—even worse, a priest. On the other side, a Jew—even worse, a woman. By the prophet's beard! How could such a thing be?*

One of the *sheshbesh* players shouted victory and broke Musa's concentration. The two pushed each other back and forth in mock jesting. Musa smiled. Somewhere close by the voice of a *muezzin* sounded from a minaret, calling the faithful to prayer. People around him began dropping to their knees, lowering their faces to the ground. Reluctantly, Musa followed suit. During his college days he got out of the strict habits of observance and still did not like the public prostrations common in the Arab world. Nevertheless, he joined the faithful of the Muslim Quarter in their late afternoon ritual.

When Musa sat back down at the table, he took a slow sip of the strong coffee and watched two young boys chase each other down the street. A young man wearing a red fez ambled by; the hat identified him as a *haji*, a pilgrim from Mecca. In Musa's view, Islam was obviously the superior religion. Though ancient, Judaism had become the religion of the old and exhausted, used to justify the claims of the Zionists and Hasidic fanatics.

On the other hand, Christianity remained the religion of the middle-aged, the people with full bellies, the faith of the indulged. Christians used Bible talk to shore up the claims and intentions of the capitalists and colonialists. In sharp contrast, Islam was a young man's faith, a source of strength to the courageous fighting against the injustices of the Western world. The Prophet had offered *jihad,* the holy war, as a tool for the young to use against oppressors. Yes, of the three great religions, Islam was without equal.

In many ways, Christians could be the most frightening, Musa thought. After all, was not their unpredictable behavior a fact of history? The worst chapter in the chronicles of the land had been written in blood by the Crusaders' swords. Hordes unleashed by the call of the pope broke through Jerusalem's walls on June 7, 1099, slaughtering every Muslim in sight and then rounding up all the Jews, locking them in a synagogue and burning it to the ground. When Saladin recaptured Jerusalem almost a hundred years later, the Muslim sultan rode in on his white horse, proclaimed peace, and offered well-being to all the inhabitants, regardless of their faith. No one was killed, tortured, or violated. *Perhaps,* Musa thought, *I should be the most leery of Kelly, the priest. after all, he is the spiritual descendant of the Crusaders.*

Focus was hard to maintain when the proprietor bustled about, cleaning up the empty coffee cups from the two men who had just left. Musa looked away. On reflection, he thought the worst problem to be Zionism. Actually, Jews and Muslims had done rather well together through the centuries. Jewish scholars and scientists were treated well during the four hundred years of Muslim rule. The coming of the Turks was a problem, yes, but they persecuted everybody. No, life would have been fine if it had not been for the fanatical ideas of the Zionists. The Zionists assassinated people in the streets of Amman.

Musa lit a cigarette and watched the young man still reading the paper. He looked up and exchanged a lone and solitary glance. The man returned to his paper, and Musa watched a Palestinian woman walk past with her child in hand. Though worn and soiled, her bodice remained bright with elaborate embroidery. Stitching on her scarf matched the color of the long brown flowing skirt. Maintaining propriety, the woman avoided eye contact.

At such moments, Musa despised his single status. Too intellectual to settle for only a village girl with no education, he had let time slip through his fingers. Some said he was too serious, some thought him too studious. The truth was he was too shy.

Musa watched the woman and child disappear around the bend at the end of the street. College had exiled him from such women. He could not settle for a mate who functioned like a maidservant with no opinions beyond the proper seasoning of the broth. He wanted a woman who could challenge his ideas, talk of complex things, and show him respect.

Then again, he could not get both feet in the world he discovered on the campus of Cornell. Aggressive, liberated coeds scared the liver out of him. Men and women living together in dorms scandalized everything he believed. Flaunting their bodies was wicked, drunkenness an evil. In the end, he had lived in the library and hurried back across the ocean with only a degree in hand.

"*Keef halak?*" the proprietor asked of Musa's health. Almost as if appearing from out of nowhere, he stood immediately in front of the table with an apron tied around his thick waist.

"*Kwayyis. Kwayyis,*" Musa answered. "Would you have a little *baklava*, perhaps? Something to tide me over?"

"Coming up." The owner hurried back inside. "I have a surprise."

For a few minutes Musa smoked a cigarette and tried to let his mind slip into neutral, but he could not keep out the one thought that returned again and again, day and night. From the moment he had heard the terrible news of David's death, he had known the tragic truth. Of all the dividing lines ever drawn in Jerusalem, the worst cut between him and Leah, even though she did not know the barrier existed.

"Try this little pastry." The owner placed the plate in front of Musa. The small but stout man had a thick black mustache. Perhaps he was of Turkish descent. "You will like the *kunafa*. The nuts are superb."

"*Shukran*." Musa took the fork from his hand and took a bite. "Yes. Excellent."

"Good. Good," the Turk said and then hustled away to the next table.

Musa plunged the fork into the pastry and watched the tines sink into the crust. Like a dagger. Like the dagger he helped stick in David's back. Even though Leah had no idea, someday she would figure it out. Perhaps Kelly would tell her. So far he hadn't, to spare her the grief, Musa imagined. But in one way or the other, the truth would come out. Only one reason existed for David Rosenberg becoming the target of an Arab terrorist. He was killed in reprisal for the attack on Arad. And the link between his name and Musa's village could have only come from one source. Uncle Hassan had leaked Musa's relationship with the Rosenbergs. The son told the father, the father told the uncle, and the uncle told the village. Death followed.

Musa pushed the sweet pastry away, his hunger suddenly gone. Pulling several bills from his pocket, Musa more than paid the check. He hurried down the street in the direction the woman and child had gone. The bitter truth was unavoidable. The Salah family had consigned Leah to an untimely life as a widow.

On this evening, Musa felt confused and bewildered. Nothing had worked out as he had expected. A scant sixty days ago everything seemed clear and filled with excitement. He was about to become renowned for an amazing discovery, a break-through in modern scholarship, a hero to his people. Two months had turned into a lifetime. As night approached, shadows fell over his hopes and dreams. He felt like a criminal, duplicitous in a crime not of his choosing. At the same time, even the daily newspapers carried hard evidence of Israeli aggression against his people. No one could look away from the injustice . . . and yet . . . a man who had been his family friend was dead . . . and he had played some part in his death.

Musa continued north on the journey that had begun an hour and a half earlier, crisscrossing his way out of the Muslim Quarter until he left through Herod's Gate, crossed Sultan Suleiman Street, and turned down Salah a-Din street, winding into east Jerusalem where Palestinians traditionally lived. His flat was a small place on Ibn Batuta, not far from the Rockefeller Museum.

As he approached the old stone apartment, Musa saw a shadowy figure sitting at the top of the five steps, the form crouched near the wall. He stopped instantly; his heart raced. A setup? A trap? Another assassin? Reprisal for David's death?

Musa looked for a tree to jump behind, a car to use as a shield. People who might help.

The front door to the building opened, and two children came out. They paused on the steps and laughed. One boy threw a soccer ball into the street, and the other chased after him. The boys had not been frightened by the person, who did not seem to try to avoid them.

Musa tried to get a better look. He inched forward. Probably the man had a backup lurking somewhere in the area. No doubt armed to the teeth. A car turned the corner and the driver flipped on his headlights. Musa knew he was silhouetted against the light. He had nowhere to hide.

Straightening up, Musa tried to walk forward with a normal, confident stride, but his mouth was dry and even the cool evening could not keep him from perspiring.

"*Misek al-kheyr*."

Musa froze.

It was a woman's voice that wished him a good evening, but she didn't sound quite as Arabic as her words. The last voice he expected to hear on his doorstep.

"Leah?" Musa asked cautiously.

"Yes. It's me."

Musa bounded up the steps. "What in the world are you doing here?"

"I wanted to talk with you." Leah looked down. "I feel terrible about the loss of the medallion. I know my credibility is still on the line."

His mind raced around all sides of the possibility. He could not ask her into his apartment. By the Rosenbergs' standards, the place was too small and meager. In addition, everything was a mess. Wouldn't be proper either. Then again, there wasn't really a restaurant or a good place to talk in the area. He was starting to feel intimidated being alone with her.

"Don't feel you have to ask me up." Leah kept her end of the conversation running. "Actually, I'd just as soon sit here and talk. Won't take long."

Musa glanced around. A few more lights were going on and

the street was quickly getting even dimmer. They would not be able to see each other very clearly. Maybe she already knew the inside story on David's death and had come to confront him.

"Why don't you just sit down here on the step, Musa?"

"Thank you." He sat on the other side next to the opposite rail. "I'm surprised to see you." He knew the words sounded stiff.

"Sure. I understand. After our translation session, I went home and read the day's paper." Leah cleared her throat. "I guess I'd missed the story of the attack in Jordan. I saw the pictures of men lying in the street." Leah stopped and inhaled deeply. "My first thought was that those men had families, friends. Regardless of what the politicians said, maybe they were innocent victims. I realized these people might even be your relatives." She took a deep breath. "After David's death, I see things differently."

Musa stared. He couldn't believe his ears.

"And then, I realized even if they weren't family, maybe you knew these people. Even if you didn't, you would have strong feelings about their deaths. I wanted to come by and tell you how sorry I am that this happened."

He fumbled for words. "Leah, I don't know what to say." Musa fell silent.

The moon rose over the trees and made her face more visible. She looked hauntingly lovely and lonely at the same time, like a crushed flower broken off and left behind when a garden is cleared out in the fall.

"Yes. Yes," he finally said. "It's hard for me, for my people not to take such things personally. I didn't know those men, but it could have been me, my father."

"Things have changed in how I see such events. Before David's death, I didn't think much about these killings. I suppose I viewed them as part of the undeclared war we're all caught up in. Today I don't see Israelis and Arabs as much as I see people. Just people. People like you and me. Our histories are different, our experience shaped by events the other has never experienced, but we're still human beings trying to get through this life with as little pain as possible."

Musa looked down the steps. "Yes. Definitely."

Leah stood up. "Well, I simply wanted to express how sorry I am about what happened." She walked to the bottom of the steps. "I'd best be on my way."

"Leah . . ." Musa reached out and then withdrew his hand. "I don't quite know how to say it . . . but I want to thank you for caring enough to say these things. No Jew—" He caught his tongue. "None of your people have ever said such things to me before. Hearing your words helps very much . . . especially tonight."

She walked away from the steps. "Good. I'm glad I came." Leah started up the street. "I'll catch a taxi at the corner." She waved over her shoulder. "As we say in my world, shalom."

"*Alayich shalom*, Leah," he called softly after her. His Hebrew, like her Arabic, came haltingly. But the greeting of peace was sincere.

Musa watched her disappear into the night. He did not go upstairs but sat back down on the top step. What a remarkable thing. Never would he have expected such an encounter. Maybe he was wrong in some of his judgments. The woman was certainly to be seen in a new and different light.

The moon moved above the trees. Children disappeared from the streets. The windows on Ibn Batuta Street looked like glowing boxes of light arranged in a symmetry that was too random to fit any pattern, and that was the way the events of the day felt. No clear way to stack them together. No one pattern or explanation made sense out of things. Leah, the Jewish widow, had scrambled the world of Musa, the Bedouin archaeologist.

28

Thursday, October 1
Tel Aviv

While Leah Rosenberg returned home in a taxi and Musa Salah sat alone in his flat on Ibn Batuta Street, a heated debate unfolded in the Mossad's secluded offices inside Tel Aviv's Hadar Dafna Building. The top five officers sat around a conference table arguing. Avraham Halevy listened intensely to the head of operations as he explained their mistake getting caught in the agency's attack in Jordan on Hamas operatives.

"Yes, yes, errors happen," the rotund executive barked. "However, let us not lose sight of our accomplishments. Remember that our foray into Arad was a stunning success," he argued. "No one squealed when we knocked off the Hayat brothers and the other terrorists in that village. We got rave reviews."

"Yesterday's headlines don't make any diference," Halevy retorted. "We can't afford even *one* mistake like what just occurred in Amman." The Mossad's director thumped on the table with his index finger. "*Not one.*"

"But there is no question about the identity of the men we hit," the white-haired executive countered. He hit the table with his fist and puckered his bottom lip. "Our information was correct. Every one of our targets was scum, murderers, leaders in Hamas's Izzadin Kassam military wing. The microfilm passed by Al-Amid identified them as the essential link between Hamas and this crazy new Islamic Revolutionary Front. Even without the recent attacks, these guttersnipes were completely legitimate targets." He squinted his eyes and ground his teeth. "They needed to go."

"That's not the issue," Halevy snapped. "The problem is we got caught with our hands in the cookie jar." He cursed violently. "Every one of you remembers what happened when the attack on Sheikh Ahmed Yassin backfired. Our enemies held rallies up and down the Gaza Strip like they were celebrating New Year's Eve. Newspapers made us sound like a pack of fools. We had the same problem after the assassination of their master bomb maker, Yihye Ayyash, 'The Engineer.' The justification doesn't make any difference. When we goof up and the press gets the story, we're the dead ducks."

The head of operations bit his lip; his face turned crimson. "Yes. Yes, we all know." He ran his hands through his black hair. The youngest man in the room, he also appeared the most nervous. "The next step will be for Hamas or these new idiots with this Islamic Revolutionary thing to respond with a wave of suicide bombings in our cities. Get ready for more attacks," he snarled.

"So, what do you make of this predicament?" a man at the end of the table asked. "What's going to happen?"

"I will be forced to resign," Halevy said with no show of emotion. "Daniel Levy's death, Uri Dori's death, David Rosenberg's death . . . the body count was already way too high before we plunged into this problem. I will be submitting my resignation to the prime minister tomorrow afternoon. The Mossad will soon have a new director."

No one spoke for a full minute.

"Director, I wish to delay discussion of your previous statement of departure for the moment." Even though he was in his fifties, the coordination officer appeared to be at least a decade younger. His close-cropped crew cut and excellent physical condition gave him the appearance of a military officer in his prime. "The fact of the matter is that we have an ominous political problem looming on the international front. Recent statements by the American president signaled an approaching shift in their foreign policy. As we all know, the Americans play under the table as well as on top. Now we understand where they are going. The Yanks are going to put big pressure on us to negotiate a 'land-for-peace' deal that includes giving up control of Jerusalem, or at least giving a big piece of the city back to the Palestinians. We give up the land, and they get the peace . . . the same old game. They will use King Abdullah of Jordan. His wife and 60 percent of his people are Palestinians. And don't forget, his father, King Hussein, controlled East Jerusalem before the war. Abdullah will come out the consummate diplomat if he supports Arafat. Anyone disagree?"

Halevy looked straight ahead without a show of emotion.

The coordination officer cleared his throat and continued. "The Vatican has already picked up this theme to further their interests in the internationalization of the city and will press the United Nations toward this end." He looked around the room. "Gentlemen, get ready. The next political front we must face will be worldwide pressure to split Jerusalem."

"The prime minister and the cabinet will never consider such an idea," Halevy snapped. "We'd die first."

"Die?" The coordination officer widened his eyes in mock disbelief. "Die? And who'd do the dying? Maybe we'll get more of what we witnessed when a religious militant assassinated Yitzhak Rabin." He reached into a briefcase at the side of his chair and pulled out a file. "This report came in this morning. Tomorrow our local hippie peaceniks will hold a demonstration on Ben-Yehuda Street, encouraging the government to take all steps necessary to achieve peace, regardless of what we give up." He leaned over the table, his voice turning mean. "That includes censoring the Mossad and declaring us a rogue terrorist organization."

The officer took a deep breath and forced a smile. "The same type of radicals who hit the souvenir place in Bethlehem will show up to disrupt the demonstration. People could get hurt before this one is over."

"What's your bottom line?" the head of operations asked.

"We've got big, big problems. Obviously. However, before we condemn ourselves too harshly, let's put the current problems in context. The real issue that must be addressed is the forthcoming drive to split Jerusalem. Everyone from the pope and Uncle Sam to the former Soviet Union and the entire Islamic world is going to be in on this play."

"Thank you for this astute analysis." Halevy rose to his feet. "I believe you are correct and that we understand the dimensions of our problems. However, at this point the Mossad's reputation has suffered significant damage. The responsibility for this loss ends at my desk. You will be the personnel that must repair the breach as I will no longer be at the helm." He paused and looked at the table. The muscles in his jaw tightened. "Thank you, gentlemen, for your loyal service during my tenure." Halevy saluted and briskly left the room.

As Halevy walked out of the meeting in Tel Aviv, about a

thousand miles away, in the capital of Libya, Saad Abu Yusef walked into a secret meeting of selected leaders from the OPEC nations. Impeccably dressed in an Italian silk suit, his robes and sandals of the desert had been changed for the best Europe offered. The ministers of petroleum, or finance, or their equivalents sat silently waiting for Abu Yusef to speak. A week earlier Saudi Arabia, Iran, Kuwait, and Libya had agreed to hold talks under the guise of discussing petroleum production quotas. Every precaution was taken to conceal the meeting.

Yusef nodded to the guards at the door to lock the delegates in the suite provided by Gaddafi himself. Because Tripoli maintained a secure seaport, some officials entered the country by way of the Mediterranean Sea, making detection of their movements more difficult. Nevertheless, no aspect of security was overlooked. A surprise attack on such an elite gathering would wreak incalculable havoc.

The Saudi minister of petroleum stood at the head of the long ebony table. "Let us be completely candid with one another." Even Abu Yusef knew how phony his smile must look. "In the past, we have often agreed to certain quotas, only to discover various members went home and did the opposite of what was pledged." He held up his hand to fend off denials. "I accuse no one but merely desire to establish an atmosphere of complete candor. Agreed?" He waited for their response.

The executives looked back and forth at one another in mock bewilderment.

"We must be forthright in facing our current predicament," Yusef continued. "And we must fully discuss the objectives of our common enemy."

"I believe I can speak for all of us," Hussein Shawahin responded. "Libya desires full disclosure. In spite of our international image we are as unsettled as the rest of you. The facts must be faced. Our adversary can topple any one of our governments. We have no alternative but to be honest."

"The war is not new," Abd Al-Hakim answered. "Iran shares the same concerns. Our problems just won't go away."

The representative from Iran held up his hand. "I know how we are perceived around the world." He shook his head. "The truth is we are the primary evidence of what can happen when these forces are unleashed."

Saad Abu Yusef nodded vigorously. "Thank you for your forthrightness. We are agreed in principle about the problem we face."

"The adversary cannot be trusted." Abd Al-Hakim pounded the table. "None of us are safe from them."

Shawahin snapped his fingers. "That quick, and they would overthrow us."

"These people are radicals, off the scale," Abu Yusef answered. "They have one burning ambition: to destroy Israel and the great Satan, America. Shawahin is correct. The Islamic Revolutionary Front would destroy us."

Solemn quiet settled over the room. No one looked at anyone else.

"Such has never been said aloud before," Shawahin continued. "If Jerusalem, our third holiest city, is bombed, then Armageddon will follow for all of us. The Israelis have enough nuclear devices to take out every one of our countries. If the Americans stop Israel, the IRF may stop subversive activities in America. What the USA did to Iraq will be a scratch, a mosquito bite, compared to what they will do to us if the Americans conclude that we raised this ferocious alligator to devour them."

"Does anyone doubt that these people are our enemy?" Abu Yusef glared as he talked. "They want us?" The Arab crossed his arms over his chest. "Should anyone in this room betray this conversation, each of our lives would be worth nothing. The problem we must face is that desperate times call for desperate measures."

"Here! Here!" Delegates rapped the table with their knuckles.

"My friend from Libya stated the issue well," Abu Yusef spoke out of the side of his mouth. "We are the most likely IRF targets if we don't feed Jerusalem to this alligator quickly. We are vulnerable. Look at each of your countries." Abu Yusef folded his arms, then dropped them dejectedly to the table. "King Fahd is too ill to govern Saudi Arabia much longer, and Hosni Mubarak is seventy. He refuses to appoint a vice president even today so that he can be finally replaced, yet the unemployment rate in the Gaza Strip is 80 percent." He ran his hands nervously through his hair. "Hafez Assad, like Yeltsin, has severe heart trouble and has diabetes as well. The truth is, not one of us in this room will be alive much after the new millennium begins because of our ages."

The group broke into grumbling and carping. Abu Yusef took a quick drink of water and stared at the floor for a moment. The mumbling and moaning continued.

Finally, Abu Yusef flipped on an overhead projector. "The time has come for us to set a course of action, gentlemen." He turned and looked at the large images on the wall behind him. "I have prepared a course of action to keep the IRF off our backs and allow our governments to function without fear of revolution." He reached into a file beside the projector and pulled out a transparent sheet. "I have a plan that is possibly our only hope to stabilize the political climate." The Saudi oil minister laid the overhead on the projector and walked to the wall.

Each of the executives leaned over the table, studying the chart.

"The first point is simple," Abu Yusef began. "Rollover. We move all Arab assets from America to the European Union with the speed of light." He pointed to the figures. "I am talking about over a trillion dollars, including 35 percent of the U.S. Treasury bills. The Korean economy collapsed when thirty billion dollars went out in a day."

"Such an action would not disappoint the Europeans," Abd Al-Hakim jested.

Abu Yusef smiled and pointed to his second point. "Oil. We will not raise the prices of oil by simply cutting production. By opening oil spigots on the day we take our money out of America, we flood the market. Crude oil fell 55 percent in two years. They did it to us. Now we will do it to them. This strategy will involuntarily shut down the infrastructure for the production of oil and natural gas in the West—putting us back in the driver's seat and driving the dollar down and the Euro up." He looked around the room. "As I said, desperate times call for desperate measures."

Shawahin began clapping, and the rest joined him.

"America will come to us in terror," Abu Yusek continued. "We will say very simply to them, 'Give us Jerusalem, and we will return to our old ways of doing business.'" He smiled broadly. "The method you prefer, America." Abu Yusek looked slowly around the room. "Our *jihad* for Jerusalem must work. This action is the only hope we have for survival. Who knows? In time, history may record that we saved the entire world from Armageddon."

"Yes! Hear! Hear!" echoed around the room.

"Of course," Abu Yusef sounded annoyed. The commotion disrupted the direction he was moving the group. Once again he folded his arms over his chest, then continued. "These IRF fanatics must secretly be told that we are helping them return Jerusalem to its rightful owners. If the IRF blows up Jerusalem, death would be a comfort compared to what our own people will do to us for the part we have played in its destruction and desecration. If we survive this avalanche, we will invite the IRF to a special gathering with us and honor them. At midnight, we will cut off their heads and hang them over our doorpost."

The executives broke into enthusiastic applause.

"Think of it. We save the Americans, the Jews, and ourselves. Not bad, gentlemen. Not bad at all. The entire world owes us praise and gratitude!"

29

Friday, October 2
Jerusalem, Kiryat Wolfson

Leah awoke with a start. For a moment, she was not sure where she was. A terrible noise wouldn't stop. Since David's death, sleeping pills were necessary but left her feeling wrung out the next morning. Leah reached for a hand that was not there and then realized the telephone was ringing.

"Shalom," she answered groggily.

"Leah," the familiar voice responded. "It's me. Musa."

"Yes?" the best reply to be mustered.

"You okay?"

"Yeah." Leah scooted up against the head of bed. "Still trying to get awake."

"You always sleep late?"

"What time is it?"

"Eight-thirty."

She slung the covers back. "Oh, no! I guess the alarm didn't go off again." She tried to stand but slipped back on the edge of the bed. "I'm sorry. I know we've got work to do this morning."

"That's why I called." Musa sounded troubled. "I think I should come and pick you up today."

Leah pushed her hair out of her eyes. "Why in the world would you do that?"

"I just got wind of a big disturbance downtown on Ben-Yehuda Street. Things may get out of hand quickly."

Leah glanced at the small calendar by the clock that never worked right. Only two days had passed since Yom Kippur, just two eternally long weeks since David's death. Time did not make a lot of sense anymore.

"You still there, Leah?"

"Oh, yes. Sorry. You were saying?"

"The Israeli Human Rights Coalition has put together a demonstration in the plaza where a terrorist bomb killed twenty-six Arabs and Jews several years ago as they were negotiating the status of Jerusalem. They've called on other peace organizations to join them in protesting the current political climate and lack of progress in settling West Bank issues. Peace Now people will be there. Left-wing supporters from the *Ha'olam Hazeh* magazine are going to show up and beat their drum."

"So, what does that have to do with us?"

"Some of my people picked up the rumor that right-wing activists are going to surface and bust up the rally, claiming the stories about a scroll and a secret message are nonsense. They'll blame everything on Palestinians when the demonstration turns into a riot. I thought you might need protection in such a climate of violence."

Leah glanced into the mirror. She looked awful. Dark circles under her eyes. Her hair needed washing. Who cared? She didn't.

"For these reasons, I am offering to pick you up if that is acceptable."

Leah smiled at the phone. "Thank you, Musa. Very thoughtful.

Maybe I should be more careful. Yes. Please. I will be waiting at the door at nine-fifteen. I promise to be ready."

Dropping the phone back in the cradle, Leah leaped out of bed, hurrying to the shower and leaving the covers in disarray.

Father Michael had been at work for an hour when Musa and Leah arrived. He barely acknowledged them as they came down the stairs and then turned back to his notes.

"You're missing all the fun going on downtown today." Leah tried to sound casual. "Apparently, the locals are rioting on Ben-Yehuda Street."

"Certainly picked a fashionable place to do it," Kelly commented without looking up.

"Apparently our discovery has a little something to do with the season of their discontent."

Kelly took off his half glasses and rubbed the stubble on his goatee. "I have been working on a small segment of the text." He used the laser pointer to underline a Greek portion. "*Khilia ete* means 'the millennium' and is placed in a strange configuration in the text."

"What do you mean?" Leah sat down next to the priest.

"At first I thought the section was concerned with a six-day period, but the more I worked with the syntax, I began to sense the actual meaning was intended to use six days as a symbol of six millennia."

"Six thousand years?" Musa frowned. "If the manuscript is as old as we think, they would have had a hard time talking about such a long period of time behind them, because the ancients considered the world to have just begun a short while before they arrived on the scene."

"Exactly!" Kelly shook his fist in the air. "You're following my identical line of reasoning. Therefore"—he leaned into Musa's face and virtually whispered—"they must have been projecting something into *the future*. Whoever wrote this could only have been suggesting something that was to come."

Leah looked blank for a moment. "Really? After all, this is the year 5759 on the Jewish calendar. Right?"

"And where does this take one?" Kelly's small blue eyes seemed to dance behind his glasses. He looked like a child waiting to spring the punch line on a joke.

"Well, if everyone operated on approximately the same system we do today"—she paused and tossed her head side to side—"give or take a little time. It would seem to mean . . . that . . . the message is for . . . now."

"Exactly!" Kelly exclaimed.

"Are you saying the scroll was intended to be a prophecy for our time?" Musa gawked incredulously. "Come on."

"As the world well knows, I'm no Bible-thumping fundamentalist," Michael bore down. "If anything, I've been accused of being a faithless skeptic, a card-carrying agnostic in a clerical collar. You won't find me claiming esoteric nonsense." He held his notes up in the air. "But I tell you this thing is about something that was to happen in Jerusalem at the end of the sixth millennium and, friends, that's where we're living *right now*."

Musa shook his head. "I find this very hard to believe. Why such a thing would be, be . . ."

"Revolutionary!" Kelly exclaimed. "Who cares what it means. Just the idea alone would turn the world of scholarship upside down. We'd be the most sought-after archaeologists and scholars of all time." He slammed his fist on the table. "Yes!"

"But what it says *does* make a difference," Leah objected.

"Look." She pointed in the direction of the center of the city. "People are out there rioting right now because of a hint of some obscure claim. If this thing is really a prophecy about our period in history, we haven't even begun to calculate the problems."

"I agree," Musa added. "We've got to get the rest of this translation hammered out immediately. I suggest we put your idea aside for the moment, Michael. Let's see if we can get the surrounding text worked out a bit more and then see where your idea fits."

Kelly smiled with the self-satisfaction of a person reaching a lifetime goal. "I just can't believe my eyes."

Leah pulled her notepad from her purse. "I worked a bit on the area where we left off last time. We had discovered a portion that seemed to speak of *u.ruwshalem emeristhe*, 'Jerusalem divided.' I worked on the section that ties to *khilia ete*, 'the millennium.'" She looked at the page. "*Ubak.hum* is Hebrew for 'will weep' and, of course, *lithois* is Greek for 'stones.' It is preceded by '*o*' or 'the.'" Leah looked up. "This part of the text is simple and certain. I find it is saying that Jerusalem will be divided, and even the stones will weep on that day."

"I came to the same conclusion last night," Musa answered. "If Michael's conjecture is right, the text would seem to issue a warning of what will follow the division of the city. Amazing."

"*Amazing* is an understatement," Leah answered.

The door opened at the top of the stairs, and one of the monks hurried down. He spoke pleasantly to Leah and Musa but whispered in Father Kelly's ear before hurrying out.

"I am sorry." Michael stood up. "Brother Raphael tells me that we have unexpected guests from Rome. Protocol demands I greet them immediately. Please excuse me." He followed the steps of the brown-robed brother back up the stairs. "Go right ahead and see what you can do without me," he called over his shoulder. "I'll be back as soon as possible."

When Kelly reached the top step and closed the door behind him, the brother was waiting for him. "Most unexpected, but I knew you'd want to know at once. We have a papal nuncio, Cardinal Mottola, waiting in the abbot's office."

Michael blinked several times in surprise. "Who?"

"Cardinal Mottola, on special assignment from the office of the secretary of state." Raphael rolled his eyes. "Big stuff, Michael. The Vatican wants to talk to you."

Michael could not fight back the smile. "Mottola! He's been the pope's man for the past five years. It's been a long time since we talked. He's really an old friend. We must hurry and see what is expected of me."

Brother Raphael opened the door for Father Kelly and then withdrew. The abbot and the cardinal stood.

"Eminence." Father Kelly bowed at the waist and took the cardinal's ring hand.

"Father Michael." Luca Mottola held open his arms. "Has it really been ten years?"

"I am afraid so." Michael returned the hug.

"One of my finest students," the white-haired prelate told the abbot. "I've followed Michael's career ever since he went wrong and got off into this archaeological mishmash," Mottola joked. "I wanted him to stay with us where the action is." He shrugged and sat down again.

"What brings you to Jerusalem?" Michael took the chair opposite him.

"You, Michael." Mottola nodded solemnly. "Word has come to us through the secret communiqué you sent to the secretariat."

"Secret communiqué?" The abbot frowned. "I am usually . . . and I might say . . . *supposed* . . . to be informed of any exchanges with the Vatican." He looked hard at Michael.

"Ah, I have created a problem accidentally." Mottola held up his hand in protest. "This is my fault."

"After all, we are an order bound by a rule of life," the abbot added.

Michael lowered his head. "I acted rashly. Please forgive me. After some reflection, I realized a certain arrogance in what I had done. Though it excuses nothing, I went to confession and repented."

"Where?" the abbot demanded.

"In Bethlehem . . . the Church of the Nativity."

"There you have it," Mottola concluded. "Things are now back in order. Do I have your permission to continue?" the cardinal addressed the abbot.

"Certainly, Eminence." The abbot seemed less than satisfied with Michael's explanations.

"This archaeological find you're working on—" Mottola shifted from the sound of a pastor to that of an inquisitor. "You actually think it might have some bearing on the status of Jerusalem?"

Michael nodded his head several times. "The scroll becomes more amazing the longer I work on it. We began with the assumption that it was the legendary Donation of Melchizedek. We are still working on that hope."

"Good. Good." Mottola toyed with the gold pectoral cross around his neck. "Excellent." The cardinal turned to the abbot. "I wish to discuss some of the technicalities of this scroll. I would not want to bore you with such details and keep you from your numerous pressing duties. Please, feel free to leave us to these insignificant scholarly details."

The abbot's face reflected the realization that he was being dismissed. For a moment he looked miffed but quickly recovered his poise. "I must make sure we are preparing a lunch worthy of Your Eminence. Perhaps, I should check with the kitchen."

"You are most gracious." Cardinal Mottola nodded politely and waited for the abbot to leave before beginning again. "Michael, my son, this is an opportune moment for both of us. Your find may well play into an important aspect of our foreign policy."

"Really?"

"If you play your cards right, there may be a very important opening for you in Rome."

Michael swallowed hard and tried to quell the surge of elation. "I remain the humble servant of the Church."

"Of course, nothing must be manipulated, and we expect you to do no more than rightly divide the truth." Mottola smiled subtly. "However, I wanted you to know fully our position on the internationalization of this city. An opportune moment is approaching for us to press our interest. Understand?"

"Yes." Michael pulled at his goatee and spoke earnestly, "I am most aware of where we are at this time in history."

The cardinal patted him on the hand. "Excellent. Should your translation help establish our position, the Holy Father would be more than grateful."

30

Friday, October 2
Jerusalem, Dormition Abbey

Musa glanced at his watch. "Michael's been gone nearly forty-five minutes. Think he's coming back this morning?"

Leah raised an eyebrow. "I'm not sure his ego could survive the truth, but we generally get more done without him."

Musa laughed, then added, "We're a better team without him, but in fact Michael is brilliant. Arrogant? Yes. Then again he's got much of which to be proud."

"Nobody's got a right to be *that* haughty, Musa. I'd call it self-absorption."

"Remind me not to cross swords with you."

Leah grinned. "I will."

"Okay, let's put together what we've got to date. Read your notes to me."

Leah studied the page for a moment. "We've considered two options for how to begin. 'Come, that which the nations behold. Dance with peace in the dust around Jerusalem's ridge.' On the other hand, we could translate it, 'Behold and tremble! Nations pretend to come to Jerusalem to make peace and dance on the mountains. But forty-eight months later the city is divided.' You've got another approach, I think."

He knew her translation was better and felt inadequate. Musa nodded and began reading. "'Come, that which the nations behold will dance with peace to make' or, 'dance with who makes peace.'" He stopped and looked at Leah. "This is where we struggle. 'The day is designated Jerusalem to weep, pride in you shall rejoice, ages of all sorrow.'" Musa shook his head. "The syntax is everything. We obviously don't have the words in the proper order. But how can we, when they're in code? We need help with this . . . big help."

Ignoring Musa, Leah retorted, "I am profoundly impressed by the use of the ancient form *Jebus* for Jerusalem." Leah used the pointer to underscore *y.buws*. "I knew this Hebrew usage existed but have not seen it in a manuscript before. The word alone validates the antiquity of the scroll." She pointed further. "Here's that fascinating little hieroglyphic *cheper*, Egyptian for 'will arise.'"

Musa leaned over the table. "Unfortunately, languages aren't my strong suit. I studied the wrong subjects in undergraduate school." He shrugged. "You're exceptional, Leah." He cupped his hand over his mouth as if confiding. "To tell the honest truth, I knew from the moment my father and I found the scroll, we'd need significant help to crack the code. I hated to admit it, but that's the truth."

"Don't blame yourself, friend. No one could master all these languages in a lifetime." Leah leaned over as if sharing a secret. "Not even Kelly the Presumptuous."

Musa laughed again.

"My husband," Leah said enthusiastically and then stopped. For a moment she looked at the table and then took a deep breath. "David was excellent in languages, but . . . he never boasted about the fact or let people know. Thought it made for a better strategy to let others think he couldn't understand them." She sighed. "David was also a very humble person."

Musa felt Leah's sudden surge of emotion and was taken aback. He did not know what to say, how to respond. The best he could do was return to the translation. "Please, allow me to map out this section in its entirety, putting both of our attempts together." He read, "'Behold and tremble! The nations dance with you, peace to make with Jerusalem, from months forty-eight celebrate with the dust of the ridge, but divided is Jerusalem, the millennium for weep stones will designated broken shall be and then arise will your pride for rejoice, ages of all sorrow.'"

"We haven't adequately factored in how Michael's discovery of the meaning of six millennia fits here," Leah observed. She sounded more subdued. "He is sure the first part of the text is a warning of something to come at the end of the sixth millennium of human existence, but I can't see where it fits together here."

"Me either." Musa pushed his notes back. "Everything is too scrambled."

Leah suddenly grabbed his wrist. "Just a minute. Look at this mess of words." She crossed her arms over her chest and stared. "Look again." Leah abruptly took the pointer and ran it back and forth across the lines.

"The ancient world was infinitely more remote than our modern world," Leah stated. "People didn't have frequent contact. Few Akkadians and Sumerians had any idea what an Egyptian was about, much less the meaning of Greek language that would come into vogue much later. Maybe no one ever ventured a guess about the meaning of the Donation of Melchizedek. What if the scroll was carefully preserved because no one could completely decipher it? The priests hid it in the Temple without any sense of what it actually said."

"Sure. The theory makes sense," Musa said. "They revered something they couldn't grasp, just like medieval peasants heard Latin used in their worship services but had no idea what it meant."

"Even with our problems in unscrambling the text, we're the first people in who knows how many centuries even to come close to the meaning." Leah beamed.

The door at the top of the stairs opened, and a subdued Kelly came down. He resumed his place at the table without fanfare.

"Everything okay?" Musa asked.

"Yes. Fine." The priest looked away.

"We've done a considerable amount of work," Musa added. "Leah's come up with a very significant theory about the inability of the ancients to understand the text fully."

"Hmm." Kelly nodded knowingly. "Good."

"Perhaps you'd like to look at our work to date and comment."

"Thank you." Kelly sounded distracted. "Let me see." He took Musa's work and stared at the page, almost as if he were not really seeing the words. Like a man with a wild monkey perched on his shoulder, Michael's attention was elsewhere. The priest blinked several times and then stared at the lines. His lack of focus disappeared in the heat of his laserlike concentration. "Yes," he mumbled to himself. "Close, but not quite there." He grabbed a pencil and began making editorial adjustments above Musa's handwriting. Minutes later, Michael put the pencil down and stared at the paper as if no one else were in the room.

"Want to give us a few clues?" Leah asked.

Kelly blinked several times again as if breaking a trance. He pulled at his goatee and started to read. "'Behold and tremble the nations that come to Jerusalem to make peace with you. You will dance with the dust of the ridge.'" He stopped and offered a caveat. "I take this ridge to mean the mountains that surround Jerusalem."

Musa and Leah nodded, although they still looked puzzled.

The priest began again. "'You will dance with the dust of the ridge and celebrate forty-eight months from the day Jerusalem is divided. But the stones will weep for the millennium, for the millennium spoken of is designated.'" Michael stopped again. "This is where the play on numbers occurs," he explained. "What seems to be six days is really six thousand-year periods. See?"

Leah shook her head. "But do you understand what it means?"

"Obviously the heading across the top says 'The Donation of Melchizedek to Avram' . . . or Abraham . . . but I don't understand how any of this fits together or where it's going." Kelly pulled at his goatee. "I'm surprised. I expected to walk out on the other side of the mystery, and now I seem to have only stomped off into the swamp again." He shook his head. "I don't know."

"Well, your ability to put the words together right is nothing short of astounding," Leah conceded.

"There's another portion I want to add," Musa said. "I think we all know the Greek word *sfralisin* for 'seals.' Leah, how do you read the Akkadian next to *sfralisin*?

Leah looked for a moment. "Oh, that means 'shall be broken.'"

"I thought so," Musa continued. "I believe the meaning is that at the end of the six millennia a very important set of seals will be broken and the sorrow of the ages will be unleashed."

"Yes," Kelly confirmed slowly. "We have here the prophetic element. Perhaps a warning, but certainly a dour premonition of something bad." Once again the priest seemed distracted, as if moving away into a world of his own making.

"But how do we know what is exactly the right word order?" Musa pressed. "What can we compare our insight against?"

"Nothing," Kelly sounded irritated. "We don't have an ancient text to use as a measuring stick. That's a big problem."

"Then we cannot find an answer using the usual scientific methods and approach," Musa concluded. "In the end, all of our scholarly disciplines fall before this obstacle. They fail us."

Kelly turned and looked blankly at Musa. "You have any better ideas?" He did not speak with rancor but sounded as if speaking from the top of a distant mountain.

Musa looked back and forth between the priest and Leah and then shrugged.

For a long time no one spoke.

Leah broke the silence. "Maybe I have an idea. We've been functioning like a bunch of human computers, with Michael seeming to have the most data stored on his hard drive. I think that's our problem."

"What do you mean?" Kelly looked annoyed.

"Whoever wrote this still thought the wheel to be a great invention," Leah answered. "Bronze and iron were high technology. In their wildest nightmares, they wouldn't have dreamed of a computer, much less functioning like one. We have to shift gears down and try thinking like they did."

"What are you driving at?" Musa shifted into intense interest.

"This script was written by people who believed intuition was vastly superior to cold, calculating logic. Their answers arose from their dreams, their gut, their instincts."

Michael's countenance changed. "I believe you are on to something!"

"These people were highly religious," Leah continued. "They expected the reader to have a similar orientation to the message, to the process, to life."

"Where are you going with this?" Michael looked at her with the same intensity with which he had probed the scroll.

"I'm not sure." Leah smiled, then looked puzzled. "The best I can do is run down a trail here. But . . ." She paused and rubbed her chin. "But we have all commented that the scroll seems to have an unexpected effect on us. Right?"

Kelly looked dismayed. "I'd forgotten that twist."

"Muslim, Christian, Jew," Leah continued. "Our traditions share a common belief in the power of inspiration, in sacred books. Why couldn't this scroll share in that same capacity?"

"But what would that mean for translation purposes?" The priest pushed her.

"Possibly, it would mean that we must participate in that same inspiration if we are to properly understand the message. In other words, we need God's help if we are to grasp the contents."

Kelly stared at her, dumbfounded and shaken.

Musa watched the priest out of the corner of his eye. "You are bothered by this idea, Michael?"

Kelly slowly shook his head. "This is the point where I started. At the Pontifical Academy we were first taught that inspiration was the key to understanding Scripture. My professors then threw that idea out the window and turned to the same scholarly methods scientists developed during the Enlightenment. We treated the Bible like a paleontologist constructs dinosaurs from little pieces of bone." He bit at his lip and removed the half glasses from his nose. "Leah is suggesting I give up what's in my head and start searching for answers on my knees."

"I'm simply following a line of reasoning," Leah answered.

Kelly slumped back in his chair. "No question this scroll has had its effect. I even went to confession over something I wouldn't normally have given a second thought to. Maybe you are right, my dear."

Musa frowned. "Where does this lead us? What's next Leah?"

"I think we must continue to translate the words, but possibly we must also seek the help of God."

"You're suggesting we pray?" Musa probed.

Kelly laughed loudly. "All this talk is quite amazing. Here I am, the priest, the professional religionist! The Christian with two thousand years of spiritual traditions carved out by the sweat and toil of monks, mystics, and martyrs. But it is Leah, the lawyer, the nonobservant Jew, who comes up with the answers I should have offered." He stood up. "You've nailed me, little woman. I accept the verdict."

Michael started back up the stairs. "Time for me to return to the midnight vigil before setting off in quest of the Holy Grail." He stopped at the top of the stairs. "What can I say? A sinner once again exposed for the charlatan that he is." He closed the door behind him.

Musa felt his mouth drop. He looked at Leah. She had a similar amazed look on her face. "What in the world was that all about?"

31

Saturday, October 3
Washington, D.C.

Rod Parkin, representative of the Brookings Institute, sat nervously beside Jamal Shurif, the aging expert from Washington's American University. Parkin's dark business suit and carefully chosen tie were meant to help Parkin, to convey a certain savvy, but the scholar still appeared younger than his twenty-eight years. He glanced around the special conference room in the annex to the White House. "Big place!" He coughed. "I'm new to this sort of procedure," he admitted. "Feel rather uneasy."

Shurif nodded. "Yes. I understand. We're scholars, not politicians." Graying at the temples and balding, Parkin's Arab counterpart looked far more experienced and equipped for their task. He pulled a file from his briefcase and spread papers on the mahogany table.

"Exactly. I study documents, not talk to heads of state. Makes me nervous to even be in the same room with such powerful people."

"I remember the first time I came in for a similar consultation,"

Jamal Shurif added. "Was I ever nervous! But you get over it. After all, they put their pants on the same way we do." He grinned. "Except for our feminine secretary of state."

"You've been a professor at American University quite a while?"

"My parents immigrated to this area from Jordan when I was only a baby. I grew up near the university, went to school there, and ended up teaching Middle Eastern studies." Jamal smiled pleasantly. "And you?"

"I came straight to the Brookings Institute after finishing my Ph.D. at Brandeis." Rod Parkin raised an eyebrow. "Never expected to do anything but pure research. Did my dissertation on the effects of Islamic fundamentalism in shaping modern politics. I was assigned to study terrorism and ended up with this responsibility today."

The outside door opened and two men stepped in. Each wore plastic receiving devices in their ears. Obviously, Secret Service. Margaret Britton, the United States secretary of state, followed them.

Parkin and Shurif immediately rose to their feet. Two other aides walked in behind her. Everyone stood at attention. The president of the United States walked briskly into the room.

"Please be seated." The president sat down at the head of the conference table. "Time is limited, so we will begin without formalities and get right to the point. Madam Secretary, what is your recommendation?"

The small, heavyset woman spun around in her chair to face Rod Parkin. "Gentlemen, you are here today because each of you is involved in studying emerging trends in the Middle East." Britton focused her intense black eyes on them like a laser preparing to melt steel. "As you were advised before you arrived, we want to know what you think are the unspoken, unpublished objectives and problems of the current Arab heads of state."

The younger man turned to Shurif with an "after you" look.

The professor pursed his lips and started gesturing with his hands before words came out of his mouth. "Let us be precise. Every Middle Eastern head of state is more afraid of terrorists than we are. Iran remains an example of what the extremists are capable of doing. I am not only speaking of the Islamic revolution in the past.

"Today, a moderate government headed by President Mohammed Khatami moves to dismiss the threats against the life of Salman Rushdie in order to end this blight on their relations with the international community. What happens? Some Islamic foundation adds three hundred thousand dollars to the bounty for killing Rushdie, raising the reward to 2.8 million. Anything happen? No, because Khatami and company are terrified of the Islamic extremists."

The president and secretary of state exchanged glances.

Dr. Shurif concluded, "I would suggest that the United States must get ready for severe economic reprisals of a similar nature unless its foreign policy adjusts to these extremist interests and demands."

The secretary of state turned to Rod. "Dr. Parkin, I believe your task is to keep up with the count on nuclear weapons in the region. The CIA informs us there are unaccounted-for nuclear devices floating in the area. Do you agree?"

Rod Parkin always coughed when he was nervous. Fighting to keep the explosion back, he nearly choked. "Excuse me." He could feel his face turning red. "My studies indicate the Russian government has sold weapons under the table and that other nuclear devices were distributed by Russian mafia sources in Kazakstan. Yes, well-financed extremist groups definitely have nuclear capacity. If they decide to use such weaponry as blackmail, the world could well be at their mercy."

The president began taking notes but said nothing.

"What do these people really want?" The secretary continued her line of questioning. She looked straight at Parkin.

"Their objectives are religious." Rod felt a degree of self-assurance returning. "Contrary to the normal and usual commercial consideration, these groups are disinterested in economic realities. In fact, the greater the cost and loss, the more motivated they become. You cannot understand their goals unless you think in purely religious terms."

"Have you heard of the Islamic Revolutionary Front?" the president broke in.

Both men shook their heads from side to side.

"How does one gain leverage with these people?" The secretary of state turned to Shurif.

"The fallacy in most policies of previous administrations is the tendency to treat them like another political problem," the professor answered. "You have nothing to offer except to capitulate on their terms. Their goals are heaven and hell. You can't do business with them." Shurif pointed at the secretary and the president. "Don't ever forget that *you* are the Great Satan. Doing business with you is dancing with the devil. They despise everything you stand for."

"Let me ask my question again." The president put down his pen and looked carefully at both scholars. "You've never heard of a new emerging group called the Islamic Revolutionary Front?"

"It's a new name for me." Rod Parkin relaxed and could answer more easily. "But you must remember the players keep shifting back and forth among various organizations. Often a group changes its name for strategic reasons. Moreover, certain leaders keep trying to create one big comprehensive umbrella to coordinate all efforts. Usually there's too much friction for such a faction to last long."

"What if someone pulled it off?" the president asked. "An

ayatollah, an imam, a general, a head of state working in the back room? What would happen should there be a successful consolidation of power?"

Rod Parkin looked at Jamal Shurif and waited. The professor finally answered. "You could be facing the most formidable adversary this country has known since World War II."

"Do you agree?" the president asked Rod.

"Definitely."

The secretary of state and the president huddled together at the table, whispering back and forth for several moments before Secretary Britton resumed the discussion.

"Let's assume for a moment that such a thing has occurred," she asked thoughtfully. "What would be a reasonable position to take in response to such a development?"

"My family came from Amman," Dr. Shurif said. "The ways of this Middle Eastern world are in my blood stream. We have witnessed the problem at a very close range. When one has an alligator in the swimming pool, it is best to keep him fed—lest he show up for a snack the next time one takes a dip. The USA has no alternative but to feed the Islamic extremist alligator, unless you are prepared to attempt to kill the beast. The last people who tried such a thing were called the Crusaders. To this hour, they remain a Middle Eastern symbol of barbaric stupidity."

"You're telling us to feed the alligator?" the secretary shot back.

"If you want your people to be able to swim," Shurif responded immediately.

"Since these people aren't interested in the usual economic bill of fare, what would you offer them?" Margaret Britton asked.

"You must settle on what is religiously important to them." Rod felt he could field the inquiry. "Since you aren't going to agree to cast the Israelis into the sea, you must find an offering more palatable to the American people, but it must touch the fundamentalist hunger."

"Give us a 'for instance.'" Britton continued her inquisition.

Dr. Shurif smiled broadly. "Being from a family that were formerly citizens of the Hashemite kingdom of King Hussein, I can tell you what would satisfy their stomachs." He paused for dramatic effect. "Offer them a piece of Jerusalem as the capital for all Palestinians. Yes, a small parcel of real estate, but enough to keep the alligator happy for a very long time."

The president abruptly stood, and everyone followed suit. "Thank you, gentlemen. Your observations have been most helpful. May we assume these conversations will be kept in confidence for the foreseeable future?"

"Yes, certainly," Rod stammered.

Dr. Shurif frowned and was not happy. Rod immediately sensed he had spoken too quickly and out of turn. The Jordanian scholar looked at the floor for a moment before answering. "Yes . . . certainly. As you wish."

"Thank you." The president nodded to both men and then left quickly. The secretary of state smiled and followed him out. The aides and Secret Service fell in behind.

Rod waited for the room to clear before turning to Dr. Shurif. "What's your take on this discussion?"

The American University professor quickly gathered up his papers and stuck them in the file. "Change is in the air, my boy. Genuine change." He smiled kindly. "Maybe we helped it along a bit." Shurif stopped and put his hand on Rod Parkin's shoulder. "Don't ever let a politician get you to agree to silence. We lost a good article or publication out of this consultation." He started to walk away. "And never forget that the president is first, last, and always a politician."

Ten minutes later the young president and the secretary of state rendezvoused alone in the Oval Office. The president leaned over the desk and rested his chin in his hands. "What do you make of their not knowing about this Islamic Revolutionary Front?"

"Our intelligence is either very good these days, or we are being misled."

"Would the Mossad do that to us?"

"Sure," Britton answered, "but I don't think so in this case. Lots of posturing going on that makes me very uneasy. Today's October third, and they've just finished twenty-four hours of intense introspection over their recent debacle in Jordan. They know they've got to come clean with us or lose credibility. Right now they need all the friends they can get. No. I think they're shooting straight."

The president leaned back in his large leather chair. "Then we've still got some wiggle time before the Arabs put us in a vise?"

"We've been picking up vibes from the OPEC countries that I don't like," the secretary frowned as she talked. "Bad signs. I think it's time for us to get back at the front of this parade before we're outflanked."

"What would you suggest, Margaret?"

"Our people have been working on an interesting idea for some time. This might just be the moment to float it." Britton shifted in the chair. Her countenance changed from the look of an astute diplomat to an amused prankster. "Let's cut them off at the pass, Mr. President."

"How?"

"You call for a new Conference on Middle Eastern Peace. We will mandate that the major topic of conversation be the status of Jerusalem. It's time we got our EU friends to turn up the heat, and by the way, let's invite the Asians and Russians too. We can stand back as Jerusalem slugs it out with the world. They are as stubborn as mules. A good hit in the head may move them in the right direction.

By simply raising the issue, we placate the Islamic fundamentalists while reassuring the Israelis we stand with them. Whatever happens, we serve our best interests while letting the smoke clear. If this new IRF is a real threat, we'll have time to calculate the best response. In the meantime, we'll get the CIA to work at sowing seeds of discord in the IRF to disrupt their unity."

The president nodded slowly and then more vigorously. "Time is of the essence. We must get this idea out on the table before anyone tries to squeeze us. It's important we don't appear to be buckling to Arab demands. How quickly can you do it?"

"Forty-eight hours enough time?"

"Margaret, you're a genius." The president extended his hand. "Well done. Get the material on my desk along with a speech. I'll go live on television. You are the majorette, and I'll be the drum major. Together we'll take this parade down a different street than anyone expected!"

32

Saturday, October 3
Jerusalem

Leah simply could not bring herself to open the office. Father Kelly had something or other he had to do at the monastery and they could not work without him, or so he thought. Musa needed to contact his parents. Nothing was left for Leah but to walk down the street in front of their house. It was a great day to be outside. Early October usually brought wonderful fall weather. Because David always enjoyed his jaunts through Jerusalem at this time of year, Leah reasoned that keeping the tradition might in some undefined way maintain contact with him.

Rather than drive, Leah caught a taxi that took her along the northern edge of the Old City until Sultan Suleiman Street turned into Derech Yericho, Highway 417, the direct route to the Dead Sea. Near the bottom of the Kidron Valley, she got out and took the side road into the Jewish cemetery. Wandering uphill, Leah wound her way through the maze of stone sarcophagi, ever heading toward that one dreaded plot of ground. Above her stood *Kever HaNevi'im*, the Tomb of the Prophets, and at the top, the ever-busy Seven Arches Hotel with its magnificent view of the Old City.

The Rosenbergs had held their family section for decades. After all, burial in such an ancient place so close to the Old City made the little parcels of land of extraordinary worth. The location was not a matter of money but ultimate prestige, a statement about the family's place in the eternal scheme of things.

Little had changed since the day of the burial. The ground had to settle before the workmen would begin constructing the slab monument. Like a hernia in the world, the mound still rose, obtrusive. Leah sat down on the cement curbing that ran along the edge of the row of graves, tucked her knees up under her chin, and pulled herself into a ball. For a long time she stared at the grave as if the initial shock had enveloped her once more.

A gentle breeze swept down the steep hillside and sent the fine powdery dust of the rocky path flying between the graves and then up toward the sky. Light danced along the tops of the chalky rock boxes that could become so very hot in summertime. The brilliant blue sky seemed unusually bright and intense, like a heavenly blanket settling over earth's final bed of perpetual rest. Leah thought on how heaven and earth, light and darkness met in this place.

An hour later she left her memorial rock on the grave and started her walk back down the hill. While the area on the other side of the road and along the Kidron brook was generally Palestinian, Leah trudged on, indifferent to possible problems even though tensions in the city remained high. Perhaps a walk past the Gihon Spring down toward the Pool of Shiloach would be meaningful.

She watched children playing, chasing one another in some sort of hide-and-seek game, the little ragamuffins darting in and out of the alleys and causeways in their make-believe pursuit of the "bad guy," the "goat." Why did there always have to be a loser, an "it," a victim? The world was not a place of justice, only retribution for losing the game.

Even to think of the idea of talking with God about such matters seemed incongruous. Sitting in a synagogue receiving inspiration from ancient customs and consolation from formal prayers was one thing, but talking to some invisible being, as if He were there listening, was an entirely different matter. As modernism's child, a descendant of the Enlightenment, she knew the possibility of being in touch with the divine was almost a cosmic joke. She always thought the stories of Moses on the mountain and conversations between the Holy One of Israel and the prophets as no more than metaphor, human justifications to give the prophetic conclusions greater weight in the chronicles of history. Leah prided herself on being the product of rationalism, not mysticism. Talking to God had never been an option.

And yet . . . as she walked alone . . . as she rambled down this ancient Jebusite hillside where the shepherd boy-warrior had first made Jerusalem his capital, she hungered to be touched by eternity. With at least three thousand years between her and this great king whose name was also David, maybe . . . somehow, someway . . . the leap could be made.

Tourists and pilgrims were already walking in and around the rocks and boulders dotting the surface of the grotto at the bottom of the hill. A few of the more adventurous had begun their trek through the cold springwater, walking back up the ancient hand-carved tunnel toward what had been King Hezekiah's water main into the ancient city of Jerusalem. *Simhat Beit Hashoeva*, the Feast of Water Drawing, had taken place here during Temple times. Ten passages from the Psalms were read while "living water" was drawn to be taken back up the hill for the holy rituals. For a brief moment she could almost see the ancients returning back to the Temple Mount with containers of holy water in hand.

Leah's recollections made the place feel alive, mystically linked with all of Israel's yesterdays, and then a more contemporary figure came to mind. Uncle Nathan Roth, Leah's very Orthodox great-uncle, had always come down to this very spot prior to Yom Kippur and turned his pockets inside out, emptying lint, coins, anything, everything on the ground, as a sign of his repentance.

Leah watched the clear brook babble out of the same cave where two millennia before a Nazarene rabbi was rumored to have given the blind their sight. Leah was ready to have hers restored.

She watched tourists listen to a lecture from a local guide and snap pictures. Eventually the pilgrims filed back to their buses and vans. And then she suddenly remembered him.

Leah had not thought of Adin Scholem for years. His family immigrated from Russia under the most arduous circumstances, and Leah came to know him at the university. Adin was a bit on the eccentric side, but no one doubted his brilliance. Although the more worldly students chided him about appearing to talk to things, spirits, entities that weren't there, Leah knew Adin did have the gift of catching glimpses of eternity. Adin became more and more religious and ended up a rabbi, teaching at a synagogue filled with a host of followers, on a side street in the Katamon area in some old neglected building.

At one time Adin had been more than a little attracted to Leah. Surely a few years would not have dimmed his memory of her too much. If Leah knew anyone at all who could tell her where the edge of eternity might be found, Adin Scholem had to be the man.

As a tourist got out, she grabbed a taxi and was on her way. Another recollection came to mind. While Adin had maintained the usual Orthodox ideas about the separation of men and women in worship and the necessity of *tzniut*, of modesty in

One intrusive thought remained. It fit nowhere, but destroyed what might have made for harmony in the sequence of events. Musa was indirectly . . . or possibly directly . . . responsible for David Rosenberg's death.

thought, word, and behavior, he had always wanted to help women relate to the Jewish faith in their own unique way, rather than simply imitating the ways of men. Scholem was rumored to still be single, lost most of the time in the back roads of study, meditation, and teaching. It was not hard to remember why she had not given Adin any encouragement.

The taxi pulled to a stop, and Leah paid the man. Adin's name was well known, and it was easy to find directions. Businesses were closed, and there were not many people on the street. She listened for a minute and started toward the sound of people talking. She quickly found her way to Rabbi Scholem's storefront synagogue. An amazing conglomeration of men, women, and children were coming and going through an old door. Sephardic Jews in black conical hats and striped Arab-style robes walked alongside Hasidim in yellow caftans, marking them as descendants of old Jerusalem families. A babble of different accents filled the air as the people chattered and talked. Young men hurried by, wearing *kippot* designed to signal they were members of a youth movement. Other congregants wore the traditional tailored look of the high Levantine style of North Africans. Here and there blond-haired European immigrant children dashed off with the black-eyed descendants of Middle Eastern Jews. Leah walked through the Noah's Ark of Judaism into the inner sanctum of Adin's domain.

Cracks ran down the sides of the dirty white stucco walls. Wooden benches filled the floor. She quickly spotted Adin at one side of the synagogue, standing with a white-and-black striped *tallit* still draped over his shoulders and lecturing to a group of young admirers. His black hair now had a touch of gray and he looked older, thinner. But the snapping eyes were the same, peering out from behind those six-inch-thick glasses that made his eyes appear to be half of his face. The long shaggy beard fit the image expected of a man of his following. More than a few long strands of gray had invaded the black forest. His high-pitched voice had not changed.

She could hear Adin explaining the nature of heaven, one of his favorite subjects decades ago. A lump formed in her throat. Leah thought briefly about the existence of an afterlife. If heaven were a reality, would her David be found there somewhere among the angels?

Adin turned and looked toward the door. He stopped in mid-sentence and looked at her. The enormous eyes became even larger, his mouth dropped slightly. In one step, he pushed out of the circle of students and bounded toward her, the *tallit* bellowing in the breeze.

"Leah? Leah Roth? My old college friend? Is that really you?"

Leah smiled broadly. "Shalom, Adin. How are you?"

The rabbi reached out and then withdrew his hand. He plowed toward a door at the side of the synagogue. The bewildered students stared, watching as their questions were left dangling in the air. "We must talk in another place. My private office." He ushered her into a spartan tiny room with a small desk, two chairs, piles of papers and books everywhere. "I know it's unusual to be alone with a woman, but I can't believe it's really you, Leah Roth."

"Actually, it's now Rosenberg." Leah glanced around at the pile of old prayer books, religious pamphlets, empty cups, napkins, paper, old newspapers, litter, and clutter. "I know you're very busy and today isn't a good time, but I did come for a religious question." She noticed a leaflet on the desk promoting a study group Adin was teaching: how to apply the Torah to the problems of contemporary women.

Adin pushed a chair toward her and sat down. "I've thought of you so many times, Leah." He rolled his eyes. "Leah the skeptic. Leah the intellect." The rabbi smiled broadly. "What could possibly bring you to see me, boring old Adin Scholem . . .?" His voice trailed off.

Leah squeezed his hand. "Dear friend, you are as intriguing and fascinating as ever. I hear so many good things about what you are doing here." She smiled reassuringly. "Adin, I've been through a very hard time and need some religious insight today. You came to mind."

"Blessed be the Holy One of Israel!" The rabbi beamed like a child lost in a forest who is suddenly found by his mother. "To think that I might be of such help to an old and dear friend!"

Leah took a deep breath. "Neither of us has enough time now for a lengthy conversation. Perhaps another day I will come and tell you of the tragedy that I am living with." She bit her lip and fought back the tears. "My question is simple. Is it possible for me to open my heart and let the light of God shine in?"

Adin looked as if she had struck him with a brick. He pulled at his graying beard and stared at her in wonder. "*Oy vey!* That you should seek such a thing." He put both hands on his cheeks and shook his head in amazement. "Leah Roth comes to me to seek such a holy thing." The rabbi held his hands toward the heavens in supplication.

"I am not worthy," Leah began, "but—"

"No one is worthy," Adin cut her off. "This is not the issue. Our task is to fulfill the yearning of the soul, known or unknown, to get beyond the shell of what we see around us and find our way to the divine realities. We must remove the outer coverings that keep us from the truth, the truth buried within the Torah."

Leah nodded her head slowly. "Today as I looked into the Pool of Shiloach and was reminded of things I had forgotten, I thought of you and your desire to know the Holy One."

"Ah"—Adin shook his finger in the air as he spoke—"that

was a *hochma*, a flash of insight. Yes, you are coming to a turning point."

"I don't know how to pray," Leah confided. "I've always been the daughter of Kant, the disciple of Nietzsche, a companion to the spirit of this age. Such a spiritual process is totally foreign to me." She looked at him helplessly. "Do I empty my mind?"

"No, no!" The rabbi shook his head vigorously. "Such is the nonsense of the Eastern mystical teachers, of Zen, of the transcendental meditationalist. On the contrary, the task is the perfection of your spirit through filling your mind with the holy words of Torah. You need a spiritual cleansing, so to speak." He leaned over as if interrogating a student and shook his finger. "Are you ready for such a discipline?"

"Yes!" Leah tried to sound as sincere as she felt. "I want to know how to proceed."

"You should go back to Shiloah and empty your heart as we empty our pockets on Yom Kippur. Just as we rid our homes of leaven before Passover, seek to be free of every defilement. Seek to have a pure heart. Listen for the Holy One."

For a moment Leah felt light-headed, almost as if the room were spinning. Yes, the air was somewhat stale in the musty old office, but Adin's intensity carried the magnetism of genuine, tangible spirituality. He was his own best example of what he taught. She knew why the rumors, which were fast becoming legends, passed from student to student. She took a deep breath.

"Leah, my dear." Adin stopped and tugged at his beard. "I do not know how to say such a thing, but I must try. There was always so much spirituality in you, but you fought to suppress it. You saw the beauty of the rose, heard the divine in the symphony. If you had not rejected what was waiting in your soul, you could have encountered the *shechina*, the holy presence, much earlier. Now the time has arrived."

The rabbi jumped up from this chair and began rummaging through the pile of books. "Ah, here it is." He held up a tattered old book. "Rabbi Jacob Emden's prayer book, *The House of Jacob*, is filled with prayers for entering into the blessings of the Sabbath. In fact, they are best offered at sundown. I want you to go back to Shiloach and read, think, and pray these prayers. Let the waters of the brook run into your mind and overflow into your soul, cleansing and purifying. Pray!" He shook his finger in the air like an evangelist on the verge of demanding repentance. "Pray! And pray again until the Torah is more real than the stream itself. Only then will you be able to truly find what you seek." He leaned forward until he was barely inches from her face and then whispered, "Only then will your heart be filled with inspiration."

33

Saturday, October 4
Old City, Dormition Abbey

Michael Kelly noticed Abbot Friedrich Hoffman appear in the entrance of the Dormition Abbey gift shop. Hoffman nodded pleasantly to the visitors and looked around the room. Shadows of the late Saturday afternoon sunlight fell across the tourists mingling around the counters of trinkets, books, and souvenirs. The abbot was obviously looking for someone.

"Might I have a word with you, Father Kelly?" Abbot Hoffman finally beckoned to him.

"Certainly." Michael left a group of admirers and followed the abbot back inside the restricted quarters of the Dormition Abbey. "Mostly Americans today," he said pleasantly. "A group from Cleveland."

Because almost everything Jewish closed on the Sabbath, tourists tended to come to the Abbey in larger numbers on Saturdays. Often Michael chatted with English-speaking groups and autographed his books on sale in the little store. He had spent the entire morning teaching a group of novices the subject of biblical criticism, and he needed a break. Michael hurried after the large man who was known for his long stride.

The abbot closed the door to his personal study and gestured toward the chair in front of his desk. A large singular crucifix decorated the bare stone walls and a plain gold cross hung above his ancient oak desk. Although Abbot Friedrich Hoffman did administrative work here, the room still looked and felt more like a monastic cell or a chapel. The spartan quarters contained only one more piece of furniture, a knurled prie-dieu with a worn leather breviary lying on the kneeler, bearing silent witness to countless hours spent in penance and supplication.

"We will be preparing for the evening compline service and the mass tomorrow," the abbot began slowly, "and I am sure you are busy with many important matters." He paused as if to carefully frame his words. "You always are."

Michael studied the imposing man sitting across from him. Four decades earlier Friedrich Hoffman immigrated from Frankfurt, Germany, to Israel and began his work as a Benedictine monk, overseeing the Church at Tabgha, the place of the multiplication of loaves and fishes in the Galilee. A most lonely assignment back in those days. The rumor was that Father Hoffman came to do his own special penance for what his race had done to the Jews. The thoughtful German had certainly learned the disciplines of solitude the hard way. No one questioned his moral authority.

"I must speak my heart to you." The abbot sounded pained. Old gold-rimmed glasses and a full beard offset the emptiness of a very bald head. "Yesterday's conversation with Cardinal Mottola left me feeling rather disturbed." He nervously adjusted his glasses upward on his large nose. "Might we speak in German? I would be more at ease."

"Certainly." Michael edged closer to the desk in order to listen more intently. Though preferring English for a serious conversation, linguistic challenges always hooked his interest. "I will do my best."

"I would not want to do anything to impede your career." Speaking German made the abbot appear more relaxed, but his words still sounded strained. "What I have to say is not prompted by any sense of competition or envy for your accomplishments."

Michael remembered the first time he had met Father Hoffman at the Tabgha Church on the edge of the Sea of Galilee. Hoffman had a minor reputation acquired from a few small articles in obscure scholarly journals. The slow-moving German had once proposed a slightly different location for the site of the Second Temple than most scholars held to. His theory went embarrassingly nowhere, but the man remained a quiet, humble servant of his calling. The abbot was a man without guile. No competitor here.

"Should this archaeological find prove to be everything that is rumored, you would bring great honor to our monastery," the abbot continued. "However, when I see a papal nuncio coming all the way from Rome to discuss this matter, I must have concerns."

"Certainly." Michael shifted nervously in his chair. The issue of his contacting Rome without the abbot's awareness did not appear closed. "I realize I made a mistake," he added hastily.

"No, no." The old man shook his head and smiled benevolently. "We have already dismissed the matter." He leaned over the desk and smiled kindly. "I have a very different concern than the maintenance of protocol."

"I don't understand."

"When I studied your face as Mottola greeted you, Michael, I recognized the look in your eyes. I have seen it before. For this reason, I wanted to speak to you." The abbot suddenly stood up, his massive six-foot-four-inch frame towering over Michael.

He was not so much fat as very large, built like a sturdy farm-hand. "I speak with you now because of what I saw in your face." Hoffman turned abruptly and glared, the kindly St. Bernard eyes turning into instruments of fire and fury. "Yes, one glance into your eyes, and I knew the devil had found a lair."

Michael gritted his teeth and fought the impulse to strike back. No one confronted him in such terms and walked away unscathed. Accusing him of being the devil's den! He bit his lip to keep from lashing out.

"Do you understand what I am saying?"

Michael shook his head, although it was merely a ploy to buy a little more time before he responded. Anger could drive him to a place he did not want to be.

The abbot straightened and peered at Michael out of the corner of his eye. "I am charged with the divine responsibility to care for the eternal destiny of every person living in this place. I speak to you now out of that concern." Hoffman began to pace. "The issue before us is not lying, stealing, or some simple sin of the flesh. The problem is always much more difficult when it is a violation of the spirit. That is the worst kind."

Michael pulled at his goatee and took a deep breath. He couldn't believe he had been found out. Then again, the abbot had a gift for spiritual perception. All those years by himself were their own reward. He had mastered his spirit and learned to see through the likes of a proud priest.

"I am speaking of the sin of *pride*, my friend. The sin of the angels." The abbot suddenly sat down and leaned over the desk. "The possibilities of fame, the promise of recognition, the hint of favor among the mighty has sparked something deep within you, Father Kelly. The light danced in your eyes, but it was not the light of heaven." He pushed back from the desk and folded his arms over his chest. "Am I not correct?" His voice rumbled as if arising from the depths of the earth.

Michael broke eye contact and looked away, searching for something outside, beyond the window, that might legitimately demand his attention for the moment, but the stained glass windows and stone walls offered no escape. He was left appearing evasive and chastened.

"I have seen visions of the skyline of Rome dancing in your eyes, Father. You could leave this little hotbed of terrorism and intrigue behind for the romantic cafes of one of the most intriguing cities in the world. I thought to myself, 'Father Kelly must decide where he intends to live the rest of his life.'"

"To live?"

"I do not speak of a bed, a room, an office, in this place or that place. I am not thinking of a domicile in Italy, Israel, or America. My question is about your soul. Where will you live inside yourself, my son?"

Michael did not answer. He no longer felt a need to deny the charge. To the contrary, he felt a sense of resignation and relief. Michael scratched his head and rubbed the back of his neck. "You are a wise man, my friend, and holy as well. What can I say when such a voice speaks to me? How can I deny the probe that is plunged into the very depths of my soul? Yes, I suppose you have posed the ultimate question. Where is the true place that my heart is at home?"

"I do not attempt to accuse you, my brother. My question is not meant as an embarrassment. I raise the issue out of sincere concern for your spiritual well-being."

"I would never doubt your intent, Abbot." Michael folded his hands in his lap like a penitent. "And you are right on target. I seem to have an incurable disease. Even within the last few weeks I sought out the Rite of Reconciliation over this very matter. Obviously, my confession was without true repentance."

Abbot Hoffman frowned and looked over the rim of his

glasses. "Please, I am not intending to sit as your judge. Compliance with my opinions is not necessary. I may not be correct in my conclusions."

Michael slipped both hands inside the billowy flowing sleeves of his large brown robe, his head dropped to his chest, and he looked at his feet. "Yes, when Cardinal Mottola came looking for me, I was quite elated. From the beginning I had hoped that this discovery would give me a certain prominence in Rome. I wanted the world to know who I was. All this I freely admit." He shifted wearily in his chair.

"You are not surprised at what I am saying?"

"Such questions would never have crossed my mind a year ago, six months ago," Michael confessed. "Then this scroll came along and I started working with people I really didn't even like." He hung his head. "Yes, I will admit it. I considered the Jewish woman and the Arab inferior to myself. I cajoled and placated them to simply get on with the work." Michael looked straight into the eyes of the abbot. "The truth is that I consider almost everyone inferior to myself." He quickly looked away and took a deep breath.

A few moments later he began again. "The project began to have a strange effect on me. As I examined it, the scroll seemed to examine me. Oh, I didn't speak of this to the others. In fact, for a while I didn't admit it to myself, but slowly I faced the truth. I was having to consider my own motives in a way I hadn't done previously."

"Ah, an exam of conscience!" the abbot observed knowingly.

"A crisis of conscience, precisely." Michael sighed. "Behavior that I formerly considered normal began to appear in a very different light. I started to recognize the jaundiced nature of my deepest motives. Most of the time I was able to set these thoughts aside, but in moments of reflection my own self-accusations and doubts could not be denied."

The abbot merely nodded, encouraging Michael to continue his spiritual exploration.

The priest rolled his eyes and held out his hands in a gesture of bewilderment. "Abbot . . .," he started, then stopped. How could he explain that his skepticism had become so enormous, his doubts so deep, that he even questioned the existence of the God he had supposedly given his life to serve? Oh, it was too difficult even to put into words. And yet . . . yet there was something about Abbot Hoffman's compassionate, nonjudgmental silence that compelled him to try.

When Michael spoke again, it was with great difficulty. "Actually, it's not just a crisis of conscience; it's more like a crisis of faith. When I first embarked on a life of scholarship, I adopted the attitude of healthy—at least in my eyes—skepticism. I prided myself on not accepting things without close examination. Yet at some point the skepticism became not just a critical eye, but an unwillingness to accept anything that could not be proved by reason. And . . . and working on the scroll has, well . . ."

"Has brought your doubts and disbelief to the fore." The abbot completed Michael's sentence. "And you've been more inclined to believe the Bible is merely the philosophical writings of ancient men, not the inspired word of God. You have even questioned your calling. True?"

"Ye-e-s." Michael slumped back in his chair, drained by the admission of something so central to his faith, to his very life.

"Our faith *is* rational, Michael. But it is also experiential. And your scholarship needn't stand in the way of experiencing God on a personal basis. It's true that some scholars have allowed their academic endeavors to deconstruct their faith. Yet others have used the same scholarship to discover or reaffirm true faith. The answers are there for you, Michael. There in your books, your scholarly articles, and your scrolls. And there in your heart as well."

The priest could not reply. He leaned forward, elbows on his knees, head in his hands. He would have preferred tears or anger—any emotion—to the vast emptiness of his engulfing self-doubt.

"I appreciate your candor, Michael. And I pray you will find the answers you need." The large man stood up and walked around his desk. "Please, feel free to stay here as long as you wish." Abbot Hoffman patted him on the shoulder and started toward the door. "Remember, it profits us nothing to gain the world and lose our souls."

Michael remained in the abbot's study for a long time, searching his heart for the answers Friedrich Hoffman had said he would find there. A verse of Scripture kept coming to his mind, one he had learned as a young child. "Thy word have I hid in mine heart, that I might not sin against thee." Michael realized that pride and ambition had been hidden in his heart, not the word of God.

He recalled what he had said the day before, when Leah had suggested they pray for divine guidance in translating the scroll. Her words had pierced his heart as well as his mind, and he had referred to himself as "a sinner once again exposed for the charlatan that he is." Quite a confession the Jewish woman had wrung out of him. It was a painful realization for Michael Kelly, priest, scholar, sinner, and charlatan. He felt his soul had been stripped bare.

An old, familiar verse from the Psalms returned. Michael, the altar boy, had once memorized, "Your word is a lamp unto my feet, and a light unto my path." The old passage came back with new meaning. The abbot had squarely posed again the old academic question that continually haunted him. Was the Bible merely the words of men, or was it truly the inspired word of God to men? And where did the intriguing gold scroll fit into the picture? Was it merely the dazzling light of a momentary opportunity, his chance to bask in the spotlight of scholarly success? Or was it also a divine word, even a personal word from God?

"The answers are there for you," the abbot had said, "in your books, your scholarly articles, and your scrolls."

Insight slowly opened a window. The light began like a tiny pinprick but quickly broadened into a sunbeam of spiritual illumination. It was no accident that a Catholic priest, a Jewish attorney-antiquities expert, and a Muslim archaeologist came to be intertwined in a project that held such promise. No more coincidence. An unseen hand brought it to pass?

And why had this unique scroll been preserved? Oh yes, it was quite ancient and if actually the Donation of Melchizedek held tremendous political and spiritual significance for Jerusalem and beyond. Had mere random chance preserved the scroll in almost pristine condition for centuries? Or was it an act of . . . a . . . sovereign God?

Michael thought of the Dead Sea Scrolls discovered by Musa's father. The rock-throwing Bedouin had unwittingly located an immense, ancient library that had been saved intact for some twenty centuries—a library containing every single book of the Old Testament (except Esther) as well as copies of several books like Genesis and Isaiah. The scrolls had survived for more than two millennia, continuing to exist in spite of disasters that had shaken the world. When the ancient texts were compared with the most authoritative Hebrew texts in use today, there was virtually no difference in manuscripts. Not a single tenet of faith had been altered by this incredible discovery of ancient manuscripts.

Coincidence? Couldn't be.

A book on the abbot's desk caught his eye. The small beautifully illuminated collection of manuscripts celebrated the work of obscure monasteries, working through the centuries to keep the sacred word alive. Monks spend their lives for the sake of these texts. No coincidences here.

"Your word have I hid in my heart," the psalmist said. Was it not the very purpose of scribes and scholars to preserve the word of God so that men and women throughout the ages could treasure the truth in their hearts? Tyrants and infidels tried to eliminate the authoritative words of Scripture, seizing and burning countless thousands of biblical texts, martyring the faithful following God's precepts. Yet Scripture endured, preserved virtually word for word from the original manuscripts.

In college he had studied and loved the classics. Only ten copies of Julius Caesar's *Gallic Wars* had survived into modern times and the earliest copy was written nine hundred years after Caesar penned the original. Yet thousands of manuscript fragments and hundreds of entire scrolls of Scripture still existed, some dating to only a few decades from the time of their original apostolic authorship. Michael reflected that there was more evidence for the authenticity of scriptural texts than for any other ancient writings.

He pulled at his goatee and rubbed his chin. Yes, the abbot was right. The answer was in his books and scrolls. All those years spent in higher criticism had dimmed his eyes to the sovereign miracle of Scripture. The tiny sunbeam of hope had penetrated his darkened heart. God's Word could illumine his path . . . and his doubts.

And then he remembered the prayer of a man desperately seeking healing for his dangerously ill son. Jesus had said to him, "If you believe, all things are possible." The man replied, "Lord, I believe; help thou my unbelief." The father knew there were no easy answers, that doubt and belief coexist in every true seeker. Father Michael and the boy's father were kin.

Michael reached out and touched the illuminated manuscript, tangible evidence of the unseen Hand that had brought him to this project and to his crisis of faith. Slipping to his knees in front of the abbot's desk, the priest brought his hand to his forehead in a slow deliberate motion. Far from a reflex, he slowly made the sign of the cross and prayed, "Lord, I believe; help thou my unbelief."

34

Sunday, October 4
Tel Aviv

The Mossad's executive committee sat silently in front of Avraham Halevy's desk, waiting for his response. He slowly returned the telephone to its cradle, pursed his lips, and stared at the desk calendar for several moments. Sunday morning. October 4. The day he had expected to vacate the premises.

The heavyset head of operations glanced at his younger counterpart, the director of coordination. Both men continued stoic stares, betraying nothing of their personal feelings. Briefcases waited beside their chairs and each had files in hand.

"I didn't anticipate assembling this group again." Halevy broke the silence. "In fact, I'm shocked." He looked at the telephone and shook his head. "The prime minister rejected my resignation." The usual demanding edge was gone from his voice, and he knew he sounded somewhat unsure of himself. "Apparently the cabinet feels that too much is unsettled for such a shift in leadership right now." He smiled for the first time in days. "For once they've even backed off blaming us for the Jordanian mess."

"An excellent sign!" the young executive exclaimed.

"No!" Halevy growled. "To the contrary, it's a bad sign that things are worse than we thought. The politicians are afraid and uncertain about which path to take. The country's *not* in a good place."

"May I personally say that I'm delighted you're still on board," the director of operations added. "I'm relieved with this turn of events, but we have little time for congratulations. Overnight we received a new response from the CIA." He pulled a report out of a file. "The Islamic Revolutionary Front is more comprehensive, bigger than we suspected. The Americans verified most of what Daniel Levy obtained. Their sources are worried too.

"The IRF is motivated by a radical religious agenda and care little for anything else. The final triumph of Islam goads these radicals on like a hot poker on their backsides. What I gathered from the CIA report is that the liberation of *Al-Masjid al-Aksa* or, as they would say, the conquest of the Aksa Mosque, is their primary objective." He pushed the pile of papers toward Halevy. "Hate is their primary tool for recruitment of the young and the means to achieve political solidarity."

Halevy took the file and quickly thumbed through the initial pages. "I'm going to have to get myself acclimated. Mentally shift gears, since I had no expectation of being here today." He folded his arms over his chest and dropped his chin against his neck. "I'll be honest. I really didn't want to be. After my army buddy Daniel Levy's death, the fun when out of this job. Then came that horrible attack on my old friend David Rosenberg. Frankly, I felt as if I'd had enough intrigue for two lifetimes."

"I understand," the operations director responded with uncharacteristic sympathy. "We're a rugged, hard-nosed pack." He cursed and thumped the table. "But the body count isn't easy to take . . . *ever*. I know, I know, we're trained to be impersonal, but every one of us has those points of vulnerability where pain slips through the chinks in the armor."

"Perhaps this is the time when I should interject what has just been verified in the last twenty-four hours," the younger man said. "I planned to submit these discoveries when the new director arrived. Obviously, this is a more appropriate moment." He handed a single-page report to both men.

Halevy quickly skimmed the page and then stopped. He adjusted a desk lamp on the credenza behind him and read the report again very slowly.

"How accurate is this?" the director of operations barked. "Are you sure of this data?"

The younger man nodded his head. "No question that the funding for the IRF has come from Saudi Arabia and Kuwait—countries we risked our lives to save from Saddam. We took his Scuds and risked the lives of our people so they could have a clean war. Other Arab countries have also poured in massive amounts of capital, allowing this group to arm themselves with nuclear weapons." He took another file from his briefcase. "Through our infiltration of the Russian mafia in Krasnoyarsk/26, we now know that they have three nuclear bombs ready to go. At this very moment, the IRF is closing a deal to obtain a fourth and final bomb that will be used to punish 'the Great Satan.' The liberation of Jerusalem will require only punishing 'Satan,' that is, the U.S., of course."

Halevy reached for the phone. "I must alert the PM immediately. I'll seek the earliest possible appointment to present this material."

"One moment." The white-haired operations director held a finger in the air. "Everything I have seen leads me to believe we can't really depend on the Americans. In fact, the threat of an atomic attack might send them running in the opposite direction."

"What are you driving at?" Halevy's old assertiveness was back.

"I believe we must also prepare a recommendation for how we should respond. The cabinet's going to want to know what we believe is an effective military posture."

"Yes, you're right." Halevy took his hand off the phone. "You have made a good point." He looked at the director of coordination. "Your thoughts?"

"We must prepare a recommendation and plan for a preemptive strike before matters worsen." A *sabra,* a native Israeli, the director was well known for his refusal to retreat, regardless of the size of the adversary. Military comrades nicknamed him the Giant Killer. He no longer looked so young. "What began as a simple punitive raid into the village of Arad has turned into a full-scale assault on the enemy. A national plan of attack should be formulated immediately. We hit them *first.*"

Not far from Arad, a Bedouin family sat inside an old dilapidated tent talking with their distinguished son. The remote wilderness area had its own way of swallowing those who ventured in too far. Only the experienced like Rashid Salah could survive in the arid badlands.

"You are doing well?" Musa asked.

"Of course, of course," the father blew cigarette smoke in the air and shrugged. "Your mother's happier out here anyway. We simply tend the goats and avoid talking with anyone." He laughed. "Of course, no one comes."

"Father, I need your advice. In order to finish this translation, I need to have inspiration from our father, Abraham. Tomorrow we will start again, and I need help." Musa gestured aimlessly, fumbling for words. "Such things are hard for me to understand."

The old man leaned back against a leather-covered pillow and stared into the fire still burning just outside the tent. His wife scurried about, cleaning the pots and utensils. Rashid watched the little flames dance back and forth across the top of the charred sticks.

"Have you studied the Koran?" Rashid asked his son.

"Yes." Musa said little more, hoping to give no offense because of his father's illiteracy. "But I am seeking deeper, more profound understanding."

"Good. Reading the Koran is very good." Rashid nodded. "Perhaps such is the best use of your education. Of course, the Koran is meant to be heard, not read," he justified himself and puffed on his cigarette. "What you must do is seek the guidance that comes from the seventh heaven. In his great night journey from Mecca to Jerusalem, the prophet touched that place and it was there that the Koran was inscribed on golden tablets."

Musa listened attentively. "Have you ever experienced holy insight?"

"I am a simple man. What would I know of such things?" Rashid shook his head and looked at the coarse rug running the length of the tent.

"Sometimes the simple are wiser than the learned, Father. You have spent decades sitting among the goats and pondering life. Please share your thoughts."

Rashid squinted. Cigarette smoke curled up the side of his face and across his yellow-stained moustache. "Often I have thought about the mirages that come when the sun is high and the heat is fierce. For a moment the camel, the sheep, and the lake look real. I would swear they are out there just beyond what I can touch. Suddenly, everything fades and disappears. The sand is empty, and I have been tricked, betrayed by the light. Do you understand?"

Musa puzzled for a moment, not sure where the conversation was going. "You must say more."

"Much that people treasure is an illusion of light. Enormous sums of money are spent on what you call chrome, or a color of paint. The glitter and shine lure the greedy and beckon the foolish like thirsty travelers chase after a lake that isn't there. A person must make sure that what they are seeking is genuine." He winked. "And that it's *really* there."

"How does one know?"

"You must wait patiently, my son. Wait and watch until the illusions fade. Do not rush into anything, but seek to make sure your own eye is single." He patted his chest. "Be suspicious of what you see from afar and have never touched."

Musa reached into the shoulder bag he had brought from his apartment. "I have been reading a book as I searched for insight." He quickly thumbed through the pages. "The author's name is Ibn Arabi." Musa ran his finger across the lines. "Here's something of what he writes. 'Listen. I profess the religion of love. Wherever its caravan turns along the way, that is the belief, the faith I keep.'"

Rashid pondered the words but said nothing.

"Father, we've had many bad experiences with the Jews. Sometimes they cut down our orchards and take the land for a road without paying. Palestinians must use different colored license plates from the Israelis, which makes them easy targets for harassment. Yes, they came to our village and killed people." Musa drew a deep breath and watched his father's face carefully. "But are these not political problems? Are not Jews *as persons* a different matter?"

"Politics makes people crazy." The old man looked out through the opening of the tent and spit in disgust. "Everyone turns into animals."

"Father, even within our religion there is division between the Sunnis and the Shiites. Obviously, opinions greatly differ. I know there are many radicals who use our faith to justify killing and mayhem, but they are not true to the teachings of the Prophet. In my college days, I learned that many religions speak the language of love, not hate."

The old man listened and nodded. "Love is never an illusion. Surely you cannot be misled if you travel in that caravan." He reached for his son's hand.

35

Monday, October 5
Old City, Dormition Abbey

As agreed the previous week, the translators assembled on Monday afternoon to start again. Leah had not gone by the law office and arrived first. Musa bounced down the stairs and was all smiles. She felt him to be unusually warm toward her. Most pleasant. For a change, Father Kelly was the last to come.

"We will forgive you for being late if you have solved the rest of the translation problems," Leah greeted him.

The priest slid down at his usual place at the head of the table. "I'm afraid I haven't given our project much thought," he conceded. "The truth is that I've been working on the problem of getting Michael straightened out." He pulled his half glasses from his pocket. "Much more difficult, I assure you, than making sense out of these languages."

Leah looked again. Nothing had changed about the scruffy goatee, the half glasses now balanced precariously on the large nose. Yet Kelly was different. Perhaps she was projecting her own new resolutions on him, but he certainly sounded more mellow.

Michael folded his hands in front of him and leaned on the table. "In our last meeting I believe we decided to set our houses in spiritual order before we plowed on. How has it gone for everyone else?" He sounded like the cautious diplomat, always letting others play their cards first.

"Very significant." Leah immediately knew she sounded more guarded than she intended. "I spent time with an old friend who is a rabbi. He gave me much to think about."

Musa looked reluctant. "I, too, have sought the spiritual path." He nodded. "Yes, I have given very serious thought to these matters."

"Well!" Kelly beamed. "We are ready to begin."

Leah held up her hand and wiggled her finger mischievously. "And you? How are things in your heart, noble priest?"

Kelly looked pensive for a moment. "I have had a very long weekend. Perhaps I can speak of it more fully later in the session." He adjusted his notes self-consciously. "Need to check a few things here before we start."

Leah took her notebook from her briefcase but watched the priest. The pushiness was gone. He did not seem to treat her as an imposed necessity. Must be a fascinating story there somewhere.

Kelly picked up the tape recorder that had lain on the table through most of the sessions. "I hope today we can come to some final conclusions about the first section. We've been at it long enough that we may want to record insights for transcription."

Musa leaned forward. "I am more than ready to begin. As a matter of fact, I have done some thinking about the end of this section." He opened his notebook. "We have this fascinating combination of Egyptian hieroglyphics, Sumerian, Akkadian, Greek, and Hebrew interwoven into what seems to be a positive prediction, but I think it is to the contrary."

"What do you have, Musa?" Leah scooted her chair closer to his and looked over his shoulder.

"*Sfralisin* or 'seals' in Greek is followed by *kasapu*, Akkadian for 'shall be broken,' and we recognize *Jebus* as being Jerusalem." He looked up and waited for acknowledgment.

Kelly nodded. "As I'm sure we all know, the first mention of Jerusalem is in Egyptian execration texts. They pronounced the name *rushalimum*, whereas in the Tel el-Amarna tablets it is written *Urusalim*. The ancient world seems to have had its own fascination with the city."

"Rabbinic writings indicate that Jerusalem will ultimately extend and rise upward until the city reaches the very throne of divine majesty," Leah added. "Don't Muslims have a similiar view?"

Musa nodded. "We foresee a heavenly Jerusalem coming down to earth. Yes. Christians, Muslims, Jews, all see a correlation between a heavenly and an earthly Jerusalem. A 'divine thread,' if you will. With this in mind, I particularly tried to decipher the last four symbols," Musa continued, pointing to the text.

Kelly looked straight at the table. The wrinkles around his eyes seemed to have deepened. He nodded his head slowly. "I am afraid we have a warning for the end of the sixth millennium that a tragic action will bring terrible consequences."

Leah thought of David's death. Was that not a seal broken? Perhaps she was presumptuous to think of her problems in the same context as this amazing text, but her "sorrow of the ages" began a little over two weeks ago.

Michael cleared his throat and pushed his reading glasses farther up his nose. "I realize we are still struggling with the entire passage, but I believe Musa has taken us to what must be the crux of this message. I agree we have a warning that, amazingly, is for our moment in history. How we finally see the meaning of the first portion is shaped by this business of scrolls being broken. Something terrible being released."

Leah inhaled deeply and silently prayed for inspiration.

"Leah, you are thoughtful," Michael broke in. "Where are you in this struggle?"

The insight slipped from nowhere. She tried to find the words. "Something just occurred to me. What would any of us do if we thought a special instruction had been handed to us to deliver to people centuries from now?" She watched the two men carefully. Both abruptly looked confounded. "No one would keep or make much sense out of a message for people three to six thousand years in the future. The only way they'd pay attention was if it had something in it for them at that particular moment. Right?"

"Brilliant," Kelly mumbled under his breath. "Of course. Christian apocalyptists are always stumbling over this fact. The Apocalypse, the book of Revelation, had to have great meaning for the first readers, or they'd never have kept it in the canon."

"So, what's the payoff for them?" Musa asked.

Leah rubbed her forehead and studied the golden scroll. "Notice we have two sections. It's unusual that the text is broken into two parts. Maybe the second part was originally first . . . or was meant to be read first by the original author."

"Yes!" Kelly's eyes snapped with enthusiasm. "Probably the metal worker inscribing the scrolls had no idea what they meant." He thumbed the table. "He would have been copying off papyrus or a leather scroll, vellum, something of that order."

"Therefore, the second part will actually make the full sense of the section we are working on evident," she concluded.

"Most excellent work." Michael leaned as far forward as possible and nodded vigorously.

"Therefore," Leah continued thinking out loud, "we might as well construct the first portion as best we can, but not worry if the sense is not completely clear." She stopped and stared at Kelly. "Or . . . or . . . the original writer might have actually constructed the text in this way to ultimately emphasize his warning in the first section!"

Kelly pulled at his beard and kept shaking his head. "Leah, you are inspired today." The priest spread several sheets of paper in front of him. "Let's see what we might have here in light of all we are saying." He studied his notes for a second.

"'Behold and tremble.'" Michael stopped. "I sense we should put a period there. Yes, I think that is a complete unit of materials. 'Behold and tremble. The nations come to Jerusalem to make peace with you.'" He cleared his throat again. "I don't have a great reason for it, but I think we should place an 'and' there and tie the lines together. 'Behold and tremble. The nations come to Jerusalem to make peace and you will dance with,' or 'on, the dust of the ridge.'" Michael thought for a moment. "Better, 'you will dance on the heights of Jerusalem.'" He took his glasses off. "Everyone agreed?"

"I think this is correct," Musa said. "What makes this thing so strange is that we have a warning of a false peace. The next section I feel says, 'Celebrate for forty-eight months, but the stones will weep for the millennium.'"

"Yes," Leah interjected. "We have not actually put the sixth-millennium fragment in the right place yet."

Kelly stared at his notes again. "What if . . . what if we said . . . ?" He scribbled something above the line. "'Behold and tremble. In,' or 'On the sixth millennium, nations that come to Jerusalem to make peace . . .'"

"There's the prophetic element!" Leah exclaimed. "But the question is, are we right? Does the date really belong at this point? That's the key question. It might go somewhere else and completely change the meaning."

"I think it should," Musa ventured. "When we add the

breaking of the seals portion, it must be prefaced by the phrase in Greek *khilia ete laloutos*, 'the millennium I spoke of.' Such a modification must refer to the earlier millennia. Therefore the phrase describing six millennia has to come at the beginning."

"Yes. Yes." Kelly's laser concentration took over. "This is precisely so. You see, we have already recognized that the warning of false peace is in some way tied to Jerusalem being divided. Hmm." He paused and stared at the page. "Could the division of Jerusalem be the breaking of the seals? The event that will make the stones weep? Maybe this is the great warning to anyone dividing the city."

Musa's mouth dropped, and he flinched. "What are you saying?"

"I don't really know." Kelly shook his head. "But it would seem the modifying clause for the meaning of the breaking of seals is the partition of the city." He rubbed his chin. "Division will loose the terrors."

Leah immediately noticed the complete change in Musa's countenance. Lips tightened, eye narrowed. He wrung his hands and cracked his knuckles.

"I am not comfortable with that translation," he finally blurted out. "No, no."

"Why?" Kelly asked indifferently. "You see a better rendering?"

"If this is correct, the Palestinians would never have a place here unless they capitulate!" He rolled his eyes. "Or we would be responsible for unleashing unparalleled havoc!" He dropped back in his chair. "Once again, my people become the victims!"

Kelly took off his glasses. "Please, Musa. We are only letting the words be what they are. A scholar doesn't always make a very good politician. We must let the text say what it says. We have to be brutally honest."

"That's easy for you to say," Musa fired back. "You've got nothing at stake in this. For me and my people, it is everything!"

The priest smiled sadly. "No, the matter is not quite as simple as you might think." He reached out and patted Musa's tightly clenched fist. "Perhaps I should be completely honest with both of you." Michael stood up and started walking back and forth in front of the table.

Leah watched the distracted priest. "Are you okay?"

"I don't want you to misunderstand me," Michael began. "Please believe that I have always worked on this project with complete honesty and integrity as a scholar. I have not offered compromised opinions. Do you believe me?"

Leah waited for Musa to nod his agreement and then followed suit. "Of course, your intentions are very clear."

"But I did betray your trust," Michael countered. "Not in what I translated, but I let my superiors in Rome know about this discovery."

Musa leaped from his chair. "You did *what?*"

"Please, please, let me finish." Michael gestured for him to sit down again. "This is one of the matters I wrestled with this entire past weekend."

"What you have done is worse than my uncle Hassan telling my village about this discovery!" Musa jabbed his finger accusingly at Michael.

Leah froze. The missing piece suddenly slipped into place. She could still hear Michael explaining that the scroll was secure and nothing of the text had been leaked to anyone, but his words evaporated in her ears. A new realization gripped her mind. Night after night she had agonized over why David should be caught up in an assassination attempt. Other than Halevy, no one knew they had the scroll. No one could have known . . . unless this Uncle Hassan had told the story. The horrible image she fought to deny filled her mind again. David lay cold on the side of the Mount of Olives *because Musa talked*.

"Please!" Kelly held up his hand. "What I want you to know is that working on this scroll has changed me in a very important way." He stopped and sat back down at the table. "Last week an official from Rome came with the veiled suggestion I use our work to further the political purpose of the Vatican. When I confronted myself, I saw how duplicitous I had been. I want you to know this is the problem I struggled to resolve this weekend," he pleaded.

"You are my friends," the priest continued. "Musa, I pledge absolute fidelity to this project. I turn my back on all political schemes in order to be completely honest in this translation and in its use when our work is done."

"And *your* uncle Hassan told the villagers about this scroll?" Leah asked with seeming objectivity.

"Unfortunately," Musa snapped. "But I—"

"And the village of Arad provoked the terrorists who attacked in Bethlehem?" She abruptly bore down. "The same terrorists that killed my David?"

Musa's dark complexion turned white. A look of startled realization swept over his face. "I meant," he stammered. "What I was trying to explain . . ." He swallowed hard.

Leah felt pain well up from the very center of her, being. The room seemed to tilt, almost to spin. For a moment a wave of nausea swept over her, and she grabbed her mouth. Kelly was saying something, but the words would not register. She felt faint and dizzy.

"Please, I can explain," Musa pleaded.

Leah glanced at Musa. He stared back in shock, his words frozen in his mouth. She tried to organize her notes but could not seem to get the papers together. She could not stand to look at him. She had to get out of there. The chair would not move fast enough. *Kick it back. Run. Just run. Anywhere. Run. Run.*

Later she remembered hearing the chair crash against the floor. The purple knot on her shin testified that she must have tripped on the steps and bruised her leg, but at the time there was no pain. Somehow she had run out of the Abbey and into the parking lot. How she navigated across the city remained a mystery. There had only been blurred street signs, nameless streets, unknown faces, pointless turns in the road. Nothing reconnected until Leah realized she had been sitting in her car for thirty minutes, parked only a block from Adin Scholem's synagogue.

36

Monday, October 5
Old City, Dormition Abbey

For a long time after Leah and then Musa left, Michael sat alone in the basement. He felt disoriented. His attempt at honesty had turned into complete chaos. How could such be? But the issue was not one of fault. Matters were far beyond something so simple and meaningless as blame. Leah had been broken in half, like a pencil stepped on by a careless boy stomping out of the room.

He placed the tape recorder back in its unused position, gathered his notes, and slowly rose to his feet. Leah's papers were still in the same disarray she left them. For a moment he looked at Musa's empty chair. The poor man had left totally distraught. The slip of the tongue was innocent enough, but Musa clearly knew his family's part in disclosing the fatal information that brought David's death.

The priest shook his head. Of course, Musa's blunder was a mistake. Never! Never would the good man intend such a terrible thing. But then again, had any of them actually intended malice? Ever? In a strange, unexpected way, each was a victim of circumstances far beyond their control. Life seemed to be filled with little accidents that changed everything. A word said here. A chance meeting there. A conversation overheard. Discovery of some lost or obscured fact and one's destiny was turned upside down and inside out.

Over the weekend Michael had reflected on God's sovereign design in bringing the scroll to light and bringing the translators together. But could so much hurt and heartache really be part of God's plan? The price of preserving God's message, if indeed, that was what they were doing, was simply too high.

Michael turned off the light switch at the top of the stairs and locked the door behind him. Instead of going to his room, he turned in the direction of the sanctuary. Tourists were already browsing around, nosing in every corner, but he slipped into a pew and sat quietly. A few strangers could not possibly interrupt this morning's journey into the troubled depths of his soul. He stared at the ceiling and studied the ornate artistry of line and color, symbol, and sign.

Magnificent as always, the nave and chancel offered their gifts of splendor, the comfort of beauty, as the starting place for his overdue spiritual odyssey. As works of art go, the church would always be worthy of any tourist's time. Today, he only wanted the harmony of design and pigment to minister to what his eyes had already seen far too much of, the disorder of distrust and doubt. Perhaps the artists' aesthetics would offer the consolations of beauty where now he only felt the ugliness of death and betrayal.

And what strange, unexpected circumstance had made him a priest in such a place as this? Was this the working of a sovereign God, or just a quirk of fate? The craggy face of the old pastor of the small Church of St. Michael, Father Kelly's childhood church, returned. Father Patrick O'Reilly had probably been exiled to a poor parish in Roxbury, New York, as a last resort for both him and the church. His sermons were as confused as the man was most of the time, but no one could fault the Irish immigrant for goodness. Like everyone else in Michael's world, Father O'Reilly was far past his prime.

Again strange circumstances. Michael was born the late and final child in the life of Leslie and Alice Kelly, lifelong Roxbury residents. Michael, the unexpected, the unplanned, must have been quite a jolt at the time the elder Kellys were thinking of plans for a secure retirement. Of course, they were good, attentive parents, but his appearing was not exactly an epiphany. Michael was summer come in the late fall.

One Sunday morning while Michael was vesting as the altar boy, Father Kelly had said, "Me boy, have ya thought on the priesthood? Nothing can give parents such joy as knowing they've raised a priest." The old man winked. "Ya'd be a fine one, lad."

Michael remembered how overjoyed his mother was at the suggestion. Probably, Father Patrick had already primed that pump before Michael got home. For the first time his father appeared genuinely impressed with something he was about.

The bubble of memories burst, and Michael's thoughts were diverted when one of the old monks entered from the side and shuffled to a side-altar. *Brother Thomas must have lived in the Abbey for fifty years*, Michael reflected. As was typical of the monk's unassuming piety, he dropped to his knees to say his prayers from the breviary. Michael admired the simple uncomplicated faith of such a thoroughly good man. With all of his own learning and skepticism, he was not worthy to buckle the old man's sandals, even though Thomas had little of which the world could take note.

Of course, that was the problem. The only thing that ever seemed to get his aging parents' attention was achievement. Never did he doubt his mother's love; they just did not connect much of anywhere except when he brought home the report card. Papa often seemed worried about whether there would be enough money for the future. However, achievement always got a smile. Yes, the priesthood was the ideal solution. What better gift could be offered to Leslie and Alice Kelly than the priesthood? And so he had forsaken the body of a woman, the passion of love, the joy of parenthood.

His birthright as a male was sold for the title of Father, the office of Doctor of the Church.

Not so long ago Leslie and Alice had been laid side by side in the Roxbury Cemetery surrounding old St. Michael's. Their approval certainly should not be needed anymore. All debts now canceled and paid—and yet, it was not so.

No, a funeral or two did not complete things quite so neatly. As a matter of fact, his old passionate yearning for affirmation had been transferred lock, stock, and barrel to the Church.

As the multicolored light of the stained glass settled around him, Michael saw the whole matter with greater clarity than he had ever known in his life. St. Peter's, Rome, the Pontifical Academy, and Cardinal Mottola were nothing more than the reincarnation of Father Patrick, Roxbury, Alice, and Leslie; all come again in new shape and size. What Michael called academic excellence was not much more than a grade school boy presenting all A's to his parents.

Although the realization had been unfolding for a long time, it was no less unsettling. His confessor probably would not call the problem sin. A contemporary psychologist would suggest only misplaced expectation, compensation for low self-esteem, no doubt. But it was sin, the sin of separation. His pride of heart, his idolatrous lust for affirmation, had fractured any genuine sense of integrity and made him a pawn in the endless game of the search for adoration.

Such issues were not solved in a confession booth or by lying prostrate before the high altar. Only in the quiet of his soul could he put to death that narcissistic self-love, that hidden piece of his own psyche that considered itself to be exceptional, entitled. He must embrace the common and settle only for his humanity. Rather than scaling the heights of fame, the true calling was to be only a child of God like Brother Thomas and Father Patrick. Not being the exceptional man but simple and single unity with all humanity must be enough for him if he was ever to be whole.

He wept for that which he could not define. The light from the clerestory windows seemed to mingle with his tears in a great healing wash. And then, as it had happened two days before during his lonely reflection in the abbot's office, a verse of Scripture came to Michael's mind. A verse from John's Gospel saying that Jesus is the light of the world. How did it go? He struggled to recall the exact words until he thought he had it right. "I am the light of the world. He who follows Me shall not walk in darkness, but have the light of life."

Jesus, the Light of the World. Until the past few days Michael Kelly had never put much stock in the claim. He had remained indefinite and blurry about what or who Christ was. As the abbot had discerned, his scholarly diet ran to devouring the Jesus of history, the Jesus of Bible stories to be dissected and disproved when possible. Jesus was a great intellectual challenge, a puzzle to be solved, but the Light of the World? That was a very different question.

And yet at this moment the light bathing his tearstained face seemed infinitely more meaningful than his lifetime of critical study. One could not capture the significance of light on a piece of paper or describe its power with mere words.

The apostle John had written that the light became flesh and shined into our darkness. This light was not an idea to be debated and discussed. It was an experience to receive. Michael closed his eyes and let the Light of the World come into his darkness. For once he pushed the old questions aside and quietly dwelled in the shadow of the Almighty.

And there, in the serene solitude of the sanctuary, the doubting priest laid down his disbelief and enountered his Savior anew. Jesus, the resurrection and the life. Jesus, the way, the truth, the life. "No one comes to the Father except through Me." More words of Jesus, as recorded by John, the beloved apostle, streamed into Michael's consciousness as clearly as the rays of light beaming through the high windows of the Abbey. Perhaps the words had been hidden in his heart, after all. Buried under all the academic clutter had lain the simple truth he was seeking, just as Abbot Hoffman had indicated.

His mind illuminated by his encounter with the Living Word, Michael suddenly saw the rest quite clearly. For reasons he could not identify, his conversation with Cardinal Mottola had left him deeply depressed. The man had offered him the yellow brick road to Rome, but at that exact moment he had found a rock in his shoe. Michael remembered returning to the basement in a nasty, glum mood, the opposite of what he should have felt. The reason had been as obscure to him as it surely was to Leah and Musa.

How could he have missed something so appallingly obvious? Mottola actually bore a significant resemblance to his father. All those years he had studied with the man, it had never occurred to him why Mottola's affirmation was so profound, so satisfying. Michael could hardly believe his own insight. Leslie Kelly had come back from the grave, wearing a scarlet cassock, and once again Michael reached out, hoping for a word of absolution from the perpetual struggle to be worthy.

When he finally arose out of the pew with trembling hand, Michael Kelly knew what he must do. He silently found his way to Brother Thomas, who was just finishing his prayers. The old man smiled kindly and struggled to his feet. Michael offered him assistance before falling to his knees and burying his face in his hands.

Life would no longer be shaped by circumstance, by happenings, by anything vaguely resembling fate. The Light would be the compass, the gyroscope, the window to the future. He looked up at the crucifix above the altar in adoration.

"O crucified Son of God, no man is worthy to follow You who does not first die to himself. I empty my heart of pride and ambition. Come, Light of the World. Illumine my path. Let me no longer walk in darkness, but grant me the light of life."

Leah waited two hours for Adin Scholem to return. Most of the time she watched his followers scurry in and out of the synagogue. Women chattered, children played, yeshiva students argued and life went on as if David Rosenberg were still alive, working at his law offices or busy somewhere in the city. Leah felt annoyed that none of them were in the least offended that her beloved lay on the Mount of Olives.

Of course, such feelings were nonsense but, then again, everything was irrelevant, meaningless without rhyme or reason. When Adin returned, the sun had gone down and evening prayers had ended. She poured out her disbelief and disillusionment over Musa's role in what caused the assassination. Adin listened with compassionate intensity, but his students interrupted them five times, breaking her story up in fragments and pieces. Finally, he stomped outside where he barked orders and then returned, locking the office door.

"We will not be bothered again," he said. "I promise."

Leah looked at this strange little man who had once been attracted to her. The thick glasses that made his eyes appear like marbles, the shaggy beard, the *tallit* over shabby clothes. What could one say? Only this. Adin had become a holy man, a man without guile, a prototype of a Jeremiah, an Amos.

The rabbi reached for her hand and then abruptly crossed his arms over his chest. "So, what are you to do with this terrible information? The friend betrayed you? Yes?" Adin covered his mouth with his long fingers. "Maybe no. Possibly a blunder beyond the man's control. We have a tragic drama playing itself out before our eyes. A play in which all the actors are victims? No?"

Leah shrugged, unconvinced.

"And the Holy One of Israel apparently has abandoned us all?" Adin hunched his shoulder and put a closed fist to his mouth, gently touching his lips several times. He pointed to the open copy of the Scriptures lying on his cluttered desk and closed his eyes. "How deserted lies the city, once so full of people! How like a widow is she, who once was great among the nations," he quoted from memory with eyelids clamped shut. "Bitterly she weeps at night, tears are upon her cheeks. 'Vanity of vanities,' says the preacher. 'All is vanity.'" He shook his head in despair.

"What are you saying, Adin?"

"Only feeling the pain, my dear Leah." The rabbi's eyes filled with tears as he spoke. "And being aware of the only thing that you can do if you want relief."

"Which is *what*?"

"Forgive. You must forgive this Musa."

Leah caught her breath. He would have more easily hit her with a board.

"You have no choice unless you want to drink the poison of hate, the elixir that turns the soul to stone."

"How can I do such a thing?" Leah pleaded. "I don't think it's possible. My husband is dead! To forgive is betrayal."

Adin shook his head fiercely and then held up his finger. "Isaiah gave us the better way. What was it that he learned through the light shining into his darkness? He heard these words. 'This is the person to whom I will look. The one who is humble and contrite and trembles at my word.'" The rabbi moved his finger closer to her face. "Forgiveness is the strength of the righteous, the *tzadikim*."

The best she could do was try to find a window to look outside, somewhere, anywhere away from this advice. Leah ended up silently staring at her feet.

"Let me tell you something I learned from the great rabbis." Adin spoke softly with gentleness. "Jerusalem is a special place where heaven and earth meet. The purposes of the divine are forever focused on this place. Because this is true, the desires of the human heart are exposed in the Holy City as no place else. Every moral action is magnified, and the result intensified." He held the sides of his face like an old woman peering into the mystery of life and death. "Who can stand before such a thing?"

His words shook Leah out of her retreat. "What in the world are you telling me, Adin?"

"Light and darkness collide and explode in this Holy City. It's always been a play of betrayals and bitter disappointments. The eternal struggle between evil and good has been, is, and will finally be fought out on this playing field." The rabbi smiled sadly. "And now the battleground is in your heart, Leah. Despicable anger, unforgiveness, and goodness cannot coexist. One must win; the other must fall. What will it be?"

Leah was surprised that she suddenly thought about the scroll. Everything Adin was saying applied, not only to her, but to something in that strange message. She felt strangely relieved.

"Forgiveness brings the light that drives out darkness," Adin instructed. "Reconciliation heals one's own soul."

Leah swallowed hard and tried to find some adequate response. None came.

"I once had to forgive you for not loving me as I wanted," Adin confided sadly. "Oh, yes, quite silly. The broken heart of a schoolboy with no right to expect anything." He waved his long fingers in the air as if removing cobwebs from the past. "I confess because of my own inordinate need to say such a thing in order to be free of its tentacles." He blushed. "Now I know the Holy One used this scenario to bring me to my life work as a scholar, a rabbi, a eunuch for the truth."

Leah smiled compassionately. "You really believe that the purposes of God find their final fulfillment here, in Jerusalem, in our hometown?"

Adin nodded his head solemnly. "The Romans crucified this Jesus of Nazareth. The Christians in turn afflicted us because of what the Romans did." He closed his eyes in bitter recollection. "The Palestinians, the Arabs, tormented the sons and daughters of Zion for coming home." Adin abruptly opened his eyes and stared deeply into hers. "And have we also not tormented the Palestinians? Where does it stop, unless each one of us resolves to forgive? The hope for tomorrow begins or ends in what you do with what is in your heart."

37

Tuesday, October 6
Jerusalem, Prime Minister's Office

Avraham Halevy knew that the cabinet had met late into Monday evening. Reasoning that the prime minister must surely be exhausted, he did not expect to be summoned so early Tuesday morning. When the 7:00 A.M. call came at his home for an 8:00 meeting, Halevy was caught off guard but quickly prepared and immediately left for the prime minister's office in Jerusalem. As soon as he arrived, Halevy was ushered into the private offices.

Ten minutes passed and no one appeared. A sudden demand to appear and then a delay could only mean something big was afoot. Halevy glanced around the office at the pictures, the usual mementos carefully chosen to give a personal touch to an impersonal room. He did not really like this prime minister much and expressed his opinions only to the closest associates. Such thoughts had a way of slipping out. After all was said and done, the prime minister remained the boss, and one did not tweak the nose of whoever sat in the big chair behind the front desk.

The door opened and a security officer stepped in and nodded politely. Avraham knew the man well and winked. The prime minister briskly marched in, looking the military man he had been. "Shalom," he said perfunctorily.

"Shalom," Avraham answered and bowed his head respectfully.

"Please sit down, Avraham." The prime minister immediately settled behind his desk. He instructed the security officer, "Give our friend the file with the notes of the cabinet meeting and then leave us."

Avraham quickly thumbed through the pages and summarized the contents. About twenty sheets of carefully detailed outlines and notes of direction. "You've been very busy," he observed casually.

"It's all your fault." The head man looked down his nose almost accusingly. "You started the ball rolling with the business about this new Islamic Revolutionary Front. The cabinet was more than a little concerned."

"Good. That's my job."

"We aren't taking the threat casually." The prime minister pointed at the report. "We've got a plan now. I want you to fully understand the intent of the three-pronged attack we're going to make on these crazies," he lectured Halevy. "The Mossad is crucial in the completing of this grand design. The entire cabinet fully concurs and believes succeeding governments will stay the course we've plotted. Understand?"

Avraham shook his head.

The prime minister suddenly cursed and shook his fist at Halevy. "We will not give up Jerusalem! I don't care what the Europeans, Russians, Palestinians, Americans, the Arab League, anyone says. We won't give one more inch of land!"

For a moment Avraham felt relieved. He smiled. "Excellent."

The prime minister looked surprised and then returned the smile. "Good! At least we're on the same page. Both of us know that the United States government can only be trusted up to a point. The White House still lives by the creed, 'It's the economy, stupid.' If the Arab world breaks the economic back of the U.S., then the current administration's close relationship with Israel becomes expendable. Right?"

"Arab nations understand this principle well," Avraham answered. "When push comes to shove, Wall Street owns the day. The Americans won't stand by us if the cost is too great."

"Correct. Self-interest is the cornerstone of their foreign policy. If this IRF group puts pressure on the U.S. to divide Jerusalem, or to turn some portion of control over to them, the Americans will capitulate in the end. Oh, they'll try to make themselves look good to us for a time, and then they'll fold."

"Nevertheless," the prime minister pushed on, "you will immediately alert our friends and allies that the IRF now has nuclear power and is completing their arsenal. We will not tolerate such a development, and the Western powers had better take note of our posture."

Avraham studied the man across from him. Tanned, graying, slightly overweight, the prime minister had more determination and sheer guts than one might have thought. Avraham would have to reevaluate his opinion of the leader.

"The gravity of this policy ought to cause the Western nations to be a bit more temperate toward us and a great deal more supportive of our position."

For a moment Avraham pondered his response. The right words were everything in a conversation of this magnitude. "What if, God forbid, one of those bombs went off in New York City or Los Angeles? I'd think there would be a radical change in perspective." He shook his head.

"I'm concerned about tiny Israel—what if a bomb went off in

Tel Aviv or Haifa? Surely they would not be insane enough to try to blow up Jerusalem," the prime minister growled. "Point two of our plan is calculated to prevent such a possibility. We will let it be known that we will make the Samson Option operational if necessary . . . if conventional means cannot guarantee our survival."

The Mossad chief stared straight ahead. He recognized, of course, the code name for the ultimate equalizer, Israel's nuclear capability. Probably no other nation knew for a fact that Israel possessed a low-yield neutron bomb. Some suspected; none knew for sure. If pushed to the brink of annihilation, Israel had the capacity to bring the roof down on the Middle East— just as Samson had destroyed the Philistines, at the cost of his own life. Developed during the Cold War, Israel's nuclear strategy called for fighting with conventional weapons as long as possible. But if faced with imminent destruction, and if the U.S. or other allies could not, or would not, intervene to prevent it . . . in the end, Israel would use its nuclear power.

Avraham pulled nervously at his shirt collar as the prime minister continued.

"We must prepare for a preemptive strike. Understand? None of us may be around to retaliate if this IRF hits us first. Avraham, you might someday be the person that tells me to push the button. Are you up to it?"

"Sir." Avraham stopped and caught his breath. "My training, my work, my commitment have prepared me for such a moment, and yet I must confess that I tremble before such a decision."

"As well you should!" The prime minister swore again. "I don't care how badly your people failed, I could not possibly make such a decision without your advice. If the moment arrives, you must be ready." He looked at Arvaham like a schoolteacher chastening a naughty boy. "Coming in here and handing me your resignation! Let's not do that again."

Daniel Levy's face came to mind, and Avraham thought of David Rosenberg. Battle images from the Six Day War emerged from the depths of his soul, and he saw men falling on either side of him. The smell of smoke and the stench of death filled his nose. Words could never express what he had seen and felt. But a nuclear attack on his nation? Unthinkable. He tightened his jaw and made a small salute.

"The third part of the plan is this Zechariah Project. I know your people are also completely on top of the plans. Where are we in this thing?"

For the first time, Avraham smiled. "Absolutely one of my favorite little assignments. Yes, everything is in place."

"Brief me on how it works."

Trying to keep a professional demeanor, Avraham fought back a grin. "Our man in Krasnoyarsk has now worked his way to the top and is the confidant of the local crime boss, a former KGB assassin named Ivan Kremikov. Our agent's family has been persecuted like all the rest of the Jews. Alexei Izhevsk's father starved to death in a Siberian labor camp. Some years ago, Alexei became an operative for us and stayed behind rather than make *aliya* to Israel. Kremikov thinks Alexei is playing the double agent for him." Avraham laughed. "He's our double agent."

"Excellent." The prime minister picked up his phone. "Send in some coffee and a bagel. I haven't eaten since last night." He hung up. "Go on. How does this fit together?"

"The Zechariah Project is so secret that only I and two other officers know of the existence of Alexei Izhevsk. Through him we have complete knowledge of what is happening with the former Soviet arsenal. Further, Kremikov thinks Alexei is working an angle to line both of their pockets and has no idea of Alexei's real intent. We know the Russian mafia has completed the deal with the IRF. Money has switched hands, and the nuclear device is being prepared for delivery.

"However, the critical mechanism has been replaced with our own fabricated computer chips. Everything will read perfectly until the bomb is set for detonation. At that moment, the electrical circuits will malfunction, burning everything up and exposing the saboteurs to extreme nuclear danger. The radicals spent millions and will only come away with junk and the possibility of frying their own people."

The prime minister sighed in relief. "You, me, the other two officers, we're the only ones who know that there's actually one less nuclear weapon out there than the rest of the world thinks?"

"Yes."

The prime minister massaged his temples. "Good. We will have our little secret." He sighed again. "Unfortunately, our enemy's capacity to destroy us is no less significant." The PM looked straight into Avraham's eyes. "Unless, of course, you and your people prevail."

Avraham stood up. "Your three-point plan will be fully operational within the next twenty-four hours. You may assure the cabinet of our complete dedication in the matter."

The prime minister nodded. "I know you haven't always agreed with my positions, Halevy. Politics is like that." He rubbed his neck and stretched. "But you're a pro, the best. Thank you. Go home and see your wife. I'm sure she misses you." He sounded genuinely grateful.

"Misses me? Not with her aim. Hits every time."

The prime minister stood and offered his hand. "Consider this assignment to be your sealed orders. Done and finished. If the hour comes that we must break the seal, there will be no turning back."

Clutching the file, Avraham hurried out of the building. The plan was masterful, deadly. High-stakes poker played Cold War–style. Winner take all.

38

Wednesday, October 7
Jerusalem, Kiryat Wolfson

Leah heard the phone but tried to ignore it. She pulled the pillow over her face. Finally, after six rings, she reached out from under the covers and picked it up.

"Sha-lo-o-m?"

"Leah? Sounds like I woke you up. Sorry."

"Michael? Michael Kelly?"

"I tried to get you several times yesterday but couldn't seem to connect."

Leah sat up in bed. The digital clock said 9:00. Sleep was now an impossibility. "Needed the day off to try and sort things out a bit." She looked around the bedroom. Clothes thrown everywhere.

"I understand." Michael sounded like a friend, not Father Kelly, the priest. "I can't tell you how sorry I am about what happened Monday. While I certainly am not able to feel your depth of pain, I know the shock was staggering."

"Turned out to be a rough day." The best she could muster.

"Are you okay?"

"Who knows?" Leah wasn't sure. At that moment drowsiness still held her captive. She shouldn't have taken two sleeping pills. "I suppose I'm a bit numb," she conceded.

"Yes. Yes, of course." Michael cleared his throat. "Leah, I want you to know something important. I spent much of yesterday with Musa. Can I be honest without violating your feelings?"

She puzzled for a second. When had Michael Kelly ever checked out her feelings before barging in? Then again, what was he going to drop on her now? She shuddered and felt more awake.

"I don't want to intrude if this isn't the right time," he continued.

"Please feel free to tell me anything you wish, Michael. I'm sure there's nothing left that will surprise me."

"Without taking anything away from your distress, I must tell you that Musa is devastated. Some time ago, he figured out that his loudmouth uncle had put the wheels into deadly motion. Apparently, old man Salah told his brother about the discovery without Musa's knowledge. He's been holding this terrible secret inside only with the greatest agony."

For a moment Leah wanted to say, "Good, great, I hope he strangles on it," but she fought back the impulse. "I see," she concluded.

"Yesterday I watched the man weep because of the grief he caused you. Please believe me. Musa is terrified to face you again."

"Me?" The idea surprised her. "Really?" Leah only thought in terms of *her* dread of ever encountering *him*.

"Musa is ready to flee to the desert and disappear forever up one of those wadis running into the Dead Sea." Michael sounded genuinely worried and concerned. "He's very depressed. I honestly fear for his state of mind if we don't get this thing turned around quickly."

Leah shook her head. Apparently there was something left in the universe to surprise her. "What are you suggesting?"

"I am calling today as an agent of reconciliation, Leah. No one could be critical if you never spoke to this man again. I would understand, but at the same time I am hoping that healing is still possible . . . for both your sakes."

She took a deep breath and looked at David's picture on the dresser and then glanced up in the mirror. Her reflection was equally disconcerting. Hair in every direction, frazzled. She looked unstrung. Dark circles under her eyes told their own tale. She quickly looked away. A painting of a medieval rabbi instructing young boys in a village synagogue hung on the opposite wall. David had collected it years ago. The rabbi could be Adin Scholem.

"You still there, Leah?"

"Oh, Michael. I know what I should do. What I ought to say but . . . but . . . I don't know if I'm up to it."

"Leah, I've searched my soul in the last several days and I can tell you it's not been pleasant. Musa is literally turned inside out in contrition. Look at us. This scroll business has become a trip to purgatory that simply won't stop. None of us can really walk away. We're stuck with one another. What else can we do?"

Leah closed her eyes. "Okay," she said through her teeth. "I suppose this confrontation has to happen some time or the other." Kicking the covers back, she swung her feet to the floor. "What do you have in mind, Mr. Diplomat?"

"Well . . . actually"—Michael's hesitancy betrayed his old calculating self—"I was thinking of gathering immediately after lunch in our work area."

"And then we can get right back to the translation after our little chat."

Michael cleared his throat. "I wouldn't be averse to working later, but the matter at hand must take precedence."

Leah shook her head and couldn't help smiling. "Oh, Michael some things change; some never change. It certainly won't be easy, but I'll be there at one o'clock sharp. I'm not promising anything, though . . . Think your boy can make it?"

"I'll be on the phone to him immediately after we hang up, and I'll convince Musa you're not coming armed with a .45 caliber Smith and Wesson."

"Are you sure? I might take one look at him and say, 'Make my day.'"

"What?" Michael's voice raised an octave.

Leah laughed. "Never take women for granted, Michael. You never know what we're capable of."

"I, I don't understand," the priest stammered.

"Try. The effort would be good for you." She hung up. Leah chuckled and looked in the mirror again. "Oh, Adin! How did you ever talk me into this?"

"You have another translation session this afternoon?" the abbot asked.

"We hope to start again," Michael said. "Things have been a bit rocky lately."

"Speaking of bumps, I understand a big announcement is coming from the Americans." The abbot reached for the power switch on the small television in his office. "We have time to catch the headlines before lunch if we act quickly."

Michael glanced at his watch and settled into a desk chair in front of the screen. The volume came up as a commercial faded. A middle-aged Israeli sat behind a news desk, holding a manuscript. "Looks like our timing is on the money."

"The entire region is buzzing this morning following the call by the American president for a Middle-Eastern Peace

Conference on the final status of Jerusalem." Scenes of Washington, D.C., and the president walking to a microphone covered the screen. "Citing new fears over the possibility of renewed military confrontation, the president forcefully stated his belief that the ultimate bone of contention is the official status of the ancient city." His statement was followed by comments from the secretary of state. The portly woman indicated the United States considered all options open and up for discussion.

A picture of Israel's prime minister took center stage. "The prime minister's office issued an immediate response, noting that Jerusalem remains the eternal capital of all Jews and that status is non-negotiable. He also expressed concern about the context of such an international conference. However, the Vatican's secretary of state quickly issued a statement indicating strong support for further discussion of the status of Jerusalem. Turning now to regional news . . ."

The abbot switched off the television. "Things are warming up."

Michael stared at the blank screen. "Maybe more than any of us can possibly grasp. Yes, we are coming to an eternal crossroads running through this city."

"Really? You don't have to be *that* dramatic." The abbot sloughed off Michael's comment. "Can't be anything more than just another international hot air venting contest."

The priest followed the abbot down the hall, listening to his running commentary on the news but thinking about the message of the scroll. He found it equally difficult to focus on the conversations going on around him during the meal and kept glancing at his watch. As soon as politely possible, he dismissed himself and left.

As his footsteps echoed off the stone walls of the Abbey, the opening words of the scroll seemed to ring out in rhythm with his pace. "Behold and tremble! Behold and tremble!" Could the scroll's warning about nations coming to Jerusalem pretending to make peace be any more timely?

Father Kelly slipped into the sanctuary, knelt, and said a prayer for the afternoon meeting. It was a new habit for him, but it felt right, especially in light of the difficult meeting ahead. He then went downstairs five minutes early to put everything in order. The light was already on. To his consternation, Musa waited in his usual chair.

"Hey, old friend, how long have you been here?"

Musa looked up slowly. "I came early lest I lose my nerve and not show at all." He hung his head. "I don't think I can face the woman."

The priest put his arm around Musa's shoulders and gave him a hug. "I understand. We're in a tough place."

"You sure she's coming?"

"Sometimes I don't think I understand one thing going on in that woman's head," Michael conceded, "but I feel certain she will be here on time today."

Musa gritted his teeth. "If Hassan had only kept his mouth shut, none of this would have happened."

The door at the top of the steps opened. Musa clasped both hands together tightly, and Michael turned slowly toward the sound.

Dressed in blue jeans, casual blouse, and a stylish black leather jacket, Leah smiled perfunctorily and put her purse on the table. "Good afternoon, gentlemen," she said politely.

Michael realized how attractive Leah was with her raven hair pulled back smartly in a French roll. The makeup did not quite cover a blue tinge under her eyes, but she was unquestionably a beautiful woman.

"Hello," Musa answered and swallowed before quickly looking away.

"Perhaps we could all sit down." Michael slipped to the head of the table like the chairman of the board.

Leah found her regular place but said nothing.

"I know this is an unusually difficult moment." Michael scrutinized both faces carefully. "Leah, your willingness to come is most admirable."

She tossed her head slightly and shrugged.

"Musa, I've heard your heart and know this isn't any easier for you." Michael searched for a key to break the logjam. "The tragic struggles tearing this land apart seem to have taken flesh in us. I feel that if we could just—"

"I'm so sorry," Musa abruptly blurted out. "I wouldn't have wished David's death for the world, much less participate in anything to cause it to happen." He started to sob. "My father doesn't even know about the attack. I couldn't tell him lest he would make the connection with Hassan." His voice cracked. "It would kill him to think our family even indirectly caused anyone's death, much less David's." Tears streamed down his face. "The Rosenbergs did nothing but try to help us. Always! David's father was the fairest man we ever knew. David was trying to help me. He was our friend. Then, then," he said choking on the words, "such a terrible end because of stupidity, arrogance." His body shook, and he held his hands in front of him, locked in supplication. "David was good to me. I will take this tragedy to my grave." He threw his head into his arms and sobbed bitterly. "You can never forgive me." The dirge arose as a desperate confession.

Michael stared at the broken man. Tears came to his eyes, but there was nothing left that he could say to either person. He pulled at his goatee and glanced at Leah out of the corner of his eye.

She sat there, staring across the table, her countenance like an unadorned wall. And then a tear started a winding trail down the side of her cheek, her forehead furrowed, her lip quivered. Leah looked up at the ceiling, caught her breath, and slowly eased out of her chair. She walked around the table and put her hand gently on Musa's head.

In all the times they'd been together, Michael did not remember ever seeing Leah touch Musa. The Arab jumped slightly and looked up, surprised not to see anyone across from him.

"We must make an end of it." Leah's voice wavered. "No more, no more retribution."

Musa's eyes widened in dismay.

"Nothing can bring David back," Leah agonized. "What difference does it make who holds the title to Jerusalem if we're all dead?" She gently patted his shoulder. "We must learn to live together, or we'll all die together."

Michael shook his head in consternation and felt a knot tightening in his throat. He looked at Musa's shaking form. The man slowly turned and looked up, not fully comprehending what he heard her say.

"Regardless of our mistakes, we all do the best we can." Leah spoke directly to Musa. "You didn't intend us harm. I don't hold you accountable." Leah reached out and gently wiped a tear from the side of his face. "Please forgive yourself, Musa. David would insist on it."

Musa rubbed his forehead and ran his hand through his hair. He opened his mouth, but nothing came out. He reached out feebly for something that wasn't there.

Leah squeezed his hand. "Be at peace, Musa. *Shalom alecha.*"

"*Alayich shalom*, Leah," Musa replied in a broken voice.

"Yes, God's shalom to all of us," Michael said. "Now we can go in peace."

39

Wednesday, October 7
Old City, Dormition Abbey

Michael glanced at his watch. "It's two-thirty. Ready to plow into the last section." He looked at Leah and Musa, hoping for enthusiasm, or at least resoluteness.

The priest bit his lip. Shifting from the intensity of personal reconciliation to the work of translation had not been easy even with an hour of conversation, adjustment, probing to see if things were truly back on track and the atmosphere safe.

"We've learned so much from the first portion that it shouldn't be so difficult to get the rest in order," Musa said. "I'm ready to go." He took out a piece of paper and a pencil to record their conclusions.

Leah nodded her approval.

"I suppose we've all been fudging just a bit." Michael grinned as he talked. "How could we not look ahead?"

Leah picked up her unopened file from a day earlier. "As a matter of fact, I have given a little thought to the first introductory sentence. Of course, we must read right to left as we've been doing, but the combination of Akkadian, hieroglyphics, and Hebrew form a sort of introduction to the whole message. *Barru* in Akkadian is both 'I,' and 'king.' Next the combination of Hebrew and Egyptian words proclaims 'of,' or, 'from,' and then the expression we all know, *Salem,* which means 'peaceful' and was the early name of Jerusalem. There it is. That's our context for the whole document. The King of Salem. The City of Peace, Jerusalem, is the sender, the source of the message."

Michael beamed. "No question about it! We're looking at the Donation of Melchizedek."

Leah used the laser pointer to underline the Akkadian *seqru.* "Here's the crucial word. We find here a combination of possibilities, but I believe they must be taken as a whole, a concept, more than a single word."

"And . . . and?" Musa leaned over the table.

"The word means 'behest,' or 'command,'" Leah continued, "but it also means 'to name.' So, this King of Salem is going to command that *something* be given or left as an inheritance and yet, at the same time, he is naming it in much the same way that the book of Genesis has Adam and Eve naming the animals."

Kelly nodded his head slowly. "Yes, for the Hebrews to name something was to describe its essence, to clarify the meaning of its identity."

"Which means," Musa broke in, "the king is commenting on the meaning of this gift as well as who owns it. Adds a special dimension to the document. A religious dimension."

"Definitely," Leah agreed. "We must draw this conclusion because of what follows. We have the Akkadian *esirtu,* meaning 'holy ground' or a 'sanctuary.'"

Michael pointed at the next line. "Even though we've been considering the political dimensions of this document, the last section clarifies the first, telling us that everything must actually be seen in a religious context." Michael leaned back in his chair. "Once again, we enter into the uniqueness of the ancient world. Nothing is secular; everything is sacred. We can't slice the world into pieces as we've done in this age of science."

Musa nodded knowingly. "For all our so-called sophistication, we're far more fragmented than they were. Time and eternity, politics and religion, were far more of a seamless garment, an essential unity in which the purposes of the divine prevailed in this world."

"Here we have the big word." Michael pointed to the scroll. "We have the early Hebrew form of *Yehova Yireh*, the 'All-seeing One,' or God."

Leah picked up the pointer. "The connecting terms in Hebrew and Greek indicate that a pronouncement, an intent, or thought is being expressed. So, we have something like the King of Salem, the city of peace, saying that he is going to say something or give something that reflects the very thoughts or intents of the divinity that we must identify as the God of the Hebrews."

"I've caught some words here that are familiar to me." Musa took the pointer from Leah. "*Jed Medu* means 'declares' and the Egyptian *en* means 'to.' This king is declaring his message to someone, but I don't get the next word."

"*Kissatu* is Akkadian for 'all,'" Leah said, "but 'all' in this context means all of creation. The king is telling the entire world his message."

"I think I've got the next part." Michael's laser-like concentration kicked in. "We have a combination of Akkadian and Hebrew saying the city, or the inner city, is the belonging or possession of *hu*, or 'him.'"

Musa stopped scribbling. "And who is 'him'?" Musa asked. "The king?"

"I don't think so," Kelly answered. "I've got a strange hunch where this is going." He looked thoughtfully at Leah. "Ever see this word used before?"

"The Hebrew structure of *hu* takes us to a different conclusion," Leah replied. "The 'him' referred to is none other than God Himself."

"I don't understand." Musa had a quizzical look.

"This ancient king of Salem was pronouncing a remarkable idea to the world and all creation," Kelly explained. "The City of Peace belonged to him in only a limited sense. Apparently, the king was passing on to Abraham the trusteeship of what the divine had first bestowed on him, and like wise, the trusteeship has been passed on through the centuries." Michael took a deep breath. "Friends, here's the astonishing message. 'Jerusalem belongs to God . . . and God alone.'"

Leah and Musa looked at each other and then back at Kelly.

"But what does that mean? I don't see it." Leah also looked puzzled.

Musa frowned. "Me either."

"Before my very eyes sit the two sides of Abraham's family. I am looking at the descendants of Isaac and Ishmael. Each of you comes with open hands to receive the inheritance of your father. And just who is it that should be judged the elder, the rightful heir?" The priest laughed sardonically. "Neither! This special place in all of the world belongs only to God. It's not real estate to be bought and sold. It cannot and must not be divided. Jerusalem is holy ground. No one can claim for themselves what belongs only to God Almighty, Yahweh. Jehovah, Yehova Yireh!"

Silence settled over the room. Kelly pulled at his goatee and stared at the scroll. His initial euphoria had turned into contemplation. Musa continued to frown. Leah drummed on the table with her fingertips and looked off into the darkness at the other end of the room.

"Most unexpected." Musa finally broke the silence. "Not at all what I expected."

"Nor I," Leah answered.

"And yet what an extraordinary statement," Michael said. "There is no question that Jerusalem has been the ancient capital of the Jewish people, dating back to the time of King David, but ultimately the title deed belongs to God. We are standing in the midst of God's city. Think what a difference it would have made through the centuries if the world had seen this place in such a light. The answer to the future lies in this scroll."

"Adin told me so," Leah spoke more to herself. "My friend, a rabbi in another part of the city, said that heaven and earth meet here. Jerusalem is holy because it exists to uniquely fulfill the purposes of God. The king of Salem was telling us to look to the intentions of the divine if we are to use the city correctly."

"I think so," Michael answered.

"No one wins," Musa concluded. "Neither side conquers the other." He threw his hands up in the air.

"We have no option but to live in peace." Leah's voice filled with pathos, longing. She smiled at Musa.

Michael let the quiet do its work. Finally, he pointed to the scroll. "You do realize that we're not through. There's more."

Musa put his pencil down and slowly leaned forward, staring at the scroll.

"Yes," Leah acknowledged.

"There is a combination of Hebrew and Greek that is relatively clear." Michael read, "*Afiemi 'Ayin 'Adam e Ethnos.* I consider the message to be, 'suffer, or let, no man.'" He looked up. "That's a collective noun meaning 'all humanity, men and women.' Okay?"

Everyone signaled agreement.

The priest continued. "Don't let humanity, any ethnic group, do something or the other, meaning that there's a warning to follow. On the basis of the divine ownership of this city, the king of Salem is about to forbid a certain action."

Leah pointed in the middle of the phrase. "*Nekama* is 'wrath' or 'vengeance.' The expression conveys an act of passion."

Michael pushed in, tracing the words with his finger just above the gold. "*Kheper*, or 'arise here, now' and the Egyptian *cher* is 'on account of.'" He stared at the metal for a moment. "'Vengeance arises now on the account of.'" He pulled at his goatee. "Something's missing."

Leah aimed the red dot of the laser pointer on one Akkadian symbol in the middle of the line. "You missed the jackpot word. *Para'u* is the expression for 'cut off,' or 'cut in two.' Get it?"

Musa gasped. "I can't believe my eyes and ears. We are warned that the wrath of God will be unleashed if the City of Peace is divided." He shook his head in disbelief. "Six millennia ago the world was warned of a false peace that would be the prelude to a terrible disaster caused by the division of the city of Jerusalem." He tossed his pencil in the air. "I wouldn't have believed in such a scroll as this if I hadn't found it myself. Astonishing. Staggering."

"Are we ready to put it all together?" Leah looked at Kelly. "You're the man with the tape recorder, the world-renowned scholar. Be my guest."

The priest picked up the microcassette recorder. For several moments he pondered the notes scattered before him. "I think I can make a fair stab at it." He switched on the machine. "Wednesday, October eighth, four P.M." He cleared his throat. "The following is the initial text of the legendary Donation of Melchizedek, first discovered by archaeologist Musa Salah, son of the original discoverer of the Dead Sea Scrolls. Assisting Dr. Salah in this translation are Father Michael Kelly and Leah Rosenberg." He hit the pause button and smiled. "I think we should record the last segment first as Leah originally suggested, as it puts the whole message in the proper context. Friends, here goes history."

Michael released the pause button. "I, the king of Salem, hereby bequeath this sacred ground and declare the intentions of the Almighty. The name of Jerusalem declares to all peoples the city belongs to God alone. Let no man or people dismember or divide, lest His wrath be released. Behold and tremble, in the sixth millennium, the nations that come to Jerusalem to make peace will dance with the dust of the ridge and celebrate forty-eight months; but the stones will weep for the millennium. For the millennium I spoke of shall be decreed, and the seals shall be broken. Jebus, or Jerusalem, shall rejoice, but in your pride you have unlocked the sorrow of all ages." Michael switched the machine off and laid it quietly on the table.

"Incredible," Leah said. "I feel as if I am in the presence of God. Simply hearing you read those words touched something deep within my soul."

"Yes," Musa whispered. "Yes, I feel the same thing. The power of a great truth is unlocked, set free, and the amazing thing is what it has already done in each of us."

"During the days of terrible turmoil, we've become people of peace," Michael exclaimed. "We started as strangers, maybe actually enemies, and we've become like a family. A wonderful divine love has not only reconciled us to one another, but to ourselves."

Leah rubbed the sides of her temples. "I can't believe how I feel right now. There's actually a sense of joy, profound joy, rising up in me. Even with the grief, I feel a wonderful sense of transcendent peace."

"We all know about my tendencies toward grandiosity and a touch of megalomania." Michael grinned as he talked. "However, at the risk of overstatement, it seems that God has allowed us to be part of one of the most extraordinary secrets of all time. What has started as an academic challenge and an archaeological opportunity turns out to be a profound privilege.

I just don't know how to express what I feel." He rubbed his goatee.

"I think we should pray," Leah answered.

Musa had already closed his eyes and placed his face in his hands.

40

Wednesday, October 7
Old City

Just as the three friends left the Abbey, the sun disappeared behind the ancient stone wall. The orange glow reflected off the golden Dome of the Rock and settled above the Church of the Holy Sepulchre. The shadow of the Western Wall lengthened and swallowed the final worshipers, davening before the remnant of the glory of Solomon.

Off in the distance an ambulance wailed as it sped off to a hospital somewhere in the city. The child vendors recognized the trio as poor commercial possibilities and hurried off after one of the final tourist groups heading for the Zion. Two Israeli soldiers stood along the wall with their rifles slung casually but menacingly over their shoulders. They eyed Musa suspiciously.

Musa smiled and watched the golden glow reflected off the ancient paving stones on Armenian Patriarchate Street, leading to the Citadel of David. "What an irony," he said. "The world is careening toward cataclysmic disaster, and yet we have found an enclave of peace in the midst of suspicion. Here we are, people of the three faiths that have been at odds with one another for centuries and yet . . . yet, we have come to a new place of respect and hope."

"My mind's certainly been changed in these last few days," Leah confessed. "Perhaps David is looking down on me and laughing at his cynical wife who now goes to the synagogue and reads the Torah. I hope he enjoys this little joke God has played on me."

The cold evening wind whistled down the long narrow alley, and Michael pulled his brown woolen habit more closely about himself. "Let's stop at a little restaurant I like, just inside the Gate, and I'm buying supper. Getting chilly out here."

"You're on!" Leah said.

Musa suddenly stopped and snapped his fingers. "I think I see something we missed. Yes, we have overlooked a very important component in what this message means. The title deed to Jerusalem belongs to God and God alone. If divine harmony is not achieved in this city as a sign to the world, then an apocalpyse cannot but follow as the powers of light and darkness collide here." He rubbed his chin and started walking again. "Perhaps the ancient writer chose the sixth millenium as his symbol of the beginning of the end because he believed if peace were not restored in people, the result would be a final collision ending everything."

"Yes." The priest held up his finger instructively. "The light of a holy God and the darkness of pride-filled human beings bent on unforgiveness and warlike anger cannot coexist. Like a match held too close to fire, eventually something will explode."

"Perhaps." Leah started and stopped. She watched a light go on in a little vendor's stand. "Perhaps the title deed to Jerusalem is also the title deed to the human heart. Ownership of both belongs to God alone. The secret of the scroll is that it can't be understood through a proud heart. In the same way, there will never be peace in our land until hearts are purified of hate and distrust."

Musa put his arm in hers and guided Leah past a large mud hole in the street. "As each of us has experienced over the last few weeks, the secret of both personal and political peace is to be found in emptying ourselves through repentance. God does direct humans toward the right path if they listen. Our task now is to help the rest of the world hear."

"Here we are." Michael pointed to a small storefront restaurant. The smell of roasting chicken and sweet *baklava* drifted out. "We have definitely come to the right place." He held the door open.

Musa waved at the Palestinian owner and they exchanged smiles. "I could stand a stiff cup of Turkish coffee, myself." He settled down at the table.

"You, Leah?" Michael beckoned to the waiter.

"Sure."

"Make it three eye-openers," Michael told the waiter.

"Feels good to be inside." Leah pulled her leather jacket tighter around her waist. "Winter's not too far ahead."

Michael leaned back into the chair and put his hands behind his head. "One task done. One left to go."

"What do you mean?" Musa asked.

"The next job is to tell the world what we've discovered in such a way that they will hear us. Sure, we can rock the archaeological world by just laying your scroll on the table, Musa. However, I don't think that's why we were entrusted with this translation. I sense a call to bring the prophetic words of the message to every nation, to all creation."

"How can we ever do such a thing?" Leah puzzled. "Sure, Michael, you've got the Vatican connection, but they're certainly not going to be thrilled to hear what you've got to say. I'm not sure many in the Jewish community are going to be thrilled either. Musa, you know the hard truth about how well this will fly in the Palestinian world."

"I think I know where to start." Michael smiled slyly. "The American president is calling for an International Peace Conference. Perhaps I can use my Vatican connections to get us on the agenda if I avoid full disclosure of the contents until we speak. Think of it! We would have a worldwide forum!"

"Sort of touches something old and corrupt in your soul, Michael. Doesn't it?" Leah asked.

The priest grinned. "God even uses reprobates."

"We must try," Musa urged. "I can see now why Jerusalem has always been such a source of rage. This place, this City of Salem, has a God-given capacity to draw out the projections of the human soul, whether they are the best or the worst. People see Jerusalem as *they are*, not as it is. Pride, prejudice, presumption have for countless centuries fostered hate, distrust, and war. We must do everything in our power to create the opposite, to bring forth love, to restore unity."

"I must speak as Leah, the attorney, for a moment. Political groups will not accept the idea of God's sovereign ownership of this city. Too much power and money are at stake. Yet I know if they don't, the stage is set for a devastation they will bring on themselves. We are caught in a vise grip of our own design."

From a nearby minaret the singing of the muezzin sounded the Muslim call to prayer. The eerie chanting floated over the Old City, summoning the faithful to their knees.

Musa smiled. "How can I not respond? Al-Aksa Mosque is close. Tonight I want to be there. I will be thanking God and praying for our next task." He stood up. "Good night, my friends." Musa was quickly gone down the narrow alley that led to the Temple Mount.

Leah watched him vanish and then sipped her coffee. "My friend Adin has some kind of women's Torah study tonight. I think I'll try to catch it. I'm sure you'll convene us in the near future, Michael. You like being chairman of the board." She smiled fondly.

"Ah, Leah! You were right. I will never again take women for granted. Well, we have no choice but to keep on this journey. God has called us to try," Michael concluded. "We simply can't get free of each other."

Women were assembled in their places when Leah entered the back door. The congregation huddled together. The cold had already swept in under the doors. Rabbi Scholem's makeshift synagogue certainly left almost everything to be desired.

Adin was already at the front, bent over the Torah scroll with a silver pointer in hand, expounding in a singsong voice.

Leah could not but think on all that had happened in the last twenty-four hours. A lifetime crammed into one day. She had looked into the ancient face of the past and seen the hideous mask of death as well as the consummate promise of hope.

Oh, Jerusalem, my Jerusalem, she thought. *What shall yet become of thee?*

Adin's voice rose as he read the passage from the prophet Zechariah:

Behold, I will make Jerusalem a cup of trembling unto all the people round about. Judah will be besieged as well as Jerusalem. On that day, when all the nations of the earth are gathered against her, I will make Jerusalem an immovable rock for all nations. All who try to move it will injure themselves . . . On that day, I will make the leaders of Judah like a firepot in a woodpile, like a flaming torch among sheaves. They will consume all the surrounding peoples, but Jerusalem will remain intact in her place.

Adin paused to catch his breath, and Leah caught hers.

At the same moment, the evening mass was beginning at the Dormition Abbey. Michael felt a particularly keen desire to join the procession of clergy, to be just one of the brothers, a singular—and, hopefully, more simple—member of the community of faith.

The massive organ poured forth the magnificent strains of the processional hymn as the congregation stood to sing.

Immortal, invisible, God only wise,
In light inaccessible hid from our eyes,
Most blessed, most glorious, the Ancient of Days . . .

Michael raised his voice in renewed fervor on the last line, "Almighty, victorious, Thy great Name we praise."

The priests and monks settled into their places, and Abbott Friedrich Hoffman, in his green chasuble, took his regular chair as the celebrant of the evening while the monastic choir continued the second verse of the hymn.

Unresting, unhasting, and silent as light,
Nor wanting, nor wasting, Thou rulest in might;
Thy justice like mountains high soaring above . . .

Michael Kelly thought of those who would dance in the dust of the ridge, the mountains around Jerusalem, the ones who would never recognize the light because their hearts were dark.

And he wondered. He pondered how close such a day might be. Perhaps he would witness it personally.

The last stanza echoed across the stone nave and filled his ears with beauty.

> Great Father of Glory, pure Father of light,
> Thine angels adore Thee, all veiling their sight;
> All laud we would render: O help us to see
> 'Tis only the splendor of light hideth Thee.

As the service unfolded, Father Michael Kelly found himself repeating the familiar words he knew by rote. Almost as if he were elsewhere, his mind raced back and forth across the events of the last several months. Where would it all go from here? What if no one would listen to them? What if this magnificent discovery would be lost in the back pages of dusty old archaeological journals, and no one would see the light? For the first time in days, Michael felt a terrible despair settle in and infect his joy.

Brother Thomas stood up to read the epistle lesson. "A reading from St. John's Revelation," the bent old man announced. "Hear the Word of the Lord."

> And I, John, saw the Holy City, the new Jerusalem, coming down from God out of heaven, prepared as a bride adorned for her husband. And I heard a great voice out of heaven saying, Behold the tabernacle of God is with men, and he will dwell with them and they shall be his people . . . And God shall wipe away all tears from their eyes; and there shall be no more death, neither sorrow, nor crying, neither shall there be any more pain: for the former things are passed away.

As he listened to the reading of God's Word, he heard a phrase echoing in his innermost being: "Jerusalem is the window of the soul through which the winds of eternity blow." Yes. The earthly Jerusalem was the window of the soul, the focal point of history; everything converged in this sacred spot.

"Behold and tremble!" the scroll warned the nations that would come here to make peace. The words of the ancient prophecy recorded on a thin sheet of gold rang as true as the passage from Revelation about the new Jerusalem coming down from God out of heaven. Yes, indeed. The winds of eternity were blowing, and Michael Kelly was standing squarely in the spot where history and eternity would soon intersect. If God had a purpose for his being here, he was ready and willing to fulfill it. Ready for his gifts and his training to be used of God to deliver His message, just as so many other scribes and scholars had before him.

"Here ends the reading of the epistle," Brother Thomas announced and sat down.

An image of the city of Jerusalem abruptly welled up before his eyes. He felt the bitterness and animosity that exploded daily in the streets and then he remembered what he had experienced with Musa and Leah. Words that he had said earlier slipped through his lips as a simple prayer. "The hope for tomorrow begins or ends in how each of us faces the contradictions in our own hearts. O God, forgiveness is the only salve that can heal the soul of Jerusalem and the heart of humanity. Heavenly Father help us, for we know not what to do."

"Thanks be to God," the congregation responded.

Michael suddenly felt as if he were going to cry. "Thanks be to God," he mumbled last of all. The joy was so intense he could not keep the tears back. Yes, he had finally done something that really counted in this world. Not for parents, not for friends, not for authorities, but for God. The peace of it all swept over him like a great wave of light. And for the first time he realized how lonely he had always been . . . because he was no longer lonely at all.

The Exciting Sequel to
The Jerusalem Scroll
The Lost Medallion

Leah Rosenberg, Dr. Musa Salah, and Father Michael Kelly know they must get their message from the Jerusalem Scroll to the world. Through Kelly's resources in the Vatican, they obtain a special place on the program of the Jerusalem International Conference on Middle Eastern Peace. Once the message of the scroll is revealed, the response from all quarters is explosive and chaotic. The trio is under attack.

The world demands the authentication of the scroll. How can it be validated? Rabbi Adin Scholem realizes what the lost medallion is! Abraham gave a tithe to King Melchizedek. The coin was a portion of his offering, the donation of Abraham! If the coin can be found and verified, the world would have to believe. But where is the coin?

The three friends race against time to find the object. Having electronically picked up conversations about the meaning of the coin, the Islamic Fundamentalist Movement enters the chase with their own diabolical intent. Can the three translators cheat death in this deadly game?

You can be the first to know. To receive a special advance publication announcement of the exciting sequel, *The Lost Medallion*, or to receive a free catalog of Mr. Evans' books and tapes, please write or call:

Michael David Evans
P.O. Box 910
Euless, Texas 76039
Phone: 800-825-3872 Fax: 817-285-0962
e-mail: memkmc@onramp.net